Murder on the
Champ de Mars

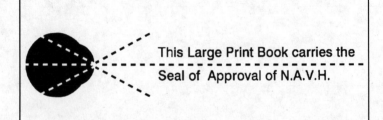

This Large Print Book carries the
Seal of Approval of N.A.V.H.

MURDER ON THE
CHAMP DE MARS

CARA BLACK

THORNDIKE PRESS
A part of Gale, Cengage Learning

GALE
CENGAGE Learning®

Farmington Hills, Mich • San Francisco • New York • Waterville, Maine
Meriden, Conn • Mason, Ohio • Chicago

GALE
CENGAGE Learning®

Copyright © 2015 by Cara Black.
An Aimee Leduc Investigation.
Thorndike Press, a part of Gale, Cengage Learning.

LIBRARY OF CONGRESS CATALOGING-IN-PUBLICATION DATA

Black, Cara, 1951–
    Murder on the Champ de Mars / by Cara Black. — Large print edition.
        pages cm. — (An Aimee Leduc investigation) (Thorndike Press large
    print mystery)
    ISBN 978-1-4104-7891-7 (hardcover) — ISBN 1-4104-7891-2 (hardcover)
    1. Leduc, Aimee (Fictitious character)—Fiction. 2. Women private
investigators—France—Paris—Fiction. 3. Large type books. I. Title.
    PS3552.L297M87 2015b
    813'.54—dc23   2015006738

Published in 2015 by arrangement with Soho Press, Inc.

Printed in Mexico
1 2 3 4 5 6 7 19 18 17 16 15

In memory of Romain Gary,
who introduced me to
rue du Bac and espresso.

For the victims of *Porajmos,* as
gens du voyage call the Holocaust,
and as always for the ghosts.

When the road bends, it's hard to walk straight.

— ROMANY PROVERB

Paris, April 1999 • Sunday, Late Afternoon
Aimée Leduc clipped the French military
GPS tracker to the wheel well, straightened
up and gasped, seeing the Peugeot's owner
standing in the shadowy Marais courtyard.
So much for being *très discrète.* She'd
blown the surveillance — now what? What
was wrong with her, making a mistake like
this? Why couldn't she shake off her postpar-
tum baby brain?

"*Un peu trop élégante* for a mechanic.
Maybe you're a *saboteuse?*" said the Vicomte d'Argenson, her target.

Think. She wasn't even officially back
from maternity leave until tomorrow, but
she'd taken the job because it had seemed
like a piece of *gâteau.* "A relative is trying
to ruin me," the *comte* had told her when
he'd hired her. "Find out who."

Now, staring across the seventeenth-
century courtyard at the *comte*'s nephew,

she arranged her face in a pout. "Just a little tracking device, Vicomte d'Argenson. You're a hard man to catch up with and I want your story." She pulled her alias's card from her clutch bag. "We journalists have to live, you know."

"*Paris Match?*" he said, fingering her card.

A little shrug sent a ripple of clicking across the metallic beading on her Courrèges-clad shoulders. She hoped this ploy appealed to the portly roué's vanity.

"*D'accord,* put me on the cover and I'll give you a story. *My* story."

"Deal." The dank late afternoon air in the courtyard chilled her, and the scent of damp stone clung to the hunting museum's walls. Vivaldi violin melodies wafted from the museum's reception, and the trailing ivy glistened in the light from the sconces.

"But I need the homing device you put under my car, *ma belle.*"

Aimée made a moue of resignation with her Chanel red lips. "I'm counting on the exclusive, Vicomte d'Argenson."

By the time she'd recovered the device and put it in his waiting palm, he'd checked the other tires.

"Damn paparazzi," he said, grinding the tracker under his heel on the cobbles.

Good thing she'd put a second one inside

his briefcase on the backseat. She activated the second tracker, smothering the click with a cough.

"My number's at the bottom. *A bientôt,*" she said, shooting him a complicit smile, and air-kissed somewhere in the vicinity of his cheek.

And with that she hurried through the tall doors, slipping the control, which was no bigger than a lighter, into the waiting hand of Maxence, Leduc Detective's intern hacker, who was posing as a valet.

She joined the *comte*'s fiftieth birthday party. Mission almost complete, she thought. She stood under the chandelier in the thronged gala, a position from which she could keep one kohl-rimmed eye on *le vicomte*. Part of her enjoyed getting back to the grown-up world and off diaper duty for a few hours. The other was tinged with guilt for going back to work full-time tomorrow.

Notes from the violin drifted up to the hunting museum's twenty-foot ceiling. To avoid conversation, she pretended to admire the decor, suppressing shudders at the antler trophies; other walls were hung with medieval tapestries of gruesome hunting scenes. Meanwhile, her target stood amongst his entourage with a glass, looking bored. No suspicious contact yet.

"Interesting scent you're wearing." A member of *le vicomte*'s entourage had appeared at her elbow. He had periwinkle-blue eyes and tousled curly hair. He offered her *une coupe de champagne.* "What's it called?"

She sniffed. Puréed aubergine. With her fingernail she scraped off the splattered souvenir her six-month-old daughter, Chloé, had left on her clutch.

"A mixture of Chanel No. 5 and my own blend." She smiled flirtatiously and passed on the champagne. Not that she wasn't tempted. But this was work. And she was nursing.

At last, *le vicomte* separated himself from the crowd and made toward the door.

"Pardonnez-moi, monsieur." In three strides she'd reached the doorway, speaking into the mic buried in her beaded collar. "Target on the move."

Maxence nodded from the foyer in his valet garb. She adjusted her earwig's volume. "He's asked for his car," said Maxence. "Signal's coming through clear. Even with your clicking beads."

As planned. *Parfait.* "You'll take over from here, Maxence?"

12

"On it."

Plenty of time to make it home, dress Chloé and get to the church for the christening.

As she passed Maxence, she took some francs from her clutch and handed them to him — a tip to keep his cover. She winked at her employer, the *comte,* and headed into the candle-lit museum foyer, where she was taken aback by a giant taxidermied polar bear, one of the *comte*'s donations to the wildlife collection. Men and their trophies! She presented her scooter's keys to the real *voiturier.* In exchange he handed her an envelope containing the *comte*'s embossed card and a check.

She slid up the kickstand with her Louboutin heel and revved her loaner Vespa — a bright turquoise model with more oomph than her own pink one, which was in the shop — while she navigated the cobbled courtyard. Too bad the damned A-line Courrèges rode up her thighs.

She could get used to this scooter's power. She gunned it down rue Beaubourg, weaving between a bus and a taxi in the street, wove around the Hôtel de Ville, then turned left along the quai, past the budding green branches of the plane trees. But a roadblock stopped traffic before she could cross Pont

Marie to the Île Saint-Louis. What now? A strike, an accident, police checking for drunk drivers? Her scooter stalled.

Tension knotted her shoulders. She couldn't make Chloé late for her own christening. She dreaded the look on the priest's face after he'd done a favor fitting them in; she'd never live it down. As the traffic cleared, she kick-started the Vespa. Finally she pulled into her courtyard on Île Saint-Louis, jumped off the scooter, and ran up her apartment building's worn marble staircase.

Aimée could handle it. *Vraiment,* she could: telecommuting part-time from her home office, she could still manage computer security virus scans and lucrative industrial surveillance. If only she could buy eight hours of sleep over the counter.

"She's got an appetite, your Chloé," said Madame Cachou as she handed Aimée a teaspoon. The sixty-something concierge had a stylish new blunt-cut grey bob. "I changed her diaper two minutes ago, then laid out the gown."

"Ma puce," Aimée said, leaning down to kiss those cheeks, and thinking again how painfully like Melac's eyes Chloé's grey-blue ones were. Those eyes reminded Aimée of her baby's father every day. As for his total

lack of interest in paternity — Aimée hadn't seen that coming.

That wasn't the only thing she didn't see coming. Chloé coughed and puréed carrot hit Aimée in the eye. Just one more of the daily surprises of motherhood, like the overwhelming protectiveness she felt toward her baby. Or how sleep deprived she could be. Aimée wiped off the carrot and hoped to God they wouldn't be too late.

By the time she'd cleaned her daughter's smiling, rose-shaped mouth and her perfect chubby fists, Miles Davis, her bichon frisé, had licked up every trace of orange from the kitchen tiles under the high chair. He'd gained weight from all the cleaning up since Chloé was born.

Her life had changed. Instead of working long hours at the office before heading out for nights on the town, now she spent her afternoons taking Chloé to the park in the stroller. There she joined the other children's mothers, who were laughing, commiserating and sharing apple juice and tips. She couldn't imagine not being a *maman, simplement*. She found herself trying to remember her own mother more and more often, the mother who'd disappeared so long ago, now nothing but a footprint on the wave-washed shore of Aimée's childhood. She missed her more than ever now that she was a mother herself.

Today, Chloé would wear the gown Aimée's mother had baptized Aimée in.

Her phone trilled somewhere on the counter behind the baby bottles. By the time she found it, Chloé had spit up all over her shoulder. Thankfully the burp cloth had caught it all. She hoped.

"We're waiting at the church, Aimée."

"Five minutes, René."

"You know the priest did us a special favor," said René, his voice rising. "Wedging us in this late on Sunday with the Easter rush."

"Five minutes," she said again, clicking off.

Aimée deftly laid Chloé on the changing table and pulled off the soiled onesie. She nuzzled her pink tummy with kisses, and Chloé cooed with delight. Chloé's sweet baby smell engulfed her as she slipped her into the lace christening gown.

She scooped up her secondhand Birkin bag, loaded it with some diapers and wipes, slipped into her cheetah-print heels and headed down the wide, worn marble stairs with Chloé on her hip.

In the early evening, the quai-side lamps' yellow-gold glow filtered through the plane trees. Below her flowed the khaki-colored Seine. With any luck, Chloé wouldn't need a diaper change before the priest started.

Around the corner, Martine, her best friend since the *lycée,* was pacing on the church steps. Martine wore a chic navy blue suit with a matching straw hat, both Italian. She pulled Aimée's arm.

"*Mon Dieu,* Aimée, everyone's waiting," said Martine. "Love your dress."

"My surveillance uniform." She hoped she hadn't missed any of Chloé's spit up.

"Only you would call a vintage Courrèges a uniform."

"Got an upscale gig," she said under her breath. "I'll need to borrow your Versace."

They entered the church and found flickering votive candles, incense and a waiting crowd near the baptismal font in a side chapel.

"You'll be late to your own funeral, Leduc." Morbier, Aimée's godfather, bent down to kiss Chloé.

"*Bonsoir* to you, too, *mon parrain,*" she said, using the term for godfather. A term she hadn't used since she wore knee socks.

Morbier, a *commissaire* and an old colleague of Aimée's late father, looked rested for once, despite the drooping bags under his basset-hound eyes. He was wearing a three-piece suit — a first. He stood arm in arm with a beaming Jeanne, his companion, all in yellow flounces. "I can't believe I held you like that once," said Morbier. He reached out and touched her hair. Her throat caught.

She was surprised to see her father's old police comrades since he'd left the force under a cloud of allegations — allegations that had taken her years to disprove. Lefèvre, an old Friday-night card-playing crony of her father's from the *commissariat*, along with Thomas Dussollier, another card player who'd attended the police academy with her father and was about to retire. Both wore police uniforms. Lefèvre leaned on a cane; Thomas's dark hair was speckled grey. Dussollier held a photo out to her: her own christening, here at this same font, Dussollier, Morbier and her papa all young men. "Jean-Claude would be so proud, Aimée." His eyes brimmed. Hers, too.

René Friant, godfather-to-be and her partner at Leduc Detective, looked relieved to see her. He wore a dark blue suit, matching cravat and cuff links. A dwarf at four feet tall, he stood on a stool by the baptismal font.

"*La voilà.* Good of you to join us finally, Aimée," said her old catechism teacher, Père

Michel, beckoning them closer.

Chloé Jeanne Renée — named for her great-grandmother, her grandfather Jean-Claude and her godfather-to-be, René — yawned. Aimée's cousin Sebastian and his wife, Regula, beamed. Regula, six months along herself, was showing her bump.

The incense tickled Aimée's nose, and the splash of holy water brought back memories. Memories of coming here with her parents, and later, after her American mother had abandoned them, Morbier taking her small hand in his and bringing her to catechism classes. As she stood under the soaring seventeenth-century domed roof, it all passed before her like old photos in a slideshow. She grabbed at tradition in whatever family memories she could find.

Just as the priest was about to begin, Martine tugged on Aimée's sleeve and pointed to a man in a black jacket striding down the aisle. His magnetic grey-blue eyes caught Aimée's. Still a hunk. A chord vibrated in her stomach.

Melac, her baby's father.

Six long months without a word, and he could still make her heart pound. He'd never even seen his daughter. Nor had he replied to the christening invitation, or called once. She noted his leanness, a

19

deeper line added to the crinkle on his brow.

She felt conflicted: both furious with him and glad that he had come. Maybe this was an olive branch that might lead to some involvement in her baby's life? But why hadn't he called, even once? Aimée pulled Chloé close, nuzzled her rose-pink cheek. "*Ma puce,* he's your father, so let's be nice."

Père Michel gave the blessing in his white cassock. She felt Melac's presence at her side as he bowed his head during the prayers. That same remembered lime scent clung to him. The ice block inside her thawed a little at the look of joy spreading over his face. He ran his finger under Chloé's chin. She cooed and broke into a smile.

"Before us, Chloé Jeanne Renée's father and mother . . ." intoned the priest. The rest of the litany was lost to her. For a moment, for this sliver of time, they were a family. Together. Aimée choked back a sob.

"Now, witnessed by her godparents, Martine and René . . ."

René nodded, his big green eyes serious. He took Chloé in his arms, a bundle of white organdy in her flowing christening dress. Then he handed her to a smiling Martine. Morbier blew his nose with a handkerchief.

Chloé emitted a startled cry at the cold holy water pouring over her head. "Brave girl, it's almost over," Aimée whispered.

And then it was. There were smiles all round and wiping of the eyes by these people who she'd grown to realize were her family.

"Being a *maman* suits you, Aimée, couture and all." Melac pecked both her cheeks. "May I, René?" he said, opening his arms. "*Enchanté* to meet you, Chloé, my little trouper."

René, ever the diplomat — or most of the time, anyway — shot Aimée a look. *About time he showed up,* she thought, but bit the words back and nodded instead.

Melac's wrists were tanned, and she did a double take when she noticed he was wearing a rose-gold serpent ring on his fourth finger. That hadn't been there before. Her insides knotted.

Back with his ex-wife?

What happened to his offer to "do the right thing"? He'd dropped off the radar almost the moment he'd made it. Not that she'd have married him, although her pride still smarted. She'd crossed him off the list, realizing there was no room for her and Chloé in Melac's life. His attentions were spread too thin elsewhere, with his injured daughter, still comatose after a school bus crash, and his high-maintenance, suicidal ex-wife. Aimée and Chloé weren't going to play second fiddle to anyone's other family.

She'd moved on. Hadn't she? Aimée's fists clenched.

"C'est incroyable," said new godmother Martine, whispering in her ear. "He's brought a woman."

Not the ex-wife, whose picture Aimée had seen. This woman was a smiling redhead, with freckles dusted over her nose. A big-boned athletic type, she wore a hand-knitted wool sweater, a woven rust-colored skirt and short boots. Not an outfit for a christening, the Parisienne in Aimée noted. Provincial, all right. The woman's gaze was fixed on Chloé.

"Meet Donatine, my wife," Melac said, his voice low. "She's helped me through a rough time. She nursed Sandrine until life support failed."

"Je suis désolée," said Aimée, realizing why he'd gone off the radar. His daughter had died. She felt terrible. "I am truly sorry for your loss. I know how much you loved Sandrine."

This Donatine woman, she now saw, was wearing a matching rose-gold serpent ring.

"Chloé's *un ange.*" The redhead gazed at

the proud father holding Chloé, drinking the sight in.

The hair bristled on the back of Aimée's neck.

"*Regarde ça,* Chloé loves her papa," said Donatine.

Melac smiled from ear to ear, rewarded by Chloé's cooing.

"*Vous me permettez?*" said Donatine. Before Aimée could prevent it, she had Chloé cuddled in her arms.

Aimée's internal alarms screeched on high alert. Danger. She wanted this woman away, far away.

"Donatine's a natural," grinned Melac. "She loves children," he added.

"Oh, I'm glad, Melac," she said, relief filling her. "You'll have a new family, move on with your life." She reached for his hand.

He pulled back. "I want to register as Chloé's father, go to the *mairie* and recognize her officially." He shifted on his boots. "Forgive me, Aimée. I meant to do this before."

"Six months too late, Melac," she said. No way was he getting on Chloé's birth certificate.

Aimée watched Donatine coo and bounce Chloé. It made her skin itch to watch Chloé babble and drool and smile.

"Donatine can't have children," Melac said. He paused. "We're interested in figuring out an arrangement. Sharing care. Custody."

Aimée's jaw dropped. Custody? Just like that?

"And where have you been in Chloé's life so far, Melac?" she said, blood rising to her face.

Melac held out his hand. "Be *juste,* Aimée."

"You think you can just waltz in like you have some right?" she said. "I've raised her without a father, without even a phone call, for six months." She wanted to grab her baby out of Donatine's arms.

Near the nave of the church, René was asking for everyone's attention. "As the proud godparents, Martine and I invite you to join us for a champagne toast at Aimée's," said René. "We've prepared a little celebration."

Melac winked at Donatine. Besotted, that was the only way she could describe that look of his. He caught Aimée's furious glare, and his intent grey-blue eyes narrowed, dispelling that gaze she'd once gotten lost in. "*Désolé.* This isn't the place to bring things up. Let's catch up at your place. Donatine's brought Chloé a present."

24

He'd crossed the line. The gall!

"Melac, I invited you as a courtesy. But you never replied."

A pall of silence fell over the church vestibule.

"You've got some nerve," she said, her voice rising. "Chloé's six months old, and you've just seen her for the first time."

"Shh . . . don't make a scene here, Aimée."

A scene? She wanted to pick up the nearest crucifix and hit him. Chloé gave a little cry.

"There's nothing to discuss, Melac." Anger rippled up her neck. "Until she graduates from university."

Melac's mouth pursed. "So you want to blow this up, make it an issue?"

"No, it's a nonissue, Melac," she said. "You're not legally recognized as her father. Get over it."

"My lawyer says otherwise, Aimée."

Panic flooded her. Was it possible? Could he get rights to her baby? A cold shiver ran down her legs.

"You're talking to a lawyer?" Shouting, she was shouting now. She felt a tug on her arm. She couldn't let go. "How dare you?"

Several older women in the pews turned toward the vestibule and stared. Donatine rocked a now crying Chloé in her arms.

Aimée reached out for her daughter, but Donatine turned away. "Shh, you've scared her."

Bitch. Interloper. "What right — ?"

Melac stepped between her and Donatine. "Like to make scenes, don't you, Aimée?"

"*Non,* Melac, you're confusing me with your hysterical ex-wife."

Père Michel's cassock swished as he moved between them. In one swift move, he took Chloé and put her in René's arms.

"*D'accord, mes enfants,* take this outside and go with God," said the Père, shaking his head.

Morbier grabbed Melac's shoulder and ushered him through the church's leather-padded door. Martine hooked an arm in Aimée's, shoving her forward and leaning in to say into her ear, "Let it go for now."

"Like hell I will."

"He's doing this to keep his new woman happy, Aimée, and it's her tactic to keep him. You need a good lawyer. I know some people."

Outside the church on the twilit, cobbled Île Saint-Louis street, Aimée's hands trembled as she watched Donatine give René a wrapped gift. Without another word to Aimée, Melac put his arm around Dona-

26

tine and they disappeared around the corner.

Aimée'd looked forward to this event, and now it was ruined. Melac had turned into a menace.

"No wonder you didn't end up with that *salaud,*" said her cousin Sebastian, snapping his leather jacket closed. He hugged her, then stepped back so Regula could. "We've got work, can't stay." Sebastian pulled on his helmet while Regula hopped onto the back of his motorcycle, her helmet already on. A wave and they'd taken off into the descending shadows. After kissing Chloé, Lefèvre and Dussollier bowed out, too.

Martine held her cell phone, a pained look on her face. "Got to go, an emergency with Gilles's daughter. Teenagers. *Désolée.*" She hugged Aimée before getting into her lime green Mini Cooper. "We'll talk later."

The christening party, now just Aimée, René, Morbier and Jeanne, reached the quai d'Anjou. Chloé's cries had turned to hiccups. Aimée settled the baby on her shoulder and patted her back. A moment later she was rewarded with a loud burp.

"Always exciting with you, Leduc," said Morbier. "Not often I'm kicked out of church."

"The nerve of him, appearing *sans* RSVP and talking custody. What was I supposed to do — smile and give my daughter to a man who's nothing more than a stranger?" Aimée's voice had risen in anger, and Chloé whimpered. Aimée stopped and kissed her whimpers away.

As she followed the others toward her townhouse, she was startled by a young man, olive-complected with curly black hair, who stepped out of the shadows by a tall green door and stopped her before she could cross the street. He wore a hoodie and jeans.

"Mademoiselle?" he said.

Her arms started doing double duty: cradling Chloé and now gripping her bag tight, too. Young Roma were notorious for purse snatching, usually working in teams. Right away, guilt washed over her for profiling him.

"Mademoiselle Leduc?" he said.

A chill rippled over her. He knew her name.

René, Jeanne and Morbier were waiting in her doorway. "Let's go, Aimée," Morbier called, beckoning her.

"Do you remember me, Mademoiselle? You and your father visited my mother when I was small," the Romany boy said.

"I'm Nicholás, remember? I go by Nicu now."

A vague memory came to her now — an afternoon at the market, years ago, with a woman and a boy who could have become this young man. French Gypsies, *les manouches*.

"I think so," she said. "A long time ago." Aimée noted the shadows under his eyes, the intensity radiating from him. "I'm sorry, but now isn't a good time," she said, about to edge past him. How did he know where she lived?

"My mother is in the hospital. She's dying." His lip quivered. "Her spirit's agitated. She can't go beyond without talking to you."

The damp quai-side pavers shone a dull graphite. She shifted on her heels. "I don't understand."

"Maman needs to let go and depart on her journey," he said. "She kept in contact with your father."

"My father?" Aimée's arms tingled.

"Her name is Drina. Don't you remember her? Don't you remember bringing us Christmas gifts?"

Then memories flooded back — chill Christmas Eves with her father, skidding on ice-kissed cobbles, her scratchy wool scarf, fingers sticky from the gift-wrapping tape.

29

They played Papa Noël, then stopped for a *chocolat chaud* at a café with fogged-up windows. Selfish and self-absorbed, her young self thought only of the *chocolat chaud* she would get at the end of those visits.

René was walking back toward them. "Any problem here, Aimée?"

The Romany boy's face closed down, completely blank.

"*Non, c'est bon.* Mind taking Chloé upstairs?" she said. "I'll join you in a minute."

With Chloé in his arms, René headed into the courtyard.

Aimée glanced at Morbier, still in her doorway with his phone to his ear. "Look, let's talk later."

Nicu pulled out a dog-eared business card — her late father's, with the old Leduc Detective logo. Aimée still had some of those left in her desk. On the back, in her father's writing, were the words, *Always come to us for help. Anytime. Anyplace.*

"You believe me now, don't you?"

Unsettled, she nodded. She felt overwhelmed thinking of the obligations she could face thanks to her father's old promises. But if her father had given his word, Aimée was honor-bound to see it through.

"Nicu, I'll visit her tomorrow in the

hospital. Promise."

A seagull cried over the river, and the sound echoed off the stone walls and cobbles.

"Can't you come with me now to Hôpital Laennec, in the seventh?" Nicu's mouth trembled. "She doesn't have much time left. Wouldn't your father want you to do the right thing?"

Do the right thing? Chilly gusts of wind, algae-scented from the Seine, whipped her shoulders.

"S'il vous plaît."

Over on the Left Bank, in the 7th arrondissement? "I can't just leave my baby."

Nicu's shoulders slumped as if the fight had gone out of him. His gaze rested somewhere in the land of grief and fear.

"Maman's suffering. She can't let go until . . ." Nicu paused. "In our culture we repair disagreements before someone passes or it will haunt us. She's insisting she must see you."

She glanced at the spot where Morbier had stood speaking into his cell phone. She didn't see him.

Torn, she clenched her fists. Decided.

"Let me take care of things upstairs," she said. "See what I can do."

She ran inside her courtyard to find

Madame Cachou's concierge loge darkened. No chance of wangling her to babysit again. She'd see if Morbier and Jeanne would stay with Chloé for a little while.

But upstairs she found her salon deserted. All but one of the champagne flutes stood unused on the table, like a row of soldiers. Silver bowls of *dragées* — those pastel-colored sugared almonds, de rigueur for a baptism, as René had insisted — sat untouched between bouquets of white roses.

She dropped her bag on the escritoire. "Where is everyone?"

"They weren't going to wait for you forever," René said. "Morbier and Jeanne begged off, and Chloé fell asleep." He loosened his cravat, put his silk-stockinged feet up on her recamier and sipped a fizzing flute of champagne. "Shame to let the Dom Pérignon go to waste." René sipped again. "Why the hell did you invite Melac?"

"How could I have known that his daughter died, or that he'd have a new woman? He would have surfaced eventually anyway. But he scared me, René. Talking about custody . . ."

"Don't you always say the best defense is a good offense?" said René. "Strike first. Hire the best lawyer."

She kicked off her heels in the sparkly-clean hallway. Her apartment was spotless for the christening party that had never happened.

Alors, she couldn't go to the hospital in Courrèges. From the armoire in her room, she picked out her black stovepipe denims, which she could finally fit into again, and an oversized cashmere sweater, and pulled them on.

Rushing back to the salon to grab her leather jacket, she said to René, "Mind babysitting for an hour? The champagne will keep you company."

"Wait a minute — you're going out?" René's eyes landed on the card in her hand. "Does this involve that Gypsy waiting out front?" Before she could reply, he'd reached for the card and read her father's message on the back. "*Et alors?* This card proves what? Don't be a sucker, Aimée. This is a trick to reel you in — they want something, and you'll end up getting ripped off. Cons like this are their stock-in-trade."

"His mother's dying. She knew my father, and she has something to tell me."

"They always do. Then they read your palm and charge for it."

René was so riled he dropped his glass. He caught it, but not before pale yellow drops sprinkled on the marble-topped table, glimmering in the light from the chandelier.

"This Gypsy kid pops up outside the door, and you believe him, just like that?" René shook his head. "I call it naïve. Do you really know these people?"

"I'm trying to remember. It's hazy, years ago. But we'd bring them presents at Christmas."

"*Mon Dieu,* Aimée! It's a scam."

Aimée couldn't help wondering whether he was right.

"Scam or not, I have to hear this woman out, René. Papa promised." She snapped her jacket closed, wrapped her scarf around her neck and knotted it.

"Still so desperate to jump on anything to do with your father?" René shook his head. "You've got Chloé, Aimée. Think of her . . ."

"Like I don't already?" But she was too distracted to argue for long: she'd had a brainwave about her father's connection to this woman, Drina. She snapped her fingers. "I've got it, René. I think this Gypsy woman was my father's informer."

Doubts cycled through Aimée's mind in time with the clicking of the escalator as she rode up to the exit of the Sèvres-Babylone Métro station. Nicu had insisted that his mother's spirit couldn't leave on its last journey unless Aimée spoke to her — but why? A guilty conscience? It was anyone's guess, since she knew nothing of Gypsy culture.

Brisk April-evening air blew around her in gusts as she emerged onto the 7th-arrondissement pavement under the red-and-white lit Métro sign. A disruption on the line had shut the closer station at Vaneau so she had to walk. Her head cleared when she caught a whiff of a woman's floral perfume on Boulevard Raspail. Across the intersection hulked the spotlit Art Nouveau façade of Hôtel Lutetia, the former Abwehr headquarters. In its famous lobby bar congregated literati who found it convenient to ignore the ghosts.

The lit rooftop letters of Le Bon Marché, the department store, shone overlooking the gated square Boucicaut. Aimée pulled up the collar of her leather jacket against the chill. Here, deep in the Left Bank, quiet reigned. She passed darkened boutiques on rue de Sèvres, emblematic of the restrained elegance of this exclusive arrondissement where the shutters rolled down early.

Boring, and lifeless on a Sunday, when hunting down an open café was nearly impossible. Not her haunt, much less that of Gypsies. Everyone who lived here had family money, a *de la* in their name, or a job at a ministry or embassy — sometimes all three. These streets sheltered enormous wealth, secret gardens and courtyards, the prime minister's residence, seats of government and a few ancient convents, now home to aging nuns.

She made her way toward the seventeenth-century Hôpital Laennec. A late-model brown Mercedes had pulled up at the curb, half blocking the crosswalk. Voices raised in argument faded in the echo of an evening bus whooshing by on the damp street.

Coming closer, Aimée recognized Nicu, his hood up. He was gesturing to a stocky man wearing a fedora. Climbing out of the car was an older woman in a long skirt, with grey braids emerging from under a paisley scarf. She was clutching the hand of a little girl in jeans. In her free hand, the woman held a covered cooking pot.

In the jumble of French and Romany, she overheard Drina's name. A problem? Was she too late? Her heart sank.

"*Excusez-moi,* Nicu, I came as fast as I could," she said, feeling awkward breaking into their argument. "How's your mother?"

"Who's this woman?" said the man, gesturing with a lit cigarette, the tip glowing orange in the dark.

"My Uncle Radu's upset," said Nicu. His

eyes were uneasy. "He thinks your visit's not a good idea."

"Didn't you say it was urgent?" said Aimée. "That she needed to tell me something?"

"Another one of your Christian do-gooders, eh, Nicu?" said the uncle. He expelled a plume of smoke, ignoring her, but he was speaking in French so that she could understand him. "Or one of your *ethnologues* wanting to document some *gens du voyage* culture? Maybe she wants to hear you recite some poetry?"

Hostile, obstructive and protective. Nicu's uncle was threatened by her somehow. Too bad.

"*Alors,* did I take the trouble of finding a babysitter just to make a wasted trip?"

Nicu shook his head and turned toward his uncle, beseeching.

"How dare you bring this *gadji* here?" Uncle Radu said.

"I don't have time to stand in the street and argue." She jerked her thumb toward the entrance and said to Nicu, "Coming?"

She took off, counted on him to follow. She realized she only knew the woman's first name, Drina.

The hospital, laid out in the form of two crosses connected by a chapel, radiated eight courtyards with gardens. Large signs informed the public that next year the hospital, which specialized in treating lung diseases, would be shut down. Aimée recalled from her one year of med school that Dr. Laennec, the nineteenth-century physician who invented the stethoscope and for whom the hospital was named, had his medical career cut short after diagnosing himself with TB too late. Ironic.

Hurrying over the worn pavers, past age-darkened courtyard walls, she reached the hospital door. The vaulted entrance — a mélange of architectural styles from several centuries — reminded her of women of a certain age, whose wrinkles and crow's-feet hinted at their past.

Nicu, his uncle and the rest of the retinue joined her at the desk.

"*Désolée,* visiting time ended an hour ago," said a nurse.

Great.

"But we're family," said Nicu's uncle. "My sister needs us."

"Come back at nine A.M. tomorrow."

The uncle gestured to the old woman and the girl. The woman set down her pot and burst into loud wailing.

"How can you tell us to leave?" The uncle spoke over the woman's crying. "She's family. It's better we bring her home. Prepare her our way."

Aimée tried to catch Nicu's eye. He was staring at his uncle, transfixed. She tapped his arm and saw him startle in fear and clutch the messenger bag hanging from his shoulder.

Had she broken some Gypsy taboo?

"Nicu?" she said.

His shoulder twitched. A nervous tic, stress? For a moment he looked lost, adrift. Or maybe hurt. And younger than she'd thought.

After asking René to babysit and coming all this way, she wasn't going to leave now. She had to find out what the woman had wanted to tell her.

"Let's not waste time," she said, keeping her voice gentle. "Which ward, Nicu?"

Another nurse had joined the fracas at the desk.

Nicu pointed left. Made a C with his thumb and forefinger.

She nodded meaningfully, and they stepped back, slipping behind the noisy group and past the distracted nurses.

She followed Nicu through the arched corridor, fluorescent light panels buzzing above the scuffed green linoleum. It was almost cave-like. The layout of the public wards looked as if it hadn't changed since the seventeenth century — halls bookended by spiral staircases and nursing stations. As they passed closed wings stretching into shadowy recesses, Aimée wondered whether Nicu's confused expression, that twitch, was due entirely to his mother's illness; she sensed there was something else on his mind.

Ward C contained ten curtained partitions, a bed in each, some open, some closed. It smelled of disinfectant. Chipped white enamel bedpans hung from the wall, reminding her of men's starched shirts. She heard beeping machines; a snore rose from behind the curtains.

Nicu looked around, put his finger to his lips and then pulled back the curtains on the left.

Over his shoulder Aimée saw an empty hospital bed; on the rolling table sat a food tray with an untouched cup of bouillon, a skim of congealed fat floating on the surface.

"Maman?" He pulled at the blanket as if there might be a woman hidden under it. "Where is she?"

At a glance Aimée took in strewn sheets, an abandoned respiratory machine and a blank heart-rate monitor with wires trailing from it. Disconnected tubes dangled to the tiled floor.

"You're sure we're in the right ward, Nicu?"

Nicu held up a menu slip with her name, Drina Constantin — a check marked next to the clear liquid menu. "I don't understand. She was here an hour and a half ago. Less."

An emergency operation? Her breath skipped. Maybe they were too late.

"Gone for tests?" she said. "Or maybe a procedure?"

"They ran tests all afternoon," said Nicu. "Her fever spiked. She was gasping for breath. I thought the end was coming. She rallied somehow. Tonight she was so tired, the doctor wanted her to rest. Why would they move her?"

Worried, Aimée didn't know what to believe. It was all so strange — the young man waiting for her in the dark, the angry relatives, the missing patient. She still didn't know why she was here. Could René have been right, was this some kind of scam? Or had this frightened boy just lost his mother? Even if he had, what did it have to do with her?

The nursing station wasn't the hive of activity she expected. Two nurses sat, their pens clicking as they filled in charts.

A middle-aged nurse looked up, her twist of hair held in place by a chipped green hair clip that matched the walls of the well-worn facility. "How did you get in here?"

"Has my mother gone for an operation?" Nicu asked.

"I'll have to ask you to leave. Visiting hours are over," she said, her voice firm.

"After I see her," said Nicu, his eyes flashing. "Please check on Drina Constantin, Ward C. Was she sent for more tests or a CAT scan?"

"I remember you," the nurse said, her mouth pursed. "She's taken her medication and is resting for the night."

"My mother's gone."

"Monsieur, please leave before I have you escorted out." She shot a look at Aimée and added, "Both of you."

"Don't you understand?" Nicu said. "Her bed's empty. She didn't leave on her own — she can't walk."

"*Ce n'est pas possible,* Monsieur. You've made a mistake."

"No mistake," said Aimée, glancing down the dimly lit corridor. One empty gurney. A tight knot of dread was forming in her stomach. "Call security. Find her doctor."

"*Attendez,*" said the nurse, sounding unhappy and picking up the phone. "Let me verify with the staff."

Judging by the murmurs and looks passing between the nurses, something was off. Aimée sat on a cold plastic chair and watched the hands of the wall clock move. She tapped her sneaker on the green linoleum. Nicu paced, then sat down on the plastic seat next to hers.

"Nicu, what's so important that your mother has to talk to me now, after all these years? What was this about?"

Nicu shook his head, his eyes clouded with worry, or maybe fear. "All she said was that it had something to do with the murder of a detective named Leduc, who's your father, *non*?"

The mystery behind her father's death, in a bomb explosion in Place Vendôme, had never been solved. Just another dust-covered file in the bowels of the Brigade Criminelle. Over the years, the only lead had been a rumor; a plane crash in Libya took care of everyone involved, and there was no one left to ask.

Aimée felt her heart pounding. "Your mother knows who killed him? Did she give you a name?"

"No name."

She fought back the image flashing into her head, his charred limbs on paving stones, one lone shoe with a foot still inside. The horror flooded back. A sob erupted from deep inside her.

"Proof," Nicu said, "you need more proof that I'm telling you the truth, right?" He thrust his hands into his pockets and pulled out a crinkled black-and-white photo, tucked it in her hand. "Keep it."

A scene of her in knee-highs, looking up at a younger version of her father, smiling; behind them a market stall with a woman in a long skirt with a young boy holding a model airplane. Nicu looked about eight, Drina a little older than Aimée now. What year could this have been?

"Tell me more, Nicu."

"That's all I know. She needed to tell you herself. She insisted."

A trio of nurses assembled hurriedly around Aimée and Nicu as a thirty-something male doctor strode toward them. "Who unplugged the Ward C patient from the machines?" said the doctor, his brow furrowed. "Why did you take her off the medication drip? I want her chart."

"We have no record of her being moved," said the nurse with the green hair clip. She didn't look stern anymore.

"I don't understand how this patient could have been disconnected without my approval and knowledge. Check the wards, the whole floor."

"*Tout de suite,* Doctor Estienne," said the nurse, mobilizing the others with a wave of her arm.

"My mother was here an hour and a half ago," said Nicu. "Why didn't someone stay with her? How was it you didn't notice she was gone?"

Dr. Estienne stuck his stethoscope in his coat pocket. He put his hand on Nicu's shaking shoulder. "As soon as I find her chart —"

"What good will that do?" Nicu interrupted.

"*Ne t'inquiète pas,* young man," said Dr. Estienne, his voice measured and reassuring. "We'll sort this out."

Sort this out? But Aimée knew that tone — they taught it in med school, for use with hopeless cases.

"Doctor, when's Drina due her next medication?"

"I don't have her chart at the moment, Mademoiselle," he said, looking her in the eye before turning to Nicu. "I checked on your mother an hour ago, after her last meds. I wanted to monitor her pain level. She will most likely be due another dose in a few hours or so, and we will have found

45

her and everything will be back to normal by then."

"Her situation's critical," Aimée said. "As you should know. Didn't you run tests today? Her son deserves to know her prognosis."

"Mademoiselle, we don't receive crystal balls on graduating from med school."

"I learned that in my first year of med school, Doctor," she said, neglecting to add that it had also been her last year of med school. The formaldehyde smell of the dissection-lab fridge, with its human organs sitting side by side with student lunches, had cured her of any aspirations to a medical career. "What's her prognosis?" she repeated.

"We're concerned about possible renal failure," he said finally. "The hemodialysis was keeping her electrolytes out of the critical range. And I'm worried that with a heightened potassium level, she's facing a fatal heart-rhythm disturbance."

Good God. A hemodialysis patient yanked from the machine.

"You gave her meds an hour ago." Nicu seized the doctor's arm. "How long does she have if she doesn't get her next medication dose?"

"Young man, we'll have this under control

46

soon," he said, in that smooth voice again.

"And if you don't?"

But the doctor was nodding at the arriving orderlies. "Search the X-ray center and lab wing," he said to them, pointing down the corridor.

He turned away from them to consult with an arriving doctor. Aimée strained to catch snatches of their murmured conversation. "If she's kept stable . . . dosed at six-hour intervals . . . fifteen, eighteen hours before it's . . . irregular heart rhythm."

Aimée inserted herself between the two doctors. "Give me the best- and worst-case scenarios," she said, lowering her voice. "Please. I might have to prepare her son."

"Best-case scenario?" Dr. Estienne glanced back at Nicu. "His mother's terminal, an advanced stage of invasive cancer. We can help her to pass peacefully, control her pain over the next few days."

"What if she's not found? What would happen to her?"

The doctor looked at Nicu, then back at Aimée. "Not that this will happen. But the other scenario . . . ? *D'accord.* Without intervention, in ten to twelve hours there will be limb paralysis, then another few hours and her heart will start to fail. Twenty to twenty-two hours, development of de-

lirium. Twenty-four to twenty-eight, sponta-
neous hemorrhaging, the respiratory system,
vital organs shut down. I'm sorry, but there
will be nothing painless or peaceful about
it."

Aimée's throat caught. Her heart ached
for Nicu, and for this missing woman she
didn't remember knowing. Her father's
informer, she felt sure now. What could she
do?

"Him." The nurse pointed to Nicu's uncle,
who'd arrived, chest heaving, at the nursing
station, with the older woman and little girl
in tow. "That's him, the man who kept
threatening to discharge the patient."

The woman let out a cry and began to
beat her chest. She rocked back and forth
on her heels, weeping.

"Never trust hospitals." Nicu's uncle's
eyes narrowed. "I told you, Nicu. And Drina
alone here — in our tradition we never let
someone pass alone. Why didn't you tell me
earlier that she was here so we could come
keep vigil?"

"I didn't know how sick she was until last
night," he said. "Today she got worse, like
I've told you already." Hurt and resentment
simmered in his eyes.

"So you talked her into leaving?" asked

Dr. Estienne.

"Me? I haven't seen her." The uncle's voice was furious. "I've been trying to get *in,* not take her out."

"That's impossible, as I've been telling you, monsieur," said the nurse. "Hospital regulations forbid anyone after visiting hours."

"And now look what's happened." His uncle stepped toward the doctor. "May the spit in your eye dry up if you've killed her."

Aimée's gaze caught on an orderly who had appeared behind Nicu's uncle. He gave a quick shake of his head. "All patients accounted for except for one in Ward C, Doctor."

She could tell from the staff's faces that they were at a loss. Not good. She couldn't just stand here, listen to this wailing woman. She had to do something.

Amid the ensuing shouting match between Nicu's uncle and the staff, no one paid her any attention. She followed the corridor until it branched in two, one hallway heading toward the lobby, the other toward the staircase. Which way had Drina gone? Had someone bundled her out, somehow sneaking her past the reception desk? Beneath the staircase on the left was a door with an emergency-exit sign over it, but a large sign proclaimed that an alarm would go off if the door was opened.

She ran toward the lobby.

"Have you discharged anyone within the past hour?" she asked at the main reception.

The long-faced male receptionist looked up. "Visiting hours are over, Mademoiselle. I'm going to have to ask you to leave."

Just what she needed. Another by-the-book hospital administrator.

"We're looking for Drina Constantin," said Nicu, who had appeared, panting, at her elbow. "I'm her son."

"Visiting hours ended," the man repeated. "We follow regulations here for health and safety. Don't you people understand? I escorted a bunch of you out already, do I need to do it again?"

The receptionist's look said that he'd be damned if he helped her or a Gypsy.

"The patient's missing. There's an alert!" Aimée pointed to the red alarm light above them. As she did so, a loud buzzing began to sound. Down the hallway, she heard Dr. Estienne shouting to the nurses.

"Please be helpful, Monsieur," Aimée said. "A simple yes or no will do."

The receptionist sucked in his breath, checked the log. "Only two discharges this evening. Inter-hospital."

"You mean they were headed to another hospital in the Assistance Publique system?"

He nodded. "But her name's not on either one."

"Then how could she have left the hospital within the last hour? Don't you monitor patients?" Aimée glanced around. No video cameras, of course; why would they keep the technology up-to-date when they were shutting the hospital down next year?

Nonplussed, the receptionist nodded. "*Bien sûr.* But it's shift change, everyone's updating charts, finishing paperwork."

"That's your excuse?" Nicu pounded his fist on the desk.

"Describe your mother, Nicu," she said, trying to keep him calm. "Show the man a photo."

Nicu reached in his messenger bag and pulled out a photo ID, Drina Constantin's permit to work in the markets. On it Aimée saw an unsmiling woman with deep-set eyes and a strong jaw, her greying hair pulled back. She looked to be in her fifties, but her birth date said she was forty-three. How she'd aged.

"Have you seen her?"

The receptionist shook his head.

Aimée worked to keep her voice rational,

51

free of accusation. "How could a terminally ill woman, presumably in a wheelchair or on a gurney, get by you?" she asked.

"Wheelchairs and gurneys pass by here all the time," he said. "We've had several transfers in the last hour, as I told you. And the lobby was crowded with departing visitors and families."

That set her thinking. Someone had probably taken advantage of the departing visitors and the shift change to move Drina. Yet Nicu and his uncle had been arguing outside the hospital entrance when Aimée arrived — they would have noticed Drina leaving, which narrowed the window during which she could have passed through.

Her mind went back to the emergency exit behind the staircase. She thought of the dark, cave-like recesses in the hallways on either side. They'd be so easy to hide in for a short length of time.

"Has an emergency-exit alarm been set off near Ward C?"

The receptionist's eyes grew wide.

She needed to propel him into action. "Can you check with security?"

"*Mais non,* no alarm's gone off."

Suddenly she felt her post-pregnancy fog clear and her investigator's instincts finally kick in. What if Drina wanted to tell Aimée who killed her father, and the killer had abducted Drina to shut her up? Perhaps she'd known the secret was dangerous, and that was why she had refused to tell Nicu the whole story. She hadn't wanted to endanger her son.

Aimée drew Nicu aside to the window by a potted palm tree.

"How long were you out front talking to your uncle?" Aimée asked Nicu.

"Five, ten minutes, if that," he said. "I'd just arrived, so had he."

"So Drina disappeared between the time the doctor medicated her, an hour or so ago, and when we entered the ward." She scanned the courtyard through the glass doors. "Would your uncle lie?"

"Him? He lies for a living," said Nicu.

"I mean to you," she said. "Could he have taken her and then pretended he'd just arrived? Would he throw a fit to deflect suspicion?"

"My uncle's a lot of things, but he's no body snatcher," said Nicu. "Tradition insists if we can't bring the dying one back home, we bring the family to the dying one. You heard him." His worn sneaker tapped on the linoleum. "We observe rituals, seek forgiveness for any wrongs committed. That's why my uncle came. Maybe he

53

wanted to settle something before she passed to the next life."

Sounded like woo-woo to her. But what question did Nicu think might have been on his uncle's mind? "What do you mean?" she asked.

"My uncle and the rest of the family were estranged from my mother. Long story."

Aimée let that go for now. "Can you remember the last thing she told you?"

His dark eyes fixed on hers. "Tonight she was passing in and out of consciousness. At lucid moments she kept saying the *gadjo* had found her, that he was back."

"Gadjo?" The second time Aimée had heard that word.

"You. Outsiders." He fingered his bag strap. "And she kept saying your name. She tossed and turned, begging me to find you so she could let go, let her spirit travel."

Did the woman have a guilty conscience? Aimée believed what he was telling her. And that he knew more. "What else, Nicu?"

He hesitated. "It didn't make sense."

Aimée's tongue caught in her throat. She forced her mouth to open, to form words. "What didn't make sense? Did she tell you about my father's killer?"

Nicu shook his head. "I didn't understand."

"Tell me exactly what she told you."

"Her words came out garbled." He looked out the window at the sky, the few stars poking out between puffs of cloud. She saw his face shutting down again, as she'd seen it do before. Direct questions had only gotten her so far. "Look," he said finally, "she begged me to find you. That's all I know."

"To tell me who killed my father," she said. "Right? To make it right after all these years?" When he didn't respond, she asked, "Why now, after all this time?"

He chewed his lip. "I don't know. *Désolé.*"

She was frustrated, but she sensed that if Nicu had more to say, he would tell her in due time. However, he might be unaware of how much he knew.

Her father always told her that informers required maintenance. They came at a cost — the cost of withholding incriminating evidence from your colleagues on the force, of looking the other way or providing favors to keep them delivering. Sometimes all three.

"I believe you," she said, trying another tack. "I think she was one of my father's informants." She tried to keep the question out of her voice.

Nicu shrugged. He didn't deny it.

"You would have noticed things, I imagine. Little things. Maybe her behavior was different after my father's visits." Nicu averted his gaze. "But he trusted her, Nicu. Offered our help. He knew she kept her promises. That's what she's trying to do now."

Another shrug. Somehow she had to break through his anguish, the shock. She scanned the lobby — a few nurses, murmured conversations.

"The *gadjo* she talked about," she said, probing. "Who could she have meant? Maybe you'd seen him before? Can you remember?"

Again no response.

"I want to find her before it's too late," she said. "But I need your help. Give me something to work with. Who knows she's here, who did she last see, where does she live?"

She sensed a stillness in him. Thinking, or shutting down? She couldn't tell.

"You came to my house, asked for my help. You insisted I come here," she said. "Why don't you trust me now?"

He looked up. "She kept saying the *gadjo*'s back, that he had found her," said Nicu. "His murderer had found her. And in her next breath, your father's name."

Aimée shivered.

"Do you have any idea who she could have meant? Have you noticed any new people around, or why she'd be at risk?"

At first she thought he had shut down again, wasn't going to answer, but then he suddenly said, "Recently . . . I've felt like we've been followed a few times."

"Followed? By whom?"

He shook his head. "I don't know. I just . . . I could tell. Someone has been watching. A man."

Two uniformed *flics* had arrived and were speaking to the security guard in the hospital lobby. The guard pointed to Nicu. All she knew was that she had to figure out what had happened — to Drina, and to her father. How, she didn't know.

Aimée palmed her card into Nicu's shaking hand. "We need to talk, but not now. Call me after you talk to the *flics*." Nicu chewed his lip. "Can you do that?"

He nodded.

The two *flics* were working their way past orderlies toward Nicu.

Aimée kept her head down, got in step with a passing nurse and slipped out of the lobby and back down the corridor. Keeping to the wall, she reached Ward C.

The crumpled white sheets showed where a body had lain. Under the hospital bed, she noticed a blue ankle sock on the floor by the machines' dangling tubes. No other sign of a struggle.

A ball of dread was forming in her stomach. She fought off that old flashback again — but once more her mind flooded with images of her father's charred remains after the explosion on the blackened pavers of Place Vendôme. And now, just like then, she was arriving too late.

Out in the corridor, she hurried away from the nurses' station and to the emergency exit. She wrapped her scarf around her palm to avoid leaving fingerprints, and then covered her ear with her other hand and pushed the bar, waiting for the alarm's shriek to blast.

Silence, except for the nighttime trilling of a starling outside in the shadow-blurred hedge. Looking up she saw snipped wire sticking out from behind the exit sign above the door. Fat lot of good the security did here.

Her shoulders tightened. The abductor had known exactly what he or she was doing. Aimée followed the dark alleyway between buildings until she found herself under a narrow canopy of trees that led to one of the ancient courtyards adjoining the hospital wings. The tall trees rustled in the rising wind. At the far end, the courtyard opened to a narrow paved lane. Aimée quickened her step as an ambulance drove by, bathing her in a flashing blue light. When she reached the lane, she saw that it led to the open gates of the emergency entrance beyond.

She could barely make it out in the dark, but because she was looking for it, she spotted an empty wheelchair shoved into the bushes at the end of the walkway. She felt around its smooth metal frame, its padded arm rests, under the cushion. Nothing. She leaned down into the bushes, running her hands over the rubber wheels and metal spokes, until her fingernail caught on a piece of cloth wedged between the wheel and its guard. Tugged until she heard a rip as it came free. Half of a blue ankle sock, a match for the one under Drina's hospital bed.

Sunday, 10 P.M.

"Fifteen years ago, Mademoiselle Aimée?" said Martin, an old informer of her father's, as he gazed at the photo Nicu had given her. Martin adjusted his large tortoiseshell glasses on his nose. Dyed charcoal hair, skin too taut and unwrinkled for his age. Martin, she suspected, had had some work done since they'd last met.

Calculating roughly based on what she was wearing in the picture, Aimée had narrowed down the year Nicu's photo was taken to 1984. "Your father, bless his soul, had so much hair then. *Bien sûr,* I had more hair, too, Mademoiselle Aimée. We all did."

Martin had never forgotten her father, who'd helped him get out of prison before he'd served his full sentence. Aimée never asked for details. Martin had a mass said in her father's name and put flowers on his grave every year on November 1st, Toussaint, All Saints' Day.

She tapped her freshly lacquered "terabyte taupe" nails on the wood tabletop. They sat in Martin's "office," the only place he took appointments: on the red leather banquette in the back room at Le Drugstore on the Champs-Élysées. He would dispense his knowledge in his own good time. And for a price.

"*Merci,* François," said Martin to the waiter in a black vest and long white apron who served Aimée a steaming *chocolat chaud,* its deep mocha color pierced by a dollop of *crème.*

"Forgive me for missing Chloé's christening," Martin said. "But I'm getting over *un rhume;* wouldn't want to spread germs to the little one."

She slid her latest photo of Chloé over the table. "Six months old, mostly sleeping through the night. She has a fondness for puréed aubergine. Go figure."

Martin blew a kiss at the photo. A wide grin broke his pock-cratered cheeks. *"Qu'elle est belle!"*

"The onesie you sent her is her favorite," said Aimée.

His eyes softened behind the large lenses. "Your father's looking down on her."

If only, she thought. Maybe he was. How

many times in the past few months had she imagined him, a proud *grand-père,* pushing the stroller beside her in the Jardin du Luxembourg? Or the two of them strolling arm in arm on the quai, Chloé on her hip?

Move on. She needed to move on. But Nicu had brought it all back, and she had a promise to keep.

Le Drugstore's mirrors reflected a Manet-like scene of blurred streetlamps on the Champs-Élysées and tree branches bent in the wind. Aimée and Martin shared the back room with only one other couple. François hummed to himself, drying glasses at the counter. Cigarette smoke spiraled from Martin's unfiltered Gauloise. Aimée tried to stifle her craving: she couldn't risk a nicotine patch since she still nursed Chloé. Sixteen months and two days without a cigarette, and she still wanted to tear the Gauloise from his hand.

Martin had no cell phone; he arranged appointments from his "nerve center" — using the pay phone in the lounge downstairs by the WC. Four rings followed by two alerted the toilet attendant, *la dame pipi,* to an incoming request for Martin. He received his clients upstairs at his reserved table. His clientele ranged from ex-cons and gang leaders to prominent officials. A conduit for both sides, he bought, sold and bartered information. His expertise and contacts were too valuable for even the *flics* to compromise. Still, he'd told her once, he had the phone swept for bugs daily.

En route to Le Drugstore, she'd called Morbier for help, but her call had gone to voice mail. Elusive as always, screening his calls. No doubt out celebrating Chloé's christening *sans* her in a restaurant and couldn't hear the phone ringing. Or maybe he'd been angry with her for stopping on the curb with Nicu, delaying the party, or for making a scene with Melac, and planned on chewing her out later in private. Knowing Morbier, though, she figured on the latter.

Niceties over, Martin raised an eyebrow meaningfully at François, who nodded — they would not be disturbed. Martin leaned forward.

"You made an appointment, Mademoiselle Aimée?" Martin had given her fifteen minutes, his usual. And she couldn't leave René babysitting all night.

She gathered her courage. Martin never liked speaking about her father's death. "An informer of my father's, Drina Constantin, a Gypsy with a small son, remember her?"

Martin's eyes were hidden behind his

thick lenses and the smoke from the Gauloise. "My memory's not that good, Mademoiselle Aimée."

"You're too modest, Martin." His knowledge of the underworld was encyclopedic. And if he didn't know something, he knew someone who did. "Think back to 1984."

"Let's say I was otherwise occupied at that time."

In prison.

"D'accord." Aimée bit her lip. "I think Drina Constantin knows who killed Papa."

She watched Martin. Looked for a movement, a flicker of his eyes behind those framed glasses. But his eyes were as still as the glass they looked through.

But then Martin heard bigger secrets than that every night.

"Et alors?" he said.

"An hour and a half ago, Drina Constantin disappeared from Hôpital Laennec. Poof, gone." She told Martin the little she knew. "The woman can't walk, she's dying."

"A Gypsy scam, Mademoiselle Aimée," he said, relaxing against the back of the seat. Like *tout le monde,* Martin distrusted Gypsies. "These Romany scam artists have been flooding the country these last ten years. The Roma keep to themselves — they would never really bring an outsider into a family matter."

That much she'd witnessed from Uncle Radu's reaction. Martin had raised a sliver of doubt in her mind.

"You watch, someone is going to ask you for money — expensive medical treatments for your papa's old informer."

Her stomach twisted. Could Martin be right? Could that be why they'd brought her into this, exploited her vulnerability, her obsession with her father's death? A classic scam. Could she have been so naïve? But no — she shook off the prejudice and doubt that came to her so easily. These were people, suffering people, not scammers. Her gut instinct told her to trust Nicu, that he didn't lie about his mother's message. She believed that the woman had been abducted by someone who wished to keep her silent. What if other lives were in danger?

"Distrust goes both ways; to them we're the outsiders," she said, putting down her cup. "I was skeptical at first, too. But the woman's got terminal cancer, and someone pulled her off a hemodialysis machine. The doctor was alarmed; I heard more than concern in the staff's voices. Whatever happened to her, it wasn't Drina's choice, and I need to help her."

Martin tapped ash off his Gauloise, unimpressed. "So her son contacts you, out of the blue, after all these years, now that she's dying?"

Aimée raised her hand to stop him. "*Arrête,* Martin. Her son's terrified. I need to find her. Look at this picture again. Do you know anything about this woman?" She put Nicu's photo down by the ashtray containing his smoldering cigarette. Took a sip of her *chocolat chaud,* giving him a long moment to think.

"*Eh bien,* I remember that coat your father's wearing. *Ça fait vraiment longtemps.* Memories."

Something had clicked, she could tell.

"Think, Martin," she said. "Did Papa talk about a *manouche,* using her in an operation?"

A drag on his cigarette, a puff of exhaled smoke. "You're sure this Drina informed for him?"

She couldn't think of any other explanation, given her father's open offer of help on the back of his business card. And that Nicu had known her address. And that it felt like something her papa would do.

Aimée nodded and set down her cup. She scooped the lace of foam off the rim. Licked her spoon.

"There are five or six *manouche* families

all the rest are related to. *Gens du voyage* clans." Martin stared at the photo. "Do you know if she belonged to the Marseille branch, or Avignon, or Berry or those in Essonne?"

She shrugged.

"That's important — there might be territorial rivalries, an old feud," said Martin. "She could come from Montreuil, in the suburbs, or from the few smattered in the nineteenth arrondissement, or maybe north of Porte de Saint-Ouen. Or have ties to the Evangelical Protestant Gypsies clustered in Essonne."

Aimée remembered Essonne, thirty minutes on the train from Paris, with its patches of farmland, horses, a medieval church she'd visited on a school trip and enclaves of *gens du voyage.*

"Does she live in an encampment? Or travel, move around?"

"I don't know." She wanted to kick herself for not asking Nicu more — insisting he tell her where they lived, how they survived. Then she remembered Drina's ID. "She worked in the markets. That's all I know. Can you help me find her, Martin?" she said. "Where do I look next?"

His face was still impassive, but she knew she had engaged him. "Who steals a dying

Gypsy from a hospital other than her own clan?"

Under the table she pressed the envelope containing the francs she'd withdrawn from the ATM into his lap. "A *gadjo* who wants to keep a secret and cover up the past."

She exited the Métro at Pont Marie, her collar up against the wind blowing off the Seine, and crossed the bridge to Île Saint-Louis. Lights gleamed in her third-floor window on quai d'Anjou. Had Chloé woken up? Was she hungry?

By the time Aimée'd run up the worn marble stairs two at a time and unlocked the tall, carved door, all she could think about was that sneeze of Chloé's this morning. A full-blown cold now? Or worse?

She tossed her jacket and bag on the hall escritoire. "Is Chloé all right, René?"

But instead of René, it was Morbier who stood at the kitchen stove by the boiling kettle. Steam fogged the window overlooking the quai.

"Shhh. She's asleep." He wiped his nose with a handkerchief. "René enjoyed a little too much champagne, so when I came back to see you, I sent him home in a taxi. Shame about the celebration." Morbier pointed to a cup. "Join me for a tisane?"

Her jaw dropped. "Since when do you drink herbal tea?"

"Jeanne sticks the tea bags in my pocket," he said, pulling one out. Miles Davis looked up hopefully from beside his water dish, wagging his tail.

Morbier had trimmed down, visited the barber, even wore matching socks these days. His new squeeze had accomplished miracles. He handed Aimée a cup.

"Your hands feel like ice, Morbier," she said.

"Cold hands, warm heart," he said, not missing a beat.

She was braced for an onslaught, but she felt too tired to deal with his disapproval after the church scene. It all streamed back: the shock of Melac's arrival; the flicker of joy she'd felt turning into humiliation when she realized he'd brought his new woman; the creeping fear of watching that woman hold her daughter; Melac's talk of custody and lawyers — it all swirled in her head. How dare he threaten her? Why couldn't he . . . but she didn't even know what she wanted from him anymore. Once she'd hoped he could be a father for the occasional weekend, but he'd disappeared from her life, and she'd shut the door on him. He hadn't come knocking until now.

Her outrage bubbled up again; she wanted to kick something.

"Don't start on me about Melac," she warned Morbier. "Not you. Not now."

"Who said I would?" He jutted out his chin. "Dig your own hole, Leduc."

Helpful as usual.

The tisane burnt her tongue, and she set down the cup. "I'm finding a lawyer," she said.

"Good," he said. She'd expected recriminations, arguments about the benefits of shared custody and how much the baby needed a father figure, but instead Morbier said, "I've been hearing things about his new woman."

Aimée blinked. Melac wasn't on the up-and-up.

"Make sure you hire a family-law specialist," said Morbier. "Like this one."

He pulled out his notebook, tore out a page with the name Annick Benosh written above a phone number and an address in the 8th.

Aimée stared at the paper on the counter. "Can I afford her?"

"I'd say you can't afford not to hire her."

Touched, she noticed the look on his face. One she hadn't seen in a long time. His guard was down; emotion welled in his eyes.

"Get smart, Leduc. For once. My great-goddaughter's involved." He dipped his steaming teabag several times. "And if anything happens to me, *alors,* there's something set aside for Chloé."

"Happens to you, Morbier? You're not threatening retirement again?"

But she knew that wasn't what he meant. If only they got along better. If only she didn't always feel like a child with him. He had been the only constant in her life since her father died.

She hugged him. Hadn't hugged him like that since she couldn't remember when. Inhaled that Morbier muskiness, so familiar from her childhood: the smell of wool, a trace of unfiltered Gauloise and — *mon Dieu* — something new. She sniffed.

"Is that Eau Sauvage, by Dior?" She sniffed again. "Another gift from Jeanne?"

He shrugged. "*Ce n'est rien,* just some experimentation with my fragrance palate."

"Fragrance palate?" Did he even know what that meant?

His thick eyebrows drew down in irritation. "It's all to do with the body's chemistry. Olfactory stimulation."

Her jaw dropped again. "Next you'll be taking vitamins, mixing protein shakes and

71

doing yoga." And the world would spin off its axis.

He stretched both hands in the air, reached for the ceiling. "They call this the *talasana,* or palm tree pose."

"Really? Yoga?" She caught herself before she said, "At your age?"

"No age limit, according to the instructor." Why did she always forget his uncanny skill for reading her mind at the most awkward moments?

"Tisane, Dior *eau de cologne* and now yoga. Wonders never cease." Or maybe he was just getting in shape to impress the sexy grandmothers at Chloé's playground. She grinned but quickly hid it. Time to be serious. She needed to find out if he knew anything that might help her find Drina Constantin. "Who do you know at the *commissariat central* in the seventh, Morbier? Does Jojo still man the desk on rue Peronnet?"

"What trouble have you gotten yourself into this time, Leduc? Does this have anything to do with the Gypsy-looking boy you were talking to after the christening?" He looked at her and shook his head. "Does it?"

She nodded.

"Go on, what happened, Leduc?" He

sighed and sipped his tisane.

Standing next to him at the counter, she told him about Nicu and Drina. Held back the meeting with Martin. After all, Morbier was a *commissaire divisionaire* and Martin an ex-con and private informer.

"Leave it alone. What's the point of bringing all this up again, Leduc?"

"A dying woman's abducted from a hospital and new information about Papa is hitting me in the face. What am I supposed to do, ignore it? Let Papa's murderer go unpunished?" she said. She slammed her hands on the counter. "Let the murderer evade justice again?"

Morbier put his cup down and shrugged. His profile was dark against the window overlooking the Seine and the quai's globe streetlamps.

"Morbier, you were Papa's first partner on the beat. Did you know this woman? Have you heard of Drina Constantin?"

"*Putain,* Leduc. Say this woman did inform for him. We had tons of informers," he said. "Why connect her to him years later? Doesn't make sense."

"She's the one who made the connection — maybe a secret she needs to get off her chest before she dies?" she said. "Some Gypsy code of honor — I don't know."

"She thinks of you while she's lying on her deathbed, Leduc?" Skepticism filled Morbier's voice.

"But someone else thought it was important, too. Someone else cares enough to try to shut her up."

"Gypsy culture's a law unto itself," said Morbier. He squeezed the teabag with his spoon. "We're talking professional thieves here. You can't believe they wouldn't steal a person if they wanted to."

Typical. The easy way out. Aimée remembered *Le Parisien*'s article the week before about police crackdowns on Gypsy enclaves.

She'd seen the encampments of *gens du voyage* off the RER B line, tin shacks hugging the rail lines, the laundry hanging from trees, the lean-tos on the other side of the *périphérique* near the Stade de France — mostly refugee Roma, the Eastern European Gypsies. Sad.

"I know the prefecture mandates workshops on the dangers of discrimination, how to avoid racial profiling," she said. "Have you been skipping those seminars again?"

"Missing the point as usual, Leduc. There's a time to realize when things are best left alone," he said, his voice thick. "There's nothing you can do for this woman, or for your father. Move on. You've got Chloé now. That's what he would want, you know that."

She knew. "But Papa offered her his help. My help. Look." She thrust her father's card in his palm. "Papa always said a person's only as good as their word." Over his wine glass, standing on this exact spot in the kitchen, a week before the explosion.

Morbier averted his eyes. "A promise made years ago? Grow up, Leduc."

Aimée winced. Why couldn't Morbier understand?

"Were you at the bombing? Did you find his melted glasses, his charred —" Her throat caught. She rubbed the burn mark on her palm, the scar had been imprinted from the smoldering van's door handle. "*Mais non,* you were . . . you were . . ." She couldn't finish the sentence. A no-show at the morgue, at the pitiful funeral. "Where were you, Morbier?"

He leaned on the counter, his fists clenched, the knuckles white. "I don't want you to get hurt. It's complicated . . ."

"Complicated how, Morbier? Isn't it about time you told me?"

But Morbier's chest heaved. He grabbed at his cup on the counter, missing and sending it clattering on the wood parquet.

"You all right?"

"Indigestion."

A cry pierced the warm kitchen air, making them both jump. It was followed by a second. The baby monitor; it was right there on the counter. She could hear Chloé's sobs, the crib springs creaking.

"We've woken her up, Leduc," said Morbier. The color had drained from his face.

Alarmed, Aimée wondered if he could be having a heart attack. "Any chest pains? Shortness of breath?"

"Leave it, Leduc. I'm fine."

"Sit down, for God's sake." She pushed Chloé's high chair aside and helped him onto the kitchen step stool. Chloé's wails rose from the counter, escalating in pitch. "Put your arms up."

"Take care of Chloé, Leduc," he said, catching his breath. "Your daughter needs you. Before you go: I'll ask around on one condition."

"What's that?"

"You keep your nose out of it, *d'accord*?" he said. "If you want my help, then it's on my terms, Leduc."

As if she wouldn't do her own nosing around. Aimée nodded.

His phone was vibrating on the counter as he waved her off.

Aimée found Chloé in a wet diaper and

tangled blanket. The window was open, and the room was cold. Chloé could catch a chill.

How could Morbier leave the damn window open in April? She was spitting mad until she remembered. Disorientation was a classic heart-attack symptom.

She took off the sopping diaper, swept up her daughter and wrapped her in a fresh blanket, kissing her tears away as she hurried to the kitchen.

"Hold on, Morbier, I'm just changing Chloé and then we'll call the doctor . . . Morbier?"

No answer.

With Chloé clutched to her hip, Aimée found the kitchen warm and empty. She rubbed her finger on the fogged window to clear it but saw only a spotlit cone of mist under the yellow sodium lamp on the empty, cobbled quai.

On the piece of paper with the attorney's name on it, Morbier had written a message: *Get your priorities straight.*

Sunday, 11 P.M.

Nicu felt someone shaking his shoulder, pulling him from his nightmare. He blinked awake, sitting up on the hard bench in Hôpital Laennec's chapel. Before him stood a white-coated hospital attendant and a blue-uniformed *flic.*

"Nicu Constantin?"

He nodded. Rubbed his eyes. "You found Maman?"

"We'd like you to come with us," said the *flic,* before saying into a small microphone clipped to his collar, "Got him."

Fear rippled through the hair on Nicu's neck.

"What's going on?" He grabbed his bag. "Is she all right?"

"Par ici, Monsieur."

The *flic* took hold of his arm.

They led him down the hospital corridor. He heard footsteps and the clatter of medication trolleys. A gurney whooshed past covered in bloodstained sheets.

With mounting anxiety he realized they weren't going toward Ward C. They'd descended a deep flight of stone steps. "You found her? Is she hurt?"

"This way, *s'il vous plaît.*" The *flic* and attendant escorted him through swinging double doors to a grey, tiled hallway. They stopped at a wide, scuffed grey door. The sign above it read MORGUE.

Mon Dieu, he thought, they'd found her too late. His stomach dropped, a heaviness like stone filled him. Apart from a curtained window, the bare room resembled a prison cell. Nicu wanted to escape.

"We'd like you to identify her and answer some questions."

"*Non, non!* It's all my fault . . ." A sob caught in his throat.

The *flic,* his grip still on Nicu's arm, looked up as the door pinged open. Instead of a doctor or a priest, a man in a leather jacket appeared, took the unlit cigarette from his mouth and stuck it behind his ear. "*Pardonnez-moi,*" he said. "Please proceed."

The attendant nodded to Nicu. "Ready?"

"Oh, I think he's ready," said the man. The cigarette nestled under a brown curl wedged behind his ear. "Go ahead."

79

Nicu's hands shook. Cold, so cold in here. A priest glided in, nodded to him.

The attendant parted the curtain. Behind the glass Nicu saw a mound covered in a sheet with only the face exposed. The stark light exposed an older woman's closed eyes, her sallow cheeks and mouth sunken in death.

Nicu blinked. "Who's this?"

"We think you know, Nicu," said the man, then inspected his fingernails. He rubbed his thumbnail on his pinkie's cuticle. "I'm Captain Ponchet. The *Père*'s here if you want to make confession. To confess how you killed your mother. A mercy killing, isn't that what you said to the doctor?"

Nicu's mouth dropped open. "What?"

"Get if off your chest, Nicu. You'll feel better." Ponchet took a step toward him.

"But this isn't my mother."

"You just said, 'It's all my fault.' I heard you. Now that'd be a good place to start."

"There's been a mistake." Nicu's stomach churned. "I meant it was my fault I didn't make her visit the doctor sooner. But I had no idea how ill and weak she'd become."

"So you helped her on her last journey," Ponchet said. "You're one of those *gens du voyage,* travelers, *non?* Gypsy culture has no room for the sick, the aged. No room in the caravan."

One more *flic* who, just like the rest, subscribed to the stereotype that *manouches* all belonged to organized crime clans. *Flics* hated Gypsies — the ones they dealt with stole, begged, pickpocketed and ran cons. People like Nicu's Uncle Radu. It was like that old joke: How do you bake a Gypsy cake? First you steal twelve eggs.

"I don't know who this poor woman is. Quit wasting my time." He read in their faces that they didn't believe him. He was just another Gypsy, another criminal to be contained by whatever means necessary.

"I'm afraid, Nicu, that this medical chart we found with her says this is your mother."

"Then there's a mistake!" He was yelling now. His shoulders were shaking, heat spreading up his neck. "Someone stole my mother's chart and planted it on this woman. Don't you understand? It's some kind of setup. The DNA will tell you. My mother's dying somewhere. She needs hemodialysis."

"She died by strangulation." Ponchet's eyes were like hard, brown stone. "Even in a terminally ill victim, we call that murder."

Fear collected in the pit of his stomach.

"My mother's forty-three. This poor woman looks eighty." Nicu clenched his

81

fists. "Where's my Uncle Radu?"

"I've seen your police record, Nicu," said Ponchet. "This will go better for you if you help us." Ponchet nodded to the uniformed *flic.* Handcuffs were clamped around Nicu's wrists. "You can tell us more at the *commissariat.*"

Jail. Not again. They'd beat him up, let him rot in the cell. Uncontrollable shaking overcame him.

The door opened on his Uncle Radu, escorted by a *flic.*

Radu took in the scene, his eyes brimming as he walked to the viewing window. He took off his fedora, then shook his head.

"I thought you found my sister," he said. "Who's this? Why the handcuffs on Nicu?"

Nicu turned to the priest. "Father, you're a man of God. Is this right?"

The priest, a young man, shrugged. "Captain Ponchet, two members of Drina Constantin's family can't identify this woman as Drina Constantin. It's not my place, but under the circumstances, I'd suggest you release this young man."

Ponchet's mouth tightened. He pulled the cigarette from behind his ear, rolled it between his thick fingers, nodded to the other *flic.* "Good point, Father. Release him. For now."

Nicu heard the click and felt the metal handcuffs tug, then loosen. He rubbed his wrists.

"Do your job," Nicu said to Ponchet. "Find her."

But Ponchet had his phone to his ear.

His uncle put on his fedora. "When did the *flics* ever do anything for us?" he spat. "We'll take care of it our way."

Monday Morning

Priorities. Aimée had priorities. Right now they boiled down to loading Chloé's baby bag for shared care, finding a project proposal she'd misplaced and getting dressed. All in ten minutes. Her cell beeped.

Merde! Where had she left it? Chloé, lying in the middle of the duvet on Aimée's bed, laughed with delight as Miles Davis licked her toes. They played this game all the time. Over the birds chirping outside the open window and Chloé's dulcet burbling, Aimée traced her phone to her leather motorcycle jacket pocket.

She saw a voice message received last night after she'd fallen asleep. *Merde* again! She hit play. Nicu's voice trembled. "The police tried to frame me." Panting. ". . . done nothing and she's still missing." His voice was low. "When we were followed . . ." Shouts and banging in the background drowned out his words. "Please meet me —"

The message cut off. Where was he?

She hit callback. But a France Telecom recording came on, telling her, "This number does not accept calls."

Her fingers tightened on her cell phone. She was worried. She wished to God she'd spoken with him last night. Had he been followed and framed by whoever took his mother?

Morbier didn't answer. *Merde, merde, merde* again. She left him a message.

She cleaned up Chloé's apricot-smeared chin, spooned horse meat from the butcher's white-paper packet into Miles Davis's bowl. By the time that was done, she knew she couldn't wait until Morbier responded. With no other lead to Nicu, she'd go to the hospital before starting her first official day back in the office.

Ten minutes later, clad in black leather pants, a silk YSL blouse (a flea-market find) and a flounced three-quarter-length wool coat by Jean Paul Gaultier, she locked the front door. Thank God the coat fit her again. Chloé, slung in the carrier on her back, drooled on her collar. "Babette's taking care of you today, *ma puce*. You remember, we talked about this."

85

She'd worked out an arrangement with Babette, her concierge's twenty-something niece, who also took care of Gabrielle, the six-month-old daughter of the new family across the courtyard. Now that Aimée was going back to work full-time, they would share care in a *garde à domicile* arrangement, alternating apartments. This week, Babette would watch the babies at Gabrielle's apartment, and her aunt, Madame Cachou, would take Miles Davis on his walks. On Babette's Wednesday afternoons off, Aimée and René would take turns, or bring Chloé to the office. Between Babette and Madame Cachou, Aimée would have backup coverage if she needed to work late. Like tonight for surveillance, Babette would take her after-hours at Aimée's place.

The carved door in the flat above the carriage house opened for them. Butter smells wafted out. A cat slinked a velvet tail across her ankles.

Chloé smiled in delight as they passed a colorful, dancing mobile. Babette, her hair up in a ponytail and an apron over her jeans, beckoned them inside with a breathy *bonjour,* followed by "Hungry?" In the light-filled, stainless-steel state-of-the art kitchen sat a bowl of ripe strawberries — small, fragrant *gariguettes,* just in season.

Aimée put Chloé in the high chair adjoining Gabrielle's. Two peas in a pod — one with light brown hair, one blonde.

" 'Don't sugar the strawberries,' my mother used to say," Babette said as Aimée set down Chloé's baby bag — biscuits, diapers, clothes and milk she'd pumped for tonight.

"My grandmother did too," said Aimée, catching the meaning behind the saying. "Is there a problem?" Already? It was only the first day of their arrangement. Babette had babysat for Aimée before and Chloé had loved her. Aimée dreaded a search for a new caregiver; this would have been so convenient and reasonable.

"Can you pick Chloé up by five on Fridays?" Babette said. "I'm taking a class. Just until June."

Aimée breathed a silent sigh of relief. That was all. *"Bien sûr."* She'd have to write that down. "Hope you brought extra bottles for tonight, just in case," said Babette.

Aimée nodded. "If surveillance runs late, I'll call."

She nuzzled Chloé, inhaling her freshly powdered baby smell. "I'd like to stay and play with you, *ma puce.*"

"Maman's off to work," said Babette, lifting Chloé's fist to wave. Aimée kissed her once more and left, riding out a powerful stab of regret.

In the courtyard she replayed Nicu's voice mail. Chilling. Could he have been calling from the hospital? She tried the number for the hospital's reception, and they put her on hold, then requested she call back after rounds. Great.

Her scooter was still in the shop, and wouldn't be ready for another fifteen minutes, so she stopped at the corner café.

"Un express double," she said to Fantine, the Normandaise wife of the owner's son, who helped out from time to time.

Fantine knocked the coffee grounds into the bin with several loud thumps and switched on the espresso machine. "Need an extra jolt? Powder not enough for you this morning?"

The street term for cocaine. Where did that come from?

Fantine pointed to her nose. Aimée rubbed the tip and her finger came back white. Babette had forgotten to tell her.

"Baby powder, Fantine." She smelled her fingers: Chloé's sweet baby smell. A pang hit her.

"Alors, you've lost weight. Look tired these days."

"It's called having a six-month-old," she said.

Aimée pulled out her LeClerc compact to touch up her face. Her dark-circle disaster needed more than quick first aid. At this rate she'd need to buy concealer wholesale and spackle it on.

"So Chloé's with a babysitter today? That Babette?"

Why did she always forget what a village it was here? And Fantine was nosey for a Normandaise — unlike the majority of those phlegmatic apple growers, notorious for their closed lips.

Fantine slid the steaming demitasse over the counter. "*C'est dur,* by yourself and all," she said as Aimée stirred sugar lumps into the espresso. "Your ex — the ex-*flic,* that one — he was going on about it last night. Said you kicked him out of the christening."

Aimée dropped the spoon. Hot brown spatters flecked her wrist. She licked them off.

"He stopped for a drink with his new woman," said Fantine, wiping the counter. Her small eyes gleamed. The gossip queen. Playing a part in what she saw as the soap opera that was Aimée's life. "That red-haired nurse."

Aimée winced thinking of Donatine's greedy arms holding Chloé.

"Sounds *merveilleux,* their farm in Brittany, sharing custody."

So Melac had hatched a plan, goaded on by Donatine. Hadn't Morbier said he'd heard things about her?

Fantine was watching Aimée for a reaction. She'd be damned if she gave her the satisfaction.

"So they like Brittany, eh?" Aimée smiled, her knuckles clenched below the counter.

"The only crime there is poaching, the air's clean and great for children, Donatine kept saying."

They were on a first-name basis, it seemed.

"Did they ask you about me, Fantine?"

She shrugged. "*Eh bien,* you know me." Fantine ran her forefinger across her mouth as if zipping it. "Melac helped my brother with that fiasco a while ago. Kept it quiet. But I keep clients' confidences."

Like hell she did. Aimée was about to tell her off when the Stella Artois deliveryman interrupted and Fantine disappeared down into the cellar.

Talk about a gossip — suggesting she coked up before work, looked too tired to handle her baby. All fodder for Melac. But

Aimée couldn't let it get under her skin. She downed her espresso, slid some francs across the counter and pulled out the lawyer's information. As she left the café to head toward the garage, she punched in the number Morbier had written down. Only an answering service.

Merde. She left a message for the lawyer, then another for René at Leduc Detective confirming their scheduled lunch meeting with a potential client — a lucrative one he had been salivating over. She had to keep the accounts and René happy. Couldn't let the search for this Gypsy derail her priorities.

Let Morbier think she'd listened to him.

Last night after she'd tucked Chloé into her crib, she'd made notes in her red Moleskine notebook, trying to come up with a plan. Right now she only had Nicu to go on, but he hadn't said much and his message worried her.

"Installed a new spark plug," said her mechanic at the garage on the tip of Île Saint-Louis when she returned the loaner. "You're good to go." He always said that.

"Merci."

Opening the scooter's seat, she took out her leather gloves and pulled them on against the morning chill. She walked her scooter over one-way Pont de Sully to the Left Bank, then keyed the scooter's ignition and drove along the river. She watched the long quai change names, growing posher as she passed through the arrondissements: from de la Tournelle to de Montebello in the 5th, to des Grands Augustins and de Conti in the 6th and Voltaire in the 7th, then Anatole France, until it became the quai d'Orsay alongside l'Assemblée Nationale; and further on, the not-so-secret Centre d'Écoute, the wiretapping center.

Always start from the target's last known location — a dictum drilled into her by her father. She'd see if she could find Nicu, and while she was there, she would check for possible witnesses to Drina's abduction.

Taking the long way round to the rear of Hôpital Laennec, she reached the ambulance entrance off rue Vaneau connected via Impasse Oudinot. Off the narrow *allée in* the hospital grounds were tucked small blossoming courtyard gardens where patients in wheelchairs soaked up the chance sunshine. An ambulance was parked with its doors open, a gurney being lifted out. The wheeled legs clicked into place, and Aimée heard rubber tires bump over the damp cobbles. She parked her scooter.

The ambulance attendant, a woman,

closed the van's back doors. Her arms were muscular in her white uniform, her short reddish hair pinned back.

"*Bonjour.*" Aimée flipped open her father's police ID, which she had doctored with her photo and name. "I'm following up on last night's patient abduction. You might have answered questions already . . ."

"*Moi?* No one talked to me."

Aimée seethed. The *flics* on top of it, as usual.

"But I heard. Terrible," said Lana, which Aimée had read on her badge. "Matter of fact, it must have happened on our shift."

Good, a talker.

"Can you run down your timeline from last night? We know two patients were discharged . . ." *Merde,* what term had the receptionist used? ". . . inter-hospital. May I see your log?"

"Inside."

In a cubbyhole of an office, which they reached by Gothic-like stone stairs, Lana pointed to an open binder. "*Voilà.* Last night at eight oh five P.M. Monsieur Dracquet was taken to Résidence Sans Souci, a fancy name for the nursing home we're partnered with in Montrouge. Then at eight-forty, Mademoiselle Ribera was taken to Hôpital Lariboisière."

"Is that usual?" Aimée asked. "I mean late-night transfers to other medical facilities?"

"Depends." Lana shrugged. "If the nursing homes get behind on paperwork, they might only be able to accept transfers late in the day. Or if a patient has an early-morning procedure, which was the case with that old spinster Mademoiselle Ribera."

That didn't interest Aimée, but it did show Lana's observation skills.

"Did you notice anything out of the ordinary last night?" she asked, pretending to consult notes in her red Moleskine. "An orderly hanging around, for example?"

Lana looked at the log and thought. "We kept the gates open, that's right, because of the two transfers. Other than that, the *quartier*'s quiet as a tomb at night. *Alors,* with all the ministries, embassies and you lot patrolling . . ."

She paused.

"Go on, Lana. You thought of something, didn't you?"

"It's nothing. We see them all the time."

"See what?"

"Like I said, nothing, but . . ."

Spit it out, Aimée wanted to say.

"There was a black car blocking the *impasse egress* onto rue Vaneau."

94

"Wait a minute, you mean blocking the ambulance exit?"

"I had to honk, which we don't usually have to do."

"Black. You're sure? Not a brown Mercedes?"

Lana tapped her short-nailed index finger on the log as if trying to jog her memory. "Black, tinted windows, anonymous looking. That's right," she said. "Rue Vaneau's a one-way street, it's quiet and that rarely happens, that's all."

"Did you see the driver, or do you remember anything distinctive?"

"I wish I had. *Désolée.* I'm working a double shift since last night." Lana was waving to someone in the courtyard. "That's my boyfriend, Naftali." She grinned. "Eighty-five years old, a charmer with a pacemaker. I call him my boyfriend to keep my husband on his toes."

"And what time did you honk at the car?"

Lana pointed to the log. "Eight forty P.M., when I left with the old spinster."

The timing fit with Drina's abduction.

"Merci," Aimée said. "Does your boyfriend's room overlook the *allée*?"

"Try asking him. His hearing's gone, but he sees like a hawk."

95

Naftali, one for the ladies despite his wheel-chair and his pacemaker, gestured her to sit close to him when she introduced herself. He had thick, snow-white hair, charcoal brows and bright green, watering eyes. He grabbed her hand and winked. "Let's make Lana jealous."

Aimée grinned and planted a kiss on his leathery cheek. His hearing seemed fine. "Only if you tell me what you saw last night."

"Saw? I saw everything. I don't sleep much." Naftali noticed her look. "Like a lot of old people, you're thinking."

"Lack of beauty sleep hasn't harmed your looks, Naftali," she said, squeezing his hand. She realized that one of his green eyes never moved. A glass eye. Great.

"Ah, Mademoiselle, you are as *charmante* as my first wife, Rosa, may the Lord take good care of her," he said, beating a gnarled fist against his heart. "But an old fart like me, I haven't had a full eight hours since before the camps."

A faded tattoo of a number showed on his inner arm, below the rolled-up sleeve of his robe. A survivor.

"It was the screaming, you see . . ." Naftali's words trailed in the air, and Aimée braced herself for another sad story of the dark times, as her grandfather had called the German occupation.

"That woman screaming in Romany," Naftali was saying. "I know, because I speak a little Romany myself."

She moved closer. "Last night, you mean?"

His good, watery eye looked far away.

"In my day the *manouches — les Tziganes, les Roms, les Sintis, les Ziganers, les gens du voyage,* whatever you call them — lived in *des roulottes.*"

"You mean wagons with wheels? Caravans, trailers?"

"C'est ça." He nodded. "Back then, during the war, whole families of *nomades* were rounded up by the French Vichy gendarmerie and put into some flimsy barracks at Montreuil-Bellay, in the Loire Valley," he said. "Me too — I got caught in Nantes along with a bunch of Republican Spaniards escaping Franco, white Russians and *clochards.*"

She squeezed Naftali's hand. Hoped this led somewhere.

"They branded us asocial types, misfits, and administered the camp under a 1940 *décret* signed by the last president of the

Troisième République," he said. "The Nazis could have taken notes: electrified barbed wire, no heat or sanitation. The camp was stuck in a field, no trees. Nothing but dirt and mud in the winter."

"That's how you picked up some Romany, Naftali?" she said, gently trying to steer him back on track.

"I had to keep my mind active," he said. "Or I'd give up."

"So what did you hear? Can you tell me about last night, Naftali? Could you understand?"

"*Les manouches* live in the moment. Incredible people." Naftali sighed and shook his head. "They sang. They shared food, the little they had. I'll never forget that. Or their loyalty. Only a quarter survived the extermination camps the Germans sent them to. *Les manouches* call it *Porajmos* — the devouring. But who even talks about them? It's always about us Jews."

A male nurse approached. "Naftali, time for your tête-à-tête with Doctor Sonia."

Naftali smiled, his mood broken. "*Zut!* But what do I have to complain about, eh? My doctor's blonde, thirty-two, legs like Bardot.

"But what did you hear last night, Naftali?"

"Ah, the bird flies into the house."

Riddles, the man spoke in riddles. But she had to keep prodding if he'd heard Drina last night.

"*Mais* didn't you say you heard the woman screaming in Romany? What was she saying?"

He shrugged his frail shoulders. "At first I thought I'd dreamed hearing that, but I don't sleep much."

The nurse leaned over, listening as he tucked Naftali's blanket into the wheelchair.

"Can you remember anything you heard, Naftali?"

"Scratch a *manouche* and you'll find superstition," he said, patting her hand, then letting it go. A deeper sigh. "When the crows in the field circled close, *les manouches* shooed them away, yelling to scare off the spirits. To them, a bird flying into the house brought death."

How did that make sense? Naftali's attention caught on the scudding clouds overhead as the nurse bent to release the wheelchair brake.

"Naftali, please try to remember," she said, touching his thin, blue-veined wrist. "A *manouche* woman was abducted from Ward C last night. I think you heard her. It's important."

"You mean a kidnapping?" He raised his shrunken left shoulder and leaned on the chair's armrest. "She was screaming about the birds, and that the boy needs to know . . . what was it? The . . . *non,* that's it . . . the boy Nicu needs to know the truth."

"Confidentiality precludes my discussing a patient or their treatment," said a young doctor. A different one.

Aimée set down her oversized Jackie O sunglasses on the desk in his office in the hospital. "But the patient's missing, Doctor. She was pulled off a hemodialysis machine. Every hour is crucial."

He checked his files. "I don't see her chart."

This wasn't working. She'd try another way in — stretch the truth. "Drina Constantin's grief-stricken son, Nicu, hired me to find his mother."

"Hired you?"

She slipped her Leduc Detective card over the desk, which was piled high with reports. "Abductions and kidnapping are my forte." She paused. "Have you seen him this morning?"

"No visitors allowed in the morning, Mademoiselle."

Where was Nicu? What could she say next?

"You wouldn't want your hospital's negligence pointed out, its credentials called into question."

He snorted. "You're threatening the Laennec, a hospital that's closing next year, Mademoiselle —" He looked at the card. "— Leduc? Confer with the police in charge of the investigation, not me."

As helpful as the reception staff.

"But Drina Constantin's life's in danger," she said. "Time is of the essence. How long can she last without hemodialysis?"

"Not for me to say." He shook his head. "Doctor Estienne, the attending physician last night, has gone off shift. Look, I shouldn't be talking to you." His pager bleeped.

"We know the abduction occurred during shift change."

"Again, I'm not the one to talk to. Doctor Estienne was in charge."

He looked at his watch. She had to stall, to get something from him. A knock came from the open door — a trio of interns stood there, charts in hand.

"We're ready, Doctor."

"Time for my rounds."

He stood up. Now she'd lost him. One last try.

"Look, I spoke with Doctor Estienne last

night, after the abduction." True. "He stressed the hospital staff would help in any way possible." Not so true. "He's more than concerned." Another lie.

He paused in the doorway. "Talk to Marie Fourcy, our public-health liaison." As Aimée joined him at the door, he beckoned to a small-boned black-haired woman with an aquiline nose who was talking to staff in the hallway. The woman, who reminded Aimée of a sparrow, broke off from the group and joined them.

The young doctor hurried away as soon as he had introduced the two women and explained Aimée's concerns.

"We've sent an alert to all facilities in the system for Drina Constantin," Marie said, repeating the party line back in the doctor's office. "As soon as she shows up, we'll be notified."

Aimée wondered what the chances of that were. "Have you spoken with her son, Nicu?"

"Her son? I haven't seen him, Mademoiselle." Marie glanced at the reports on the desk. "But from what the *flics* told me, you'll get nothing out of him, unless it's something he wants you to know. People like him send people like you in circles."

No sympathy there. But Aimée'd get

nowhere fast if she accused Marie of prejudice. She'd have to try something else.

"Marie, can you help me understand some
things here? I don't get why Nicu would
have brought his mother to this hospital unless they lived in the *quartier.*"

"Gypsies, here in the seventh? With the
prime minister?"

She'd wondered that too.

Marie rubbed her brow. "*Bien sûr,* we
maintain our public ward, as all hospitals
do. Laennec was founded as a hospital for
incurables." Marie shrugged. "My job's
coordinating public health outreach," she
said, by rote, it seemed to Aimée. "The
more integrated and assimilated *manouches*
are musicians or those working the markets."

Markets. She remembered Drina Constantin's market-vendor ID from last night.

"I need Drina Constantin's address."

"I can't give you that, of course," Marie
said. "Her son hasn't given it to you? I'm
not surprised. Even the integrated Gypsies
take off in a moment. Roaming's in their
blood."

Some public-health liaison this Marie was.
"The alarm wires to the back fire-exit door
of Ward C were severed last night," Aimée
said, pretending to consult her Moleskine,

103

which she'd opened to her to-do list. "One of Drina's socks was found beside a wheelchair that had been abandoned near the emergency entrance at the back of the hospital. It's clear that Drina Constantin was abducted by someone familiar with the ward layout, someone who blended in." Or anyone who had cased out the hospital and its slipshod security, but she bit her tongue. "If that doesn't point to staff, Marie . . ."

"Haven't you consulted the *flics*? They questioned the staff who were on duty last night," she said. "Each of them has accounted for their whereabouts last night pre- and post-shift."

Yet no one had questioned Lana the ambulance driver.

"So how did the abductor get in?" Someone had probably watered the plants, as her father would say — bribery. "Perhaps a wad of francs to an orderly to disconnect the alarm? Maybe even to bring the patient out to the ambulance alley?"

"I personally vouch for the three orderlies on duty last night." Marie's small eyes narrowed. "One of my husband's cousins; the other two have worked here ten, fifteen years and will retire when we close."

Alors, Aimée thought: if it wasn't a paid-off hospital employee, then a keen observer.

104

Behind Marie's head a hospital directory was pasted on the wall by a list labeled USE-FUL NUMBERS. That gave her an idea.

"Here's my card," said Aimée.

Professional courtesy demanded that Marie give hers in return. Didn't it? Marie made no move.

"May I have your card in case I need to reach you?"

"*Désolée,* I'm all out."

Liar. One was stuck above her head on the corkboard.

"Consult the *flics* if you have any further questions," Marie said, an arch tone in her voice. She showed Aimée to the hall, closing the office door behind them. "I've got a meeting."

So far she'd gotten little: Naftali overhearing Drina's shouting about birds, and Nicu needing to know the truth; Lana's recollection of a black car with tinted windows.

Aimée followed several paces behind Marie until she entered a ward; as soon as she did, Aimée backtracked down the hallway and slipped back into the office, praying the woman wouldn't return. Standing behind the door for cover, Aimée took Marie's card from the corkboard and consulted the wall directory, then on the desk phone dialed 09, the extension for Admissions.

"I'm Marie Fourcy, calling from Doctor Estienne's Ward C station. We're unable to locate a patient's records. Drina Constantin. Can you give me her contact information?"

"You've got the files," the admissions clerk said.

Great. "Her chart's missing, that's the problem."

"Your problem. We processed the patient yesterday upon admission and sent the records down to you at . . . eighteen hundred hours."

She had to get something. Thought back to Nicu pulling out the market work permit. "*Bon*, what's the patient's address?"

"Address? You should have it."

"But of course you've kept a copy in Admissions, *non*?"

A sigh. "When the messenger comes I'll send it . . ."

"*Merci beaucoup*," Aimée interrupted. Noises came from the hall. The rubber wheels of a trolley, approaching voices — *merde*! Couldn't the woman just hurry up and cooperate? "But the *flics* in the hallway want her address."

"This is their second request." Her voice rose in irritation. "I've got to process pending admissions, I told them."

Aimée heard footsteps outside the door. "*Bon,* just give me an address so I can keep them happy."

"*Attendez,*" she said. "There's a pile here to go through."

The footsteps came closer.

"*Voilà.* Thirty-nine Boulevard des Invalides."

"*Merci.*"

"What are you doing here?" asked a nurse.

Aimée hung up the phone as noiselessly as she could and turned around. Managed a shrug. "Stupid me, I left my sunglasses on the doctor's desk."

A moment later she'd escaped into the corridor, not looking back.

With an idea forming in her mind, she headed to the service rooms she'd noticed. The laundry steam seeped through a wall vent. She followed the ramp through swinging doors labeled LAVERIE and UNIFORM PICKUP.

Inside she saw lockers and canvas carts heaped with soiled sheets. Detergent and stale coffee smells wafted from a table in the corner with a *cafetière* on it. She could hear loud voices from the changing room for male staff.

Aimée reached for a staff newsletter on

the table by the coffee stains. *"Excusez-moi,"* she called into the locker area. "I'm with Department of Requisition checking on stock. Reports have reached us about thefts in staff locker rooms and in the laundry."

"Tell me about it," said a man who stuck his head out. "Lost my windbreaker, my uniform, even my ID."

She nodded, controlled her excitement. "As recently as last night or today?"

He shrugged. "I come back to work today after two days off, my locker's been cleaned out and I have no uniform. It's making me late for my shift. Why don't you people investigate?"

"Oh, I will," she said.

Her phone vibrated in her pocket. A number she didn't recognize. Nicu, finally!

But it was the lawyer's secretary calling to book her appointment. "She has an opening tomorrow afternoon."

"Nothing sooner?"

"Call it lucky a client cancelled and I can fit you in, Mademoiselle."

"D'accord, merci." Aimée scratched the details into her Moleskine. "My baby's biological father is making custody claims."

"Oh, she knows."

She did? "But how?"

"The *commissaire*," said the secretary. "Just to alert you, the biological father's attorney has contacted Maître Benosh."

Aimée's heart dropped. Already? "But I'm just making the appointment. How could he know?"

"You'll need to confer with Maître Benosh."

What was Melac plotting?

"Tell her he hasn't recognized his daughter. His name's not on the birth certificate."

"That's another thing," the secretary said. "Maître Benosh requests you bring your daughter's birth certificate and *livret de famille.*"

And hand them over to Melac's lawyer? No way. "I don't understand. I'm her client. Isn't she supposed to work for me?"

"The paperwork's standard. Again, you'll need to discuss the details with Maître Benosh," said the secretary. "Or do you want to cancel?"

Torn, she paced. Her fingers gripped the cell phone so tight in anger she almost cancelled the appointment then and there. But she needed a lawyer, fast — and Morbier said this lawyer was the best. She knew better than to ignore a tip from the *commissaire.*

"Keep the appointment," she said, her

insides churning.

"Maître Benosh insists that you have no contact with the biological father before your appointment." The phone clicked off.

Her cold hands clamped together in fear. Melac meant business.

Then her phone rang again — Nicu this time. Within a minute she had arranged a meeting and headed to her scooter. Her hands were shaking. For now she had to put Melac aside, stuff down her fear of custody over Chloé. She could deal with this. Couldn't she?

And a dying woman who'd begged to see her about her father's murder — missing. She noticed the time on the wall clock as she left the building: 9:40 A.M. Drina had been missing for more than twelve hours.

Aimée parked her scooter on the curb outside side La Pagode, where she'd arranged to meet Nicu. La Pagode, a rose-colored nineteenth-century Japanese pagoda, had been built by the director of Le Bon Marché as a "folly" for his wife. A few months later, the wife left him for a chauffeur.

Now La Pagode was an art-house cinema with ivy trailing the walls. Drooping willows canopied the tea tables nestled in the

110

Japanese garden. It lay quiet and deserted, apart from Michel, the projectionist, who waved to her while sweeping the lobby. Maïs, the house cat, slinked past the pair of ceramic dragons guarding the stained-glass door to the cinema.

Nicu wasn't there. She tried to take deep breaths under the paulownia tree's curved branches. Did her best not to worry that Melac was running more than one step ahead of her. This *jardin de rêves,* an exquisite jewel of the Japonisme craze that had swept that epoch's *haute bourgeoisie,* had been her haunt during maternity leave. She'd brought Chloé in a sling on her chest to two o'clock matinees and a silent-film festival with accompanying piano. Music put her baby to sleep, even in a theater.

Wistfulness filled her. Her mind went back to drinking green tea in the garden as Chloé gummed a teething biscuit, entranced by a butterfly hovering over a stone lantern. A faded memory of coming here years ago with her mother floated through her mind.

She'd fight Melac if it took everything she had.

And then she remembered, this was her first day back in the office. Time to quit daydreaming. No way she'd make it to Leduc Detective in fifteen minutes to open

111

up. *Merde!* But she could handle it, couldn't she? Still plenty of time to prepare for the late lunch meeting. She called the office and left Maxence a message that she would be working from home until the lunch meeting with René. But where was Nicu?

Nicu's voice jolted her out of her thoughts. He was wearing the jeans and hoodie from last night; dark circles pooled under his eyes.

"Over here," she said, pulling out a chair for him.

Nicu sat down. "The *flics* tried to frame me for murdering my mother, accused me of performing a mercy killing. Set me up as the suspect, showed me a body in the morgue. It looked like an eighty-year-old woman, and they claimed she'd been found with Drina's chart."

Planting evidence on a corpse. Incompetence or desperation? In either case, worse than she'd thought. The *flics* would never find Drina in time.

She checked her Tintin watch. More than thirteen hours since Drina's abduction.

"Listen, Nicu." She recounted what she'd discovered last night: the alarm wires that had been cut on the hospital's exit door, Drina's sock lodged in the spoke of a wheelchair by the ambulance alley, the ambulance driver who had observed a dark car blocking the *allée,* Naftali hearing a woman screaming in Romany, the theft of a staff uniform from the locker room.

"*Et alors?*" said Nicu, his voice thick. "The *flics* do nothing."

"That's the work of a pro, Nicu." She took Nicu's shaking hand over the tea table. "Who was Drina frightened of? Who can you think of?"

"I don't know."

Nicu, no more than a kid, was in shock.

She had to reel him in, get him to focus. "You need to think. We don't have much time, Nicu," she said. If Drina was even alive. "That man you said had been following you. Can you remember anything? Clothing, an accent, tattoos?"

He rubbed his eyes, distracted. "*Maman* kept jabbering."

"Jabbering what?"

"I don't know," said Nicu, his lip quivering. " 'Sister,' she kept saying. Her sister, maybe?"

"Her sister, your aunt?" Aimée asked. "Where is she?"

"Passed on a long time ago. Death's a taboo, we don't speak of the dead. But she said she couldn't meet God without telling me . . ."

Exasperated, she tried to get him back on

113

track. "Think back to the person who was following you, Nicu."

"The *gadjo* came back, she said. He came back. That's all."

The metal garden chair bit into her spine. She took a deep breath to calm herself, then coughed at the mingling smells of fetid drain and drifting pollen. Think, she had to think how to investigate from here. "Nicu, we'll start with Drina's apartment on Boulevard des Invalides. Go from there." And look for what? But she had to start somewhere.

He looked at her blankly.

"Apartment? *Maman* lives in a caravan in Avignon. She only comes to Paris sometimes, to do the market."

"So what's the address she used at the hospital, on Boulevard des Invalides? Your place?"

"*Moi?* No. No idea. I crash at the artist squat under Pont Alexandre III," he said. "But I know the atelier she uses to repair cane chairs. I could take you there."

Now it made sense. At almost every street market, *manouches* could be found hawking services to re-cane chairs, a disappearing art.

Every minute counted. "What are we waiting for? You've got the key?"

114

He pulled a key chain from his pocket.

"My scooter's out front," she said.

She waved goodbye to Michel. With Nicu sitting behind her, she eased off the brake, nosed the scooter onto the street and took off. The *quartier* was quiet. In the words of Martine's *tante,* who owned a shop on rue du Bac, behind these walls, *entre cour et jardin,* lay secrets big and small.

Aimée hoped the atelier held some hint as to Drina's whereabouts; she needed to find her before it was too late to learn anything about her father's killer.

Nicu directed her past the modernist UNESCO building, the grounds of the École Militaire and the enclave of antique shops known as Village Suisse. After Avenue de la Motte-Piquet, she wove among traffic on crowded Boulevard de Grenelle under the overhead struts of the elevated Métro, which rumbled above them. Line 6, her favorite line, with its uninterrupted view of the Tour Eiffel.

Following Nicu's directions, she turned in to Passage Sécurité, a narrow lane of one- and two-story buildings off the broad boulevard. At one end of the lane stood a tall housing block, at the other the grey rivet-dotted Métro structure. On the crumbling stucco wall below the blue sign reading *VOIE*

PRIVÉE, a rusting metal sign said *PLOMBERIE, CHAUFFAGE.*

"Here." Nicu jumped off and inserted a key into the padlock on the grey wooden double door of a small warehouse with butterscotch stucco. Bits of torn newspaper flew through the alley — giving it the abandoned feel of a wind tunnel. She shivered. Not a place she'd choose to frequent.

Inside the musty, skylit atelier was a scene of chaos. Cane chairs overturned, metal tools and empty paint cans littering the cracked concrete floor. The place had been trashed. Pillows slit open, down feathers clumped and matted in a wet corner. Someone had been searching for something. It was the work of a pro.

And it sickened her. Nicu had gone to the back *courette,* a postage stamp–sized courtyard. Aimée saw a white camper van parked there, its door open.

Her breath caught. Could Drina be hiding here, or even be here as a captive? She reached in her bag for her Swiss Army knife, flicked the blade open. "Watch out, Nicu."

But Nicu came back, shaking his head. "How could they do this?" he said, a stricken look on his face.

Aimée closed her knife. "More impor-

116

tantly, Nicu, why?" she said. "What were they looking for?"

Inside the small caravan, pots and pans, blankets and clothes littered the floor. The cooktop had been overturned, and a bottle of vinegar broken, leaving a dry residue and a tangy odor. The built-in seat and covers had been slashed with a knife.

Nicu picked up a wooden toy wagon that fit in his palm. He spun the small wheels, which were decorated with a metal band. "She loved these. I carved them for her. The old Gypsy wagons, *les roulottes.*"

"Nicu, if your mother had something that proved who murdered my father, where would she have hidden it?"

Nicu's shoulders were shaking. "Face it. She's . . . passed." He shook his head. "I thought I'd know, feel her departure. What does it matter now?"

Was he right? Had she been beaten to the finish by the man who murdered her papa — again?

"We don't know that. Until we find her, we search. Think, Nicu. Where else would she hide something?"

He gave a shake of his head.

"Don't you at least want to try your best? How can you give up any hope of helping her?" She wanted to mobilize him. But this

117

kid was in shock, his mother likely dead. Pity mingled with her determination. "I'm sorry, Nicu, but please try to think of where she'd keep money, valuables."

"*Bon,*" he said, catching her urgency. "At the market she'd keep her cash and account books in the caravan. She'd customized it." He went back into the atelier and returned with a screwdriver, which he used to start unscrewing one of the caravan's outside panels. Nothing inside. He tried the next one. "This could take a while, Aimée."

He was focused now. No good her standing here wasting time.

"I'll ask around in the café, the shops, see if anyone noticed anything. Call me."

"There's no phone here. And I don't have a cell."

She remembered seeing a phone booth, rare enough these days, half a block away under the elevated Métro. "Use the phone at the Métro." From her wallet she took out a phone card. "Plenty of credit left."

The heating-system shop next door was shuttered. At the corner café, she caught the waiter's attention amid loud shouts directed at the horse races on the *télé* screen overhead. A shrug when she asked about Drina, the atelier. More shrugs from men at the counter. The produce-shop owner, stocking only tomatoes, shook his head. She glanced at her phone. No call from Nicu yet. Up and down the block she'd gotten the same story — no one had seen anything, no one had heard anything. No one wanted to get involved with a Gypsy.

She had more luck on the opposite corner at the tailor's.

"I know who you mean, the Gypsy," said the thin old man, hunched over a thrumming sewing machine as he guided fabric through it under a harsh desk light. "Keep to themselves, those *manouches*. Thieves."

Great, another bigot. "Monsieur, this woman canes chairs. She is an artisan, not a thief."

"*Et alors?* Enough of them are. One pickpocketed me on the Métro last week. I filed a report and the *flics* just laughed at me."

"I'm sorry, but this woman's dying," she said. "She was abducted from the hospital, her atelier's been trashed. People here don't want to know or to help. Do you know anything that could help me find her?"

"You don't look like a *flic.*"

"I'm not." She took out her PI license. "Did you notice anything unusual this morning or last night?"

"What's it worth, Mademoiselle Columbo?"

119

A smart ass. But she didn't have time to shake him down, there was no love-thy-neighbor feeling in this *quartier.* "This look right?" She put a fifty-franc note on the fabric.

"Why don't you sweeten it?" he said.

She forced a smile. "Give me some juice to sweeten. Do you remember seeing someone at her atelier?"

His foot paused on the sewing-machine pedal as he put the note in his shirt pocket. "My back window upstairs looks onto the passage. Two or three nights ago, looked like the *flics* were there. Unmarked car."

The *flics*?

"And you know this how?"

"My son-in-law's a *flic* in Nantes. Did a stint plainclothes."

"Go on," she said.

"Odd, I thought, seeing *flics* by her place. Then I see her coming from the Métro with a shopping bag. She stumbled, her bag fell. Looked ill, I thought," he said. "Left a few minutes later, her hands empty."

Drina had been well enough to walk. "Like she'd dropped something off, that's what you mean?"

He nodded, not looking up, guiding the fabric under the punching needle. The hum of the machine filled the small shop.

"Can you remember what day this was? The time?"

He paused. Lifted up his foot and thought.

"I'd just eaten dinner. Spaghetti *vongole.* So Saturday."

"Why did the unmarked car strike you, Monsieur?"

"Nothing's open. Barely anyone walks there at night." He pressed his foot on the pedal. The machine hummed to life. "But there was someone watching the street."

"How could you tell?"

"Who stands smoking on the corner in the rain for an hour?"

So the night before she went missing from the hospital, Drina returned from the Métro and someone watched her. She'd left something in the atelier, according to the tailor. Hidden it?

Her phone rang. "*Merci,* Monsieur." She slipped another fifty-franc note down.

She stepped outside the tailor shop to take the call and headed toward the passage.

"*Oui?*"

"Where are you, Aimée?"

"Coming from the tailor's. He noticed someone watching the street two nights ago. What have you found?" She turned into the short passage and saw Drina's locked atelier.

"You need to see this. There's half of

Drina's notebook." He sounded excited.

"I'm coming," she said, breaking into a run. "Let me get my scooter."

"I'm at the phone booth on the corner, under the Métro."

She got on her scooter, popped the kick-stand and inserted the key with the phone still to her ear. "What's in the notebook?" she said as she started up the alley.

"You'll see. Names, numbers, places. It's torn. It's sort of like the notebook she keeps accounts in."

"Anything you recognize, Nicu?"

"I don't know. Lots of numbers . . ."

"Phone numbers, Nicu?" she interrupted, trying to crane her neck above the traffic. An old Fiat pulled in front of her, taking its sweet time.

"Ah *non,* like she enters her sales. Five hundred francs every month" — a horn blared, cutting through his words — "entries end in June 1989."

The year Aimée's father died. Going on her assumption that Drina informed for her father — maybe a record of payoffs?

"What names?"

Over the line she heard scuffling, shouts. Alarmed, she sped up. "What names, Nicu?"

"Where are you?" he said, terse and distracted.

Traffic had ground to a halt at the red light.

"Right down across the street. Stuck in a wall of cars and taxis." She fumed inside as a passing bus shot diesel exhaust in her face. "Tell me, Nicu. What are the names?"

"Fifi, Tesla. The last entry says *Tonton JC à six heures du soir Place Vendôme.*"

Her gut churned. JC? Like Jean-Claude? Papa had died in the bomb explosion in Place Vendôme.

"I found something else, there's pictures. My . . ." His voice cracked. "Come to the corner . . ." The rumble of the train overhead drowned him out.

"Pictures of what, Nicu? Please, can't you tell me?"

Only the rumbling of the Métro. Her stomach knotted, her knuckles whitened as she squeezed the handlebars.

"Can you see me?" she yelled into the phone over the noise of the busy two-lane boulevard. So much traffic.

The call had clicked off.

Two cars zipped past her, honking at each other. She saw him now standing at the Métro's stone pillar support. He waved. She motioned for him to wait, she'd come to him. A van pulled up between them, and she watched more traffic block her way.

Buses, cars, trucks, scooters — everyone going somewhere. The Métro added to the urban cacophony.

Her heart was pounding. She felt so close to knowing the truth about her father.

The traffic thinned.

In the crowd of people that had suddenly assembled at the corner, she couldn't see Nicu anymore. She pulled up. Then she saw why the people were huddling. Nicu lay half sprawled against the pillar, bleeding. His face frightened, he reached out to her.

Non, non . . . It couldn't . . .

Someone in the crowd shouted, "Anyone a doctor?"

Aimée dropped her Vespa to the ground and ran toward him. His ripped hoodie was red with blood. His lips moved.

She heard a man on a cell phone demanding an ambulance. She pushed her way past a young woman bending toward him holding out tissues. Aimée knelt down besides Nicu. He was saying, "My bag. They took it."

"It's all right, Nicu," she said, smoothing down his damp matted hair with her shaking fingers.

"Drina . . . you don't understand," Nicu said.

"I'm a doctor," said a man's voice, "let

me through."

"Don't understand what, Nicu?" she said.

"Not my mother . . . why didn't she tell me?" His trembling hand reached up to unzip his bloodstained hoodie. She saw an envelope in his shirt pocket. "I found this. Read the . . . take it."

Numb, she took the envelope from his pocket as she felt the doctor move her aside.

She watched as the grey-haired doctor pressed his hands together against Nicu's chest to staunch the blood. "Tell the medics to prepare for a deep puncture from a knife wound to the left sternal border. Ribs involved, possible internal bleeding." The doctor looked up. Shouted. "Now!"

The man nodded, still on his cell phone.

Aimée shook off the cloud of horror and scanned the crowd. "What happened?"

"The boy was standing right here at the curb —" said the young woman, bloody tissues in hand.

"*Oui,* there was a blue van," interrupted the woman next to her. "The boy was pulled in. I saw. Next minute, he stumbled out here and fell."

"Yes, I saw too . . . he shouted at them. Then the van pulled away in seconds. It cut across the walkway — drove like *un fou.*"

The doctor leaned back on his knees. "No pulse."

Good God, she'd gotten Nicu killed. Guilt flooded her. Then alarm. Was she next?

If something happened to her, who'd take care of Chloé?

She stepped back. Voices in the crowd blended into one around her. "*Oui,* a van stopped, the door slid open . . ."

"*Mon Dieu* . . . The boy was staggering, he knocked my shopping bag . . ."

"Clutched his stomach . . . the van took off. I didn't get a look."

Aimée made her hands move, righted her scooter. Tried to put the key in the ignition. Her fingers, sticky with Nicu's blood, kept slipping. Bile rose in her throat.

Get away. She had to get away right now.

Somehow she managed to walk her scooter to the street. The whine of a siren pierced her ears. Lights flashed; an ambulance pulled up on the corner. She flipped the ignition, revved the handlebar and weaved into the traffic.

Three streets later she pulled into a square. Blood — good God, her hands were covered in blood. And then she leaned over just in time as her stomach heaved, over and over until nothing more came out.

She forced herself to clean up at the

fountain, wash the blood and bile away. But washing it away wouldn't take Nicu's blood off her hands.

When the shaking stopped, she sat on the grass and opened the envelope, stained with bloody fingerprints. Why hadn't he put this in his bag?

In it she found two black-and-white photos. The first was of two young women, one holding a baby. Written on the back was *Djanka, Drina, Nicu.* The next was of a young couple squinting into the sun, the man's arms around the woman, who was holding a baby. On the back was written *Djanka, Nicholás and Pascal.* With them was a creased, much-folded birth certificate. *Nicholás Constantin, date of birth June 12, 1977.* Under "father" it was blank, and in the mother's column were the words, *Djanka Constantin, aged 24.*

If Drina wasn't Nicu's mother, who the hell had he just died for?

Monday Morning

Roland Leseur hung the framed iridescent butterfly on the office wall in his ministry, beside his brother Pascal's commendation from *le président.* A *Phengaris arion,* the latest addition to his collection, the violet blue of the insect's wings reminded him of Françoise's eyes. He let his gaze pass over the collection. These winged creatures, suspended as if caught in flight, made his heart quiver. Little else did these days.

"Excusez-moi, Monsieur le directeur." Juliette, his ministerial assistant, entered through the tall door, accompanied by a whiff of something citrus. Afternoon light glinted off the Seine through the window, catching in Juliette's short, nut-brown hair, which glowed like her smile. "Jacques from *Libération,"* she said. "He wants a quick word."

Fresh faced, young enough to be his

daughter, idealistic like he'd been. Like they'd all been once. Even Pascal.

"Put him on, Juliette."

But Jacques — mid-forties, like Roland; balding and thick waisted, unlike Roland — stood in the doorway. "Roland, can you give me five minutes?"

Roland was inclined to refuse, but he shrugged as Jacques helped himself to a seat on Roland's Louis Philippe office chair.

"Why not, Jacques?" He pulled out that smile he'd perfected over the course of years in the ministry, as a *haut fonctionnaire.* Jacques, a socialist, wrote for the left-leaning *Libération* — not Roland's choice of newspaper — but he was a respected journalist. "Hold my calls for five minutes, Juliette," Roland said. "Ever seen my collection, Jacques?"

"*Bien sûr,* Roland," he said. "But I'm not here for that."

Never one for small talk, Jacques.

Jacques's gaze drifted over the framed butterflies, but lingered on Pascal's 1978 commendation. Pascal, the youngest *député* in the history of the Assemblée Nationale.

"Please take this as coming from a friend," Jacques said. "I've known you, what, twenty years?"

Roland nodded. "Twenty-one. We met at

Pascal's funeral."

Jacques's hand went to his forehead, shading his eyes for a moment. Then he looked up, his thick brow furrowed. Jacques was genuinely worried.

"*Et alors,* it's serious. Why are you here? Get to it, Jacques."

"Off the record, you understand." Jacques leaned forward. The Louis Philippe chair creaked. "You're a friend, I knew your family. This concerns Pascal."

"My brother?" Roland said. "Talking from beyond the grave?"

"Roland, I wanted to warn you," said Jacques. "You won't like this, but the editor's going ahead with an exposé."

"Another scandal?" Roland folded his arms and leaned back in his chair. "What do you ever print but scandals?"

"There's a memoir coming out. *Libération* is going to run an accompanying article about governmental corruption, and Pascal's mentioned. Often."

Roland's jaw clamped. "He died twenty-one years ago. Such old news, your editor must be desperate."

Jacques twisted in the chair. He took his case and stood. Roland had never seen this seasoned journalist look so uncomfortable before.

"Bad idea, let's forget I came," said Jacques. "I'll let you get back to work."

Worried, Roland shook his head. "Please tell me what you feel I need to know. I'm sorry, I see this isn't easy for you."

Instead of sitting back down, Jacques walked to Pascal's framed presidential commendation, then to the window overlooking the Seine. His bald crown shone in the sun. Perspiration glimmered on his neck.

"Minister Chalond's former teenage boy lover wrote a memoir — not even that scandal-worthy, given that Chalond's long dead and the remaining family all senile. This now mature man has cirrhosis of the liver." Jacques paused.

"Pascal? Gay?" Sunlight slanted onto the Aubusson rug and warmed Roland's arms. *"Au contraire."*

"The issue being that he serviced others in the ministry as well. Others who are very much alive." Jacques paused. "It has other implications. This boyfriend heard pillow talk and gossip, attended dinners. He overheard deals being made — promised ministerial posts, do-this-and-the-ambassadorship's-yours favors, bribes disguised as foreign-delegation junkets."

Roland folded his arms tighter against his chest. "So? Why would the public believe a boy prostitute with twenty-year-old stories?"

"The issue, Roland, is that the exposé was thoroughly researched, all allegations verified. Pascal led two of those foreign delegations."

Roland shrugged. "That's all part of the public record, Jacques."

"Cover-ups can still do damage twenty years later. They're a threat to certain officials. I know Pascal was your older brother and you —"

"Idolized him? Say it, my father always did."

Jacques averted his gaze. He pulled several stapled sheets from his case, set them on Roland's desk. "I never gave you this, Roland."

Roland didn't want to look. Wouldn't. Then his eye caught on ". . . honeypot sting . . . police hush money . . . homicide of Pascal's Gypsy lover . . . reputed 'suicide.' "

Good God. The fear he'd smothered all these years made him break out in a cold sweat. His arms tingled and blood rushed to his head. Dizzy, he gripped his desk, knocking the papers to the floor. Could it be true? Had Pascal's suicide been a murder?

"I just didn't want you blindsided," said

Jacques. "I'm sorry. It goes to print next week. I heard rumors of an investigation."

Roland bent to pick up some papers, trying to recover. "I'm having my attorney read this."

"Wouldn't matter," he said. "He's got media lined up. Matter of fact, he is the media."

"What the hell does that mean?"

"Charles Frenet, aka the teenage lover, is the former announcer on RTL. He's been paid off to keep this quiet all these years, I imagine. Now he's broke, wants a new liver. The interviews go live day after tomorrow."

"I'll stop him."

"Good luck with that." Jacques shot him a meaningful look. "Françoise's husband's name came up. There are implications . . ." Jacques sighed. "What you *can* do is warn Françoise."

Monday, 11 A.M.

Aimée's empty stomach was knotted in fear. Her raw throat hurt and she was trembling. She tried to piece the implications together as she sat on a bench under a canopy of linden trees. Her mind spun.

She had sent Nicu to his death.

Focus. She had to focus. Drina was still out there. Whoever she was.

Put it together, her father had always said, piece together the puzzle. If you fail, try again. And again.

Half a notebook. Drina now fourteen hours gone and counting; her limbs would be ceasing to function.

Loose ends — she only had loose ends. Names and a few family photographs. And without the notebook, which she'd never had a chance to see, it led nowhere. She had zero.

Nothing to follow up on.

Chloé depended on her. What kind of fool was she, putting herself in danger like that? And she'd found nothing but a trail of smoke and names.

Part of her wanted to run away from the whole damn thing. Erase what had happened. As if she could. If she stopped now, whatever Drina knew about her father's killer would go with her.

Her father's words came back to her from an afternoon at the park long ago when she'd fallen off the swing. "No pity party, Aimée. If kisses don't make the tears go away, be a big girl, put on the Band-Aid." Her ten-year-old self that afternoon needed to put on a brave face and get back on the swing.

If she gave up now, Nicu's death would mean nothing. Any chance of finding her father's killer would disappear.

She hitched her bag over her shoulder. Time to put on the Band-Aid, get back on the swing and fit the pieces of the puzzle together. If she didn't, she could be next.

Number 39 Boulevard des Invalides, the address from Drina's hospital record, stood three stories high opposite the nineteenth-century Saint-François-Xavier Church, amid the green stretches of Place du Président Mithouard. This was the stomping ground of France's titled families, and it oozed privilege. *Pas mal,* she thought.

Drina Constantin had given this as her address. A friend's place, maybe? Where she received mail? Worth a try. And if she came up with zero, she'd figure the next thing out from there.

One of the tall, dark-green double doors yielded to her touch. She found herself in a covered *porte cochère* with a directory listing the names of priests and one monsignor. No listing of Constantin.

She strode over the moss-veined cobbled courtyard to look for the concierge. There was only an office of the nearby Lycée Victor Duruy Christian youth association with a FERMÉ sign in the window. Frustrated, she turned to leave. Just then, she heard a scraping noise from behind what she had assumed was a wall covered in thick wisteria. Looking more closely, she realized it was a fence, and from behind it was coming the scratching of dirt accompanied by a grunt.

"Il y a quelqu'un?" She entered a gate and followed the gravel path into a garden the likes of which were not often seen in Paris. Stone walls splotched with white and yellow lichen enclosed a profusion of budding

plants, red-button flowers, a weeping willow, trellised vines.

"Dump that in the compost pile." A man's voice.

A man with a white-collared black shirt that looked like a priest's, tucked into Levi's, poked his head up from a bed of large, yellow-petalled daisies. Perspiration beaded his flushed face.

"*Excusez-moi,* Monsieur le curé, but a woman named Drina Constantin listed this as her address."

He shook his head. "Just us black frocks here at the rectory."

Rectory? Drina had given a false address. A dead end.

An enticing minty floral scent filled her nose. She'd love to have a garden like this for Chloé to play in. *Dream on.* But there still might be a clue here, something to point her toward the next place. "Perhaps she worked for you. Does that name ring a bell?"

"Constantin? No one here by that name."

No need to complicate the story she told to the priest. "It's vital that I find someone who might know her — and she did give this address, after all. Can I talk to your concierge, the staff?"

"Madame Olivera's in Portugal. She does

everything; we're a bit lost without her."

Bees buzzed in the hedge; a butterfly alighted on a budding jasmine vine.

She racked her brains for anything that could link Drina to a rectory. With so few leads, she couldn't afford to miss a single thing. Then Nicu's uncle's words came to her: " 'Another one of your Christian do-gooders, eh Nicu?' "

"Does Saint-François-Xavier do charity work?" she asked, clutching at a straw. "Sponsor programs for the needy? Maybe that's the connection."

"Hmm, our Christian society volunteers with upkeep of the church," he said. "They started this garden — quite something, all plants with the theme of our Lord." He put down the hoe and pointed with pride. "Those silver seedpods under the flowering purple look like coins, which is why the plant is called 'the pope's money,' *monnaie du pape.*" He grinned. "Those red cascade spindle trees over there we call *bonnets de prêtre,* 'priest's caps' — the branches provide charcoal for drawing. And of course there are the bonnet daisies, these *pâquerettes,* for our Easter altar."

Fascinating, but she didn't have time for the religious meanings of flowers. This *Père* had tried to be helpful, but he hadn't given her anything yet, and she could tell he wanted to get back to the garden.

"How about any outreach to Gypsies, *les manouches?*"

He picked up his hoe. "*Mais oui,* we work with the Christian Helping Hands program. Through them, we hire *les manouches* to re-cane our *prie-Dieu* prayer kneelers, repair the rattan chairs. We've got a church full of old things, you know. Even a mural of the Tintoretto school."

Finally. Her persistence had paid off.

"How can I contact these *manouches,* Father?"

He grinned, wiped his perspiring face. "I'm just the gardener today." He lifted a pile of weeds into the wheelbarrow. "Madame Uzes runs that Christian Helping Hands program. She'll know." The priest fished a card from his wallet. "Here's her number. She handles *manouche* programs. Talk to her."

Walking back toward her scooter, she dialed the number for Madame Uzes, only to hear it ring and ring. Didn't the woman have voice mail? As she was about to hang up, a recording came on and she left a message.

On top of everything else she found a traffic citation stuck to her speedometer dial.

139

Merde! She hadn't noticed the stenciled white letters CCDM, designating a ministry parking spot. Fuming, she stuck the ticket in the seat compartment with all the others.

Two nuns crossed the street in front of her, their blue habits flying as they hunched against the wind. Aimée released her scooter brake and took off, veering right. The sun fought through the clouds, scattering patches of light over the gold dome of Napoléon's tomb at les Invalides.

Sun and clouds, bright and dark, like the feelings warring inside her. Every few minutes she checked her rearview mirror for a van, worried that it was following her now. That she'd been seen. Nothing. Think, she needed to think this through. Told herself anyone doing a hit on Nicu would be long gone.

At the stoplight she reached for the Moleskine in her bag and came back with a tiny white onesie. She thought of Chloé's mushroom nose, how it crinkled when she laughed. A twinge of guilt hit her, so sharp it twisted her stomach. She didn't want the dark side of life anymore; she was done, really done, with criminal investigation. Yet her father's promise bound her — and now, so did Nicu's murder.

One thing at a time. Prioritize.

Her phone rang. Babette's number. Panic flooded her — an accident in the high chair, or had Chloé's sneeze turned into pneumonia because that window had been left open last night?

Calm down. "*Oui,* Babette?"

"Morning nap time, just turning off my phone and letting you know," said Babette. "New mothers get anxious. If you can't get through, it's because the girls are napping, *d'accord*?"

Aimée felt sheepish. "Thank you for calling, Babette." Aimée could hear the tension in her own voice.

"First-day-back jitters, eh?" said Babette.

Little did Babette know.

"Watch out, Aimée," called Maurice, the vendor at the kiosk on rue du Louvre. He pointed to the dog dump on the pavement.

Missing it with a quick step, she grinned. *"Merci."* Thought for a moment. "I need eyes on the street. Interested?"

"As in . . . detective work?" Maurice's eyes widened. An Algerian War vet, he'd lost an arm but still stacked his stock of newspapers and magazines faster than someone half his age.

"If any blue van lingers or parks here," she said, sticking a fifty-franc note in his

141

pocket, "you let me know, *d'accord*?"

Maurice raised his one arm, touched his brow and saluted. "At your service."

Inside the grilled door of the Leduc Detective building, she slipped on the wet tiled floor. Caught herself just in time. Madame Fortuna, the new Portuguese concierge, was kneeling, rag in hand, soaping the stairs.

On the elevator ride to her office she thought of her next step, where to look for missing pieces of Drina's puzzle. Her mind went to her father's files in the cellar, causing her to turn straight back around.

"Bonjour, Madame," she said to the kneeling concierge. "I need the key to the cellar."

" *'Scuse, non comprends.*"

A hard worker, this concierge, but her French left much to be desired. Aimée mimed turning a key in the lock and pointed to the cellar door.

Two minutes later she was descending into the bowels of 18 rue du Louvre, glad for the concierge's spare set of keys. She hadn't been down here in years and never remembered where René kept their copy.

Years ago, when her grandfather had left the Sûreté, he'd formed Leduc Detective and made a name for himself as a private investigator. Later, Papa, forced out of the police, had joined him and never looked back. Their history, the legacy they had left her — a detective agency in its third generation — gave her an enormous sense of pride and a mostly empty bank account.

In the cellar she hit the old porcelain light switch. A bare bulb shone on several taped-up cardboard boxes, an old army-green metal file cabinet of her grandfather's and two orange Plexiglas chairs circa the seventies. Not much.

She hoped to find anything at all on Drina Constantin — an informer dossier, maybe an old address. It would be a start.

The smell of old paper and tobacco from her grandfather's cherry pipe hit her when she opened the metal file. The folders here were dated from the late thirties to the late eighties. She'd personally dated and labeled all these boxes after transcribing their contents. But if there'd ever been a file on Drina Constantin, it was gone.

Another dead end. Disappointed, she wanted to get out of the damp packed-earth cellar. She thumbed one last time through all the yellowed dossiers inked with her father's spidery black handwriting. Wedged at the back of the drawer was a thick pile of newspapers. With one hand she pushed them to the side; with her other she felt around behind them. The brittle, yellowed newspapers, editions of *Libération,* crackled, the edges nibbled by silverfish. She glanced at the dates: 1978.

Shivering in the cellar's dampness, she put the newspapers in an empty cardboard box, lugged it up the stairs and locked the arched wooden door behind her.

On the ground floor, the *rez-de-chaussée,* Madame Fortuna was still working away at the stairs, so Aimée took the wire-cage elevator. It was just big enough to accommodate herself and the box.

Again the elevator wheezed up to the third floor. She hit the entry code at Leduc Detective's frosted-glass door and entered. She hung up her bag and her coat, noticing the cloth diapers stacked on the layette. Had she ordered these?

Maxence looked up from his desk, which adjoined René's. He wore his usual attire: Beatle boots, black turtleneck and stovepipe denims. He took off his headphones and swiped his bangs from his eyes.

"Welcome back. What are you doing here?"

"This." She plopped the box on her desk and wiped her brow; the office radiator had gone into overdrive, giving off a summery heat. It either worked overtime or not at all. The nineteenth-century woodwork on the high ceiling and the marble fireplace — the repository for their shredder — shimmered in the pale midday light.

"Thought you were working from home until your lunch meeting with René," Maxence said. "Two minutes ago I faxed you three contracts René needs you to look at right away."

Great.

"He's with a client, awaiting your response." Maxence handed her the originals.

Aimée scanned the contracts. "What's with the diapers?" She pointed toward the corner with the crib, high chair and mobiles that now decorated René's desk.

"René thought better safe than sorry."

René thought of everything. Not for the first time, she wondered if his inner parent ruled their lives too much. A vase of fragrant white freesias and a welcome-back card sat on her desk.

"Sweet, Maxence. Thank you," she said.

"René's idea." He winked. "I guess all your telecommuting and last night's surveillance didn't count."

She sat at her desk under the framed original of her grandfather's detective license and a photo of her father. It felt good

145

to be home.

"How's the *vicomte*'s tracker feed?"

"Incriminating. I transcribed his itinerary and bolded the juicy locations." Maxence smiled. "Invoice updated and on your desk."

Already? A whiz kid worth his weight in the dark chocolate he consumed — a provision of his paid internship.

She flipped through his paperwork — at this rate they'd need at least two more evenings of surveillance. Another big, fat check awaited. It never ceased to amaze her how members of the same family nipped and bit each other's heels.

She read through the contracts as quickly and carefully as she could, signed two and circled a clause on the third. "Tell René this needs more clarification."

While Maxence turned back to his work, she spread a plastic bag on her desk and the newspapers on top of it, and got to work.

The 1978 *Libération*s chronicled the news of the day: Jacques Brel's death; the birth of the first test-tube baby; President Giscard d'Estaing's "close" friendship with the President of the Central African Republic Jean-Bédel Bokassa, who'd proclaimed himself emperor; in Tehran, the shah of Iran fleeing the country after a year of protest; ex-*légionnaire* Bob Denard and his mercenaries staging a coup in the Comoros islands; some whiffs of scandal relating to an Assemblée Nationale *député*'s suicide.

"Que c'est ancien," said Maxence, looking admiringly at the culture section she had open. He wiggled his non-existent hips, shot one arm in the air. "Le Travolta." *Saturday Night Fever* had been playing in the cinemas.

The silverfish had damaged the edges, but tucked between the back pages was a plastic folder whose contents were pristine.

Could she be imagining it, or did it smell like her father? His pine cologne? How she missed him.

Her insides twisted. It all came back to her again — the reek of secrets surrounding his death in the bombing, the silence of those she'd thought of as his friends and colleagues. She had tried to put it behind her for so many years, but she had failed. Now she knew the only way to get over it was to find out.

She thumbed through the contents of the plastic folder, the pages covered in his familiar scrawl.

A 1978 *procès-verbal,* her father's signature at the bottom. The police report consisted of a witness statement from a military cadet, from an equine detachment, detailing his discovery of a body, female, in the grassy

147

moat surrounding les Invalides early on the morning of April 22, 1978. A homicide.

Why hadn't this file been with his others?

Attached to it was a grainy photo of the crime scene, the body covered with plastic, only the victim's black hair visible, twisted and matted in the grass. A diagram showed the position of the body, in the grassy walled ditch at the right corner below the small square Santiago-du-Chili. Above it was a row of cannons, and beyond, the familiar dome of les Invalides, Napoléon's tomb. Good God, she'd passed by there today, gone past les Invalides hundreds of times; it was a busy thoroughfare. She shivered, imagining such a violent death at this iconic monument.

The victim, listed as *sans domicile fixe,* had been identified two months later by dental records obtained from the Berry region. A Djanka Constantin. She grabbed the edge of her desk. Nicu's birth mother had been murdered only a year after he was born.

She had to concentrate, put these pieces together. In the course of the investigation into the homicide of Djanka Constantin, her father would have questioned Drina, a family member, most likely, maybe a sister or cousin.

Further digging in the plastic file revealed a Leduc Detective in-house case memo from 1985, labeled NORLAND, GEORGES: a missing person's investigation. Reading it, she discovered standard surveillance findings of an operation conducted over a week in the Saint-Germain-des-Prés *quartier* — seemingly unrelated, until she spotted a dated list of sightings of Georges Norland at the market. A note on the list read *de la part de Drina de ma liste de tonton.* The proof Drina worked for him. He'd put Drina on a *tonton liste* — an "uncle list," a way the *flics* paid their informers and protected them, like "uncles," from others on the force. But by 1985 he was long out of the force. It was significant that he'd kept Drina on a private payroll as his informer.

Of course, her father had brought Christmas gifts, like a *tonton,* to show how much he valued her, to keep those ties strong. But informer perks went beyond money. Could informing have won Drina security — for herself or those close to her — maybe even for the mysterious child, Nicu?

And what would Drina Constantin know about who was behind the explosion that killed Jean-Claude Leduc?

Noon. Fifteen hours since Drina's abduction.

Cold prickles ran up Aimée's spine.

She turned back to the file and came up with an autopsy report. Djanka Constantin had been twenty-four years old; she had no known belongings. She had died by strangulation.

Next was a photocopy of what looked like a torn drink receipt that had been recovered from the victim's pocket. She peered at the letters and made out a name: LA BOUTEILLE AUX PUCES.

"Maxence, see what you can find on La Bouteille aux Puces," she said. "Whether it's a bar, a *resto* or a shop."

Maxence leaned back. "But it's famous, Aimée. It's a club in Saint-Ouen. *Le temple du jazz manouche.* It's totally iconic."

"*Vraiment?*" she said, puzzled. "Thought you liked the Beatles?"

"Les Beatles, *le jazz,* I love it all. Why do you think I moved here? Quebec has no music scene." Maxence ruffled his mop top with his fingers, excited. "Django Reinhardt played La Bouteille aux Puces all the time with the Quintette du Hot Club. It's been around for, like, sixty years."

Aimée thought back to the area by the flea market. From her childhood she remembered the Gypsy encampments, *bidonvilles* — it had been a shantytown before the

Stade de France was erected last year.

"Can you do some digging? See if the club had any police troubles circa 1978?" she asked.

"On it."

She could make it there and back before her late lunch meeting with René. Aimée pulled out her *plan de Paris,* found the Métro stop closest to the flea market at Porte de Clignancourt. "I need to get going," she said.

"Call and check that La Bouteille's open first, Aimée." He dropped his notes on her desk. "Couldn't find much."

The voice recording at La Bouteille aux Puces gave their hours as 2 P.M. to 2 A.M.

No way she could make it there and back in time.

"Nice to see you in early on your first day back, Aimée." René strode into the office wearing a charcoal double-breasted suit and a strange, pinched smile.

Weren't they meeting at Café Marly overlooking the Louvre's pyramid to wine and dine a prospective client? Didn't she have more than an hour until their lunch?

"René, *écoute . . .*" The words died in her throat as a tall, broad-shouldered man in his early thirties followed René into the office. He was carrying a pigskin briefcase in one hand, and he reached to shake her hand with his other.

"Marc de Brosselet, with Villeroi Frères," he said. "Apologies for just showing up, but I begged your partner, Monsieur Friant, to let me visit. He indulged me."

Indulged him? How could René bring him here on her first day back in the office? Her desk was a mess of papers and files awaiting attention — some way to impress a potential client with a hundred-thousand-franc contract. *Merde.* She wanted to kick him. Her bare feet scrambled under her desk, seeking her high heels. Too late to change into the Dior suit hanging from the back of her chair. She hadn't even applied mascara.

But her manners kicked in, and she caught his handshake. A firm grip.

"Monsieur de Brosselet's interested in how we work, Aimée," said René, straining to maintain his smile. "The nitty-gritty."

Now she really would kick René. He wanted to see nitty-gritty, did he? She hoped her leaky breasts hadn't stained the silk blouse she hadn't had a chance to change out of. Pads, where were her pads? Too late now.

To top if off, she noticed a dust ball in the corner. The cleaning lady must have missed that corner last night. Or for the last month.

"We like to get a feel for a firm before we make decisions."

So all this would go in a report to board members, shareholders, those men in suits who had no clue about computer and corporate security apart from what they saw on the *télé*.

René's smile froze as de Brosselet paused to inspect the diapers. Chloé's crib. The stuffed animals.

"Interesting," he said. "I gather you bring your baby to work?"

No running or hiding now. No doubt he'd ask whether they could perform under pressure and on deadline with an infant in the office.

"That depends on the project and my hours," she said. "But under normal circumstances, Chloé, my six-month-old, stays with a child-minder." Lame. "But it's my name on the door, Monsieur."

"*Pardonnez-moi,* but I'm curious about this diaper service, Didee Wash. Do you recommend them?"

She nodded. "René thinks they're the best in terms of hygiene. He surveyed all the cotton diaper services in the Paris region, and Didee's the only one who uses an organic alternative to chlorine."

"Good to know," de Brosselet said. "My

wife's pregnant. And good to know you're a thorough researcher, Monsieur Friant."

She relaxed. What was that Oscar Wilde saying? *Be yourself; everyone else is already taken.*

"Please sit down, Monsieur de Brosselet," she said, moving Chloé's stuffed dinosaur and pulling out the Louis XIII chair for him. "Maxence, can you make us three espressos?" Maxence leapt to his feet. "He's our intern from the Hackaviste Academy, where René teaches," she explained. "We'll show you how our small but innovative firm works, and how we get results that larger ones don't."

"Can you make a system hack-proof and totally secure?"

She shot a look toward René. "Let's show Monsieur de Brosselet the Veleda project to give him an idea of our services," she said. "Monsieur de Brosselet, this is pre-operational, but it's three-quarters realized, and I think a good fit to show you and Villeroi how we adapt security as needs arise."

René, mobilized into action, was nodding as he opened his desk drawer. "We're constantly adapting, refitting, retooling," he said. "Microdots — remember them? — were once the safest storage, reams of info on the head of a pin. Use once and destroy.

Efficient for single use, but static. Computer security can't be static."

René opened the file and began to shuffle through, so Aimée took the reins.

"Changing and evolving is our forté," she said. "One day a firewall is secure. The next day, it might be full of holes. You need a security system that is constantly vigilant, that roots out any sign of unexplained probing," she said. "Malware's insidious. All it takes is one click on a link from a customer's compromised email account to penetrate your system."

"You mean hacked? How can you tell?"

Had it happened to his firm?

"We work with people who've been hacked every day," she said. "And we're selective about who we take on, Monsieur de Brosselet. In your case we'd perform a threat assessment to see if we could address your needs."

De Brosselet opened his briefcase, took out a notepad. From the way his broad shoulders bulged through his pinstriped suit jacket, it was clear he worked out. "How would that work, exactly?"

"We would attempt to break into your system to see where your weaknesses are. Then we would fix them."

"Isn't hacking against the law, Mademoiselle Leduc?" De Brosselet smoothed a crease in his trousers.

"That's a technical grey area these days."

"So where do you draw the line?"

A tad too inquisitive? She threw René a look. He put his hands together in supplication, so she kept talking.

"Monsieur de Brosselet, the British have been undertaking security operations in this way since 1994 under protection of the Intelligence Services Act. And you think our own government hasn't been doing the same thing? I say we need to keep up with the hackers. Or hire them ourselves — just like the government does." She smiled. "You didn't know that, did you? That's the truth, and the other companies won't admit it. They hire hackers for security purposes; it's the cheapest way to get the most sophisticated programmers. And we do the same."

He grinned. "You're outlaws."

"The Internet's like the Wild West these days. Does your firm want to be left behind? Can you fight back with a club when your opponents are using laser guns?"

René piped up. "Too many times we're hired after the fact. Statistics show it's not *whether* your firm will fall under cyber attack but *when* and *how many times* your vulnerabilities will be exploited."

De Brosselet crossed his legs. "As you must know, Villeroi's a family firm, old school — handcrafted products, world renowned. I married into the family, took my position ten years ago."

Aimée nodded. Villeroi was on a par with Hermès, but the true cognoscente believed Villeroi's wares were the more finely crafted. She'd lusted after a bag herself, but Villeroi never showed up at the flea market.

"Counterfeiters are stealing our designs, destroying our market," he said. "You come personally recommended." He recrossed his creased trouser leg. "By my uncle, the *comte.* Seems you're working for him."

Yet another nephew? Aimée rewound her memory but she didn't recall de Brosselet's name among the *comte*'s family members. Or on the board of the *comte*'s engineering firm. She'd have remembered that even with baby brain. Had René forgotten to do his research? Or was this a lie, an attempt to infiltrate the *comte*'s company?

Maxence turned from the espresso machine with a raised eyebrow. René had gripped the back of his ergonomic chair. *Merde.* They couldn't play both sides.

"We can't speak to that, as you must understand." She paused, hating to pull away from such a lucrative client. "We'd need to explore for any conflict of interest," she said. "I don't want to waste your time, Monsieur de Brosselet, but I'm afraid . . ."

"My family allegiance would cloud things?" He grinned. "My uncle's quite taken with you, you know. But feel free to ask him."

Wary, Aimée wondered if she'd read him wrong. It wouldn't be the first time.

"Excusez-moi." Aimée pulled out her phone, dialed. A moment later, after a quick query, the *comte* confirmed there was no conflict of interest.

"He's my sister's boy, got his own inheritance. From the right branch of the family, if you get my meaning, Mademoiselle," said the *comte.* "Snag his contract if you can, his firm's loaded."

"Merci."

She clicked off, caught René's gaze and nodded.

"Villeroi's looking to safeguard our communications system worldwide," de Brosselet said, consulting his notes. "Can you convince me Leduc Detective would do a better job of providing a comprehensive computer-security system than the five other firms bidding for the contract?"

Aimée knew all their rivals, competitors with large offices and lots of people power.

"Monsieur de Brosselet, your designs and sensitive data could be stolen in myriad ways," she said. "That's why we cover all the bases, not just the technical ones. Maybe someone's walking out with designs the old-fashioned way and photocopying them. Or someone's bugging the phone of the president of the company. Which is why we're experts in surveillance and counter-surveillance."

René's eyes popped.

"And of course we'd do computer security as all the other firms do," she said, stirring her espresso.

"Interesting. How many employees do you have?" de Brosselet asked, smiling as he accepted a demitasse from Maxence. *"Merci."*

"Who you see and Saj, our permanent part-timer."

"I'd like to meet him."

"Of course," said René, shooting Aimée a look. "He's on assignment in India right now."

Assignment? More like meditation retreat.

She wished she'd prepared more. "We keep lean, if that's what you're asking. And we bring a special skill set to the table. My background in criminal investigation provides an unusual list of contacts, freelancers I trust for certain types of surveillance."

"Lean works if it delivers, Mademoiselle Leduc," he said.

She smiled at him and nodded to a wide-eyed René. "Shall we get started?"

Several hours later, René stood and stretched. "I've done my bit on the proposal. Your turn, Aimée. Think we hooked de Brosselet?"

"Time will tell. That is, if I finish these last projections."

"Lean, I like that." René grinned. "We're a lean machine."

She glanced at the time. She had a surveillance coming up, but there was still so much to do. No return call yet from Madame Uzes. Nor had she heard from Morbier. No chance to follow up on La Bouteille aux Puces for information or on Nicu's uncle, who should be questioned. And Drina Constantin, wherever she was, was running out of time, if she was even still alive.

"What's with the old newspaper? *Qu'est-ce que c'est,* Aimée, a *procès-verbal* and a torn drink receipt?"

Then an idea surfaced. "Remember that book you gave me, *Mamans Can Have Lives, Too?* It says delegate when your plate's full."

René nodded. "*Bien sûr.* It's a best seller, so it must work. Delegate away."

She wrote out La Bouteille aux Puces's name and address and slid it across her desk to him. "Sit down a moment. Let me explain."

She did.

"Delegating?" René shook his head. "That's asking me to go on a wild Gypsy chase. And it's personal."

"Who else would I trust with this, René?" she said.

"You think I can figure out what happened twenty years ago from people who lie for a living?"

"You're right," she said, seething inside. "A racist's the wrong person to ask. I'll figure it out myself."

Her phone rang. Morbier.

She turned away from René. *"Oui?"*

"How's the little princess today?" Morbier asked.

A little shiver traveled down Aimée's arm. Her father had called her that.

"She loves apricots," she said. "And splattering them on the wall. Today's her first care day with Babette. But that's not why I called and left you a message, Morbier. Are you all right?"

"Fine," he said, dismissive. "Speaking of calling, have you contacted that attorney?"

"Seems Melac's attorney contacted mine

before I'd even made an appointment. Not good, Morbier."

She knew René was listening to her conversation. The office behind her had gone too quiet. Him overhearing this was the last thing she wanted.

"Hold on, Morbier." She put her hand over the phone. Turned. But no René.

Had he stormed out in a huff?

She couldn't think about that right now. She needed to fill Morbier in, find out what he'd discovered.

"Leduc, I'm tied up testifying at the tribunal. It's the first time I could take a break. Make this quick."

Last night he'd promised to help her. For a moment she debated how much to share, decided on the bullet points: Nicu framed, his call, Drina's trashed atelier, the possible link to her father's murder.

"Back in trouble, Leduc? You broke your promise to me," Morbier interrupted. "What's going on in your mind these days?"

She figured that was rhetorical.

"Phfft." An angry expulsion of air came through the line. "Quit playing Wonder Woman and jeopardizing my efforts to find the Gypsy."

"Wait *un moment,* Morbier. Your efforts? Like what? Don't hold out on me —"

162

"I'm following up," he said. "And I can't talk about it here. *Tu comprends?*"

Before she could voice her fear that Drina's life was ebbing away, he hung up. She hit callback.

"Leduc, I'm going into court." Morbier's tone was ice-cold.

"Promise you'll tell me what you hear and I'll —"

"Keep the promise you've broken, Leduc?"

"Something like that. Morbier, the poor woman's condition's deteriorating every hour."

Pause. "I've called in favors from a surveillance contact in the seventh. Put my neck out. My contact's on it as we speak. It's promising, but I don't know any more."

"Promising?"

"Keep your skirt on, Leduc."

She heard a door slam in the background.

"Please don't disappoint me, Morbier," she said. Begging, she was begging now.

The phone cut off. She hated to admit it, but he was right. She needed to prioritize. She had come within footsteps of a murder this afternoon — what would happen to Chloé if she let herself get hurt chasing whispers? She had to trust Morbier, at least for now. How many times had he gone to bat for her, saved her *derrière*? More than she cared to remember.

She sensed a presence behind her in the office, whipped her swivel chair around. René had slunk silently back in and was sitting with his back to her in his customized ergonomic chair. A minute of silence lengthened to two. When René got really angry, he retreated behind a wall of silence. She was in big trouble.

She'd have to eat her pride. Time to make peace.

"*Désolée,* René," she said. "Call me out of line. You're right, I don't want you thinking —"

René jumped off his chair. "That you're crazy to get mixed up in this when you've got Chloé to think of? That you're giving Melac ammunition for his custody case? Next he'll accuse you of terrorism, going vigilante."

Implying that she was like her mother. Was she? Guilty heat spread up her neck.

"How much did you hear, René?"

"Enough to know that —"

"I went to meet Nicu," she interrupted, her breaths coming short, like pants. "To help him find his mother. Not to watch him bleed to death under the Métro, René." Her throat caught. "And it was my fault he was killed. My fault because I insisted he keep looking so I could find Papa's killer. When he found her notebook, they stole it and killed him for it. On top of that, Drina's not even his mother."

René's mouth widened in an O. "That part I didn't hear."

She'd kept it from Morbier, although she was unsure why. Maybe she didn't want to delve that deep into the details, feel the guilt of Nicu's death again.

"Aimée, this whole mess gets more *compliqué* at every turn."

"Like I don't know that, René." She looked up at the time. "It's four P.M., nineteen hours since Drina's abduction, twenty hours since her last medication. Without it she's suffering."

René shook his head. "If she's even alive, Aimée. Get realistic. She's gone, and her supposed secret about your father's murderer has died with her."

"Maybe she's gone." She sighed. "But her secret isn't, René."

"Face it. Time's run out. Drina's out of the picture, and her son who's not her son, too." He plopped down, adjusted the height of his custom chair. "I had too much champagne last night." He rubbed his temples.

"Then you need this." She reached into

her drawer, found her Doliprane and threw him the packet. "Not that you look hungover or anything." She paused, couldn't give up. "There's more, René."

"Do I really want to hear this? And does it even matter?" René sighed. "You're going to tell me anyway, aren't you, Aimée?"

He was always a good sounding board; she did want to hear his take. She began with Drina's notebook. René listened, swallowed the paracetamol and sipped green tea.

"Fifi and Tesla?" he repeated when she told him the names Nicu had read her. "As in a poodle and the scientist Nikola Tesla?"

"Code names, René. For who I don't know." Just then, at that moment, she wanted it all to go away. To go home to Chloé, give her a bath, play with the bubbles.

René's face softened. "You okay, Aimée?"

"I miss Chloé." Suddenly she realized that her blouse was wet. "*Merde,* I'm leaking."

After a trip to the WC and an application of mascara, lip liner and some Chanel red lipstick, life had improved. Priorities. She had priorities.

What they were, besides Chloé, she still had to figure out.

Back in the office, René said, "When's your appointment with the attorney?"

"Tomorrow. She requested Chloé's birth certificate."

"*Une formalité,* I'm sure," said René, looking grim. "Stay calm, Aimée. Morbier told me the lawyer's good. The best."

"So you two are talking behind my back?" She balled up an old fax and tossed it at him.

René kicked it back to her. "Only for your own good."

She held up the torn drink receipt from La Bouteille. "So far it's the only lead I've found."

René shook his head, pausing his fingers on the keyboard. "Not this again."

"It's related, René, part of a puzzle I can't find a way into."

"*Mais* everything you've said, Aimée, it's all conjecture. Too many ifs — if this woman's alive, if she's related to a woman murdered twenty years ago, if there's a connection to your father. What does it even matter now?"

"Not just any woman." She took out the envelope containing Nicu's birth certificate. Set it by René's keyboard. "Djanka Constantin, aged twenty-four. My father investigated her homicide. René, it's all connected but I don't know how." Then the tattered black-and-white photos she'd found in the envelope. "Here's Nicu as an infant with Drina and Djanka — see, it's labeled. Both Constantins. Look at their cheekbones. Tell me they're not sisters."

René stared. "A beauty, Djanka."

She had almond eyes, an alertness captured by the camera, which had caught her lifting her baby's feet in the air, a half smile parting her lips. A young woman full of life. A hint of the seductress.

The looks had certainly gone to her instead of Drina.

"*Alors,* this woman, my father's old informer, insists on seeing me, but gets abducted before I arrive. This boy she raised as her son finds her notes mentioning my father, he's knifed to death and the notes stolen — all within fifteen hours. I want to know who —"

"You haven't asked the important question, Aimée."

She was surprised to hear the note of interest in René's voice. But he always liked a puzzle — she'd hooked him.

"What do you mean?"

"Who's this Pascal in the second photo? Besides being Nicu's father?"

Not that hungover after all. "You're right, René. Nicu's uncle would know. The one who wanted to bring her back from the hospital."

A sigh. "Then I guess it's up to me to ask him." René took his custom-tailored Burberry trench coat from the back of his chair, donned his fedora. "Need to look the part, eh?"

"You mean it, René?" she said. "You'll help?"

"Time to hear some hot *manouche* jazz. Ferret around, look for the uncle." He took the photocopied receipt, Maxence's notes on La Bouteille, the photo and Nicu's birth certificate from Aimée's desk. "Call it delegating. Let me work on this. You finish the proposal, don't blow tonight's surveillance, and prepare for the lawyer."

Monday Afternoon

The grey-whiskered German shepherd lying on the cracked brown mosaic tiling at La Bouteille aux Puces growled as René entered. *Merveilleux.* Already irritated by having had to trek through the flea market in the drizzle — he'd had to park blocks away — René was less than thrilled with the bared teeth and wet dog smell in the dim Gypsy café.

Good thing he kept a packet of Chloé's teething biscuits in his pocket. He tossed one to the dog, who chomped down. And begged for another.

They parted as friends, and René continued past the blown-up photos of Django Reinhardt and Hot Jazz posters. The walls were stained pale yellow from nicotine. He doubted La Bouteille aux Puces had changed much since Django's time. Or that the woodwork had been scrubbed since then. Near the WC stood a wood cabin marked TÉLÉPHONE — rare to see one of those these days.

"Madame Bercou, *n'est-ce pas?*" René smiled with his most determined charm at the older woman behind the counter. "You've owned the café a long time, I understand."

The woman, wearing a violet scarf tied over a long braid and a blue cardigan under an apron, looked down at him. Squinted. Then shook her head.

Not a graduate of Gypsy charm school.

Had ownership changed hands? Or had Maxence gotten it wrong? He'd wasted his own time trying to keep Aimée from getting even more involved in this goose chase. But he'd driven this far, gotten his pant cuffs wet and he'd give it another go before he left.

"*Un express, s'il vous plaît,*" he said, trying to think of how to start a conversation, ease into questions. "Make it a double, Madame."

René climbed up onto the stool. Slipped. Wished he'd worn his loafers with the non-slip leather sole.

She set a demitasse cup under the chrome machine. Brown, work-worn hands, swollen rheumatoid knuckles — every slow movement looked painful.

He felt a twinge of compassion. His hip dysplasia pained him in the damp. What he wouldn't give for a cortisone shot right now.

Playing on the sound system was a recording of a twanging guitar with *la pompe,* the signature Django rhythm. On the walls, notices advertised nightly music. Photos of Django Reinhardt everywhere with his thin mustache and guitar held by the two fingers he played with, the deformed rest of his hand just visible. Gypsy cafés were the province of men, but the place was empty. Too early for the evening crowd, he figured.

"Madame?"

"*Attends,* need my hearing aid." She stuck a small beige plug in her ear as she stepped from behind the counter to face him. Took his measure. "No auditions here." Before he could open his mouth, she shrugged. "They're held under the big tent up from Place de Clichy."

As if all dwarves wanted to audition for the circus? Typical.

"That's not why I came," he said.

"Have it your way, *mon petit,*" she said. "So the music, you came for the music, eh?"

Not at all, he was about to retort. But it was a place to start. *"Bien sûr,"* he said with a smile, hoping to finesse it. "My nana loved this music," he said.

It was true. The speakers were playing "La Mer" now and the sound of Django's haunting guitar strains had brought back memories of his grandmother. Nana used to play Django records on her phonograph. He remembered how she set the needle on the vinyl, the scratchy sound, the burst of guitar. She would grin and hug him, and they would dance with a dish towel to *Hot Jazz.* He had only been four when she died, but he remembered sitting with her as she lay in a big feather bed with iron railings. Nana's thick grey bun had been tied with ribbon, her drawn face fully made up.

"She danced to Django's songs even in the kitchen," said René.

The woman set the wobbling demitasse of steaming espresso on the counter. Pushed the sugar at him.

"Who didn't?" she said, wiping her hands. "Everyone has Django stories. Ah, the stories. The old men drag them out at night; people like to remember." She winked. "Duke Ellington sat here and played with him."

René sat up on the stool. "Duke Ellington, here?"

"Everyone came to play with Django." Her eyes danced. "Not bad for a self-taught guitarist who never learned to read or write, eh?" She turned away as if stopping herself. Afraid of letting her guard down. Typical Gypsy, he thought. Close-mouthed to outsiders.

"*C'est vrai?* I thought I knew a lot about Django, but I didn't know he couldn't read or write." He hoped he hadn't laid it on too thick. "You mean he couldn't read music?"

"Django couldn't even take the Métro because he couldn't follow the signs." The woman was warming up again. "He took taxis, or walked if he'd gambled away his money."

"Must have been quite a character," said René.

A shrug. "Volatile, temperamental. An artist. Lived in his caravan or camped in hotel rooms."

René's foot tapped to the beat. It was infectious. For a moment he wondered if his nana had swung on this tiny dance floor in her youth.

He snapped out of it. This was a long enough trip down memory lane. He needed to find out about Djanka Constantin.

"Since you know so much, maybe you can help me," he said, hoping the change of subject didn't come off as abrupt. "Twenty years ago, in 1978, a young *manouche* woman named Djanka Constantin was murdered. Her killer was never caught. A drink receipt from La Bouteille was found in her pocket. Were you around then?"

"Me? *Non.*"

"Don't you remember hearing about it?"

She grabbed a towel. "That's a long time ago."

"Do you remember her family?"

A quick shake of the head. "Three francs fifty."

The Gypsy wall had descended, shutting him out. *C'était typique, ça.* Overcharged him, too. *Alors,* what else did he expect?

All this way only to find a deaf old woman, a shrine to Django and memories of his nana. But he sensed the woman knew more than she was letting on.

The dog growled. He heard a smack on the window, hoots of laughter. He turned around to see egg yolk dripping down the outside of the café's window. Two teenagers in rain slickers gave off snickers and taunts.

By the time the woman had grabbed the dog's leash and gotten to the door, they'd run away.

From the stool he could see the yellow smears on the window, watched her rub the stains off with a towel. Spit over her shoulder into the gutter.

Not the first time, René figured.

"Have you complained to the *flics*?" René said when she got back.

She shrugged. "We say it's better to turn sideways in the wind."

A Gypsy aphorism that seemed to cover a lot of bases. But he could use this to open her up.

"Me, I'm an outsider, too," René said, looking up from his cup. "Picked on, excluded in the village where I grew up. I took up martial arts and earned a black belt to compensate." He rarely shared these details. "My life's not so different from yours, Madame."

If the woman heard him, she didn't let on. His attempt at solidarity fell as flat as the eggshells she'd swept into the gutter.

"*Et en plus* you saw me, a dwarf, and assumed I had come for a circus audition," he said. He hated playing the sympathy card, it went against his grain. But he needed to reach out and get her to relate. "It's not like I can disguise my appearance."

She reached for a clean dish towel. "When the road bends, it's hard to walk straight, *mon petit,*" she said.

A crack in the wall. Good. He'd push.

"Can you help? Isn't there anyone who might remember Djanka?" said René. "A

176

long-time client who would have been here in the seventies, or the old owner?"

"What's it to you?" she said.

"I'm helping a friend."

"What do you care about something that happened twenty years ago?"

"Djanka's murder was filed away, forgotten. The *flics* didn't care, she was just a Gypsy," he said. "But it matters now to Drina, her dying sister, who's been abducted from the hospital. Drina's life is in danger, and I believe the secret of her location is linked to Djanka's unsolved murder."

He'd made the last part up and hoped it worked. Sitting up on the stool, he rubbed his cold hands. Had he convinced her?

"Come back later and talk to *les vieux,*" she said.

And waste more time trying to pry open sealed lips? He needed a less vague promise of help.

"Tant pis." René felt in his pocket for his billfold. "So young and full of life, only twenty-four years old, a beauty, this Djanka. See." He slapped the photo and a hundred francs on the zinc. "This help?"

The woman pulled her glasses from around her neck.

"Wasn't called Djanka back then."

René's spine straightened. His stool

creaked. "So what did you call her?"

"Aurélie."

"You knew her?"

"She sang, her husband played guitar. He died in a fire in their caravan."

"Pascal?"

She shrugged. "I don't remember."

"Pascal's not a typical *manouche* name, is it?"

She gave a sideways grin. "What's a name to us? We have many: three, four . . ."

As many as a particular situation demanded, René knew. He had read the newspapers — last year a Gypsy crime king had been sentenced, but six months into his term, the *flics* discovered it was his brother serving in prison.

"So she used Aurélie as a stage name?"

"Wouldn't surprise me. Anyway, I never saw her after her husband died," she said. *"C'est tout ce que je sais."*

He contained his excitement. Now he had something to tell Aimée.

"Funny," the woman continued, "you're the second one to ask in as many days."

Another person had come sniffing around? He was getting somewhere. Excited, he tried to keep his voice level. "A *flic?*"

"Not my business, *mon petit.*"

But she'd labeled the man, René could tell.

"It matters to me if I'm not the only one asking," said René. "Tell me what this person asked you about."

She shrugged. "Didn't stay long after I told him I'd never heard of her. Not my type of person," she said. "You, you're different."

He had gotten her to identify with him after all. And maybe the other *mec* hadn't left a hundred-franc note on the counter.

"Can you describe this man?"

"Ugly mug. Chain-smoked."

René sucked in his breath. He was getting somewhere all right. "Old, young?"

"Been around." Her face broke into a lopsided grin.

"So any scars, tattoos?'

She had a calculating twinkle in her eye. "A man must put grain in the ground before he can cut the harvest." She extended her palm.

He deliberated. Made to feel around in his pocket. Waited.

"Maybe in his sixties, thick eyebrows," she said, "a smoker, as I told you."

Could be anyone. He decided to move on and slid another hundred francs onto the counter. "I've heard in Romany culture, families insist on taking care of dying relatives. *C'est vrai?*"

"*Selon la tradition, oui,*" she said.

He wished he could remember Nicu's uncle's name, the uncle Aimée had mentioned. He decided to keep on trying. "Then why would a brother abduct his sister from the hospital and lie to her son?"

"That's not our way," she said. "Families prepare the traveler by keeping vigil at the bedside. We fear vengeance if wrongs aren't righted or forgiveness not granted before a person departs on their journey. Never happens. *C'est tabou.*"

If what she said held true, this put the Constantin uncle in the clear.

"Then who would?"

"I could ask around but it'd cost you."

More? No chance of help from the goodness of her heart, if she had one.

"*Les gens du voyage* move around," she said. "Things get *compliqué.*"

And René had little time. He took out three hundred francs — the rent due on his garage — and put a hundred and fifty on the counter with his card. "Half now. Half when I meet anyone who knew her."

His gaze caught on the Cirque Gitane poster beside the mirror. He recognized the uncle's name now — stupid, it had been staring him in the face the whole time. René jerked his thumb at the poster for the Constantin family circus. "Radu Constantin I'll talk to myself."

Monday, Late Afternoon

Aimée ran into her apartment building's courtyard, her flounced wool Gaultier coat damp from the drizzle. She wished she'd thought to pack her umbrella — then immediately felt racked with guilt for even thinking of such a thing and wished instead she hadn't sent Nicu to his death. But those thoughts would get her nowhere. The pear tree's budding leaves dripped on the lichen-laced cobblestones.

Only enough time to grab her laptop for tonight's surveillance and zip back to the office in the waiting taxi. Not even a moment to kiss Chloé, who was napping across the courtyard.

Someone stepped out from the shadows under the eaves near the mailboxes. Startled, Aimée almost dropped her bag in a puddle.

It was Donatine. The last person she wanted to meet. Melac's squeeze . . . *non,* his damned wife.

How the hell does she have the gall?

"Aimée, it's been bothering me since last night. There's been a terrible misunderstanding," said Donatine, her face concerned. Her long red braid snaked over her belted wool jacket. Shielded by an umbrella, she was dry from her rouged cheeks to her ankle boots. A perfect provincial. She was clutching a package with the brand-name Bonpoint, the chichi baby store, under her arm — "We got off on the wrong foot; please let me explain."

Aimée could feel words bubbling up in her mouth. Words like *Why did Melac choose you over me and his child?*

"My lawyer doesn't want us in contact," she said instead, determined to keep her hands in the pockets of her coat. Otherwise she'd swat this woman out of the way.

Donatine stepped aside. "*Bien sûr.* This package . . ."

"I don't want anything from you," she said. "No conversations, no gift, no trouble."

"Hear me out for two seconds, please," Donatine said.

"I'm sorry." She struggled to keep her tone businesslike. "My lawyer instructed me not to talk to anyone concerned."

"Melac thought that with your job you'd

183

welcome our help. I'm a nurse."

She was smart, this woman, inserting herself into the equation like this. Persistent.

"I'm sorry he never RSVP'd and that he's ignored the baby — your beautiful Chloé," said Donatine. "In your place I'd feel threatened, too."

Threatened. That about summed it up. And maybe a little jealous, too, though she'd deny it. The best defense was a good offense, her father had always said.

Aimée attempted to hold her tone even. "You're a stranger to me. *Désolée.* As I've said twice now, we can't be in contact."

And if you keep pushing me, I'll kick your kneecaps and ruin those ugly boots.

Donatine's pink-glossed mouth quivered. "It would mean so much to me if we were friends."

"What do you want, Donatine?"

Besides my baby.

"Melac's determined to reach a custody arrangement. Instead of tearing Chloé's life apart, let's discuss this together."

Together? A stranger, a desperate woman unable to have a child and glomming onto Aimée's? She'd neatly inserted herself into the equation again.

"Isn't it up to Melac to try to make things right with me?"

184

Why are you here instead of him?

"This doesn't have to go the legal route, Aimée. I tried to persuade him that you'd listen to reason, want the best for Chloé."

Fear flared up her spine. This Donatine spelled more than trouble. Determined, intent, single-minded — Aimée could relate. *Be smart for once.*

Think, think. In less than six months, the woman had met and married Melac, who had been on the rebound and gutted after his daughter's death.

Yesterday, life had been good apart from puréed carrot spit-up on her shoulder; then Melac had barged in with a barren wife, claiming rights to Chloé. No leg to stand on, she'd thought, but now she wasn't so sure. Then Nicu and her father's murder resurfaced . . . all at once.

"Aimée? Aimée?"

She came back to her damp courtyard and this grasping woman as she felt a package shoved into her hand.

"I don't want your gifts," she said. "Or for you to contact me again, Donatine."

"Then I'm sorry, Aimée. I wanted you to understand. I was hoping we could avoid the difficult route," she said. As she left, she added, "It's not my gift, but one from a

185

Monsieur Dussolier. I found it under your
mailbox."

Monday, Late Afternoon

René locked the Citroën's door and trudged up the cobbled passage, cursing the humidity under his breath. He winced at every step on the uneven, rain-slicked cobbles. Damn dysplasia flared up every wet spring. This season was the worst yet.

A baby's cry pierced his thoughts. Chloé? Brought back to earth, he turned around and saw a man soothing a little bundle in a stroller, tucking in a blanket.

Little Chloé took his breath away. The first time she'd clutched his thumb with her tiny fist, she stole his heart. All he wanted to do was protect this tiny thing, hold her and hear her gurgles. When she spat up banana on his new suit, he'd worn it like a badge of fatherhood. At the dry cleaner's, pride filled him when the owner smiled knowingly. "Ah, babysitting your goddaughter, Monsieur Friant? Nothing to fear — we're used to this kind of thing. I'll have your jacket looking like new tomorrow."

So many recollections of his childhood had surfaced in his mind — normal, according to the American parenting book: your new baby brings up primordial instincts and memories that you relive to relate to your growing infant. He kept a baby book for Chloé, as the American book suggested — even gave one to Aimée for Chloé's milestones: her first real smile that didn't come from gas, when she took a bottle instead of the breast, her first solid food.

A car horn blared in his ear. He almost jumped out of his skin. Stupid, he'd been daydreaming in the middle of the street.

He should forget these feelings, move on with his own life instead of helping Aimée live hers. But much as he tried, he couldn't get past them. Like his feelings for Aimée, which she'd never reciprocate. He was nothing but a best friend to her. And now the godfather of her child. Her child with damned Melac.

By the time he found Cirque Gitane in the large lot up the hill behind Place de Clichy, his hip was throbbing. The large blue circus tent took up more than half of the empty lot. Caravans were parked, surrounded by wall remnants from a Paris long

188

past, lines of washing flapping between them in the breeze. The odor from a steaming pile of fresh horse manure made it feel, for a moment, like a countryside fair. The long, unsmiling look he got from a middle-aged *manouche,* who stood smoking and polishing the fender of a Mercedes, didn't make him feel welcome.

Why had he agreed to Aimée's plea to search out the Gypsies? But he knew why — between her guilt over Nicu's murder and this loyalty to her father's old promise, she'd risk getting herself into even more dangerous situations. Not if he could help it. And he relished the challenge of this Drina puzzle — if he could solve it, maybe Aimée would stop being so distracted and get back on track.

René made his way through the caravans. The smells of cheap oil and frying onions emanated from one of the small caravans gathered around the Cirque Gitane tent. Two young boys with curly black hair ran around yelling, playing tag. A young woman wearing a pink jogging suit and a red scarf barked something at them. The boys, ragged pant cuffs trailing on the wet dirt, laughed. She filled a pail with water from the outdoor water tap, a green metal *robinet* by a wall.

"Excusez-moi," he said. "I'm looking for

Radu Constantin."

The two boys smiled at him and he was sure he saw them eyeing his cuff links. *Little thieves.* He pulled up his arms before they could get at them.

"Shouldn't you be helping your mother?" he growled and shook them off.

The woman barked at them again. In a flash they ran away, laughing, and she disappeared inside the open flap of the circus tent with her heavy pail. René followed.

Sawdust, the wheeze from an accordion — he felt immediately sucked in by the intimate draw of the big top. He remembered Saturday afternoons from his childhood, the first time he'd ever seen a grown-up man like him. The man had had a red nose and frizzy yellow hair, and he kept tripping over his big shoes, to the audience's delight. Terrified, René had hidden behind his mother. Would he end up a clown?

Now, he shivered in fascination. Colored lights masked the seediness, disguised the ratty curtains. He watched a rehearsal in full swing: candelabra-lit ringside violins and accordion players, trapeze artists, acrobats twisting like snakes, fire jugglers, tightrope walkers glistening with sweat, the clacking hooves of the dancing goat — it felt all so familiar, and it took him back to those small-tent Gypsy circuses in the countryside.

"You're looking for me?" A man in his shirtsleeves, wearing a fedora, rings on every finger, took René's arm and steered him outside onto the jagged cobbles.

"Radu Constantin?"

He nodded, his dark, unsmiling eyes taking the measure of René. "Auditions ended last week. Who told you to come here?"

Dwarves and circuses again. René's anger mounted. What did Drina and the old murder of Djanka have to do with Aimée's father's death? — that was the real question. Spitting mad now, he'd had enough. He pulled out his Leduc Detective card.

"Let me get to the point, Monsieur Constantin," he said. "How does your sister Djanka's murder twenty years ago connect to Drina's abduction?" He lifted the photo and shoved it in the man's face. "Nicu dragged my partner, Aimée, into this. Now I want answers."

Radu Constantin stepped back, startled. Gravel crunched under his feet. "That busybody he brought to the hospital — that *gadji* — I knew she'd cause trouble."

Lines of washing whipped in the wind, an eerie echo traveling between the caravans.

From inside the big top came the whine of violins. "We perform tonight. I'm busy."

"Twenty years ago, Aimée's father investigated Djanka's murder." René ad-libbed before Constantin could interrupt him. "After her sister's death, Drina raised Nicu as her own. But in the hospital yesterday, on her deathbed, she told Nicu about his real mother. Showed him his birth certificate." René hated lying, but this followed close to the truth. As much as he figured it would.

"How's this your business? Anybody's business but ours?" Radu Constantin shouted.

René knew he had to keep going. "Drina said she had a secret to tell Aimée about her father's murder. *Phutt,* before she could — she's abducted."

"What craziness comes out of your mouth?" Radu's dark eyes flashed. "My sister Drina is . . . how you say . . ." He searched for the word. "Like at the airport, in transit. Her soul's not at rest. Leave it alone. We take care of things our way."

"But Drina's missing, gone, *non?*" Exasperated, René wanted this man to see reason. "Now, with Nicu's murder . . ."

Radu Constantin suddenly put his hands over his face. Rocked back and forth. Then

192

he lifted his hands up to the sky, folded, as though in prayer.

René sighed. "I'm so sorry."

Radu hadn't known.

A few seconds later Radu seemed to come back down to earth and looked at René. "He's not family," he said dully.

René's brain stalled. These disparate events Aimée seemed hell-bent on connecting jumped all over the place. Yet if he didn't press and learn more while Radu Constantin stood towering over him in a black cloud of anger and despair, when would he? "You mean his real mother, Djanka, or Aurélie, wasn't family? Was Nicu's father a non-*manouche*? Pascal?"

"Leave us alone." Radu Constantin motioned to the middle-aged man René had seen polishing his fender before. The man set his rag down in a pail, lit another cigarette as Radu disappeared back into the tent. Shrugged.

"You heard, let's go."

"Is he always like this?" René asked the man, whose cigarette was hanging out of the corner of his mouth.

"I just married into the family," he said, the reek of alcohol coming from his pores. Glinting blond stubble on his chin and blond hair slicked back, he looked like the odd man out in this group. He stuck a pack of matches in his pocket and walked toward René and motioned him down the alley.

For one who hit the bottle so early in the day, his feet were steady on the cobbles. Still, that didn't exactly make him a reliable source of information.

"I feel terrible about spilling what happened to Nicu," said René. "But I don't understand him. Or his reaction. We only want to help, can't he see that?"

"Forget getting anything out of them, believe me." The man was turning into a conversationalist.

"I'm an outsider, eh? They're not going to talk to me, they'd rather let a poor woman die while they handle it on their own, *c'est-ça?*"

"Don't try to figure them out. Not healthy."

René bristled. "Doesn't he care that his nephew was murdered this morning?" René knew Radu did care — he'd seen the emotion rocking him. But he wanted details.

The *mec* chucked his still-burning cigarette into the running gutter. René heard a *thupt.* "Feuds round here can go back generations."

René stood at the corner, the sky oyster-grey beyond the mansard windows lining

194

narrow Passage de Clichy. The *mec* ducked in a doorway to light another cigarette. His gaze darted down the passage. Satisfied no one was on the lookout, he leaned forward.

"Drina's sister was shunned. Went by Aurélie and slept with a *gadjo* — a non-*manouche*."

"This Pascal, Nicu's father . . . Where is he?"

A quick shrug. "No idea. They threw her out." Engulfed in the *mec*'s smoke and red-wine fumes, René wished for a big gust of wind. A tornado. "That's what happened to the sister. Never mentioned. She's dead to them. Her kid, too."

Not according to what Aimée had seen. René tried to digest this.

And then, without warning, the *mec* strode away. René ran up the street as fast as his throbbing hip let him.

"Wait, Monsieur . . . ?"

The *mec* kept going.

"Monsieur? Monsieur?"

Before he hit the corner of Passage de Clichy, the *mec* turned.

"They're cursed."

Monday, Early Evening

"Where are you, Aimée? I need to load the equipment," Maxence said on the phone. "The reception starts in half an hour, it's an early one tonight. I need more setup time for surveillance."

Merde! She might have ruined the surveillance job because of her chat with goddamn Donatine. No time even to open Dussolier's gift for Chloé.

"In a taxi, I've got my laptop now." The rain had stopped, thank God. "My scooter's parked by the office. Meet me downstairs at the curb."

"*Quoi?*" he said. "Do you still have to change? It's a diplomatic event this evening. Proper attire and all."

"Bring me what's hanging in front of the back office armoire," she said. "Make sure it goes with the pearls in my desk drawer."

Ten minutes later, down on rue du

Louvre, Maxence stuffed his surveillance equipment in the Vespa's rear storage unit. He unscrewed the baby seat, clipped and bungee-corded it to the back, climbed on and held the clothes hanger with one hand while Aimée roared off.

Aimée changed while Maxence set up. After an hour at the party, she and Maxence had what they needed: recordings of the *comte*'s sister-in-law's conversations and photos of the guests she'd hobnobbed with — a Spanish attaché (her current lover) and the Belgian CEO of a rival to the *comte*'s family firm. Aimée could only speculate at this point on whether the *comte*'s sister-in-law or any other family members were passing on insider knowledge of his engineering firm. The *comte* feared plans for a hostile takeover of the family business. Their surveillance work entailed furnishing documentation to the *comte* and letting him decipher their evidence. Things were looking up — if "up" meant finding out your sister-in-law might be scheming against you.

The fading apricot twilight glowed over the Pont Neuf. Aimée could just make out a pale quarter moon, like a fingernail, half obscured by a nest of low clouds hanging above rue du Louvre's jagged rooftops.

Maxence hefted his equipment from the

scooter's case onto the pavement.

"The sister-in-law looks good for the saboteur," he said. "But I wouldn't rule out the *vicomte* from yesterday afternoon. His nastiness quotient matches hers."

She nodded, her mind elsewhere. Throughout the surveillance she'd struggled to focus on the job. Tried not to think about Nicu's half-open eyes, his mumbled last words as the Métro rumbled overhead. Her hands covered in his blood.

"Tomorrow night we can look forward to the *comte*'s cousin, more seamy goings-on," said Maxence.

She shouldered the rest of the equipment. "I'll take this upstairs." Time to check Leduc Detective's virus scans. And to change her clothes.

Ten minutes later, after checking the virus scans and setting the system to run the next cycle, she changed out of her Chanel. Back into her black leather pants, high tops, and, from the armoire, a ribbed, metallic, Lurex Gaultier tee. Shouldn't René have checked in with a progress report on la Bouteille by now? She switched her phone back on and noticed the message from Madame Uzes. Hit callback. Busy. She tried René. Busy.

Didn't either of them respect call-waiting? Almost twenty-two hours since Drina's abduction. Delirium would be developing.

Madame Uzes had left her address on the message. Should Aimée just hop on the scooter and talk to her in person? Checking, rechecking and following up — no matter how small the detail — was what investigating was all about, as her father had drilled into her. *Les petites choses* — the little things that added up. But she'd promised Morbier to stay out of it.

Morbier's phone went to voice mail.

She couldn't twiddle her thumbs waiting while the woman's life ebbed away. She knew the odds were against her, but if any chance existed of saving this woman after she caused the death of her son — or nephew — and finding out who killed her father at the same time, she had to pursue it. There was more at stake than Aimée understood.

She grabbed her vintage beaded clutch — faster than reloading her big bag — keys and leather jacket before she changed her mind.

Leafy branches hung below the lights on the boulevard, sending speckled shadows over the cobbles. Lush foliage smells filled the 7th, the greenest arrondissement in Paris with its squares, parks and gardens, public and private.

She parked her scooter at Madame Uzes's address, a stone Haussmann building the color of butterscotch with several stories of identical wrought-iron balconies on Avenue Constant Coquelin, a misnomer for the one-block dead-end street.

Aimée pressed the buzzer. No answer. She pressed it again.

"*Oui?*" A young girl's voice.

"Madame Uzes, *s'il te plaît,*" she said.

"Who's this?" the girl said.

Aimée leaned closer to the speaker and took out her Moleskine. "Aimée Leduc. She left me a message. The priest at Saint-François-Xavier referred me —"

The door buzzed open. "Fourth floor, left."

Not needing the exercise for once — since she'd been nursing Chloé, her pants slid off her hips — Aimée took the shaking elevator up. She reapplied Chanel red to her lips, blotted them with a café napkin and dabbed the napkin to her cheeks for color.

On the landing outside the apartment door stood a group of older women in a flurry of cheek kissing. No mistaking the hovering scent of Joy by Patou, one of the most expensive perfumes in the world. Or the uniform whitish-blonde coifs these women wore, each of them sporting a discreet fleur-de-lis, with a ministerial emblem or two pinned on the lapels of their cashmere jackets. This was the domain of generals' and ministers' wives, a rare breed that existed only in the *quartier* surrounding the École Militaire and les Invalides. *Très "ancien régime"* types who exuded an understated elegance that money couldn't buy.

Not her crowd. Now or ever. Yet these women — not one under sixty — freshly *maquillées,* coutured and coiffed, earned her grudging respect.

Every last one of them turned the full beam of their attention on her, the outsider in their midst, as she clutched her scooter helmet and vintage bag. She felt like a counterfeit in the land of Hermès.

"*Pardonnez-moi,* I'm looking for Madame Uzes," she said. "*Désolée . . .*"

"The tradesmen's entrance is round the back," said a voice from the crowd.

Welcoming, too. The wrong day to leave the Birkin at home. Yet her success depended on playing to their noblesse-oblige instincts.

"Mademoiselle, you're looking for Belle, my niece?" said a woman in the apartment doorway, her white-blonde hair pulled back in a chignon. Chic and soigné. "We're all

Uzes in the apartment — confusing, I know."

"Madame, the priest at Saint-François-Xavier referred me to her as the head of the Christian Helping Hands program. She left me a message with her address. I'm sorry to intrude, but it's vital."

She saw a relaxing of couture-clad shoulders, almost heard a collective sigh of relief.

"Then come in, wait *un moment,*" she said. "I'll join you before my friends and I are off to an evening reception at the *musée . . .*" Madame Uzes lowered her voice. "*. . . that racy Dali retrospective.*" One of the coiffed pack fanned herself with her hand, her diamond tennis bracelet flashing on her wrist, as if to say "racy" wouldn't quite cover it.

Dali, racy? Maybe in 1963.

"*Merci,* Madame," Aimée said, making her way through the group toward the door. Sanctioned and approved now by the ladies, she heard murmuring as she passed: ". . . all that volunteering . . . that handsome young priest . . ."

She was shown into a wood-paneled salon, where she faced a glaring girl of about eleven or twelve years old in a pleated wool skirt and matching blue cardigan, with white socks and black Mary Janes. A de rigueur outfit for the *7ème* — one that had last been in style in the fifties everywhere else.

"Maman's left me with the old dragons," she said, shooting a look at her great-aunt back at the door. "Good thing you've come. Now they'll have something to talk about."

Aimée could just imagine.

The girl pointed to her helmet. "You've got a scooter?"

Did a little rebel's heart beat inside the cardigan? Aimée sensed a possible mine of information.

She smiled. "It's pink. I'm Aimée. And you?"

"Lisette. The only things that drive down this street these days are hearses," Lisette said. "That's the only way people get out of here."

"Where's your mother, Lisette?"

"Maman's at a meeting. She's always at meetings."

"That's right, *ma chère,*" said the elder Madame Uzes, joining them. "My niece Belle took over a monumental job. She spearheads that program, Christian Helping Hands."

"Isn't that where she works with *des manouches*?" Aimée asked.

"*Bien sûr,* she sponsors a program for

Evangelical Christian Gypsies. Outreach in the spirit of Christian fellowship, open to all Christians. It's rather like an agency that helps create or find jobs for them using their artisanal skills."

Aimée couldn't believe her luck. With a little insistence, she'd find a lead to Drina.

"Nobody knows how to do that work anymore, Maman says," Lisette informed Aimée. "And they're cheap."

Aimée remembered her father's colleague, who had been stationed at the *commissariat* here in the 7th, saying that the *haute bourgeoisie* would walk three blocks to save a franc on mineral water like anyone else. He'd meant it as a compliment.

"May I consult the list of artisans in the agency records, Madame?"

"Ah, I wish I could help you, but Belle handles all that. *Je n'en sais rien.*"

She needed to see those records. "Would you mind calling her? I hate to bother you, but it's important. It's concerning Drina and Nicu Constantin."

"Do the Lord's work, *mais oui, je comprends,*" she said and picked up her cell phone, a small graphite model. Hit speed dial, then shook her head. "Never picks up, my niece. Perhaps come back tomorrow."

Tomorrow would be too late. "You

wouldn't know an address for Christian Helping Hands, would you?"

"*Désolée.* Talk with Belle."

Nothing came easily. Disappointed, Aimée handed her a card. She noticed the gilt chairs with their faded upholstery and the sagging tapestry on the far wall. This fossilized place reeked of threadbare wealth. Antique military memorabilia cluttered the glass cabinets lining the hall. Several families, or a whole encampment of *manouches,* could live in this space in comfort.

"Lisette, will you turn off the lights?" said Madame Uzes, gesturing for them to leave the room.

Frugal, this Madame Uzes.

In a swirl of Patou, she joined the rest of her cronies at the door. Aimée needed to reach this Belle; she hung back, thinking in the hallway, where Madame was putting on her cashmere scarf. "Madame, *pardonnez-moi,* but may I use your *salle de bains*?"

"Lisette can show you . . ." The rest of her reply was lost in the buzz of the ladies' conversations and laughter.

"Why not? I'm just going downstairs to sleep at my cousin's." Lisette made a face.

As she followed the girl down the hallway, Aimée asked, "Do you remember your mother mentioning someone named Drina?"

"My mother, *oui*. But it's my big sister Rose who thinks Nicu is hot," she added with a wide smile. "Rose is weird," Lisette said. "Nicu would never be into her. He's from a different world."

Aimée stopped in her tracks near the bathroom. Nicu's face, his blood on her hands, came back to her. "Did . . . does Nicu come here often?"

Lisette shrugged. "Nicu delivered some church kneelers a few days ago," she said. "When he left, my mother and sister had a big argument. I didn't hear it all."

Aimée's high heels creaked on the worn parquet floorboards. "Is Rose . . . does your sister have a relationship with Nicu?" Aimée's heart ached. Was someone going to have to break the news to a teenage girl that her forbidden boyfriend had been killed?

"It's never going to go anywhere between her and Nicu," Lisette confided. "The Gypsies keep to themselves, my mother says. She says Rose should just give up on it already." Lisette opened the creaking door to another hallway. Chill and unheated. "I hate living here." Lisette's voice rose, petulant. "We have to, Maman says. It's the economy."

No doubt the Uzes family, like others in this tony *quartier,* held on with a desperate grip to the big family apartment, worn around the edges; most of its value would be eaten up in inheritance taxes if they tried to sell.

"I think the economy's stupid." Lisette's small eyes challenged her. "Do you?"

Aimée needed to steer this opinionated trainee grown-up in ankle socks back to her mother and sister's argument. "Can you tell me anything else about Rose and Nicu? Or what your mother and sister argued about? I bet you heard a lot."

Lisette's eyes gleamed. "And if I did? What's it to you if Nicu wanted to go out with Rose after church?" Lisette paused at the bathroom door.

"You're smart, I can tell. Mature for your age. You understand a lot," she said, hoping to make the girl feel important. "Even your mother's relationship with Nicu and Drina." Aimée paused. "Did you know that Drina's in trouble?"

Lisette's eyes widened. "Trouble? Like arrested?"

"Why do you say that?"

"Maman thinks Gypsies steal, even if she pretends she trusts them," Lisette said. "Is that why you're here?"

"Lisette. Drina's been a victim of a crime. I can't say any more. I'm sworn to secrecy."

Lisette's mouth gaped open.

"Can you tell me anything about what your mother and Drina talk about?"

"But they only talk about boring things, church stuff. Maman keeps the records of the *manouches* who work with the church."

Alert, Aimée nodded. "Bet your mother has the information on her computer."

"Computer?" Lisette scoffed. "Maman's old-fashioned; she writes everything down."

Even better. Aimée smiled. "Does she have an office? Maybe Drina's information is in there. Why don't you show me? Then I wouldn't have to bother her or your great-aunt."

"Lisette!" Madame Uzes called out. "We're leaving, you'll have to go downstairs now."

Even with an old-fashioned name and outfit, there was nothing old-fashioned about the way Lisette winked at her. "If I help you, will I get a ride on your scooter?"

Aimée nodded. "And we'll keep this between ourselves, *oui*?"

"Tantine, the lady's still in the *toilettes,"* shouted Lisette, pointing Aimée toward the next high-ceilinged room and mouthing, "Desk drawer." "I need to use it, too. Don't

208

wait, I'll go to my cousin's in a minute."

The front door shut.

In the office sat an eight-legged Mazarin desk with two tiers of drawers, an antique in need of varnishing. Lisette, who had followed Aimée in, opened the drawers and showed Aimée bank records, rubber bands, insurance statements — a wealth of information, everything but a Christian Helping Hands file.

On top of the desk lay the stub from a medical-bill, next to it, a vase of daffodils.

No personal planner. No address book. No diary.

"Can you remember where your mother might have put it?"

"Guess she took it with her," said Lisette.

Aimée's eye caught on the name on the medical bill; stub: Clinique Saint-Jean de Dieu. A small private Catholic hospital and clinic in the area. At one time the 7th arrondissement had more churches than hospitals; now she figured it went the other way. "Was she going to a doctor's appointment?"

"No, why?" Lisette said, peering at the bill. "Oh, that's for my great-uncle. He's at that hospital. He's on a special diet, so she has to pay extra."

On the stub, today's date was circled, and

someone had written a check number in the corner. Aimée leaned forward and touched an ink blot on the blotter; a black smudge came back on her thumb. Not quite dry. "Does your mother go to drop checks off at the *clinique* in person? Like, could she be there now?"

Lisette shrugged.

"Don't you want to wear my new scooter helmet tonight on our ride?" said Aimée.

"Bien sûr." Lisette grinned.

After five minutes of driving up and down the tiny dead-end street on Aimée's scooter, Lisette went up to her cousin's. Time was running out, and she had to act fast and get all the details right. She'd wangled a phone number for Rose out of Lisette, but was disheartened when it turned out to be the number for a phone at a student café; the young woman who answered said, "Not here," and hung up. She called René again. Only voice mail. Frustrated, she left a message.

Aimée held out small hope she'd find Madame Uzes at the *clinique,* but she had to do something. Follow any connection.

As she rode toward the *clinique,* she thought about this *monde privé* of the privileged elite, and about the *manouche*

210

community she was trying so hard to track down. They were two different worlds, ostensibly opposite, yet they had so much in common, Aimée thought — they were both secretive cultures, worlds hidden from outsiders; their inhabitants proud people who kept to themselves. Not that Aimée was going to let pride or secrecy stop her from getting to the bottom of this.

Nicu, with his whole life ahead of him, murdered as a result of her fixation on her father. Who next?

She checked her side-view mirror at the intersection. No blue van, no car trailing her. And in front of her was only the lamplight filtering through copper-beech branches onto the zebra-striped crosswalk. The light turned green and she gunned the engine.

More than twenty-three hours now. René was right, Drina was probably dead by this point, and Nicu had been silenced forever. The pros, whoever they were, had accomplished their task. Her father's death had been walled over, Drina's secrets had disappeared with her. Aimée was left stumbling in the dark — again.

Cold night air hit her cheekbones and she double looped her scarf with one hand. Thoughts played in an endless reel in her head. Her father's tangled secrets, which she now knew must be linked to at least two but maybe three or more other murders besides his own, were a vast incomprehensible net descending on her. And in her bones, she knew she was the only one who could unravel the knots. If she wanted justice for her father — and for Nicu, whose life had been cut short for no reason; and for abducted Drina, who had probably died in excruciating pain; and for the mysterious Djanka, whose murder had been buried so many years ago, because no one cared about a dead Gypsy — she would have to figure this out herself. No other choice, whatever Morbier said; whoever had killed Nicu knew she was involved. And it terrified her. Made her knees wobble on the scooter.

For a moment she wondered if she could do this. Chloé depended on her. *Mon Dieu,* her baby was just teething. René's accusation spun in her head: "*. . . crazy . . . giving Melac ammunition . . .*" Would she turn into another version of her mother, the obsessed seventies radical turned CIA agent who'd gone rogue, dealt arms, ended up on Interpol's wanted list — and abandoned Aimée as a child?

The two didn't equate. No comparison to her mother, she told herself, as she always did. She chewed her lip, tried to push those thoughts aside.

Aimée had to make it right. She would. Count on it. And she'd make René cover her back.

Aimée smiled at the dark-haired young woman at the billing desk at Clinique Saint-Jean de Dieu. Her second hospital in twenty-four hours. And they weren't exactly her favorite kind of place to hang out.

She set her vintage clutch bag on the counter. "*Ah non,* have I missed Madame Uzes again?"

"She's a patient, Mademoiselle?" The young woman turned to consult her computer screen. Over her shoulder Aimée could make out what looked like patients' names in columns. Room numbers. If only the young woman would angle the screen to the left, Aimée'd get a clear view.

"Her great-uncle is, and she takes care of his supplementary dietary needs. I'm running late; she must have been by to pay already, *non?* Perhaps she's still here?"

"*Attendez,* I'll check." A few clicks. "Yes, she took care of Corporal Uzes's bill. If that's all?"

"I wouldn't bother you, but there's a problem with her daughter's babysitter. How long ago was she here?"

"My colleague took care of this. Looks like ten minutes ago."

"Maybe I can catch her if she's visiting the corporal. Which way is that?"

The young woman hesitated.

Aimée snapped open her clutch, pulling out her lipstick tube as if to apply it before going. "It will only take a moment," she said. "Which room is the corporal in?"

The young woman caught the eye of a colleague hunched over the opposite computer screen, phone to her ear. The colleague shook her head. "I'm sorry, *clinique* policy forbids me to give out that information."

Aimée tipped her clutch bag. The contents — mascara tube, keys, Chloé's teething ring — spilled behind the woman's computer. "Oh, I'm sorry. But I understand."

The young woman gathered the spilled contents and put them in Aimée's waiting hands.

"Oops, my lipstick . . . I think I see it. Behind your computer."

"Where?" The woman leaned forward, reaching behind the screen. Still blocking Aimée's view. If only she'd lean a few more . . . "*Désolée,* but —"

"There, see?"

The woman bent down.

Over her shoulder Aimée scanned the

display, noting the corporal's room number.

"I can't find it, Mademoiselle."

"Oh, I'm so dumb," she said, tapping her forehead with the palm of her hand, "my lipstick's right here. *Merci!*"

Room 314 — spacious, high-ceilinged and warmed by soft lamplight — overlooked a dimly lit garden that stretched half a block, if not more. Amazing, all the green spaces hidden behind walls in this *quartier*. But the room was empty.

Merde! Too late.

She was about to leave when a gnome-like figure entered the room, his gait crab-like. A grey suit hung from his frame as if he'd shrunk inside it. He must have been in his nineties, but his face was smooth, waxen. *"Quels idiots."* He shook his head, grabbed Aimée's arm. "They're counterattacking, *ma petite.*"

Startled by his grip, Aimée caught the gaze of the woman behind him. "Madame Belle Uzes?"

The woman nodded, shot Aimée a long-suffering look. "My great-uncle thinks it's 1917."

Madame Uzes guided the corporal to a chair. Her eyes narrowed. "You're not the

215

new social worker, I've met her. Who are you?"

That gave Aimée an idea. "*Mais non,* I'm the health program liaison. I'd like to ask you —"

"Where's your badge?" Madame Uzes interrupted. "How did you just walk in here?"

Aimée quickly rummaged among her alias cards. Found what she was looking for. "I'm Marie from Hôpital Laennec," she said, handing her the card she'd taken off the office bulletin board.

"Don't start on this again. I told Doctor Estienne Great-Uncle's doing well here."

Doctor Estienne? A coincidence? But Aimée was distracted by the old man thumping his gnarled fist on the table. "Retreat, I tell you. We must reach safety before the mustard gas!" the corporal shouted.

To Aimée's horror, he tugged his chin, which slipped off, revealing the lower half of what had been his face, now a deep cavity of rippled pink skin with a hole for a mouth. From beside the chair, he pulled a khaki green gas mask, which he then fitted over his disfigured visage.

One of *les gueules cassées,* the broken faces, maimed in the Great War. They had been a fixture of her childhood growing up — every *quartier* had them, although there weren't many left anymore.

"The mustard gas, *ma petite,* let's go," he said, motioning to her.

Sad. Her mind went back to the old Loterie Nationale tickets her grandmother had bought to support the rehabilitation of *les gueules cassées* in the old châteaux formerly requisitioned as field hospitals. A few were kept to house remaining severely disfigured soldiers, providing the grotesque a refuge from the public. Many of the generation who'd lost their youth, ideals and faces preferred to live among their own kind. Others wore masks to avoid horrifying children.

"Get the supply wagon, the one with wheels," he said. "Didn't you hear me?"

"After your dinner, Great-Uncle," Madame Uzes said, matter-of-factly. "You know how you like the way the nurse cuts up your *steak-frites.*"

Dinner served this late in a hospital? Or was it part of his special treatment?

"I don't want my *soupe à l'oignon* cold again," he said petulantly. "They always forget."

"We'll warm it up, Great-Uncle," she said.

A nurse appeared at the door, clucked.

"Having one of those evenings, Corporal? Let's go to the garden before we try dinner again."

And as quickly as he'd appeared, the gnome scuttled out wearing his gas mask.

"Madame, this doesn't concern your great-uncle," said Aimée.

"Good. I'm not moving him." Madame Uzes, tall like her aunt, wore Chanel pumps and a beige cashmere sweater set. She sat down and glanced at her diary, seeming pre-occupied. "If that's all, Mademoiselle?"

Great — the woman she'd lied to in order to see wanted to dismiss her. Well, that wasn't going to work. Aimée sat down in the adjoining chair.

"The priest at Saint-François-Xavier told me you're in charge of Christian Helping Hands and you employ *les manouches.*"

"*Et alors?*"

"I need Drina Constantin's address, contacts, any information you have that will help me reach her family members."

Madame Uzes looked up from her agenda. "Talk to her son, Nicu."

Aimée hesitated. "You don't know? He's dead."

Madame Uzes blinked. "What do you mean?" She snapped her diary shut. "But I saw them both a few weeks ago."

"I'm sorry. I thought you knew."

"Knew?" Shock showed on her face. "When? What happened?"

Aimée's knees trembled. "Murdered this morning, the police have the details."

Madame Uzes dropped her diary. "That's terrible."

Aimée swooped it up and handed it to her. "But you can help, *non*? There's no time to waste."

"Help? But how?" Madame Uzes shook her head. "A Gypsy killing? Some vendetta, you mean. I can't believe I let that young man into our home."

Great.

"You misunderstand, Madame," said Aimée. "Drina was in her last days; she had been put on hemodialysis at Hôpital Laennec. Last night, someone unplugged her from the machines and abducted her. Nicu was trying to find her."

"Drina disappeared?" Madame Uzes gasped. "But I don't understand."

"Every hour she's missing brings her closer to death. Any information you have will help. Can you tell me how you used to contact her?"

Madame Uzes thumbed open her diary. "That's the only address I have, a workshop near the La Motte-Picquet–Grenelle Métro stop."

The atelier on Passage Sécurité.

Back to zero. She'd thought she might find something more here. But she had to give it another shot.

"Tell me about the last time you saw Drina and Nicu," she said.

Madame Uzes thought. "Nicu delivered the kneelers, furniture Drina had repaired."

"Did they have a helper, anyone else with them?"

"How would I know?" she said, bristling. "*Désolée,* I don't mean to be unkind. I just spoke with Drina for a minute. My older daughter showed Nicu where to put the furniture."

The one who had the hots for him. Rose. The one who argued with her mother.

"To tell you the truth, I didn't notice much, I'm sorry," said Madame Uzes.

Only the hired help, Aimée thought. Gypsies.

Madame Uzes had the grace to look ashamed. "We try to bridge the differences," she said. "Spread Christian fellowship and encourage those like Drina to join a cooperative."

"I need to know every detail. What's your daughter's number?"

"Why? This has got nothing to do with her."

Au contraire, according to her little sister Lisette.

"Better I talk to her than the *flics,* don't you think, Madame? This is a murder investigation now."

She wrote it down with a quick nod. A different number from the one Lisette had given her. "Rose attends l'Institut d'Études Politiques de Paris."

The prestigious *grande école* nicknamed Sciences Po, in the 7th. Aimée stuck the info in her pocket.

"Please try to think back to when you last saw Drina. It's important, Madame."

Madame Uzes shook her head. "But it doesn't make sense."

Aimée's ears pricked up. "Have you remembered something?"

"That's right. Now I remember." Madame Uzes stood up. "The time before last was when I saw Drina at church, maybe two weeks ago. Drina didn't look well, but she wouldn't listen to me. Hated hospitals. I urged her to see Doctor Estienne, a specialist who's treated my family."

Nicu must have listened and taken her to Laennec. But that only led her back to the beginning. "Doctor Estienne treated her,"

221

Aimée said. "But she was abducted from Hôpital Laennec last night during a busy shift change."

"But Doctor Estienne's established a private practice here, in the next wing. He practices out of his own clinic, affiliated with Saint-Jean de Dieu," said Madame Uzes. "Our foundation helps with medical bills, private supplemental care and meals if needed. Why wouldn't Nicu bring his mother here?"

Aimée wondered that too.

Outside the window in the now-lit garden, Aimée saw the great-uncle rooting in a bed of peonies while the nurse tried to restrain him.

"*Désolée,* I've got to go," Madame Uzes said. "He's digging trenches again."

Five minutes later Aimée found Dr. Estienne's clinic in the next wing. So far she'd impersonated a family friend and a health liaison. She prayed the nice woman in billing wouldn't ask Madame Uzes about her daughter's trouble with the babysitter. She needed to talk to Dr. Estienne and find out as much as she could before the staff cottoned on to her.

"Doctor Estienne's at a staff meeting," said the receptionist, a young man this time, wearing thick-lensed glasses. "Then he has a patient."

"How late do evening clinic hours run?"

"I can fit you in at eight forty-five."

That would be twenty-four hours since Drina's disappearance. She glanced at her Tintin watch. Less than half an hour.

"You said you're a new patient?"

She hadn't, but she nodded and accepted the clipboard and forms.

"*Oui,* I'll wait over there." She took the clipboard to fill out on the lantern-lit clinic *terrasse,* which overlooked the private garden. Easy to keep a lookout from here and intercept Dr. Estienne before his patient. Here in the quiet, she tried the number Madame Uzes had given for her daughter Rose.

Monday Night

Rose Uzes ignored her ringing phone.

"What if it's Nicu? Answer it, Rose," said Robert. "My film's finished, and he's up next."

Nicu didn't have a phone. Annoying. "It'll just be my stupid little sister." Rose clicked her phone to vibrate without even glancing at it. "Nicu's here somewhere," said Rose. She scanned the dank artists' squat under Pont Alexandre III, a former boathouse. Didn't see him. "He promised."

"Late, he's always late," said Robert, hitting the lights to scattered applause.

"I'll find him," she said, picking up their protest flyers.

She made her way among the graffiti artists, a hip-hop DJ anxious to spin, a few of her fellow students from Sciences Po and the odd local. A reluctant Nicu had agreed to speak. He'd promised her.

Yet, as usual, Nicu was late. "I operate on Romany time," he always joked with her.

Robert's award-winning documentary film, *Le voyage des Manouches,* which highlighted the illegal destruction of encampments outside Avignon, had brought a raised fist or two from the crowd and shouts of, "*Liberté, égalité, fraternité* — now!"

Where was Nicu?

Without a *manouche* to speak to the truth of Robert's film, they'd have to figure something else out. And soon. Meanwhile, Robert stepped onto the metal boat rig, a makeshift stage.

"My film shows you what happened in Avignon. We can't let the same thing happen here. March with us in protest tomorrow at the *mairie* of the seventh arrondissement," he said. "Social housing in the *quartier* is mandated, and encampment rights for travelers should be, too."

"*Et alors?*" A voice shouted. "Where's my rights? I've waited three years for housing."

"We need your voice, too. Everyone should be heard tomorrow," said Robert. "Join us. The policy the *mairie*'s pursuing blatantly violates city requirements and your housing rights as well as the Roma's. This report's statistics prove it." Robert took a sheet and read: "*A wide disparity has been found in compliance and non-compliance with required social housing. The seventh arrondissement provides only between one and two percent available social housing in contrast to arrondissements in northeast Paris, which make up the maximum required twenty percent stipulated for the city."* Robert lifted up the paper. "See for yourselves. They'll get away with it, like they do every year, unless we demonstrate."

Marco, a graffiti artist, stood up. "I say we claim ground on the Champ de Mars."

A few snickers in the crowd.

"Why not? This is the greenest arrondissement in Paris," Marco continued, wiping his forehead in the humid air. "There's space for everyone, not just the ministries and the elite."

The concrete rumbled under Rose's feet from the nearby underground RER train. She hated the squat, especially the mildew, resin and oil odors from the boats that pervaded the atelier space. She glanced around, again wondering why Nicu hadn't appeared. So unlike the Nicu she knew. She shivered, remembering the feel of his warm arms holding her under the duvet the other night.

"The film's advisor's joining us tonight," said Robert. "He'll talk about his life, the *manouche* nomadic tradition, the musical heritage and Gypsy jazz —"

"Romanticizing the Gypsies?" interrupted a balding man wearing a duffle coat. He stepped out of the crowd. "Free spirits? Music lovers? Pah, all clichés. I live here. Talk to my neighbor. Our street's had three break-ins, all by eleven- and twelve-year-olds. The Roma teach kids to steal." He shook his head, clucked in disgust. "They use their own children."

Marco stepped forward. "You're right, they're being used. Used and victimized by the system that's kicking families out on the street. Where can they go, how can they survive? Don't they have a right to live as they wish, like we do?"

Two other men joined the man in the duffle coat. "By stealing? Nothing justifies robbery, the filth and garbage they leave behind in the encampments, the begging."

"But you see, it's a vicious circle. If we made it easier for them to access our social services and education —"

"Education?" The man was shouting. "But their children drop out of school!"

Rose noticed several figures in hoodies moving toward the center of the crowd. Filing in behind them on the paths they had cleared were skinheads with tattoos on their necks, brass knuckles glinting on their fists.

Robert jumped down to face the trio who'd pushed their way forward.

"Living in squalid caravans and stealing?" The duffle-coat man was saying. "That's a lifestyle to promote?"

More shouting. Any minute, Rose realized, a fight would break out. She edged backward, nervous, frantically looking for Nicu under the coved stone arch. Earlier, she'd been wishing he would show up, but now she was hoping he wouldn't.

Her phone vibrated, and this time she answered. Her sister. "Why don't you pick up?"

"I told you never to call. Quit bugging me, Lisette. Tell Maman I'm studying."

"Maman's out. Least of your worries. Your boyfriend Nicu's in trouble."

"He's not my . . . what trouble?"

Glass shattered in the crowd. The raised voices drowned out her sister's reply.

"Lisette?"

She clicked off, searching through the crowd. She had to warn Nicu, get him out of here if . . .

She was shoved hard from behind, and her leaflets scattered to the concrete as she fought for balance. Marco and the graffiti artists were facing off against the skinheads.

"You're talking about a people that's been persecuted, disenfranchised and run out for centuries," Marco was shouting.

Rose's chest felt tight in the humid air. Angry mumblings and red perspiring faces surrounded her. Why couldn't people discuss this reasonably?

"This is a complicated situation, with a long and entrenched history," she said, raising her voice to be heard and earning herself some dirty looks. "There's no simple solution. But if we all work together, the entire community will benefit, not just *les manouches.*"

"Quit with the bleeding-heart excuses," the duffle-coat man said. "If they live here, they need to follow the law like you, me and everyone else."

"Who says they don't?" Marco shouted. "You can't jump to conclusions about an entire group of people based on one or two members." He'd climbed onto a chair now and was speaking to the crowd. "How can these people trust a country that rounded them up and put them in internment camps during the war?"

Looking around, Rose realized her friends from Sciences Po had scattered and gone. The shouting was escalating. She felt a hand close around her ankle, then she was tumbling to the ground and into a whirl of arms and legs. Afraid, she yanked her leg free and crawled, panting, to a peeling boat hull. She pulled herself up. The entrance doors were open, three steps away. If she could just reach them, she could get out of here.

Then her foot caught on something, and the next thing she knew she was landing on her knees and elbows on the damp concrete and staring at the trailing black laces of a pair of military boots.

Monday Night

The white trailer by the exit to the Ségur Métro stop looked out of place, René thought, with its sign reading MADAME RANA: *Chiromancie; Tarologie; Médium; Voyante du Passé, Présent et Avenir; Spécialiste des Photos et de l'Écriture.* Quite a varied clientele she must get here, René figured; she was right on the border of the chichi 7th arrondissement and the more proletariat 15th.

From Gypsy café to circus to a damn fortune-teller. Madame Bercou, or whatever name she went by, from La Bouteille aux Puces, had called him and given him this fortune-teller's address. He'd paid enough for it. Now he wanted answers. But what could a fortune-teller, who lied for a living, tell him about the Constantins?

The well-lit street lay deserted. He knocked on the clean, white trailer door.

"Madame Rana?"

"Un moment, s'il vous plaît," came a voice.

A few minutes later a woman, in what René recognized as a cobalt-blue Givenchy wool coat like one Aimée had in graphite, descended the trailer's steps. A Maltese peeked out from her matching leather tote. She disappeared around the trailer in a mist of Guerlain.

"Entrez," came the voice.

Inside the caravan, the decor favored purple and red; the walls were padded, cushion-like. A young woman stood before a purple-draped table. She wore a long skirt with small mirrors woven into the fabric, an embroidered peasant blouse, gold hoop earrings and plenty of eyeliner. A little too much for René's taste.

The young woman sat down before a brass tray, shuffled a deck of tarot cards. To her right was a display of quilled feathers and satiny, polished hematite stones that invited one to touch. For a moment he visualized Chloé, who put everything in her mouth these days, choking on one. A chandelier of black glass hung from the ceiling, and a clump of sage smoldered in an abalone shell. He fought the urge to cough and run out of this bordello-like herbal cocoon.

"A tarot reading, or your palm?" She

looked up with a rehearsed smile. "Or for you I'd suggest throwing the stones. The stones respond to magnetism, your will and courage."

Choices, choices, choices.

She looked to be in her midtwenties. Too young, from what Madame Bercou had told him. "You're not Madame Rana."

"It's prepay." She gestured to the sign indicating the type of credit card taken — Carte Bleue — and the manual credit-card imprinter, the kind known as a "knuckle duster."

René sat down, sinking into the purple fabric. "I've prepaid via Madame Bercou at La Bouteille. *Comprenez-vous?*"

The words turned her red-lipsticked mouth into a moue of disappointment. "It's my mother you want. She's out."

"D'accord." René met her gaze. "I'll wait."

"Could take all evening," she said, peering out of the curtained window resembling a ship's porthole. "And I've got standing appointments, clients booked until late. *Désolée.*"

He'd been kicked out of better places than this trailer, with its polyester curtains and IKEA candles.

"You do report your earnings *au fisc,* I suppose?" he said. "Display your business

233

license somewhere? I assume you pay the three percent surcharge for bank cards?"

"We have an arrangement, the *flics* know we're here. So you can't scare me by threatening to tell them. Not that it's any of your business."

Payoffs and protection. René would have to use something else for leverage.

"But I'll tell you this for free," she said. "I see bad things in your aura."

"Yours, Mademoiselle, doesn't look that good either."

She grabbed his hand, splayed out his pudgy palm. "Hmm, a split love line." She looked up, her thick eyeliner creasing at the edges of her lids. "Must hurt, loving a woman who thinks of you as only a friend."

René blinked. How did she know? He pulled back his hand and tried to recover, sitting back on the purple cushions and crossing his legs. He thought of a comeback. "Too bad Drina Constantin's death will make her brother Radu get nasty. Especially when he hears you refused to help."

The girl became very still, her hands frozen in the act of picking up the deck of tarot cards. On top was the skeleton holding a scythe.

"*Maman,* wake up." The girl stood and pulled back the curtains behind her to reveal an alcove with a berth like you'd find in a train sleeper compartment. A middle-aged woman with a hairnet over a black bun sat up and yawned.

"*C'est le petit.* You deal with it. I need a manicure."

With that, the girl pulled on ankle boots and a short fur jacket and flounced out.

René knew these two charlatans couldn't see the future, didn't have second sight. He hadn't come for a palm reading. Still, he stole a glance at the lines on his palm as the elder fortune-teller made her way to the chair across the table from him.

"Madame Rana, if we could cut the social niceties and get to the point."

She scratched her neck. Stretched her legs. Yawned again. "So, *mon petit,* a love potion to make her fall in love with you?"

If it were that simple, he'd have tried long ago.

"That's not why I'm here, Madame."

As you well know, he thought, but instead he set one of the black-and-white photos on the brass tray. "Djanka Constantin, aka Au-rélie; her son, Nicu; and her sister, Drina. Tell me about them. And if it's something I haven't already heard, I'll make it worth your while."

Professional now, Madame Rana consulted a thick book labeled APPOINTMENTS. Waddled over to the trailer's door, flipped the sign to *FERMÉ* and sat down.

She glanced at her watch, a faux, rhinestone-encrusted affair with a Chanel logo. On second thought, René reflected, given the bright sparkle and her clientele, it might be authentic.

"You get ten minutes," she said. "My second cousin married a Constantin. There's been bad blood between our families since the war. One of those things." She jutted out her chin, pursing her mouth as if to say *go figure.* "*Alors,* my second cousin lives in Montpellier, down south. No friends of ours, this branch of the Constantin family. Djanka didn't exist to the family anymore, according to my cousin's wife —"

"Didn't exist? How's that?"

"Shunned. At least that's what I've heard."

He knew that. "Did that happen after she had her baby?"

"I'm telling you what I know, not what I don't."

René backtracked. "What about the boy's father?"

"In prison. Never came out."

Caught her in a lie. According to Madame Bercou, he'd died in a fire.

She noticed his look. "They came up with

236

a story about burning in a caravan to protect the boy."

"So that would explain why her sister Drina, presuming they're sisters, raised Nicu as her son. To protect him?"

"Our people take care of our own."

"This bad blood . . . who else did the Constantins feud with?"

"Feud?"

"Besides your family, I mean . . ."

Her tone got defensive. "You shouldn't speak about things you don't understand. These disputes are generations old."

René knew the woman had something on her tongue. "But was it a feud that caused the family to shun Djanka? Or her baby?"

"All I heard is that the sister, this one, she informed to the *gadjo.*"

René gave a little sigh. "Tell me something I don't know, Madame Rana."

"My cousin's wife said they found her in a ditch outside les Invalides."

"She went by Aurélie, didn't she?"

"Her stage name, and she had a lover while her husband sat in prison."

Who must have been Nicu's father. It fit with what the *mec* who'd married into the family had intimated.

"A lover?" He showed her the other photo. "This man, Pascal?"

Her glance grazed it. "I don't know names."

"How did she know Pascal?"

"Before my cousin's time."

Sitting atop his deep cushion, René struggled to reach his bag and pulled out the birth certificate.

"Yet on this birth certificate there's no father listed. Shouldn't the husband in prison be listed as the father?"

She shrugged.

"You're saying this lover Pascal, a non-Gypsy, is the father?"

She shifted in her seat. Rubbed the instep of her bare foot. "I'm saying nothing."

"*Bien sûr*, but it's possible . . ."

"Possible. But I didn't say that."

"So in your culture it's better for a child to be illegitimate than a *gadjo*?" René's thoughts sped, jumped ahead. "A way to protect family honor while the husband's in prison. That it? Then the family take it into their hands to kill her — an honor killing?"

She growled. "There haven't been honor killings for centuries, *mon petit*. We're not primitive. Time's up."

"I'm paid up for one more minute, Madame Rana."

She sighed. "What does all this matter now?"

Aimée thought it mattered.

"Let's just say this twenty-year-old crime might be linked to Drina's disappearance last night. Tell me more."

Madame Rana checked her watch. "My cousin's wife wants a rice cooker, one of those Japanese ones — you flip a switch *et voilà*, perfect rice."

"So you're saying that's extra?"

"You're a mind reader, *mon petit*."

René pulled out his checkbook, hoping it was worth it. They settled on a price. He took out his pen.

"What happened later?"

"The lover's long dead," she said.

Easy to say. "I need more than that. You mean Pascal?"

"My second cousin's mother-in-law, passed on now, told my cousin that after Djanka's murder the sister and the boy hit the road. Went out of reach."

"Djanka's murder sent them into hiding? Why?"

Madame Rana shrugged. "Facing a bad wind makes a wise one turn back, *mon petit*."

More Gypsy sayings.

"You're sure the child's father — the lover, Pascal — is dead?"

"Long departed. That's all I know." All of

239

a sudden her eyes fluttered then rolled up into her head so he could see the whites. A feather fell off the wall and floated in the air. Like a sign, René thought, not that he bought the woman's act.

"*Mon petit,* your business looks bright tomorrow. Good fortune. And I see a baby in danger."

"Chloé?" René tensed, then remembered that this was all fake. He seethed at this woman trying to take advantage of him.

"The *gadjo* tries to tie up a loose end."

He leaned forward in spite of himself. "What loose end?" When she didn't reply, he said, "Drina Constantin? Is she the loose end?"

"Drina's impatient for her journey. To join her boy."

Tingles ran up René's neck.

A knock sounded on the door.

"Time's up."

Monday Evening

Rose Uzes's voice mail recording instructed Aimée to leave a callback number. Frustrated, she did. As she checked her own phone for messages afterward, she heard the receptionist call the doctor by name. There he was. Dr. Estienne. She reached for the clipboard to go back in and try to catch him.

"Has that hemodialysis adapter arrived?" she heard Dr. Estienne ask as he passed through reception.

Her antenna up, she paused in the doorway.

"Check on why the delay . . . the patient needs . . ."

Aimée couldn't hear the rest.

Doctor Estienne was hurrying toward the next corridor. "I'm late."

The receptionist called out, "You've got an eight forty-five P.M. walk-in after your meeting, Doctor."

But Dr. Estienne had disappeared through the swing doors.

If it itches, scratch it, her father used to say. Madame Uzes's phrase "it doesn't make sense" rang in her head. If he was doing hemodialysis work here, why wouldn't Dr. Estienne treat Drina at this private clinic, especially since the foundation would pay the supplemental fees? Drina hated hospitals, she'd said.

In the darkness she headed over the gravel path bordering the lawn that faced Dr. Estienne's clinic. She paused before she reached the flower beds and peered through the lit windows. Four of the patient rooms she surveyed contained older men in wheelchairs eating their dinners from trays.

Halfway down the garden stood an old stone *pigeonnier* fashioned into a shrine with a statue of Saint Jean. Beside the last window she found the loosely replanted peonies where the corporal had dug his trench. Her eye caught on a glint in the clumps of dirt. A coin?

She took out her penlight, shone it. Something that looked like a small disk with a metal band around it caught the light. Did the corporal keep treasures, like a child, in his trenches?

Her curiosity piqued, she picked it up: a tiny wheel carved in wood. She felt her heart contract. She dug through the fresh clumps, getting dirt under her fingernails. And then she felt it, pulled it out with a slow, careful motion.

A small wooden wagon, one wheel broken off. One of the wooden Gypsy wagons Nicu had carved for Drina.

Drina had been here. Maybe she still was. That meant Doctor Estienne had been lying. Who else? Doctor Estienne's colleagues from Hôpital Laennec? Madame Uzes?

Her phone rang — Morbier. He could wait. She silenced the call. Time to scratch that itch. Aimée had to follow her gut. And not get caught by the staff.

From the jasmine-trellised gravel walkway, a ramp led to the rear of the white-walled wing. The corridor was narrow, with small rooms for patients off both sides. Antiseptic-smelling and basic — unlike the great-uncle's room. The ventilation system thrummed. She padded past open doors on both sides — most of the beds were empty; one contained an old man on a respirator — then a larger common room on the right occupied by old people nodding off in wheelchairs, where a muted *télé* was playing the news.

243

A door opened and shut down the hall. She ducked into the common room. She heard murmured voices, but the footsteps continued past. Aimée looked around, but none of the wheelchairs' occupants had even opened their eyes. She heard the door to the hallway swing open, the footsteps trail away.

She knew she might regret this, have to lie her way out if she was caught, but she remembered the wooden wagon and knew she needed to see who was in that last room. The one with the closed door, the one the footsteps had come from.

After a quick scan of the empty corridor, she tiptoed out into the hallway and down to the last room. She opened and shut the door without making a sound.

Lying on the bed was a shriveled woman covered in white blankets, her shallow breaths punctuated by the rhythmic flow from the artificial respirator. Dim light illuminated the sparse grey braids spread over the pillow. Seeing how the cancer had ravaged her, had turned her into an old woman, Aimée gasped. But these were the same dark, deep-set eyes she remembered from photos, and from those visits fifteen years ago: there was no denying this was Drina Constantin.

The door opened.

She dove behind the bed and slid underneath it in time to see white clogs on the linoleum. The fluorescent light flickered on, shadows moved.

"Plug it in there." A woman's voice. "Near the floor."

Lying on her stomach, she tried to make herself small. She saw the outlet an arm's length away and panicked. Thick fingers fumbled for the outlet. Then she heard a snap. Several clicks.

The machine thrummed to life. A moment later she heard the flick of a switch. "We need to refill the oxygen containers . . ."

"You're noting this down?"

"Everything. As instructed." The door opened and closed again. They'd gone, leaving the light on.

Aimée crawled out from under the bed, her heart pounding. They'd be back any moment.

"Drina?" She touched the wrinkled cheek — cool. The sunken eyes remained closed. "Maybe you can't hear me. It's Aimée, Jean-Claude's daughter. Nicu said you wanted to see me, to tell me about Papa."

No movement. Just the pumping sounds, in and out, of the machine breathing for Drina through the tubes in her nose.

"Drina, you wanted me to make something right. I know you can't talk, probably can't hear me, but if you can . . ."

Only the rhythmic *schwa, schwa* of the pumping air.

"Drina, I found the *roulotte* Nicu carved for you. See?" She lifted it out of her jacket pocket. Put the little three-wheeled wagon in Drina's stiff hand.

Aimée curled Drina's worn fingers around it. "I'm sorry, Drina." At least Drina looked peaceful, in no pain.

Of course the woman couldn't hear her, and she didn't know if it was true. But she said it anyway. "Nicu loved you like his mother, Drina."

The fingers tightened around the wagon. A hard, bony grip.

Drina's eyes opened. Her wide-eyed stare revealed dilated pupils. "I remember you . . ." Her hot, shallow breath wheezed, crackled. Aimée leaned in, putting her ear near Drina's moving lips. "You weren't big then. Jean-Claude said take care . . . make it . . ." Her whisper faded.

"Make it right, Drina? How?"

Drina's eyes fluttered. "They want to keep me quiet . . . but I promised him . . ."

She struggled, seemed to be gathering her strength, determined. Her whispers were

246

labored, and she gripped Aimée's other hand tighter.

"Promised Papa what, Drina?"

"You should know . . . I saw those men in Place Vendôme. Who notices a begging Gypsy except to shoo them away? But now they know. But they find . . . me."

Aimée's chest heaved.

"You were there, Drina? On Papa's surveillance?"

A nod. "Always toys for Nicu, he'd do that. Said if anything . . . tell his little girl . . ." Drina's hoarse whispers roared in her ears. "They covered up Djanka's murder, blew up his van . . ."

Drina lapsed into Romany. Desperate, Aimée squeezed Drina's hand. Cold, now so cold. "You mean Djanka's murderer killed Papa?"

Rattling sounded in Drina's throat. More Romany, for a minute or two this time.

"Please tell me in French so I understand . . . Drina?" She rubbed Drina's arm. "Why, Drina?"

Drina's Romany trailed off. The only words Aimée caught made her blood run cold.

Tesla. Fifi.

"Who are they?"

Drina's eyes blinked open. Stared at

Aimée. Her pupils pinpoints. "You know."

Drina's grip loosened. Her lids lowered halfway. Aimée felt a presence, hovering, suspended. A current of air lifting her, pulling at her.

"Mademoiselle, Mademoiselle," a voice was saying. "She's slipped into a coma. You can let go now."

She came back to the room, to the humming machines, to the hand cupping her shoulder. To a young nurse's nodding face.

"She's letting go now," said the nurse. "You should too."

Shaken, Aimée looked up at the young nurse, her thin face full of understanding. How long had she been there?

"I wrote down her words, the fragments I could make out," said the nurse. "Like I was told."

Like she was told? Aimée's pulse quickened. On the side table lay a notepad.

"Who asked you? You mean someone was waiting for her to confess something?" Yet Drina had just told her they wanted to keep her quiet?

"I don't know," the nurse said. "I just did what the doctor asked. I wrote the Romany words as they sounded, but they were garbled."

"I'm sure you did a good job," Aimée said,

picking up the notebook.

"Doctor Estienne's coming back, he'll want to see it."

"I'll give this to him myself, thank you."

"The orders were —" said the nurse, starting to protest.

"Changed, Nurse." She pulled out her cell phone. Hit René's number. "I'm handling this now."

"But Doctor Estienne and the *monsieur* —"

"*Quel homme?*" The nurse went to leave but Aimée caught her arm before she could reach the door. She could hear René's tinny phone voice answering her call, but he would have to wait. "Which *monsieur?* Tell me before I report you for illegally recording a patient's dying words."

The nurse's eyes batted in fear. "Who are you?"

"Special security."

"Like the *monsieur?*"

"That's all you need to know. We don't wear uniforms. I need to verify this, give me his name."

"Let me go," she said, her voice rising. "I had nothing to do with it."

"To do with what?"

Dodging past Aimée, the nurse reached for her pager from the nightstand and hit some buttons.

Aimée grabbed it. *Merde.* She had to get the hell out.

"Cooperate and I'll see you're not arrested."

"Arrested? But the *monsieur*'s with security at the ministry."

"Which ministry?"

The nurse's pager beeped in her hand.

"The ministry — that's all I heard."

Think, she had to think how to get the nurse to identify this man. "You're talking about the security team, the one with glasses, right?"

"Glasses . . . *non,* the man from Toulon."

Toulon? "You recognized his accent?" The pager was blinking. Get out, she had to get out of here. Now. "*Bon,* keep this to yourself."

And with the notepad under her arm, she slipped into the hallway, walking as quickly as she could without running.

She pulled out her phone and called René back.

"*Allô?* Aimée? Who were you talking to?" René said. "I tried calling, but your phone —"

"René, just listen. Can you pick me up on rue Oudinot?"

"Rue Oudinot? I'm close, but what's going on?"

"Just hurry. Now." She clicked off, striding purposefully. Not looking back.

"Mademoiselle, Mademoiselle!" a voice shouted.

But she kept going and broke into a run. Then out the swinging exit doors at the back, into the chill, dark air of the garden, keeping to the shadowed wall.

A starling fluttered in alarm from the bushes.

The gate was locked. The garden was surrounded by a high stone wall, trees. No way out. Her heart pounded. Floodlights flicked on, illuminating the lawn. Shouts carried through the air. She ran to the nearest tree — a ginkgo — stuck her bag down the front of her jacket and climbed. Climbed to the higher branches, scraping her nails and fingers while pulling herself up, wedging her feet in for purchase and slipping on the smooth bark.

"Over there. She's up in the tree."

Chloé's face flashed in front of her eyes. Those trusting grey-blue eyes. She needed a mother, and not one in prison — which is where Aimée would be if this *homme* from the ministry caught up with her. If she was lucky. Summoning every bit of her strength, Aimée grabbed the highest branch, hoisted

251

her weight and swung her legs over to the wall ledge.

On the other side of the wall, a dark, quiet street. With no time to think or prepare for the impact, she jumped, aiming for the roof of a truck parked on the sidewalk, hoping she'd only end up with a few broken limbs.

She landed, her legs buckling and her body crunching the metal. She slid and slipped down the dust- and leaf-covered windshield. Her jacket caught on the wipers, and she felt her sleeve tear. Nothing hurt. Yet. Moments later, she climbed off the truck's hood and ran.

At the end of the street, she saw the distinctive cat's eye headlights of René's Citroën DS. Any moment now, they'd catch sight of her, realize where she'd gone. She pumped her legs. Panted as her rib cramped. Taking a breath hurt. Go, she had to keep going.

The Citroën's front passenger door swung open. She jumped in and René took off, gunning the engine, before she could shut the door.

"Did I see that right — you slid down the windshield of a bakery truck?" René took a sharp turn onto rue Vaneau. Braked and swerved, avoiding a truck.

"Well, I didn't have the keys to get in, did

I?" She panted, catching her breath. "Get the hell out of here, René."

"Why did I ask?" René turned on the police scanner clipped under the dashboard.

Her rib throbbed. "Anyone behind us?"

René checked the rearview mirror. "Not yet."

"There's a cover-up, René. Drina told me."

"And I had my palm read," he said.

Monday, Midnight

Two figures huddled in the shadows on a bench on the Champ de Mars, the Eiffel Tower glimmering yellow-orange through the trees behind them. Low-lying mist shrouded the deserted park's gravel paths.

"There's a little trouble."

"More than a little trouble on both ends." Tesla lowered his voice. "The big mouth's going to print with his tell-all memoir."

"That's my problem, I've handled that. Everything's under control." The other man pulled his coat collar up against the chill. "You need to take care of your end."

Tesla turned, his gaze sweeping the gravel path. "Don't worry."

"Do I need to remind you?"

Tesla shook his head.

"We've dealt with these things before, haven't we? Or have you lost your touch?"

"That was years ago, I don't do that now."

254

"Then you'd prefer Larco and my people to handle it?"

"*Shhh,* no names."

"He gets overexcited. You know what I mean, *non?*"

Tesla punched the bench.

"Is that a no or a yes?"

Tesla's shoulders heaved. Why, why hadn't he refused years ago? "Just kill me now."

"So you want our friend to . . . ?"

"*Non,* Fifi." Tesla sighed. "Like always, you win."

Monday, Midnight

Aimée walked into her salon, patting Chloé's back after feeding her, a clean burp cloth over her shoulder. "Alerted the troops, René?"

"Media's on board." René sat on the recamier, his laptop beside him, his cell phone to his ear. Candles flickered on the sideboard.

Chloé burped loud and long. "*Et voilà, ma puce.* Back to sleep."

René gave Chloé an approving goodnight kiss.

After tucking Chloé in with the hand-crocheted blanket, Dussolier's gift, Aimée rejoined René, sitting cross-legged on the floor.

"I've informed *Le Parisien* and three other tabloids with twenty-four–seven on-call paparazzi." He glanced at the time. "Any moment now the news hounds will arrive to catch Uncle Radu's Gypsies wailing at the clinic, the final goodbye," said René. "It'll be a circus, all right."

Aimée could just see it.

"Martine's on board," she said. "She's pitching all her contacts. Her angle is going to be calling out the Ministry of Health, the medical issues, the implications with the hospital boards." She leaned back and stretched. Bad idea. Her rib hurt and she climbed onto the couch. "She's even going to tap her contact at *Le Monde*."

They'd filled each other in while Aimée took notes in her Moleskine — René's visit to La Bouteille, Radu's reactions, the fortune-teller; Aimée's hunt for Madame Uzes and trip to the *clinique;* Drina's last words. They had hashed out the implications over green tea — someone very high-profile seemed ready to do anything to prevent a scandal. But what scandal?

René had come up with a strategy to bring Radu Constantin into the mix and alert the media, which could create a safety net of sorts around them. Everything was in place. But there were still so many things Aimée didn't understand.

"One thing bothers me, René," she said, pulling out Chloé's teething biscuits from between the cushions she'd sat on. "Nicu was dead to the family. But I saw Radu and Nicu arguing at Hôpital Laennec. They didn't look estranged." She paused. "How did Radu react to the news Nicu had been murdered?"

"He was hurt, shocked. I saw it in his eyes," said René. "Guilty, you're thinking? The Constantin clan shunned Djanka for having a half-*gadjo* baby while her husband was in prison. Maybe after she died that shame was transferred to the child and the sister, who raised him?" René sipped his green tea. "Or maybe Radu only pretended. Maybe he sent them into hiding, fostered the idea of a feud, to protect them. Weren't they afraid Djanka's killer was still after them?"

"True," she said, "and apparently he was. I wonder if there's anything in this?"

She showed René the Romany words and phrases the nurse had written down in Drina's last moments. It wasn't much to go on.

"Even if it's translated, Aimée, this won't tell us the men's identity," said René. "Tesla, Fifi . . . Drina only used their code names."

True again. She hated to admit it, but she had nothing.

She needed to read all her notes over

again. Pore over each detail, check and recheck. See if there were any coincidences. The necessary tedious side of investigation.

But that thought shook something loose in her memory. "Wait a minute," she said. She opened her laptop and pulled up one of the 1978 issues of *Libération* that she'd had Maxence scan from her father's file. "Look, René." She enlarged the article on the suicide of a *député* at Assemblée Nationale. "Notice the suicide's name?"

"Pascal? That's a leap." René paused, shaking his head. "How many tens of thousands of men named Pascal were there in Paris in 1978?"

"But the fortune-teller told you Djanka's lover's death forced Drina and Nicu into hiding."

"*Et alors?* How can you connect that to this *député* named Pascal? It's not even a coincidence — you're pulling names out of an old newspaper."

She disagreed. Especially since the newspaper had come from her father's file. "Let's just check, *non?*"

"Going to communicate with ghosts now?"

"*Grand-père* kept every *Paris Match* for the last fifty years before he died," she said. Scandals, love affairs, real news — it was all there in *Paris Match.* "It's bound to be in here."

"What's bound to be in there?"

But she'd gone to the library, moved the wooden library ladder, climbed up to scan the dusty shelves. On the top shelf, she found four weekly issues from April 1978.

She dusted them off with her scarf, stepped down, and brought them back to René, plopping down on the recamier next to him to thumb through them.

She checked the index of an issue with a still-young Johnny Hallyday on the cover. Page 34.

"Where are those photos, René?"

René rolled his neck. "Back in the envelope by your laptop."

But she didn't want to handle that envelope, couldn't bear to touch it again. So much dried blood. Nicu's blood.

"What's the matter?" he said, noticing her look.

"It's my fault, René. If I hadn't . . ." She paused. "But I did. For what? In the end, Nicu died for nothing. I found Drina, but her message was too cryptic. It did nothing to help solve my father's murder."

Or to lessen this feeling that she'd jumped from hot coals into the flame.

Feeling hopeless, Aimée rubbed her aching shoulder. Chloé had gained weight.

René reached for the envelope. "You're tired. Me too. We'll go over this tomorrow," René said, setting the photos on the table.

But if she didn't check now, it would bother her all night. She turned to the article on Pascal Leseur, an up-and-coming *député*. Pascal's funeral was splashed through *Paris Match*'s society section in agonizing photographic detail. Photos of his apartment, the grief-stricken family on the steps of Saint-Roch Church, the small cortege to the cemetery in the Berry, the family estate and cemetery. There was one photo of Pascal Leseur, taken when he was a baby. Bizarrely, there was not a single photo of him as an adult.

"It was a long shot, Aimée. You tried."

So tired, she felt so tired. It had all suddenly hit her: Nicu, Drina. A great sadness filled her. She sank back against the sofa.

"But," said René, his eyes on his laptop screen, "according to the ministry database, his brother Roland holds office in D'Orsay, the same one Pascal did before becoming the youngest *député* in the Assemblée Nationale."

She was too tired to worry about it anymore tonight. The next moment, her eyes drooped closed.

René draped Chloé's wool baby blanket over her shoulders. Kissed her forehead. But she was oblivious.

Tuesday Morning

Since the day Françoise slammed the door on him twenty years ago, Roland Leseur had spoken to her only once: at the UNESCO reception celebrating one of her ambassador husband's postings fifteen years ago. Yet he thought of her every day.

He'd kept up with her movements all this time: from embassy to embassy, the return from Venezuela, her husband's funeral, the family townhouse on the Champ de Mars, her new grandchild, the fact that she shopped at the markets on rue Cler every Tuesday.

Today, like clockwork, she emerged from the family-owned *fromagerie,* La Fermette, with her straw basket. Her step was that of the young woman he remembered.

From the corner of rue Saint-Dominique he watched her exchange a *bonjour* with the fruit seller, then stop at the florist's and emerge with a bouquet of violet-blue delphiniums. He remembered how the color matched her eyes.

How often had he stood in line outside that cheese shop? Debated, trembling, whether to approach her. To smell whether she still wore the same *parfum,* l'Heure Bleue by Guerlain.

All the women he'd tried to forget her with paled beside Françoise.

He'd heard nothing yet from his lawyer, who was examining the article for defamation and libel. It was only a matter of time, he knew, before the story came out. He'd do anything to keep it quiet, but how long could that last? Sooner or later, the past would resurface. Françoise needed to be warned. No declarations of love or attempts at happily ever after — he simply had to protect her.

As he watched, she turned back on rue Cler. Forgotten a purchase? But a moment later she turned right and was swallowed up by the throngs on rue de Grenelle. He hurried, cursing himself for not finding the courage to grab the opportunity. At broad, tree-lined Avenue Bosquet, where the Tour Eiffel's iron latticework poked above the zinc-roofed buildings, he missed the traffic light and got caught behind a bus in the crosswalk. By the time it had passed, her khaki trench coat and trailing scarf had disappeared in the crowd.

Determined now, he ran through the bus's diesel fumes, dodged taxis and made it to the other side with horns blaring around him. He knew where she was going — home — but she usually went down rue Saint-Dominique. He pumped his legs, but there was no sign of her on the pavement. Where could she have gone?

He poked his head into the café, the cobbler. Not a trace.

Passing narrow rue du Gros Caillou, a sleepy passage of low buildings that had once been workshops and housing for construction workers building the Tour Eiffel, Roland heard laughter.

"*Merci,* Madame," said a smiling woman on the doorstep of a framing atelier. It was Françoise, holding a square wrapped in brown paper.

The next moment she'd taken off down the street.

Roland ran after her, and finally got the courage to call, "Françoise, Françoise!"

She turned at the crook of the street, where it bent left like an elbow. Her smile was edged with confusion. Her face was older — yes, his too. But apart from the few wrinkles and the fact that her thick hair that pulled back from her face was now a lustrous winter white, the twenty years didn't show. Premature white hair aged most women, but on Françoise it highlighted her sculpted cheekbones and unlined face.

"Roland?" She dropped her basket, scattering cheese and delphiniums in the cobblestoned gutter. Her mouth quivered.

"*Désolé,* I didn't mean to surprise you, but . . ." He tore his eyes away from her face. Picked up her things. Wiped them off on his trousers.

"Didn't we agree never . . . ?"

"You're in danger, Françoise."

She leaned down and their fingers brushed over a tomato. Hers were warm.

"Danger? Melodrama doesn't become you, Roland. You know about Gerard's death, I'm sure."

A long, painful illness. She had nursed her husband herself, while still taking care of their daughter, who had been deaf since childhood.

"My life's on an even course now," Françoise said. "Not that you've asked. My daughter's receiving treatment in London and now my oldest daughter's child —"

"I want to protect you." Roland took her hands. "And them."

"Protect? From what?" Her shoulders stiffened. "What in God's name, Roland, have you let out of the bag?"

More like tried to keep in the bag. "Pascal, us . . . I had to warn you."

"This is all a ruse," she said. "What you really want to know is whether Gerard knew of our affair. Whether your brother betrayed you to his best friend."

He'd always wondered. "*Alors,* when you refused to see me, what else could I think, Françoise?"

"Naïve, you always were naïve, Roland." She sighed. Pulled her hands from his and brushed back her hair. The sun slanted down on them, casting a shadow from a lantern like a black print on the limestone. The deserted street echoed with her ringing phone. She looked at the display. "I'm late. But yes, your saint of a brother told my husband about us. He couldn't keep his mouth shut, especially when he'd been drinking." She noticed the look on his face and sighed. "You still idolize Pascal after all these years, don't you, Roland?"

"I still think of you every day after all these years," he blurted out. "I loved you, still love you, Françoise."

Françoise turned away. Shook her head as if to shake his words away, then combed her

267

fingers through her hair. Like she always used to do after making love. He remembered the arch of her back, how velvet soft and warm her skin felt. The familiar gesture made him ache inside.

"For years I've kept my promise, never intruded into your life, only watched from afar."

"So you had me under surveillance? What, waiting for your chance to swoop in?" The left side of her face was shadowed by the hanging ginkgo branch from a street-facing garden. "You're a dreamer, Roland. Wake up. Whatever happened between us . . . that's ancient history."

Roland waved her words away. "Françoise, listen to me. I'm here because I need to warn you. What if Pascal didn't commit suicide?"

"You're implying someone murdered Pascal? But there was an autopsy, a cause of death. Autoerotic asphyxiation, wasn't it? But the papers were paid to keep it quiet."

How could she think that?

"After the cremation, the autopsy report disappeared. My father wouldn't talk about it."

"Murder? I don't believe it." Françoise shook her head. "For once open your eyes, Roland. Pascal couldn't face the repercussions of what he had done, the blowback that was about to level his career, *et . . .*" Her voice tailed off. *"Désolée."*

Roland's hand shook. "Françoise, I did things, things I shouldn't have."

"No more than anyone else, I'm sure," she said. "You're still trying to protect Pascal, but he played politics, made enemies by the dozen. It caught up with him, and he took the easy way out. Why is this all coming up now? What's changed at the ministry?"

This wasn't going how he'd expected. Why wasn't she taking it seriously? "You mean who cares now, Françoise?" His voice rose. Someone above slammed the shutters on their window. He took a breath. "Someone who stands to gain something. That's who." He showed her the *Libération* proof sheet.

"Always playing Pascal's pawn," she said, looking at the sheet. Her hand shook. "Your brother with a Gypsy lover, blackmailing the higher-ups, bribes disguised as delegation junkets? Amazing how Pascal can still stir up the *merde* even from beyond the grave." She shifted the basket on her arm. "Don't let them use you."

"But Gerard's mentioned here, too," said Roland. "You need to know things will come out — things people will do anything to cover up."

Françoise sighed. "It'll be squashed before it can reach the press as usual. Stay out of it. Don't bother on my account, Roland. What you call protection, I call guilt."

Tuesday Morning

Aimée rose at 6 A.M. with Chloé, and despite minor diaper leakage, by 8 A.M. they had walked Miles Davis and bought a copy of *Le Parisien* at the *café tabac.* And she'd drunk two double espressos. If only she could ingest sleep in demitasse-sized shots throughout the day, she might survive.

Chloé had woken up several times last night. Bleary-eyed, Aimée had consulted the *bébé* bible the *mamans* at yoga swore by, a book by Dr. Françoise Dolto. The respected pediatrician and psychologist insisted every *bébé* can sleep through the night, be trained to use a spoon and exhibit rudimentary table manners by six months old. Otherwise it was the parents' fault. Well, clearly it was Aimée's fault.

The adamant Dr. Dolto insisted that one needed to talk to one's baby and explain to her that she shouldn't wake up at night.

271

Reason with a teething six-month-old? Aimée was supposed to practice *la pause:* "pause a bit" before going to the baby instead of responding immediately to her cries, because the child needs to learn patience. And she was meant to try that with her little siren wailing at 3 A.M.?

Now, with her two double espressos downed and the world starting to take on some clarity, Aimée had the paper open in front of her, Chloé nestled at her side with cold compresses soothing her teething gums.

She noted that the article about Drina's abduction took up part of *Le Parisien*'s front page. In the sidebar were photos of Radu and his extended tribe filling the clinic's courtyard, human rights groups brandishing placards condemning ethnic inequality. Another photo showed some anti-elder abuse activists marching to the prime minister's residence, l'Hôtel Matignon, a few blocks away. Bravo, René. The headline was splashy: GYPSY KIDNAPPING SCANDAL ON PRIME MINISTER'S DOOR-STEP IN EXCLUSIVE 7TH ARRONDISSE-MENT.

Exaggerated, and not the most intellectual take, but it worked. She loved *Le Parisien*.

The kidnapped woman, the article read,

had passed away during the night, shortly after she was located by authorities at a different hospital from the one she had disappeared from. Did she die as a result of trauma from her abduction? Her doctor, a Dr. Edouard Estienne, had left for a medical conference in Prague and could not be reached for comment.

Convenient.

The coverage went on. There was on ongoing inquiry into the death of a young *manouche* man reported to be her adoptive son in a stabbing nearby. Police were investigating a known hate group in the area.

The sick feeling washed over her again.

Nicu's young life cut short. All her fault.

What would her father have thought? His daughter had ended the life of the little boy they had brought Christmas presents to. Gotten that little boy killed because she was so selfishly determined to answer her own questions.

She had to pick up the pieces, fit them together into a whole picture. Otherwise, Nicu had died for nothing. But even with Drina dead, Aimée was hardly out of danger. Priorities, she reminded herself. First she had to take care of the rest of her life.

After leaving Chloé with Babette, Aimée finished the addendum to the proposal for de Brosselet and emailed it to René. Plenty of time to prepare for the appointment with the attorney that afternoon.

What to wear? Earth mother or business-woman?

She chose the latter. Opened her armoire, slid the hangers draped with vintage Givenchy and worker's overalls aside in favor of a Dior pencil skirt and an agnès b. silk blouse just back from the dry cleaner's. A slim tuxedo jacket, silk tights and heels completed the outfit.

She returned to the old *Paris Match,* still spread open on her floor. On her hands and knees, she scrutinized Pascal Leseur's baby picture, putting it next to the one of Nicu in Djanka's arms and then squinting to see if she caught a resemblance. Hard to tell. She looked again, studying the background. Something jumped out at her in the baby photo of Nicu. Something she'd seen before.

She turned the page of *Paris Match* to the picture of the Leseur family château, the cemetery on the grounds. She recognized it now. Those matching garden urns that topped the stone wall, bearing the letters LS and the Leseur family crest. The urns on the wall in *Paris Match* were dead ring-ers for the urns in the background of the "family" photo of Djanka, baby Nicu and

Pascal. Proof the photo had been taken in the Leseur garden.

She shivered at the implication: Pascal Leseur had been Nicu's father. She grabbed her phone. Time to talk to Pascal's brother.

Roland Leseur's administrative assistant took her appointment request with an I'll-get-back-to-you-don't-hold-your-breath attitude. For now, Aimée would call Martine.

But first she checked in with Morbier.

"Leduc, I'm going into court," he said, his voice gruff. "Another day of testimony at le Tribunal de Grande Instance. I'm the main witness, and I'm turning off my phone. If my contact turns up something I'll let you know. Meanwhile you'll have to hold your horses."

She'd found Drina herself without his help. "Might want to take a look at *Le Parisien,* Morbier."

But he'd clicked off.

She fought off her irritation. *Hold your horses.* Such an old-fashioned phrase.

But . . . horses. Why hadn't she thought of that before? Going through her father's old file, she took out the military cadet's brief statement and the crime-scene photos of Djanka Constantin's body in the Invalides moat. The École Militaire, only a Métro stop away, held the military stables.

275

It was where she'd learned to ride.

She made several calls. Revised her schedule for the morning, confirmed her afternoon appointment with the lawyer, and shot off an email with instructions to Maxence before heading for the Métro. After a twenty-minute ride, she handed in her ID at the sentry post outside the École Militaire's limestone façade, pocked with bullet holes from the fleeing German soldiers in '44.

The complex was a living museum. The École Militaire had been founded by Louis XV, with a nudge from Madame de Pompadour, as an academic college for officers from poor families. The campus had mushroomed, overtaking the farmlands of Grenelle to conduct training maneuvers on what would become the Champ de Mars, named for Mars, the Roman god of war. Napoléon, who had been a cadet here, had graduated in one year instead of the usual two. Or so went the legend as passed on to Aimée by her riding instructor.

Horses clip-clopped over the cobbles by the stables, their breath came out in puffs of steam in the crisp air. The aroma of fresh hay by the fenced dirt riding ring reminded her of Thursday lessons after *lycée.* Little had changed.

Upstairs in the office, Commandant Thiely — her former instructor, now in charge — grinned. "How's my former equestrian?"

She kissed him on both cheeks. "Wondering about a little future equestrian of my own. Chloé's only six months old, but I know how much competition there is for places."

He grinned. "Wait until she's fourteen, Aimée. I'll make sure she's a shoo-in." He glanced at his watch, a reminder he was squeezing her in. "On the phone you mentioned an investigation?"

He sat down, gestured toward a thick-legged chair.

"I'll take but a minute of your time." She sat and put the crime-scene photos on his desk. "Nineteen seventy-eight. Remember this?"

He pulled down his glasses from the top of his head. Clucked his tongue. "The moat at les Invalides." He nodded. "One of my cadets found her. Gave a statement."

"I know." She leaned forward. "But I need more. I need to talk with him."

"He made commander in the army." Thiely shook his head. "We lost him in a NATO ambush in Sarajevo."

There went that idea.

"Is there anything you can tell me, any

277

detail you remember?"

"That's a long time ago." He sat up straight in his hard-backed chair. "You know I'm retiring after thirty years of service, Aimée. Best years of my life."

Was he brushing her off? Perhaps not, but from his tone she sensed something else going on.

"Do you remember anything about this cadet's reaction to finding the body?" she said. "A brutal strangulation, a young woman's body discarded in the moat. Did any fingers point to him or other cadets?"

"Cadets at l'École Militaire?" he said, his brow furrowed. "You don't shit in your front yard — sorry — with a four-star general living right across the street."

She nodded. "What theory went around?"

"Didn't make sense."

He did remember. "In what way?"

A sigh. "What's it to you, Aimée?"

"My father investigated this case. Came up with nothing. There's been a recent murder, and there's a connection." She'd keep it to that.

Another sigh. "To us — nothing official, mind you — this had a paramilitary flavor." Thiely tented his fingers. "Lots of rumors. *Des barbusses.*"

"*Barbusses?*"

"That's what we called secret agents, hired guns for dirty jobs back then."

"What we'd call a black-ops contractor now?"

He shrugged. "A botched job. Bad intel, that's what I heard, but back then, as now, the bureaucrats ran the show. Those know-it-all Napoléons with degrees," Thiely said, disgust in his voice. "The ones who take a course and equate that with ground and field experience. A military classroom's no match for the reality." Thiely snorted. "But that's the water we swim in now."

Bureaucrats running the show, warring factions in the military hierarchy? Aimée wondered how that fit. If it did.

"Any name associated with the rumors?" Aimée asked.

"My cadet might have heard. But too late to ask him now. If there was something, Aimée, you don't want to know."

"I do want to know," she said. "My father investigated this woman's murder —"

"Not for long," Thiely interrupted. "They shut down the investigation."

Thiely was telling her something.

"Meaning?"

"A homicide on military ground warrants a military investigation," he said. "But we never heard of one."

Odd all right. No time now to sift through the implications, but she made a mental note to revisit.

"One more thing," she said. "At that time, had you noticed Gypsies around here?"

"Here? No way. Not then or now. Except those protesters, some longhairs who want to set up camp for them on the Champ de Mars."

"So you're saying a mercenary might have used this as a dumping ground?"

"Old rumors, which I shouldn't have shared." Thiely stood. "I have to get going. I've got a stable full of ninety-plus skittish colts to check on: their feed, their hooves. And I'm just talking about the cadets." He smiled.

Something came to her. "Sorry, last thing. According to this, your cadet discovered her body at six A.M. on a morning ride. No guards on the perimeter?"

He shook his head. "The *café tabac*'s still there, kitty-corner. I do remember that the *café* owner, questioned at the time, had noticed nothing."

"Think of the weather conditions."

"I don't remember."

"If it had rained that night, she'd be soaking." Aimée pointed to the photo. "But the report states her clothes were damp where they'd been in contact with the grass. Don't those sparkles look like dew on her hair?"

Thiely nodded. "Always dew on that grass. The horses try to lick it."

"Merci."

Aimée double knotted her scarf against the wind off the Champ de Mars. She took out her phone, called Maxence at the office. "Can I put you on hold, Aimée?" he asked.

No time. "I'll call back and leave a message. I want you to check something out."

That done, she jumped on the Number 28 bus at the École Militaire and rode for two stops on the long, tree-lined block. At les Invalides, La Tour Maubourg, she descended and walked along the fawn-colored brick-topped wall to the small square facing the moat. The weak sun broke through scattered puffs of clouds. The eighteenth-century cannons, verdigrised with age, pointed toward the Seine. She used to climb up on them; every kid did. On her right, along the grass-bottomed moat, she recognized the lichen-covered stone wall — and the corner recess where Djanka's body had been dumped. Little had changed in twenty years. Aimée took out the photo, imagined her father when he was called to the scene, what he'd have thought, how he'd have looked at the crime scene. Tried to think how he would.

The ringing of her phone cut into her thoughts.

"Aimée, I've got something to tell you," said Martine, her voice breathy, excited.

"So your contact at *Le Monde* bit?"

"Meet me at fifty rue de Varenne."

In Martine parlance, that signaled urgent. Aimée scanned the boulevard for a taxi. Saw one and waved to it.

"Tell me *Le Monde*'s interested in covering Drina's abduction and you'll make my day," she said, opening the taxi door.

"Working on it. Got a call scheduled with a senior editor. And I'm learning Italian."

"Italian? For a moment I thought you were in love."

"That too."

Aimée hurried past the ten-meter Ionic columns and over the checkered marble tile of the neoclassical former Hôtel de Galliffet, now the Istituto Italiano di Cultura. A gem of an eighteenth-century mansion in the heart of Faubourg Saint-Germain. Its secluded lawned garden, fringed by marigolds and purple hollyhocks, took up most of a block.

Smells of something wonderful drifted

from an open window. She was starving. Doctor's orders required her to eat three meals a day while nursing. How could she have forgotten?

She followed her nose to the cooking school downstairs, a long room with an open window. Shuddering almond-tree branches dropped pale pink blossoms through the windows and onto the old floor tiles. Martine, wearing an apron, grinned from next to a blue AGA stove.

"Hungry?" Martine spooned a heap of something from an earthenware casserole onto a blue faience plate on a long counter. "Try this white asparagus — it's only in season for three weeks — with a *farrotto primavera* with prosciutto. I'm experimenting for my class project."

Aimée perched on a stool, inhaled the tomato, caramelized onion and basil smells.

"This better be good, Martine."

"Try it."

"I mean whatever you dragged me out here to tell me." She grabbed a fork and took a bite of the *farrotto;* it melted on her tongue. "Amazing. I'm starving."

Martine's cheeks bloomed. She was wearing minimal makeup for once, and her streaked blonde hair was pulled back with a clip. "Eat."

Aimée's best friend since the *lycée,* a career-driven journalist, had turned into an Italian mother before her very eyes.

She obeyed. Finished off the whole plate.

"I broke up with Gilles," Martine said.

About time. His ex-wife lived in the flat below them and would barge in with annoying regularity.

"So who's putting roses in your cheeks?"

"Gianni," she said. "He's delicious. Last month I was covering Italo-French relations. Met Gianni here at the cultural institute." Martine tore off part of a ciabatta and put it next to Aimée's plate. "Long story, but after a big fight with Gilles yesterday, a last-straw kind of thing, I packed up lock, stock and armoire."

"And you're just telling me now?" She couldn't ignore the hurt spreading inside her. Didn't they tell each other everything?

"What was I supposed to do, come and stay with you while you have Melac and his witch woman on your back?" Martine took her hand. "I'm at my aunt's around the corner on rue du Bac."

"Handy. You're welcome *chez moi* anytime. Chloé's mostly sleeping through the night." She chewed the bread. "I'm also considering switching from espresso to cocaine."

Martine nudged her and pointed out the window. "Look, there he is. Gianni's showing some diplomats around."

A voice came wafting in from the tall windows: "Adjoining the embassy you'll find the cultural institute which houses the Italian library as well as exhibitions, musical soirées and cooking classes. Here, in the former residence of Talleyrand, where he met a young Napoléon . . ."

The tall, broad-shouldered man with black curly hair waved to their window and flashed a big, white-toothed smile at Martine. Aimée blinked. He could have stepped out of Italian *Vogue* or *L'Uomo.*

"Not bad, eh, Aimée?"

"He fills out the Armani suit, Martine." She tapped her forehead. "Anything up here?"

"Enough." Martine grinned. "And don't worry, I checked. He's got a cousin."

Did the cousin look like him? Aimée wondered.

"I'm trying to engineer the four of us having dinner this week."

Aimée felt a flush up her neck. Martine was always trying to set her up. How long had it been? Between Chloé and starting back at work, she rated sleep higher than romance.

Aimée wiped her mouth. "I'm all for your new relationship if it means you'll cook like this for me."

The warmth and aromas gave the school's kitchen a homey feel. She looked around at the glassed-off section with its stacked ovens, tendrils of tagliatelle in the baking area hanging from racks, and a chef deep in discussion with his white-aproned students.

Maybe she could take a cooking class. But then maybe she could go to the moon — if only she had the time.

"*Alors,* met with Maître Benosh yet?"

"You knew?"

Martine's eyes narrowed. "She's the best. As Chloé's godmother, I recommended her to Morbier."

Interesting that Morbier had passed her off as *his* contact.

She couldn't keep anything from Martine for long. Told her how Donatine had waylaid her and she'd been dragged into a conversation.

"Don't miss the appointment. *Mon Dieu,* she's booked for weeks, months." Martine set down her wooden spoon. "But back to the Italians. I can count on you for dinner with Gianni and his cousin, *non?*"

"Nervous, Martine?"

"Can I?"

Aimée still hadn't found her father's killer, or Nicu's; she faced a probable custody battle with Melac, and her ribs ached from landing on the bakery truck.

"Only if you promise me that the hospital ethics article on Drina gets traction. Raises questions, an investigation."

"Don't worry. He owes me a favor. Big time."

"Look at these, Martine."

Martine loosened her apron, leaned over the kitchen counter as Aimée spread out the photo and the old *Paris Match*. "See the Leseur château, those distinctive funeral urns? You'll notice the same urns in this little family scene."

"Et alors?"

"I'd say the Assemblée Nationale *député* Pascal Leseur fathered the Gypsy boy, Nicu, who Drina raised." Aimée pointed to the names written below — *Djanka, Nicholás and Pascal.*

"That's all the proof you've got?"

She gave Martine a brief rundown. "It's all heating up. Haven't you heard any rumors lately?"

"Ancient history, Aimée." Martine studied the photos, tapping her spoon on the dish. "But interesting history. There's a tell-all memoir by a former minister's young boy-

287

friend that got pulled, I heard. First there was going to be a *Libé* exposé, then there's not, then a few copies appeared on someone's desk anonymously."

"What's the connection?" She could tell something had clicked in Martine's mind.

"In our business that means we all know the story exists, but no one can use or quote it. But as you know, Pascal Leseur's dead and so are most of the other people involved."

"Pascal Leseur's mentioned?"

Martine nodded then wiped her mouth.

"And a Monsieur X. It's news for a day, then *phfft,* over. I haven't read it. That's from my connection at *Le Monde.*" Martine gave a knowing nod. "*Alors,* Leseur's in the memoir, but again, it was twenty years ago — who cares now?"

Hadn't Thiely almost said the same thing? Advised her to leave it alone?

Well, she cared. "Drina was abducted and Nicu murdered because someone wanted them silenced. Someone high up. So memoir or not, this story is still hot. And Drina was trying to tell me with her last words that Djanka's murderer killed my father, Martine. Pascal Leseur's linked to this."

"All happening here in the most chic and exclusive *quartier* of Paris?" Martine's voice dripped with sarcasm. "*Très discret* and full of the elite — why, even the Monoprix tucks its sign out of sight."

"There's a Monoprix in the seventh?"

"I'm quoting Yves Saint Laurent; he lives around the block from it."

"If YSL shops at Monoprix, then . . ." Words failed her.

"But you could have hit the mark, Aimée. After all, this might be a chichi *quartier*, but it's home to ministries, and we all know there's nothing more seedy than what goes on behind politician's doors." Martine crinkled her nose. "That special *odeur de corruption.*"

Aimée's phone vibrated in her bag. René.

"All good with de Brosselet, René?"

A horn blared in the background. "We need to meet." She heard the stress in René's voice. "Maxence is with me."

"Can't it wait?"

"De Brosselet accepted the proposal, and he's ready to sign contracts. Before he changes his mind I need your approval." René sounded nervous like he always did before closing a deal. "Now, Aimée."

"*Attends.*" She put her hand over the receiver. "Anywhere here René and I can take a few minutes in private?"

"On one condition."

289

What now? "Join your cooking class? Use all my *free* time to start taking Italian classes with you?"

"Promise me you'll make an effort with Gianni's cousin."

"If I can stay awake."

Martine pointed to a window above. "Good. The room directly above this one's free — my Italian lesson starts in half an hour. Use it till then."

The tall-ceilinged classroom was lined by cases of Italian books and large windows whose frames were carved with wreaths of oak and laurel. An adjoining salon, with mirrors on every wall and a tromp l'oeil mural of a blue sky and clouds painted on the ceiling, contained a life-sized statue of the Marquis de Galliffet.

"Can anyone listen in on us here?" Maxence asked, looking around. His leather boots creaked on the herringbone wood floor.

"Doubt it," Aimée said. "Just don't speak Italian. Where's René?"

"Parking." Maxence set the printout on the teacher's oak desk. "Here's the meteorological report you requested. Scattered showers around ten P.M. on the night of April twenty-first, 1978, then again around one A.M. on the twenty-second. The dew forms roughly an hour before sunrise. So say five A.M."

Given the dew on Djanka's hair and her damp but not soaked clothes, she must have been dumped in the moat at les Invalides between 1 A.M. and 5 A.M. Aimée knew her father must have figured that out. She felt like she was late to the party. Twenty years too late.

She sifted the information in her mind, fixed on the fact that the military had been denied the right to investigate — unless they'd hushed it up themselves. But why? And who'd trump the Ministry of Defense? No one in her address book.

She sat down on the teacher's desk. Thought.

The classroom's radiator hissed. A feeble sputter of heat blew out and then died.

"Look, Aimée, according to this *Paris Match* article," said Maxence, pointing to her copy, "Pascal Leseur's suicide was discovered by the cleaning lady on the morning of April twenty-second. The same day Djanka was found strangled in the moat at the École Militaire."

"I know. And it must connect." Aimée mulled. Buttoned her tuxedo jacket up and wished she was back in the inviting warmth

291

of the cooking-class kitchen.

"Alors?" said René, putting down his briefcase and joining them.

Aimée filled him in on what they had learned.

"But this Pascal Leseur committed suicide," René said, stabbing the *Paris Match* page with his forefinger.

"If Djanka's the mother of his child, I'd say the fact that they were both discovered dead on the same day is more than a coincidence."

"And if Leseur's suicide wasn't a suicide, and they were both murdered . . . Good luck proving that twenty years after the fact." René wiped a fallen almond leaf off his lapel. It drifted, twisting in the sunlight, to the hardwood floor. "We've got work to do, Aimée."

"But this matters, René. It mattered enough that they pulled my father off the case. Even the military were denied an investigation on their own turf."

"Says who?" René snorted in disgust. "They hush stuff all the time."

"No denying that. But my former riding instructor has no reason to lie. I believe him. And Drina was trying to tell me that it's the reason my father was murdered ten years later. And now one other innocent person

292

has been killed, poor Nicu Constantin. That means it matters to someone, René; that someone still thinks it can be proved twenty years later, and is afraid of what will happen if it is. And I'll find out who."

René opened his case, shaking his head. "You call that a connection?"

"Big players," said Maxence, nodding. "You think someone took out two hits twenty years ago and has been trying to cover them up ever since?"

"You're on the right path, Maxence," Aimée said. "Say Leseur, an up-and-coming politician, was the target, Djanka a secondary target, or maybe killed because she was a witness . . . Years later, something surfaces, my father makes the connection to an old case . . ."

Maxence interrupted, excited. "So whoever they are, they need to cover up the murders again, so they take him out." He smiled, brushed his long bangs to the side. Noticed Aimée's wince. "I'm so sorry, I meant . . ." The alarm on his watch suddenly played a techno version of "Strawberry Fields Forever." "Oops, got class. Meet you later, Aimée. I'll set up the surveillance equipment for tonight's reception — it's an early one."

What a jewel Maxence was.

"Before I forget," he added, "de Brosselet left this for you."

From his backpack Maxence pulled out a mottled-*gris* pig-skin Villeroi Frères bag. Soft as butter. Her heart fluttered. "I guess he liked the diaper service tip."

"At least there's some good news," said René, spreading out the contract pages. He handed her his Montblanc pen. "Sign here."

As Maxence left, the open door let in a flurry of cold air. The repeated notes of a piano being tuned in the adjoining salon were momentarily louder and clearer until the door closed again.

As she placed the cap back on the pen, there was something niggling at her, just out of reach. What had she been trying to remember? Something she'd meant to make a note of before. Something to do with *manouches*? Why hadn't she written it down instead of relying on her *bébé*-addled brain? "René, what do they call people from that region where you went for a healer?"

He'd once tried a *guérisseur,* a healer, in the countryside for his hip dysplasia.

"Peasants? A step below provincials? Superstitious dullards who go in for witch-craft?"

"Quit *le snobisme,* René." She handed his pen back to him. "I mean what are the natives called?"

"Ah, you mean cross-eyed inbreds? Otherwise known as *les Berrichons.*"

"That's it, René. They're Berrichons. From the Berry." Now she'd remembered what she'd been chasing — Djanka's autopsy. "The dental records used to identify Djanka Constantin were sent from the Berry."

"What's this got to do with the price of butter, Aimée?" said René, returning his Montblanc to his jacket's inner breast pocket. "Nobody cares about the Berry, not even les Berrichons. Everybody who can get out, does." He took a copy of *Le Figaro* from his briefcase and slapped it on the desk. "Look at this, rumors of a shake-up at the quai d'Orsay involving a ministry official from le Berry. They even make it into the government. See?"

"By ministry official you mean Roland Leseur, brother of Pascal. Nicu's uncle. That's the connection." She pointed to the photo in *Paris Match* and the "family" with the matching urns.

René shook his head. *"Et alors?"*

The computer on the teacher's desk, a chrome affair, yielded to her guest-user request. A moment later she'd navigated to the Ministry of Foreign Affairs site.

"It says the Leseur father was awarded the *Légion d'honneur* for his Resistance work in the Berry." Was that the Leseur connection to *les manouches*? Did it go back to the roundups and the camps? She scanned the site further, saw that it listed the ministry's official conferences and meeting schedules.

She glanced at her Tintin watch. 12:30 P.M. She logged off the classroom computer.

"If Roland Leseur won't call me back, I'll go to him."

"You can't be serious."

"Could you work on translating Drina's Romany? I'll call you later."

René stuck the signed contract in his briefcase. "Maurice saw a blue van on rue du Louvre this morning. Promise me you'll be careful, Aimée. If only for Chloé's sake."

She nodded, a shiver rising up her neck.

Martine met her in the salon by the statue of the Marquis de Galliffet. After a two-minute huddle, she ran down the marble steps, armed with Martine's new press pass. On rue de Varenne, beside the plaque stating that the American writer Edith Wharton had lived here, she hailed a taxi.

"Quai d'Orsay," she said. No one bothered to call it the Ministry of Foreign Affairs.

The taxi driver, a mustached man of about sixty, peered at her in the rearview mirror. "Which entrance?"

"Press entrance, *s'il vous plaît.*"

Aimée flashed Martine's badge and got through security without a hitch at the Ministry of Foreign Affairs. But when she arrived at the press briefing it was already coming to an end. Chairs scraped back and a microphone whined like a siren, making her cover her ears. Several officials, identifiable by the ministry "uniform" of navy blue suit, blue shirt and red tie, filed down the few steps from the dais.

She recognized Roland Leseur from his photo in *Le Figaro:* mid-forties, tall, black hair shot through with silver, long face, prominent nose. He spoke to an AFP reporter while a photographer stood by. Aimée caught a few phrases. "As we outlined in the briefing, those Roma, citizens of Romania, Albania and Bulgaria . . ." She lost the thread as someone pushed in front of her — a reporter and a technician from RTL, the radio network. "We're working on agreements with these countries, among others in Eastern Europe, who've proved extremely helpful. The Roma situation differs from that of the *manouches* born in

France . . ."

"How can you make that claim, even while native *manouches* are being resettled like *immigrés*? The protesters on the Champ de Mars . . ."

She didn't hear the answer. By the time she caught up with the reporters, Leseur had disappeared.

"Where's the next briefing?"

"Briefing? The minister and his cronies went to play squash." The RTL reporter laughed. He wore round, owl-like brown glasses and a wool jacket with elbow patches. He ran his gaze over her legs. "New to the pack, eh?"

She nodded. "I need more for my story."

"Good luck with that. They're off to the sports center to flex their muscles for one another."

"Sports center?"

"Talk about green," he said, happy to lord it over her. "Under the Assemblée Nationale. Off-limits to us. But if you wait outside for a few hours, they'll deign to recycle what they've already spewed out, and you'll get points from your editor for persistence."

Like she had the time for that?

But she smiled. "Guess I've got to learn the ropes; I appreciate the tip."

He sidled closer. "Plenty of time for a

drink. What do you say? By the way, I'm Allert de Riemer."

By the time they'd reached the café across the street, she had a plan.

"*Un cocktail?*"

"This early?"

She nodded. "But come on, there's not really a sports club under the Assemblée Nationale, right in the Palais Bourbon. You're joking, right?"

"Don't believe me then."

"You mean the ministers just walk across the quai in their gym shorts?"

Allert smirked. "There's an underground walkway. They don't even come up for air. Normal people's air."

"Some kind of tunnel?"

"Used to be a Nazi bunker, part of the ammunitions storage carved out of the old Palais Bourbon wine cellars."

She grinned, switching to her full-on flirt. "Be nice, don't tease a newbie. You were a beginner once, too."

"I bought you a cocktail, didn't I? What could get nicer than that?"

He leaned in. His hot garlic breath hit her ear.

"If you're so nice, where's the entrance to this Nazi bunker?" asked Aimée.

"*Rez-de-chausée,* make a left at Talley-rand."

She hit the VIBRATE button on her phone. "Oops, my editor. Be right back."

He pulled her close. She tried not to breathe in. Wished she could plug her nose. "I'll be waiting, big eyes."

"You do that."

Out on the pavement, she stood with the smokers, her phone to her ear, and grinned at him. A moment later she'd edged out of view behind an old couple walking a labrador. She crossed the pavement and reentered the ministry. One minute later she'd found the marble bust of a lush-wigged Talleyrand. The man got around.

She stuck the press pass in her pocket, pulled out her clear-framed glasses and the soft leather Villeroi bag that almost melted under her touch. Folded the file with the *Paris Match* under her arm, put her phone to her ear and joined several people going into a door.

A guard was checking security passes. *Merde!* She mingled, talking intently and in a low voice into her phone, which she'd put on mute. Moved forward with the crowd.

"Pass, Mademoiselle?"

She looked down at her chest. "*Mon Dieu,* must have left it on my desk. Upstairs.

Pardonnez-moi." She spoke into the dead phone. "*Un moment,* Monsieur Leseur." She cupped the phone with her hand as if to muffle the words to the speaker on the other end. "Monsieur Leseur needs his file right now. Can I just bring it to him?"

The guard motioned for her to wait.

"*Oui,* Monsieur, you mean *le ministre* needs it?" she said in a loud voice, back into the phone. "But I forgot my pass, and I'm hoping this nice gentleman will . . ."

People behind her shuffled their feet. A few coughed. Even the guard was annoyed at the line.

He waved her through.

She followed the two women ahead of her with their heads bent in conversation. Halogen light strips illuminated the coved stone walls of the surprisingly broad tunnel. A young buck, messenger bag strapped around his chest, wheeled by on his *trottinette,* a silver metal kick scooter, his Converse-clad foot pushing off the ground with a rhythmic *cheut.* A warren, this place, with tunnels branching off right and left, signposted for the cafeteria, the Assemblée Nationale.

She kept her eyes peeled for Leseur, thought up a story. Ahead of her she saw a sign reading: *ASCAN. ASSOCIATION SPORTIVE*

ET CULTURELLE DE L'ASSEMBLÉE NATIONALE. open to députés, assistants et fonctionnaires de l'assemblée, aux fonctionnaires et agents publics de l'administration.

And then in small letters it read: AND OUTSIDERS.

Well, she qualified as an outsider. So did any member of the public — that's if anyone could find this place. Didn't she pay their salaries with her taxes? Time she collected.

"Bonjour." She smiled at the young woman at the desk. *"Désolée* to bother you, but it's urgent. I have a time-sensitive file for Monsieur Leseur. Please notify him — he's on the squash court."

"Monsieur Leseur? Non."

"But I was told —"

"Escrime. The fencing court." She picked up the phone. "A file regarding . . . ?"

A swordsman. If she got his ear, it would only be for a few minutes. "From the press briefing. He'll understand."

The woman at the desk nodded. "Go ahead to the old arsenal."

"Merci."

In a large windowless room painted white, with fencing-club flags hanging from the walls and white lines painted on the blue floors, helmeted and grille-masked figures parried and thrust, riposte after riposte. A

302

metallic smell hung in the close air. It was like stepping into the eighteenth century, except that each time the sword tip touched an opponent, bright purple bulbs lit up on their vest.

"Mademoiselle?"

Roland Leseur, in a form-fitting grey fencing outfit, helmet hanging from a strap on his arm, stood at the men's locker-room door, waiting for her. The clashing of swords, the almost balletic steps, the grunting and tang of sweat sent a shiver of unease up her back. "They know not to disturb me here."

"I'm new, Monsieur," she said, saying the first thing that jumped into her mind. She held up the file. "May we talk in private, please?" she said.

His brow furrowed in annoyance. "In here." He checked inside the men's locker room for people, then closed the door after she entered. "Make this quick, my partner's waiting." Leseur stood in the narrow changing-room aisle beside a metal locker, open to reveal his jacket hanging up, a briefcase, keys, wallet, a cell phone. He flipped open his briefcase and took out a pen. "You need something signed? Why didn't Juliette bring this down herself?"

"*Pardonnez-moi,* Monsieur, but . . ."

"Please show me what I need to sign."

"See, not sign," she said. "This." She put the *Paris Match* on a bench and pointed to the splash on Pascal's death.

Annoyance turned to wariness.

"You lied to find me." His low voice vibrated with anger. "Why are you here? Tell me who you are before I have you thrown out."

She stuck her Leduc Detective business card into his gloved hand.

"Forgive me. It was the only way I'd get a moment of your time, and it's a matter of life and death," she said, speaking fast. "My father investigated the homicide of Djanka Constantin in 1978. They pulled him off the case, but he never forgot it. Later he was killed in a bomb explosion — murdered to keep him quiet about whatever he had learned about Djanka Constantin."

He shook his head. "Not my concern, Mademoiselle."

"Your brother Pascal's body and Djanka's were discovered only hours apart," she said. "Information has come to light that strongly suggests that the two deaths are connected."

"Stop right there." He stepped back. "I don't know what you're talking about."

"I think you do, Monsieur," she said. "A painful event. I'm sorry to insist, but —"

"My brother took his own life," he said, his voice wooden. "I'm not interested in all these lies and slander appearing years later. Now if you'll move aside and let me return to the *piste.*"

How could she keep him there?

"The memoir and the *Libé* article, you mean?"

"Damn reporters dredging for scandal. They hired you, didn't they?" Fear crinkled the crow's-feet edging his eyes. He shook his head. Was that pain or sorrow on his face?

"I'm a detective, Monsieur."

"And you had my ear. Now you don't."

This wasn't going well. Scrapes of metal and shouts of *en garde* came from behind the door.

"My journalist friend says the *Libé* article's been pulled. Nobody will ever read it," she said. "Please just help me understand how your family in the Berry knew the Constantins. Two minutes."

She read the surprise in his face. "But what does it matter anymore?"

Time for the truth. "There's a piece of the puzzle no one will give me," she said. "A piece of information I need to solve my father's murder."

"I don't see a connection, Mademoiselle."

"Maybe you're right. Maybe I'm wasting your two minutes," she said. "But if I don't look for the piece, I won't know." Determined to reach him, she took out a photo of her father. Her favorite, of him leaning over a puzzle. "My father, Jean-Claude Leduc. Think of a crime like a puzzle, he'd say. Gone almost ten years. His death unsolved, murderers never caught. Don't you wish you could reel time back in and see your brother?"

He studied her card. "It was all in my father's time. During the war."

His guard down now, he fiddled with his fencing mask. His father's time? Something stuck in his memory, she could tell. She had to keep the momentum.

"See, there's a connection," she said. "Wasn't your father a decorated Resistance hero? Did he save the Constantin family, hide them from the Germans in the Berry?"

Leseur shrugged. "For years the *manouches* traveled by our land, on the old routes. My father let them camp at the lake when I was small. They played such music at night; I'll always remember their horses and painted caravans, the fish we caught." He stopped himself. "But the old Constantin — we called him the Gypsy King — he relayed Resistance messages to the maquis hiding in the forests."

"Underground, you mean?"

"They called it the Gypsy mail via forest trails," he said. "Markers like a broken branch or twisted twig, signs in nature. Who even talks about them now?"

Who even talks about them? Naftali's words.

"My father worked with the Gypsy King throughout the war. For years after, they'd come in the summer. My father even attended his Gypsy funeral in the sixties. *Non,* maybe it was in the seventies."

"So you knew Drina and Djanka as children."

He paused to think. Something opened up inside him. Memories of a happier time?

"But that's years ago. My parents sent me away to boarding school." Leseur leaned against the metal locker.

"Help me understand, then, why the Constantin family shunned Djanka for having your brother's baby." Ready with the photo — *Djanka, Nicholás and Pascal* — she brought it out from the old pages of *Paris Match* for him to see.

The phone inside his locker vibrated with a long buzz. Leseur ignored it, his face etched with hurt and longing. His lips moved. No sound came out.

"*Pardonnez-moi,* Monsieur, but what did you . . . ?"

"I said, who understands Gypsies?" He didn't deny that Pascal was Nicu's father.

"Nicu was murdered yesterday. In broad daylight, by professionals. A hit."

Leseur stiffened. "I never knew the boy." After a moment, he said, "They sent me away."

"What secret stretching back to Djanka and your brother could still be important enough to need covering up and to have caused my father's murder?"

His phone beeped: a message alert. He averted his eyes.

"Why are you so afraid, Monsieur Leseur? Is someone threatening you?"

His bony, gloved fingers grabbed her arm. "Get out." He shoved her aside.

She grabbed at the open locker door to stop herself from tripping.

"Is there a problem?" A red-faced man appeared at the locker-room door, pulled off his face mask.

Leseur moved forward, letting go of her arm. She stuck her hand in her bag, rooting through mascara tubes, her phone and mini-packs of baby wipes until she found what she was looking for.

"*Zut,*" the man said, looking at her, "don't

tell me the press got in here?"

"Press? Non, she told me she's a . . ." He caught himself before saying detective. *"Ce n'est pas important."*

Aimée took advantage of Leseur's distraction. Stuck the centime-sized tracker into his wallet fold.

"This woman's made a mistake," said Leseur, turning back to Aimée. "She's leaving."

She rubbed her arm. Leaned into Leseur's ear and whispered, "Tell me. Or I'll make a scene in front of your friend."

Sweat broke out on his brow. His hand shook. What was he holding back?

But by now her fame had spread throughout the fencing *piste,* and politicians in tight-fitting gear were crowding through the doorway, eager to expel the stranger in their midst. When she looked back at Leseur on her way out, a jacket over his fencing outfit, he was clutching his briefcase and speaking into his cell phone. The next moment, he'd disappeared through the far exit. She clicked the button to activate the tracker.

With only fifteen minutes until her appointment with the lawyer, Aimée looked down the tree-lined quai for a taxi.

"Mademoiselle Leduc, this way, *s'il vous plaît.*"

A suit wearing dark sunglasses stood at the curb by a black Peugeot with tinted windows, the door open and the engine purring.

"There must be a mistake — I haven't reserved a car," she said, raising her hand to hail a passing taxi.

"The ministry's internal security chief has a few questions," he said. "I've been instructed to escort you."

Pictures of the recent past flickered through her mind: the garden at the *clinique,* the sliver of light as Drina's door opened, her sunken eyes, the nurse Aimée spoke to. The locker room and Roland's pained expression.

"I'm afraid I can't oblige. I'm late."

He opened his suit jacket to reveal a badge on his hip.

The skin on her knuckles whitened as she clutched the strap of her Villeroi bag. "Impossible, I've got a meeting." She stepped back, her heel catching in a cobble crack. Tried in vain to pull it out.

"Which you will of course reschedule, Mademoiselle."

Her heel wouldn't budge. Perspiration broke out on her neck. He bent down and with a practiced flick of his wrist unwedged her heel. Then took her arm. "One doesn't

keep the ministry waiting. Let's go, shall
we?"

"Where?"

"I'm sure you'll find out."

Those fencing politicians had tracked her
down quickly.

Tuesday, Early Afternoon
For the second time in as many days, René knocked on Madame Rana's caravan door. In front of the nearby UNESCO building — an ugly modernist hulk, in René's opinion — rows of daffodils nodded in the breeze. At the Haussmannian limestone apartment building to his right, the concierge watered the red geraniums in her windowsill pots.

Impatient, he knocked again.

"Un moment."

René paced by old dented Peugeots parked on the street. *C'est typique, ça,* he thought in disgust. Here in the 7th, people either drove a junk heap or were chauffeured around in company cars. Determined not to show off or invite scrutiny — so revealing of the hypocrites in this sealed world.

Two minutes later, the door opened on a

312

man wearing a pinstriped suit and wrap-around sunglasses. He descended the steps and got into a black Audi waiting on the curb. No doubt a ministry official or ambassador — nice to know the fate of the world lay in such hands and in Madame Rana's crystal ball.

"A palm reading, *mon petit?*" Today she wore an aqua caftan.

"I brought you a present."

Madame Rana smiled like a satisfied cat so that her eyeliner curved up at the edges. *"Entrez."*

She thought she'd hooked him. But he hadn't come to have his palm read.

"I'm here for a translation," he said, sitting down in the boudoir-like trailer. "Do you understand Romany?"

"Romany spoken in Albania, Romania? Or the German, Italian or Spanish dialects?" she asked. "If I don't know, I know someone who does."

"How about the dialect the Constantins use?"

"And what will I get for that?"

René opened the Monoprix bag hesitantly.

"You brought me a portable foot massager and spa?" said Madame Rana, smiling at the box. "Like my sister's. *Merci.* My cousin's wife is looking forward to the rice cooker, by the way."

René set down the notepad bearing Drina's last Romany words. "It's written phonetically by someone who didn't understand what was being said, so I hope it makes sense."

She sighed and took his palm. Before he could pull it away, she clucked. "Oh, *mon petit,* you're having second thoughts about that love potion?"

Then something occurred to him. Did her reading stop at palms? "Can you read this?" he said, tapping the notebook.

"I went to school," she said, defensive now. "You think I'm a moron, slow-witted?"

The more agitated she became, the more her penciled brow furrowed.

"Django couldn't read, and look at what amazing music he created," René said, worried he'd alienated her. "I just need this translated so I can understand."

After another glance at the notepad, Madame Rana looked up. She checked her Chanel watch. "You don't want to know what this says, *mon petit.*"

"Yes, I do," he said, frustrated. "More? You need more money?"

She pushed the notepad back at him over the purple-draped table. And then the foot-massager-spa box as well.

René doubted much scared Madame Rana, but he saw terror in those made-up eyes. "What's the matter?" he said. "What does it say?"

"You give power to words when you say them," she said. "And I will never say them. It's a curse." And before he knew it, she'd pushed him out the door with his present.

Tuesday Early Afternoon

"We're informal here, Mademoiselle Leduc; there's nothing official about it." A dimpled smile as he handed her his card — Daniel Pons, Chef de Sécurité, Hôtel Matignon. On the tall side, early forties, russet hair parted in the middle. His round face reminded her of a potato. "Off the record. *Un café?*"

She nodded, stifling her unease. Pons poured from the *cafetière* into a demitasse cup. At her feet sat a wooden crate, leeks spilling out of it onto the floor. Next to it was a Styrofoam container marked COQUILLAGES DE BRETAGNE — ON ICE.

"Off the record? Is that why we're sitting in the prime minister's kitchen?"

"*Exactement.* Napoléon said an army marches on its stomach. So do the ministries."

Backroom intrigues weren't her thing.

Pons pushed the sugar bowl toward her. *"Du sucre?"*

"Merci," she said, checking her watch. "I hope this won't take long. I'm late for an appointment." She wished to God she'd gotten through to the lawyer. She'd called, frantic, but the line had been busy. Now she was a no-show.

Pons shook his head, an understanding look in his eye. "You're just here to clarify a few things, you understand."

She helped herself from the bowl of mixed brown and white cubes. Bipartisan sugar, she thought; it covered both bases — politically correct. In front of her was a chalkboard mounted on a cabinet with the day's dinner menu. The prime minister's upcoming five-course meal made her mouth water.

Another man entered, grey haired and slightly stooped.

"My colleague Grévot," Pons said.

First rule: play dumb. Not difficult. "What's this about?"

"At the prime minister's residence at Hôtel Matignon," said Pons, "we like to stay on top of things."

"Why am I here?" She wished he'd spit it out. A bad feeling thrummed in her stomach. She thought of the front page of *Le Parisien* — had they somehow connected

317

Radu Constantin's protest and the activists who marched here to her?

Pons set several grainy black-and-white photos on the stainless-steel counter. Photos of her running down the side street toward rue Oudinot last night.

Pons thought he could prove something? Blurred printouts taken from CCTV? Something told her to hold back for once, to stay calm and bite her tongue.

"I apologize for the poor quality: it's from CCTV coverage," said Pons. "But you know how that is, Mademoiselle, from your line of work. It's hard to make an identification based only on such photos."

She focused on what looked like a gravy stain on the wall telephone. "Why are you showing me these photos?"

"Word has reached us that you're a person of interest, Mademoiselle, who visited a patient in the nearby medical facility on rue Oudinot. And for security reasons —"

"What security reasons?"

"We're not at liberty to release that information, Mademoiselle," said Grévot, leaning forward.

It clicked now. Drina's abduction from the Laennec, the nurse at the *clinique* noting her words down . . . She remembered the *monsieur* the nurse had mentioned, who was waiting on Drina's incriminating last words. Was she looking at the *monsieur* now? What if this went higher up the food chain than she had ever imagined?

She had to get out of here.

"We know you were at the *clinique.*"

"*Moi?* Because you saw a blurred figure in the CCTV footage?"

Her father's rules ran through her head: Don't manufacture an alibi or you'll look guilty. Keep them off target, make them tell you what they know. Save an alibi as your last resort.

No one at the *clinique* knew her real name — she'd given Marie's card from Hôpital Laennec to Madame Uzes, and had lied to the receptionist at billing, at Dr. Estienne's clinic and to Drina's nurse.

She shook her head. "Wrong person, Monsieur." She stood. "If that's all?"

Pons and Grévot exchanged glances. The fragrant bouquet garni simmering on the stove made her stomach growl. Hadn't she just eaten?

"I'm afraid not. We have a witness from the *clinique* who can identify you, Mademoiselle Leduc."

The receptionist? Drina's nurse?

"Back up, Monsieur Pons. A witness to what? A crime?"

"Take a look, *s'il vous plaît.*" He spread out that day's *Le Parisien.* "The clinic suffered a near riot last night. We know because it happens to neighbor the Ministère de l'Outre-Mer."

The ministry responsible for a few centuries of French colonialism.

"L'Hôtel Matignon was mentioned —"

"I just saw that," she interrupted. "Now you're worried about your reputation. Picking me to blame. Why?"

She waited for them to pick up her challenge. Silence. She glanced at her Tintin watch. She'd fight her way out of here, even if she had to start throwing the copper pans and fancy Le Creuset cookware.

"I think that security which deals with the ministries got caught with its pants down for abducting a dying Gypsy woman," she said, taking her bag. "Her family should press criminal charges against all involved, if they haven't already."

Pons exchanged a look with Grévot.

"Robbery, Mademoiselle, is a crime."

Her fingers clenched on her bag strap. The notepad. *"Alors,"* she said, thinking fast, "I'm a little confused. In our judicial system, the police investigate robberies, not the prime minister's security office. Then again, if this woman was kidnapped by a ministry, she must have had important secrets."

"No doubt she did, Mademoiselle. But that's not our *terrain;* we had no knowledge of this woman until last night," said Grévot. "You've got us wrong. We don't like what's been stuck on the soles of our shoes, if you get my meaning."

Surprised at his candor, she swallowed hard. She believed him.

Her collar was sticking to her neck. "The time stamp on your blurry photo says ten P.M. I was home feeding my six-month-old."

With René driving like a speed demon, they'd walked into her apartment at 10:17. She knew because she'd paid Babette extra for staying past ten.

Silence except for the sounds of the pot bubbling and the sparking of the gas burner on the professional stove. She'd talked too much. She'd given an alibi.

Pons pulled a ringing cell phone from his pocket. Answered.

She wished she'd just replied to their questions. Kept it simple. Now her hands were shaking.

A balding man rushed into the kitchen, tying an apron around his middle. "Holding a convention in *ma cuisine? Sortez!*"

She'd use this diversion to escape. "*Pardonnez-moi,* but I'm late."

Pons clicked his phone off and blocked her before she could reach the door. "Of course. We apologize and appreciate your cooperation," Pons said.

Grévot picked up the thread. "However, you understand that we work in the spirit of inter-ministerial cooperation."

Like hell. You lick the heels of whoever's top of the heap, she almost shouted, itching to leave.

She gave her bag a purposeful yank higher up her shoulders. Pons showed her to the door, but not the one she'd come in through.

"*Désolé,* Mademoiselle — one more thing," said Grévot. "We'd like you to leave through the *salle à manger.* Just to eliminate you from the inquiry. Clarification only."

Her knees shook. Did they have a witness? Staff who would recognize her, nail her? Her lies must be written all over her face. What could she do?

"Nervous tic, Mademoiselle?" said Pons, guiding her into the *salle à manger.*

She'd shielded her eyes, squinting at the bright sunlight streaming through the floor-to-ceiling windows in the pale green ante-room. Her mind raced, thinking, trying to come up with a way to alter her looks.

"The light hurts my contacts. I've got to

take them out." She turned away, rubbing her eyes, then fished around in her bag. She always kept a quick disguise. A moment later she'd put on the large, black-framed glasses again.

"I usually wear these." A sigh. "But today I've got a meeting, so I went for contacts. The curse of astigmatism."

Lame, but the best she could do on short notice.

In the *salle à manger,* a nurse wearing a white uniform stood near a serving table crowned by a silver tureen. So nineteenth century — she was even holding her nurse's cap in her hand like a supplicating commoner in the palace.

Perspiration broke above Aimée's upper lip.

"Ninette's from the *clinique,*" said Pons and turned toward her. "Ninette, does she look anything like the woman who, to quote your statement . . . ?" Monsieur Pons pulled out a piece of paper from his lapel pocket. ". . . threatened to report and arrest you if you didn't cooperate and stole a patient's medical papers, despite your protestations? Who told you that your previous orders were changed and that, quote, 'I'm handling this now.' Is that correct?"

Word for word. Aimée swallowed. A dry,

hard swallow that stuck in her throat.

"Something's different," said Ninette, the nurse. "Her glasses."

Great.

"Take them off, please, Mademoiselle Leduc."

The woman was backlit against the bright windows, and Aimée stepped closer to see her. She was older, plump-cheeked. Not the same nurse.

A setup.

"Of course," Aimée said, taking them off. Calling her bluff. "Shouldn't you be wearing your hospital badge on that uniform?"

"Not out in public, on the street," Ninette said.

"Yet you wear a uniform. Let me see your nursing-staff identification."

The woman blinked.

"It's at the *clinique*."

"So you're prepared to swear an oath to that in front of a judge? Right now?" she said. She turned to Pons and Grévot. Locked eyes with Pons. "If you want to pursue this further, we do it at the *commissariat*." She strode toward the door. "If that's all?"

She didn't wait for their answer.

Aimée reached the attorney's secretary,

explaining that an emergency had detained her but she was en route. Snapping her phone shut, she hurried through the court-yard. Double looped her scarf, her shaking subsiding to a dull tremble.

"Aimée, you all right?"

Hearing the familiar voice, she turned around. Her father's colleague from the police academy, Thomas Dussollier got off his bike in the courtyard, his face flushed from exertion. He kissed her on both cheeks, gripped her hand and leaned into her ear. "I came from the *commissariat* as fast as I could. I'm sorry I wasn't in time to warn you before the vultures got you."

She blinked. "I don't understand."

"I heard via my network in the seventh you'd been brought here for a *tête-à-tête,*" he said, his voice low. "Lèfevre's out of com-mission — his leg's acting up again — so Morbier asked me to help you. But an old bull like me lags behind the young bucks, not that I like to admit it."

"You're Morbier's connection?" Why hadn't he confided in her?

"Forgot to tell you, eh?" Dussolier read her look. "Don't be so hard on him, Aimée."

She glanced at her watch. Hurry, she had to hurry. "But I have to go."

"Attends un moment." Dussollier took his

325

briefcase from the bike's basket. "Try to understand, Morbier's tied up as the star witness in that Corsican case. He's testifying behind closed doors and keeping your name out of the case."

Now she remembered the sting he'd talked her into doing last year — handing off a memory stick containing faux court files at that café in Montparnasse. He'd promised her immunity if she helped him set it up, sworn there'd be no court appearance, no giving testimony in the judges' chambers. She knew if the Corsican mob got her name, either tomorrow or a year from now, she'd answer the door to a bullet.

He was protecting her. And Chloé. And he'd drafted Dussollier, who was on the eve of retirement.

"You're family, Aimée," Dussolier was saying. "Once family, always family. We take care of our own."

We take care of our own — like the Gypsies. Yet the Gypsies had shunned Djanka and Nicu, and the *flics* had drummed her father out, stained him with a corruption charge that took her years to disprove.

"So Morbier asked you to help me out. Have you discovered anything?" she asked, again glancing at the time.

"*En fait,* Morbier said to keep my ears open, poke around," said Dussollier, chaining his bike to the ring in the wall. "I'm looking into it."

"Whoever killed Papa and Djanka Constantin abducted Drina." She tapped her high heel. "I explained all this to Morbier."

"He told me." Dussollier straightened up, expelled air. "And you came up with this theory how?"

Theory?

"Drina kept the proof in her notebook, which Nicu was murdered for at the Métro. That was the start of it, anyway."

All her fault. She put her shaking hand in her jacket pocket.

"Anything else to go on?" he said. "Didn't Drina give you more at the *clinique?*"

Startled, she stepped back, shaking her head. Her elbow hit the stone wall. "But how do you know . . . ?"

"You can thank Doctor Estienne for the information Drina gave you. According to my sources, he abducted Drina and kept her in his *clinique* for observation — got paid off. Aimée, that's common knowledge at this point."

The slime.

"Where's Doctor Estienne?"

"Long gone, they say. Someone's gunning

327

for you, Aimée." Dussollier looked around the courtyard, lowered his voice. "I can't do much to help you without some names, can I?"

Should she tell him? She needed help. Decided to trust him.

"Tesla and Fifi," she said. "Ever hear Papa mention them?"

Dussollier shrugged. "Informers?"

She'd keep her theories to herself, see what he came up with. "No clue." Shook her head. "Can you use your contacts here in the seventh to find out their identities, Dussollier?"

"I'll do what I can before I bow out of the force, Aimée," he said. "Pitiful, eh, but I'm all you've got for now. Tell me what else I can do."

She nodded. "Scratch beneath the surface at the Ministry of Foreign Affairs, dig for rumors — old and new — on Roland Leseur and his brother, Pascal."

"*D'accord,* leave the heavy lifting to me. I know people. And people who know people, *compris?*" Dussollier took her face in his hands. "Let this *vieux* do his last bit of police work. I'm old, but I'm not out of touch."

His warm hands, cupping her face the way her father's used to. How she missed him.

"I sent you the invitation." Dussollier kissed her forehead. "You're coming to my daughter's engagement party, *non*? My wife insists; she won't take no for an answer."

She got a taxi on rue du Bac in a panic over the time. Dussollier had been so intent on talking to her that she hadn't felt she could get away, but now she was close to forty minutes late for her meeting with the lawyer. She called Maître Benosh's office and the secretary put her through to the lawyer.

"Where are you, Mademoiselle Leduc?"

"*Je suis vraiment désolée.* I was called to an unexpected security meeting at l'Hôtel Matignon. I'm in a taxi."

True, sort of.

"I'll see you in fifteen minutes then."

Thirty minutes later — the road had been clogged with a large demonstration — she ran into Maître Benosh's office. The building lay across from square Louis XVI, home to the Chapelle Expiatoire, the site of an annual royalists mass in honor of Louis XVI and Marie Antoinette, whose guillotined bodies were dumped here.

She fought to catch her breath. Her heels sank into the wine-red carpet of the waiting room. She noticed a man near the secretary. Melac. He stood by a black lacquer Chinese cabinet, his gaze locking on hers.

"So you decided to show up."

"*Moi?* What are you doing here, Melac?"

"A little detecting of my own."

Merde. He'd been a homicide detective at the Brigade Criminelle until a year ago. Still had connections.

"Leave it to the professionals, Melac."

"Nothing wrong with getting a grasp of the playing field."

"Here? At *my* lawyer's office, at *my* appointment?" She wanted to spit. "Why the hell do you think —"

"I'm impressed, Aimée," he interrupted. "Your child's welfare is on the line and you show up late as usual."

Tired, irritated and conscious of that uneasy chord still vibrating in her stomach, she refused to argue and waste words. "I was called to l'Hôtel Matignon."

His grey-blue eyes — so like Chloé's — narrowed. "Like I believe that?"

"Like I care? Reasons of state security, Melac. I had no choice. Now if you'll excuse me . . ." She headed toward the receptionist to check in.

"Maître Benosh is seeing her next client. Your appointment's been cancelled, Mademoiselle," said the receptionist.

Panic-stricken, mired in this deep carpet, she felt helpless.

"Mademoiselle Leduc, we need to re-schedule." Maître Benosh appeared in her office door, trim in a navy suit and medium-high heels. Her dark shoulder-length hair was bobbed.

"But Maître Benosh . . ."

"It's okay." She smiled. "Tell my assistant to shuffle things around and fit you in as soon as possible."

The door closed. Aimée turned around to see Melac pausing at the double doors leading to the black-and-white tiled foyer. "Since you're so bullheaded, we'll work this out at the magistrate's," he said. "Recognizing my daughter's a done deal. A formality."

"Good God, Melac, she's six months old. Her place is with me, her mother."

"When it fits your schedule," he said.

"My life centers around Chloé," she protested.

But Melac had shut the door.

She rescheduled, begging for something sooner than the day after tomorrow. Impossible, the secretary told her, handing her a manila envelope left for her by the "gentleman."

■ ■ ■ ■

Dejected, she topped up her expired Métro card at the station, squeezed through the doors of a Line 9 train just before they closed. Finding a seat as the train took off, she opened the envelope.

An album of photos of Melac's Breton farmhouse, a sketch of the playground he'd build beside the farmhouse's organic garden, photos of Donatine's loom, where she carded and spun wool from their herd of sheep. The wholesome country life.

Aimée's shoulders slumped. She almost missed changing at Chaussée d'Antin–Lafayette.

Thinking about Chloé's prospects filled her with feelings of inadequacy and guilt. All she could offer Chloé was a sweet childminder, Sundays in the Jardin du Luxembourg and love. Like her father had done. It had been good enough for Aimée . . . hadn't it?

On rue du Louvre she checked for a blue van. Nothing. Maurice's kiosk was closed for his coffee break. She entered the office, set the alarm. It was deserted for once — Maxence was at the Hackaviste Academy, René dropping off de Brosselet's contract according to the Post-it on her desktop screen.

She brewed espresso as the radiator hiccuped to life after a good kick. From the half-open window overlooking rue du Louvre came the hissing of bus brakes. Four large screens ran data on René's desk.

Doubt gnawed at her. What kind of mother was she? Why did she feel guilty when 90 percent of mothers in Paris worked?

But she couldn't dwell on that right now.

The *chef de sécurité* at l'Hôtel Matignon and his colleague were out for her. She doubted their questioning stemmed from the usual police incompetence. Dussollier knew people — every savvy *flic* did — among the back-scratching old boys' network behind the corridors of power. And she hoped he'd use them.

She remembered what Nicu had told her about the body he'd been shown in the morgue — a body the *flics* had claimed was Drina's. They had tried to frame him. Just as Pons had attempted to frame her today, along with the supposed nurse. Were the two things connected?

Setting the steaming espresso on her desk, she called her friend Serge, a pathologist at the Institut médico-légal, to see if he could shed any light on who'd been behind the morgue frame-up. Why hadn't she done this sooner? No answer. After two tries she reached the pathology department.

"Serge? Attending a medical conference in Prague."

The same conference Dr. Estienne was supposedly attending?

The sun filtered through the window, warming the back of her neck. Her three further inquiries at different departments of the morgue all suggested she consult the Brigade Criminelle. She got nowhere.

Frustrated, she wanted to kick something. Kick this shadow behind her father's death. The shadow who'd paid off Drina's abductor, Dr. Estienne, and had Nicu knifed under the Métro.

The ringing of her cell phone interrupted her thoughts. A number she didn't know.

"Oui?"

"Marie Fourcy?" asked a young woman's voice. "I'm trying to return a call from someone named Marie Fourcy who works at Hôpital Laennec."

It could only be Rose Uzes, the one with the hots for Nicu. She'd left her a message after Madame Uzes, under duress, had coughed up her daughter's number. In case Rose checked with her mother, Aimée had used Marie's name, so it would match the card from Hôpital Laennec she'd given Madame Uzes.

"Rose, I need to speak with you about Nicu Constantin."

A quick intake of breath came over the line. "He's . . . dead, my mother said. She's furious with me . . ." Another intake of breath. Choking sobs.

Aimée waited, guilt rippling inside her.

"Rose, I know this is so hard for you, but you might be able to help —"

"*Non, non,* you don't understand," said Rose. Her voice quavered. "I was arrested last night."

"Arrested? Why?"

"Nicu promised to speak at the rally last night." Her words came thick and fast: this was clearly a young woman in need of a sympathetic ear. "He never showed up at the squat. Things turned ugly, a bunch of skinheads showed up, racist types. We knew it was a setup to turn a peaceful meeting into a brawl. The *flics* hauled us in. My friends bailed me out. Now Maman's livid that I'm involved with the demonstration for *les manouches.*"

"Hold on . . ."

"We're demonstrating against hate crimes. Like what happened to Nicu," Rose said, her voice breaking. "There's a vigil tonight at the spot under the Métro . . . the spot . . . you know . . . where it happened."

Aimée did know. Visualized Nicu's arm reaching for her, the blood.

"We drafted a petition at Sciences Po against the violence and hate crimes. We're getting signatures and taking it to the *mairie.*" Rose took a breath. "But why am I telling you all this? My mother says you work for the hospital. Why did you want to speak to me?"

An activist — rebel hearts did beat in the daughters of the Uzes family.

"Rose, I won't share anything you tell me with your mother," she said. "I can't. I lied to her. I'm a private detective looking into Nicu's murder and his mother's abduction. But you might have vital information that could help me uncover the truth."

Pause. "Why should I believe you since you've already told me you're a liar?"

"It was no hate crime, Rose. I was there." Pause. "Come meet me and tell me what you know. Eighteen rue du Louvre. Sign says Leduc. Third floor, right. I'll have an espresso waiting."

"Nicu had been accepted at the Sorbonne for next semester. Religious studies. He's . . . he was an Evangelical Christian,

336

you know." Rose stirred her espresso with a shaking hand. "I can't believe . . . Such a waste."

Aimée nodded. Rose was tall, like her mother, with long, straight brown hair. In her boots, tailored jacket and denim skirt, Rose looked like any other Sciences Po student. She'd worn sunglasses to hide her red-rimmed eyes.

"Didn't Nicu live in that art squat, the place where the fight happened?"

"Sometimes."

Quiet all of a sudden, Rose looked away.

"Nothing you say goes any further than me, okay? Please, Rose, I need information, and holding back doesn't help me work out who took his life."

"You won't tell my *maman?*"

The last person she'd tell. Aimée shook her head.

Five minutes later, Rose's secret emerged. She'd given Nicu the key to the *chambre de bonne* in the Uzes's building so he could stay there when it was cold. *That's all,* she insisted, but her blush said otherwise. It didn't seem like that blush had much to do with what Aimée wanted to know. "*D'accord,* your secret's safe. Did Nicu talk about where he grew up, why he came back to Paris?"

"*Non*, we mainly talked about rights for *les manouches*."

Maybe Rose did, but Nicu hadn't struck her as political. Sheltered, and a bit naïve, Rose seemed a product of an ancien-régime family with a social conscience.

"We're going to publish an essay of his in the Sciences Po newsletter."

"An essay?"

"I helped him. But it's in his words. Robert used some of the material in his Avignon documentary. Nicu talks about *les manouches* and music. He was a really talented musician." She sniffled. "He talked about how his mother's struggles helped him find God."

"Did he mention his Uncle Radu, who runs a circus?"

"The one he called a liar? Nicu had little to do with his extended family. When he was little, they threw them out. He and his mother had to hide."

"Did he say why?"

Rose shook her head. "I don't think he knew."

"Any idea why Nicu came back to Paris?"

"Work? For his interviews at the Sorbonne?" Rose shrugged. "What did you mean when you said Nicu's murder wasn't a hate crime? That you were there?"

Aimée uncapped an Evian, sipped. It wouldn't do to get this girl in more trouble; her arrest last night was more than enough. Her name had no doubt made it onto a list at the *commissariat*.

She gave Rose an edited version.

"Hit men?" Rose gasped. "I don't understand why anyone would target Nicu. He is . . . was . . . gentle, non-violent."

"That's what I'm trying to find out. Can you remember anything that seemed off with Nicu in the last few days? Or anything that stuck out as strange?"

But Rose had dissolved into tears. "How could anyone do that . . . ?"

"Please, Rose. I need your help."

She had to persist, get something from this girl. She pulled out the snapshot Nicu had given her. "Rose, look at this picture. That's me, my father, Drina and Nicu. He must have been about six or seven."

Rose wiped her eyes. Stared. "That's you? Whoa, your hair is so eighties."

Aimée felt older by the minute. "Rose, I should tell you that Nicu asked for my help because —"

"*Mais oui,*" she interrupted. "I saw this. He liked him, your father. That's right, I remember. Nicu told me how his mother . . . yes, she had an arrangement with your

339

father. She hid until your father told her it was safe."

And then once her father had given Drina the all clear, she became his informer. But it brought her to more questions — Who was it Drina had been collecting information on? Who were Fifi and Tesla, and what secret did they want to keep so badly that they had resorted to murder?

"Aimée, don't you remember all this?" Rose was saying. "You're in the picture."

Aimée wished she remembered. "What else did Nicu tell you? Anything else about my father?"

"He felt sorry for Drina, Nicu said."

Sorry he couldn't solve her sister Djanka's murder even after he'd been pulled off the case? So like her papa.

Rose was standing up. "I've got class, then I'm working on the newsletter and trying to get petition signatures."

Think; she had to remember what kept slipping from her sleep-deprived brain. These days she was so quick to anger, to jump into things and reflect later — but then she'd always been this way, as René often reminded her. Only it had gotten much worse since Chloé. Could it be post-partum? She grabbed at the question swimming through the grey matter. An idiot not

340

to think of it sooner.

"When did you last see Nicu?"

"We spoke on . . ."

"*Non,* Rose, I mean in person — when and where?"

"Sunday, *non,* Saturday he met me in the courtyard at Sciences Po."

"Did he mention Drina, her sickness?"

"He was going to meet her, to convince her to go to the hospital. That's all. I had an afternoon lecture." She pulled her bag onto her shoulder.

"So he seemed sad?"

Rose nodded. Thought. "But it wasn't just about his mother, Drina had told him she didn't have long. There was something more than that. I don't know. Nervous and worried." Tears welled in her eyes.

"Nervous because he sensed they were being watched?" Aimée took Rose's hand. "He told me someone had been following him."

Rose's lip quivered. "I thought . . . he always . . ." She shook her head. "I thought he was just being paranoid. Gangs pick on Gypsies and beat them up. I've seen it happen at the market, the Métro." Tears slid down her face as she shook her head. "But he wasn't paranoid. I was wrong."

Rose's phone trilled. She glanced at it. "My mother."

341

"Think back, Rose. Picture Nicu in the courtyard at Sciences Po the last time you saw him," said Aimée. "Where you were standing while you talked, the people nearby. Close your eyes. Can you describe what you remember?"

Rose muted her phone. Closed her eyes. "I remember . . . the white blossoms of the *marronniers* on the stone wall. We walked over the squished blossoms in the courtyard. Gross. Nicu waited while I went to my locker to get my books. But when I got back, he was leaving, going out the court-yard gate. He saw me. I waved, but he didn't wave back. I figured he'd remembered his appointment with Drina. He was terrible at keeping track of time."

He didn't wave back because he wanted to protect her.

Afternoon sunlight pooled on the herring-boned wood floor. A horn blared from below on rue du Louvre.

Rose opened her eyes, which shone with tears. "That's the last time I saw him."

"Who did you see, Rose?" Aimée forced herself to breathe. Count to three. "Because you did see someone, maybe behind him? You do remember."

Rose blinked. "I don't know. Maybe at the gate?" Pause. "That's right, he left right

342

behind Nicu. I didn't think anything of it."

"Can you describe him? Maybe another student, or did he look like a teacher?"

"I'm not sure."

One of René's monitors started to beep. Time to re-loop. She walked over and double-clicked a key. Walked back to her desk and turned back to Rose.

"Think, Rose . . . try to think back to what he was wearing. You can, I know, because you remembered he left right behind Nicu."

"Maybe older, maybe a suit?"

"That's good, Rose. What else?"

"All I remember thinking is that he might have been someone's grandfather."

Prioritize.

Time to summon her sleep-deprived, hormone-addled, overstimulated brain to order. Get a handle on what Rose had told her and make sense of Nicu's murder. Draw the big picture. She needed to make a time-line, visualize and connect the events. If she could work through her anxiety about Chloé, the pain in her ribs, and her tired-ness, and make connections, assemble the pieces, she'd get the whole.

She taped a roll of white butcher paper, courtesy of the butcher who sold her Miles Davis's horsemeat, to the wall. Then she closed the window against the noise, took her colored markers and wrote down names, grouping them according to what she'd learned:

Constantin clan: Gypsy King, Radu, Djanka/Aurélie, Drina and Nicu.
The Leseurs: Resistance patriarch, Pascal, Roland.
The Leducs: Papa, Aimée.
The Uzes: Aunt, Great-Uncle, Belle, Rose and Lisette.
1999 incidents: Hôpital Laennec abduction, faux body in the morgue, Nicu's knifing, Drina's last words at the clinique.

Then she graphed a timeline beginning in 1978 with Djanka/Aurélie's murder and Pascal Leseur's supposed suicide. She taped the two black-and-white photos roughly where they'd fall on the timeline.

She tried to make connections. After ten minutes she sat down and stared. So far, she'd drawn a series of crisscrossed lines. What had she missed or forgotten?

She added Dr. Estienne, Ninette the faux nurse, Pons and Grévot, the mystery grandpa at Sciences Po. Under a question mark she wrote *Tesla, Fifi.*

She rubbed her eyes, filled with shame

and guilt. Imagined the struggles Nicu had faced. How Drina had raised him in hiding, then worked at the market, caning furniture and informing for her father to put food on the table. Somehow Nicu had pulled himself up and got accepted to the Sorbonne, his whole life ahead of him. Her father had promised their help, yet when Nicu had asked her for it, she'd failed him.

Her brain stalled.

Walk away, her father would say. Let it simmer until your mind clears. She had a business to run — it was her second day back in the office and she had only another twenty minutes to check and program their daily anti-virus scans before Babette would bring the girls so she could nurse Chloé. Then she'd have to change and head out for tonight's surveillance.

Before she forgot, she left Maxence a detailed phone message about how to remotely hook up Roland Leseur's tracker feed. Thank God she'd had the backup tracker ready and primed for tonight's surveillance. She counted on Maxence to bring another, and keep it from René. These trackers cost a bundle.

Aimée cuddled with Chloé on the recamier in the office, fighting sleep. Chloé's warm fingers tightened against her clavicle, her eyelashes fluttered and her intent mouth sucked like a little machine. Aimée's shoulders sagged; her lids were so heavy. She wanted to let it all go and surrender to sleep. But she couldn't. The red marks on her arm from Leseur's grip still showed, her bruised rib hurt and her thoughts whipped like a gale through a wind tunnel. Enveloped in Chloé's sweet baby smell, she must have nodded off. The next thing she felt was a coldness. An emptiness. She sat up.

No Chloé in her arms. Good God, had she dropped her baby? She reached down to the creaking wood floor. Only the heels she'd kicked off. Was this a nightmare? She shook her head, splashed mineral water from a bottle on her face. She was awake.

"Babette?"

No answer. Only her deserted office, the door to the hallway open.

Panicked, she adjusted her Agent Provocateur bra and noticed the envelope propped on her desk, addressed to *"Aimée Leduc"* in that familiar angular handwriting.

Melac. He'd come in and taken a nursing Chloé from her arms. The snake stopped at nothing.

Shaking with fear and anger, she ran in her stocking feet to the open office door.

Grabbed her coat . . . *non,* she had to read what was in the envelope first.

A notice summoning her to appear at an appointment with his lawyer; the notice stated that a nonappearance could force a court-ordered one. Stealing her baby and threatening a court order — he couldn't do that. She doubted it was even legal.

What did legality matter? Her baby was gone. *Chloé.* She had to get her back.

A moment later she stood on the landing, hyperventilating in front of the wire-cage elevator shaft, stabbing the button. Scrolling with frantic fingers through her cell-phone contacts for Melac's number. *Merde,* she'd deleted it.

"Bonsoir," said the smiling man who stepped out of the elevator.

Her eyes brimmed, her lip quivered. Waves of helplessness washed over her. "Please, you have to help me . . . quick . . . my baby . . ."

"Ah, Benoît, you're early." Babette stood wiping her hands outside the WC in the hall. On her hip was Gabrielle, shaking a rattle, and in front of her was the baby stroller with a smiling Chloé. Aimée's knees turned to jelly as relief washed over her.

"We had a spit-up and diaper change times two, so I just took care of the girls here in the WC." Babette flashed a look at Aimée. "You just missed the fun, Benoît."

Benoît, Gabrielle's father, whom she'd never met. And now she looked a fool. A neurotic fool.

"Are you all right?" he asked.

"Sorry, I must have dropped off and woken up disoriented."

"Glad you tried that power napping we were talking about, Aimée." Babette smiled meaningfully. "If you've gone into a deep REM state, ten minutes' sleep is like an hour. Snap and you're ready to go."

Aimée nodded, feeling like an idiot and desperate to repair her first impression. Gabrielle's father would tell his wife she was unhinged.

"Sorry to come early, but my last meeting was near here," he said, adjusting his messenger bag, "and I'm watching Gabrielle tonight."

She liked him — tall, bright eyes, lean hipped, longish brown hair. He wore a white shirt under a jean jacket; not the stuffed shirt of an academic that Madame Cachou had painted Gabrielle's father to be.

"Please come into my office; I should introduce myself. I've met your wife, Carine. I'm —"

"I know who you are," he said, averting

his gaze.

She cringed inside.

"But I'm Gabrielle's uncle."

"Uncle?" So then maybe . . . available?

"Pardon?" he said.

Good God, had she said that aloud? It was then she noticed the runs in her black stockinged feet, her undone blouse buttons and Babette beckoning her to the WC.

She was leaking.

After Benoît had departed and Aimée had given Chloé a goodnight kiss, she returned to the WC. She cleaned up and applied concealer and mascara, then outlined her lips with a brown pencil and filled them in with Chanel red. Took a moment thumbing through the booklet Babette had pressed into her hands as she left — *The Ten-Minute Power Nap Will Change Your Life* — before hunting in her back office armoire for the right outfit. Found it and changed into black fishnets and a classic little black Chanel number paired with the beaded vintage fuchsia Schiaparelli bolero. She finished up with a few dabs of Chanel No. 5 on her pulse points. Tonight's surveillance was at the place the *comte* had called a "clubhouse for polytechnicians." But everyone referred to polytechnicians, the elite egghead graduates of the École Polytechnique, by their nickname, "les X."

She glanced at the power-nap bullet points. Ten minutes and ten minutes only of deep-cycle REM sleep made one fresh and alert. Powerful people and celebrities existed on power naps: CEOs who worked 120 hours a week, models jetting to runway shows around the world — even John Lennon swore by them when he was writing music.

Le Beatle? Maxence would eat this up.

Alert and refreshed after her nap — however long it had been — she now felt ready for battle with Melac. She shot an email to Maître Benosh, detailing Melac's lawyer's demand. Next she prepared for the night's surveillance by reading the dossier on the target, the *comte*'s cousin, an engineer. With all that accomplished, and for once already *macquillée,* dressed, spritzed and ready, she still had half an hour to spare.

A little time to try to make some headway on Drina, Djanka and Nicu. She turned back to the timeline on the butcher paper.

She kept coming back to the same question: Why had her father been pulled off Djanka Constantin's murder investigation?

It felt like something was staring her in the face. *She had to go back to the begin-*

ning, go over each detail. Then she'd see what she was missing.

She opened her red Moleskine, scanned her notes. Thinking about Roland Leseur, she tried to make sense of his anger. What did he know about what had happened to his brother twenty years ago?

She cut out the 1978 *Paris Match* pages on Pascal's funeral and taped them next to Roland Leseur's name. A scenario spun in her mind: Had Roland murdered Djanka years ago out of rage with her for bringing down the family? Had Pascal threatened to legitimize Nicu? Could Roland have killed his own brother and made it look like a suicide?

A long shot.

What secret was so big it was worth killing over twenty years later? And what did it have to do with her father? Then Drina's words came back to her — *You know.*

"Don't you have surveillance with Maxence, Aimée?" René walked in and draped his tailored Burberry raincoat over his chair.

"Ready and waiting."

René studied the butcher paper. "Playing pin the tail on the suspect?" He shook his head.

"What's wrong, René?"

"You missed the lawyer's appointment,

n'est-ce pas?"

"And I rescheduled it for the day after tomorrow. Sit down. Let me explain."

René rubbed his forehead. "Not this again."

"Five minutes, René, please."

He sat, pumped up his ergonomic chair and spun around to face her. "Five minutes, Aimée. Then I've got to work on de Brosselet's project. A paying project, if I need to remind you?"

"D'accord." Pointing to the timeline, she told him about all the information she'd gathered that day, including Roland Leseur's reaction to her questions, her meeting with Rose and the frame-up at l'Hôtel Matignon.

"The prime minister's security had you on CCTV?" His brow furrowed. "I don't like it, Aimée."

"Think I do?"

"And I haven't helped you much," said René. "All I got from Madame Rana was expensive fright. She wouldn't translate."

While René told her about his visit, she reapplied her mascara. Nothing they'd learned seemed to have gotten them anywhere.

"Why not go with the simple scenario?" René said. "A jealous Pascal murders his

352

lover, Djanka, dumps her in the moat — it's not far from the quai d'Orsay. Then, guilt stricken, he commits suicide. The family pays hush money to close the investigation. End of story."

If it were that simple, why had Drina been abducted? "Not end of story, René."

"*D'accord,* say the younger brother pays a hit man to kill his brother, reasons unknown, and his lover Djanka, too," said René. "Drina takes Nicu, her sister's son, to protect him. They melt into the countryside —"

"Hold on, René. From what Nicu told Rose, my father gave Drina the all clear and she and Papa struck up an 'arrangement' for her to inform. Then Nicu was murdered for her notebook containing proof."

"All these years later? All these years after *your* father's death? Didn't Nicu tell you she lived in Avignon now?" René leaned back in his chair. "Tonight's edition of *France Soir* details the police investigation into Nicu Constantin's 'hate' murder by right-wing youths who targeted Gypsies at the Métro."

She shook her head. "Too convenient. Whoever murdered him stole the notebook, too."

"So what, then? Roland Leseur's so des-

353

perate to keep the secret of his brother's affair that he hired a minion to kill the son after all these years?" said René. "*Non,* he'd call up a pal at the Ministry of Defense and request a black op to handle it." René stretched his arms over his head. "That scenario work for you?"

"You read too many thrillers, René. Yet you're right, there's a black-op flavor to it." Hadn't Thiely at the École Militaire intimated the same thing?

"How many years has he had to tie up a loose end? This is dangerous, Aimée — for you and Chloé. Let it go. Your five minutes are up," said René as Maxence entered with his equipment. He hooked up the remote and plugged it into René's bank of receivers.

"All systems go, Maxence." René scanned the screen, looking at a moving green dot. "Wait, why has this been activated already?"

Aimée pulled out her scooter keys and winked. "Roland Leseur. I put a tracker in his wallet. Now we'll see if he goes and visits the Ministry of Defense."

Aimée stood in the small round salon upstairs at the Maison des Polytechniciens, the magnificent early eighteenth-century building where the reception was being held. This land had once belonged to Queen Margot, and the building had later been owned by Louis de Béchameil, after whom the sauce was named. De Béchameil had persuaded Jean-Antoine Watteau to decorate his *hôtel particulier,* and Watteau's painted ceiling remained — a whimsical panoply of frock-coated monkeys on swings. During the Revolution it was the seat of power for the *quartier:* later in its history it was the headquarters of the national medical academy, a museum and a center of a movement for the French Renaissance. Finally École Polytechnique acquired it, "for their alumni," as the hostess informed her, "and also available to hire for weddings and DJ parties in the vaulted subterranean cavern."

Maxence had reprised his role as car valet, and was standing downstairs in the entrance hall, beside the *escalier d'honneur,* a winding staircase with smooth dark-wood banisters and filigree swirls. The conservative crowd — not one of them under fifty — drank and mingled. After a half hour of surveillance, sipping *jus de pamplemousse* and nibbling crudités, she'd begun to suspect the *comte*'s imagination at work. While his extended family talked behind his back, nobody seemed to have it in for him and his company. The *comte*'s cousin, the engineer, was short and mouse-like, with weak blue eyes behind thick-lensed glasses and a prominent nose — the only prominent thing about him. He seemed even less of a threat than the other members of the *comte*'s family. After all this surveillance, it appeared simply that the *comte* exhibited a paranoid streak.

But not her call — the *comte* was paying her for surveillance, and she'd deliver. She took careful notes in her head as she scrutinized each of the engineer's conversational partners. So far there had been a middle-aged man with a protruding chin and an elderly dame. Judging by the advance guest list, a *monsieur* from a Geneva-based pharmaceutical company and the engineer's mother.

She sighed. She'd forgotten how tedious surveillance was. She walked over to the staircase and shot a glance down to Maxence at his post in the foyer full of black and white marble. Murmured into the stamp-sized microphone clipped inside her beaded bolero. "All quiet on the western front?"

In her earwig she heard Maxence clear his throat.

A signal. Alert now, she readied her palm-sized camera. The *comte*'s cousin must have called ahead for his car. A moment later she followed him as he headed downstairs with his mother, still deep in conversation with the Swiss man.

If she hadn't had her camera ready, she'd have missed it. On the staircase the engineer whipped something from his pocket. When they got to the marble foyer, he reached to shake the man's hand. Hiding the camera as best she could behind her hand, lens aimed through her parted fingers, she snapped as many pictures as possible. After the handshake the engineer's hands were empty. Caught that, too.

"Target's handed off to protruding chin," she said softly into the mic. "Monitor and stall the protruding chin until I reach his car."

"*Oui, Monsieur,* the light blue Peugeot?" Maxence was saying for her benefit. "That's parked at the far end. If you'll take a seat on the recamier, *s'il vous plaît.*"

She brushed past Maxence, heard the car keys drop into her open beaded clutch. Two minutes later she'd installed a tracker in the rear left wheel well, clipped a mini microphone to the car's interior clutch stick base and passed the keys, wrapped in a fifty-franc note, to the waiting *voiturier.*

Maxence arrived at her scooter, which was

parked under the eaves of the concierge's loge, still in his valet attire. "Activation complete?"

She heard a double click as the blue Peugeot started up. "I wouldn't have picked *le vieux,*" said Maxence. "The one with the rheumy blue eyes and bad breath."

Just in case the *comte* had any other suspicious encounters, they stayed through the end of the party, which turned out to be a short affair. An hour later they were done.

"It's never the ones you expect, Maxence." She turned the key in the scooter's ignition and revved the engine, and they shot into the night. "Never." And it made her think.

After dropping Maxence at the Métro, she paused at the curb by a café, took her phone off mute and checked for messages. Nothing from Morbier or Dussollier. Should she call Dussollier, check in?

Her phone rang. René.

"I've got the feed recording," said René. "Interesting. This engineer's the *comte's* cousin?"

"*Exactement,*" she said. "The engineer cousin handed off something to a Geneva-based pharmaceutical company."

"*Voilà,* the Swiss man's conversation is coming in loud and clear," said René. "He's listening to classical music and he's talking percentages and shares he's about to acquire from the *comte*'s cousin in the company. Sounds like he'll get enough for a majority holding."

"Proof *parfaite*. Back up the recording, make a copy. I'll write up my notes and download the digital photos. We'll deliver a nice package to the *comte* tomorrow." She reached for her helmet. "What about Leseur's tracker? Any activity?"

"Only typical evening activity for a middle-aged *homme politique*. From the Assemblée Nationale, Leseur walked to his local Picard, for a gourmet frozen dinner, I imagine, then to his apartment off Boulevard Saint-Germain."

She almost dropped her helmet on the cobbled street.

"You followed him, René?"

"No need. This tracker does it and works more smoothly than a melting brie," said René. "I followed him visually on my computer."

"How? Does this involve some new geekoid program, René?"

"You should see it, Aimée." His voice rose with excitement. "It's a prototype in development. It overlays a visual onto a street map — it shows everything, monuments, landmarks, *restos,* shops."

359

"Sounds amazing." A streetlight cast a furred yellow glow through the trees. Outside the Métro entrance, people sat at the café terrace under a spreading awning.

"My friend invited me to alpha-test it for his new company," said René. "It even pulls his location from the Internet and plugs it into its programming. I've got Leseur's address, Aimée, which I cross-checked after hacking into the ministry's site."

Seemed René favored Leseur for the murderer. And René had more, she could tell by the energy in his voice. He loved new toys.

"So what else does your wonder program tell you?"

"Most *hauts fonctionnaires* live in state-furnished apartments, you know, at the taxpayer's — our — expense. But not Leseur. This program pulls up property records and owners. His family owns two apartments in the same building off Boulevard Saint-Germain."

"Where are you going with this, René?"

"His brother Pascal Leseur committed suicide in one of them."

Shocked for a moment, she wondered what that could signify. If anything. "I'm surprised they didn't sell it."

"Sell in the Faubourg Saint-Germain, the

most desirable part of the seventh? Where all their neighbors are aristocrats?"

Aristocrats with threadbare apartments, like the Uzes. Laughter, the slam of a door as a couple got out of a taxi.

"But getting back to murder over suicide: Roland had proximity, if not motive, since he lived upstairs," said René. "And he could dump his brother's lover in the moat."

She remembered Leseur's reaction to her questions: as if he had happy, fond memories of the sisters. On a practical level it seemed possible that he'd killed Djanka and Pascal, but she wasn't convinced about motive.

"Wasn't he younger? Might he have been away at school? Can you check on that?"

Silence except for clicking.

"René?"

"Hold on, I have to restart. My connection's slowing down."

Great.

"Give me a few minutes." She heard René suck in his breath. "Almost forgot, a Martin called for you. He said you knew where to find him. I hope this means —"

About time.

"Call me when you're up and running, René."

■ ■ ■ ■

A curl of cigarette smoke rose from between the fingers Martin tented on the table at his banquette in the back of Le Drugstore. "Let me tell you a love story, Mademoiselle Aimée."

An expensive one, considering what she'd paid Martin for information.

She nodded. Took a sip of Evian, mindful of the old framed poster opposite that showed two fishermen on a riverbank opening their *bières*. The caption read, WATER? THAT'S FOR THE FISHES.

"This love story," said Martin. "It goes back to Victor Hugo and his hunchback. Remember Esmeralda, the seductive Gypsy? Well, during the war an alliance was formed in the Berry countryside."

She nodded again. "You mean between the Gypsy King and the Leseur patriarch, who was part of the Resistance."

"*Tiens, tiens,* you already know. Why did you ask for my help?"

"Keep going, Martin, I'll tell you when I don't know."

Martin sucked on his cigarette. Tapped the ash into the Ricard ashtray. "The alliance continued long after the war, and a

362

few alliances formed under the sheets, too. If you understand."

"Pascal Leseur fathered Djanka Constantin's child." She sipped her Evian.

"Then I owe you a refund . . ."

"*Désolée,* Martin. I won't interrupt your love story again."

"For all this Pascal's faults, and it seems there were many, he loved her. Had loved her since they were children. A *grand amour.* And he loved the boy. To prevent a scandal . . . well, I don't know the details, but your father hid her sister and the child. Later she informed for him, *mais* then she disappeared again, this time to Avignon, after your father passed."

Martin would never say "murdered."

"She was afraid, that's why — because she saw Papa blown up in the explosion. She told me, Martin. Told me as she was dying. She knew his murderers. Who are Fifi and Tesla?"

"Ask Radu Constantin." Martin flicked his ash. "He's waiting for you outside in the Mercedes. My next appointment's here, Mademoiselle Aimée. Kiss the baby for me."

"*Merci,* Martin." She pecked him on both cheeks. Wished she didn't want to suck up the smoke from his smoldering cigarette butt.

At the corner of the Champs-Élysées, Radu Constantin leaned against the hood of his brown Mercedes, smoking. Like he had at the hospital, he wore a fedora. He appeared more haggard, with deep pouches under his eyes. "*Le petit* said you found my sister before she went into a coma."

Sounded like he had a problem with that. She pulled her bolero tighter. "We alerted you as soon as we could. Didn't you get to the *clinique* in time . . . ?"

"She'd departed on her journey." He removed his fedora. Put it to his chest. Wind whistled and shook the overhead plane-tree branches. He looked up. "You broke our tradition, violated our customs."

She shivered. A sign? For a moment she wondered if Drina stirred in their midst. But she had to get past this woo woo.

"I'm sorry, Monsieur Constantin. Truly sorry." She shook her head. "Instead of blaming me, what about the doctor who was paid off and her abductors? Hold them accountable, not me. Demand an investigation into her case. Get to the root of this and insist on prosecuting the guilty."

He pulled *Le Parisien* from his coat pocket. Shoved it in her face. "You think the press gives us justice? That this works?"

"*Pas du tout.* But it doesn't hurt. What

you did protesting last night was instrumental in bringing this to public attention. It makes the people responsible nervous. Makes them sweat."

A snort. "As if that will ever happen."

"Don't you want to make the system, however flawed, work in your sister's favor? Like it never did during her lifetime or your nephew's." She couldn't read his expression. "Hadn't she returned because of her illness, because she needed her family?" Aimée tried her hunch, moving closer to Radu. "To say goodbye? But it had to be on your terms, *non*? Wasn't that why you and Nicu argued?"

"Stop." He raised his ring-weighted hand. The thick gold band on his pinkie glinted under the streetlight.

He did blame her. No understanding shone in his face — not that she expected any. He'd lost a sister and a nephew, after all. She could feel his numb grief — but she also sensed that it was partially rooted in guilt over the past.

"What did my sister say in the *clinique*?" His voice rose, whether in fear or suspicion, she couldn't tell. "I know she spoke to you."

Should she hold back or tell the truth to this irrational man who resented her? Blamed her? If she walked away, like she wanted to, it would get her nowhere.

"I expect information in return, Radu. It goes both ways, or you wouldn't be here. Martin told me."

He hadn't. But if Martin had gotten him here, Radu wanted something — and that "something," whatever it was, was her bargaining chip.

He jerked his head in agreement.

"She witnessed my father's murder years ago. Told me to 'make it right' and find those implicated. She gave me two names — Fifi and Tesla. Martin says you know them."

"That's all? You broke our traditions for that?"

She'd have understood disappointment, but where was the bite of anger in his voice coming from? What did he expect? "So I broke your traditions, some taboo," she said. "To me, murder's a taboo. How about you tell me how you know Fifi and Tesla."

"That's years ago." He put his hat back on his curly black hair.

"I'm listening."

He opened his car door. "Why should I tell you?"

She almost kicked the door shut. Playing hard to get and lying — well, she could play that game, too.

"Guess you don't want to know what your sister said about you."

Radu Constantin paused, his coat lapel bent upward in the wind. A shrug of what she took as defeat. "*Non,* that's all scattered with the wind. Like her spirit. Gone." He opened the car door. Paused. "She mentioned those names."

Aimée's breath caught. "What did she say about them?"

"That's why she had to hide, she said. That's all." Radu averted his eyes. "I blamed her for mixing with *gadjo,* like always, and refused to help. Then she disappeared."

He'd shunned her when she'd asked for help.

"But why had she recently come back to Paris?"

"To make her peace, to depart among her people. But the *gadjo* found her." He looked up at the night sky hazed by clouds. "Me, I wanted her forgiveness."

And she believed him.

Aimée stood for a long moment watching the Mercedes disappear into the cars on the brightly lit Champs-Élysées. Radu Constantin's sad case was one of too little, much too late.

Her phone vibrated in her inner jacket

pocket. René.

"Leseur's on the move, Aimée." She heard him clicking the keyboard in the background. "He's going down rue du Bac. Now he's turning onto . . . rue de Grenelle. Maybe he's walking his dog . . ."

"Or maybe not, René." She plugged in her earphones, put on her helmet, keyed the ignition and revved the engine. "Guide me from the Pont de l'Alma. I should be crossing it in three minutes."

"Sure about this, Aimée?"

"Keep talking, René."

René directed her remotely, keeping tabs on Leseur, who maintained a brisk pace.

"Where did you really get this little toy?"

"My real-time simulation prototype?"

"Talking geek again, René? Did some gamer friend with military contacts ask you to alpha-test this?"

"Not military, *non*. My Silicon Valley friends." He pronounced it *Zeeleekon Vallée*.

"You got in trouble with them before, René, *n'est-ce pas?*"

And had to escape the *vallée* on a drug plane. But no need to bring that up.

"Leseur must have jumped into a taxi," said René, excited now. "He's passing les Invalides."

"I'm on Avenue Rapp." Tiled Art Nouveau façades flew by.

"Take a left at Avenue de la Bourdonnais to intercept him at rue de Grenelle."

She stretched out her arm to signal a left turn and almost got clipped by a speeding Alfa Romeo. Centimeters from losing her hand to a red bullet with Italian music blaring from the open window.

Shaken, and feeling more wary of Italians than she had before, she kept to the right.

"He's going straight on rue de Grenelle," René was saying, "passing . . . *non,* slow down, it's hard following on the screen . . ." A few clicks. "Veer right . . . it's a one-way. Make a right on Grenelle which becomes rue Belgrade." A few moments later René shouted, "He's stopped at the Champ de Mars! In front of it. *Non,* beside it."

"Make up your mind, René. Tell your cursor to behave."

"Make a sharp right on avenue Deschanel and go up to rue Marinoni. It's a narrow street leading to the Champ de Mars."

She caught the green light and zipped right, cutting in front of an approaching *camionnette.* Its burst of honking made her almost jump out of her skin.

"*Le voilà.* I see him getting out of a taxi," she said. "He's paying." She held her breath, hoping he wouldn't find the centime-sized tracker as he riffled through his wallet. Then again, he might mistake it for a coin. "René, he's going to the front door of . . ." She pulled over, squinting through her helmet's visor. "One-four-three rue Marinoni." A limestone mansion with an Art Nouveau tiled façade, its tall windows framed by iron scrollwork. "Find out who lives here. Could be an embassy, but I don't see a plaque or flag."

Trees blocked much of her view, so she idled the engine and checked the time. Leseur might stay an hour, several hours — who knew?

"Checking the address out, Aimée. Takes a minute. Call me back."

But it was less than a minute before she heard the door open, footsteps on the short rise of stairs and voices. She peered between the trees, catching sight of Roland Leseur and a woman walking past the grilled fence. She couldn't make out the woman's face in the darkness, just a shock of white-haired ponytail. The woman held a leash with a trailing Westie following behind.

At 9 P.M. Leseur had taken a taxi across the *quartier* to walk a dog with this woman — a friend? Not his sister, because her research had told her he didn't have one. A

370

liaison? Aimée killed the engine, grabbed a knit cap and thin windbreaker from under the scooter seat, stowed her helmet, the Schiaparelli and pocketed her keys. At least the oversized windbreaker covered the Chanel.

She'd lost them now. *Merde.* But with a dog they couldn't have gotten too far. The Champ de Mars stretched from the Tour Eiffel, with its tourists and pickpockets, down this way, which was a popular family spot in the daytime: there were pony rides and a marionette theater, and tree-lined gravel pathways favored by *les joggeurs.* At night it was a different story, according to Morbier — a famous rendezvous spot for assignations in the bushes.

She followed raised voices down the gravel paths of the Champ de Mars, through a stretch of darkness; the only light came from the diffuse radiance of the Tour Eiffel, which was partially obscured by trees. The damp stones crunched and felt cold under the soles of her shoes.

Finally she spotted Leseur, seated on a bench next to the woman holding the Westie's leash. She darted behind a tree. Heard them arguing but couldn't catch the words. Leseur leaned forward, trying to embrace the woman. His lover?

371

A rhythmic *crunch, crunch* on the gravel path and the bouncing beams of a jogger's headlamp made her duck into the bushes. Leseur was angry; he was shouting now, although she couldn't make out the words. Through the parted leaves, as the passing jogger's beam flashed over the scene, she recognized the 1978 *Paris Match* Leseur was brandishing at the woman from the photo of the younger Johnny Hallyday on the cover. The same edition she'd found in her grandfather's collection the night before. The *Paris Match* with the photo spread on his brother Pascal's funeral.

She hit René's number on her phone. "Found out who lives at that address yet?" she whispered. "René?"

"*Attends*, Aimée, my connection's slowed," he said. "Why the whispering?"

"I'm on the Champ de Mars, trailing them. Leseur's arguing with the woman who came out of the house with her dog. Who is she?"

All of a sudden, the woman threw the *Paris Match* down on the bench. She stood up. For the first time, Aimée caught her face in the dim light; tears glistened on her prominent cheekbones. Then she pulled at the dog's leash and hurried away.

Leseur sat, his shoulders sagging, dejected.

Should she accost him? But what did she have to say to him? All she had now were theories.

"I'd say it's Françoise Delavigne, widow of the former ambassador to Venezuela. She has recently put one-four-three rue Marinoni on the market," said René. "The Delavigne family seems to have plenty of other property — including a flat in London where she's been living with her daughter since her husband's death. Let's see, that was about six months ago." René sucked in his breath. "That help?"

"She treated Leseur like a spurned lover," said Aimée. "There's more to this. Some connection to Pascal Leseur." Otherwise why would he have flashed the *Paris Match* featuring his brother's funeral in her face?

"Hmmm. Gerard Delavigne, her dead husband, graduated from École Nationale d'Administration, previously served in the ministry at quai d'Orsay," said René.

Think. How could that be connected?

"I taped the *Paris Match* spread to the timeline. Can you check the funeral photos for Gerard Delavigne?"

"Hold on, Aimée." A pause as she heard René crank down his chair. The scrape as he pulled the step stool to the wall. Why did she always forget that things that were simple for her were difficult for him? "I'm looking at the *Paris Match* funeral photos . . . *Et voilà,* a G. Delavigne is listed as a pall-bearer. Her husband?"

"I'd better ask her," she said, backing out of the bushes to the path. "Keep monitoring Leseur's tracker in case he leaves. *Merci,* René."

She clicked off, took out her earphones. Hurrying, she kept her head down and reached the next tree-canopied *allée.* On the winding path toward the dark outline of the marionette theater, the Westie sniffed and watered the bushes. How should she play this?

"*Excusez-moi,* Madame Delavigne."

The woman gave a sharp turn on the gravel. Her scraped-back bright white hair revealed a makeup-free, tear-streaked face. Her cheekbones were sharp, her skin completely unlined except for some faint traces of smile lines. A classic beauty. Her lips quivered.

"Who are you? *Non,* I know. You're from *sécurité.* Never give up, do you?"

"Did my windbreaker give me away?" Aimée said the first thing that came into her head. There was an orange *Sécurité* logo on the collar; she'd appropriated the wind-breaker from a security job she'd done several years ago. At least it gave her an intro.

"You've probably been listening to everything we've said," Françoise said. "After all these years, can't you just leave me in peace?"

"*Désolée,* Madame Delavigne, but —"

"You're all the same," she interrupted. "Whatever branch or unit. Can't you just stop hounding Roland? We deserve some privacy."

So there was history here. An intimacy. The woman already resented her, so she might as well jump right in. Test her hunch that this was somehow connected to the tell-all memoir Martine had told her about.

"The blackmail threat's real, Madame Delavigne."

"Blackmail?" Her voice carried under the branches. "Roland's naïve, a fool sometimes. Leave him alone. His brother was the manipulator, not him. Why bring this all up again, so many years later?"

Françoise Delavigne pulled a tissue from her pocket, blew her nose. Wiped her eyes. The excitable unattended Westie rooted in the bushes.

"Not for me to say, Madame." Aimée racked her brain for how to steer the woman toward Pascal Leseur's death. "But his brother . . . ?"

"Pascal? Pah. Just like your bosses on the quai d'Orsay." Françoise Delavigne had assumed Aimée worked for the ministry's internal surveillance team. Not the first time she'd encountered a member of that team, judging by her reaction. "Clutching at power, backstabbing, manipulating." She'd warmed up, breathing fire now. "Roland's brother excelled at that. That's what did him in. Not our —"

"Affair?" Aimée interrupted. "Or was it Djanka Constantin's murder?" Held her breath — she'd either hit the truth or gone off in left field.

"Our affair, of which you've evidently been informed, ended long ago."

But she hadn't denied the link to Djanka's murder.

"Pascal Leseur fathered Djanka Constantin's child."

"Et alors?"

"Pascal's and Djanka's bodies were discovered within hours of each other." Now she tried her hunch. "So at Roland's insistence, the *flics* were pulled off the investigation, and now twenty years later he's being blackmailed over the cover-up."

"Cover-up? I don't doubt it," she said, matter-of-fact. "But not on Roland's end.

Roland can't admit Pascal kept secrets, dirt on his colleagues at the ministry. Suicide, murder?" Shook her head. "I don't know. A tragedy. That's what my husband always said."

She thought again. A staged suicide as René had suggested? She thought of René's theory. That would have been a convenient way to dispose of a backstabber like Pascal, as Françoise seemed to think of him. And Drina knew too much, so her father . . .

"In case you think any of this has anything to do with me or Roland, you're way off course," Françoise was saying. "Leave him alone. My husband never gave a fig that Roland I were lovers. Gerard's mistresses were numerous . . . *enfin,* until the Parkinson's really took hold." Françoise shook her head. "Not news to your bosses. Postings in foreign countries were a good cover for his indiscretions, and for a slow-developing disease. Your people were always so good about getting us out of the way. Which was what this has been really about, hasn't it?"

Aimée didn't know what to say. Just nodded.

"Your bosses would have done anything to keep my husband quiet." She jerked at the leash. "Well, it's all over now. Gerard's dead and whatever he knew went with him.

Tell your boss I don't care, let the papers and publishers print what they want. It's twenty years ago. I'm just a forty-seven-year-old grandmother who's living in London to help my daugher get treatment."

"But Madame, you and I know the powers that be — then and now — have a lot to lose. Especially whoever was involved in the cover-up."

"*Exactement,* Mademoiselle. You came here to give me a warning, *n'est-ce pas?* Tell them it's received loud and clear, and not to count on me giving a damn."

No wonder this savvy Françoise spoke with such candor. She'd been navigating these waters for a long time. She gave Aimée a sideways look. "You look intelligent. But I'm a terrible judge of character. I picked the wrong man to leave." She paused. "Think about where you work. Your paycheck comes from men afraid to lose power, driven by fear. Like Versailles — nothing has changed in two hundred years. They're all vengeful backbiters."

"You mean appointed officials," Aimée said, angling for names. "Like who?"

"Men afraid of a Gypsy taboo," Françoise said. "Would you believe, grown men terrified by hocus-pocus?"

The Westie barked. Before Aimée could

ask more, it had dragged Françoise around the hedgerow and into the path of a jogger. Françoise stumbled and swerved, just avoiding a collision.

Barking louder now, the Westie pawed the dirt by a clump of bushes. "What's the matter, Filou?"

Aimée took out her penlight. Shone it on the undergrowth.

The dog yelped and pawed in the bushes behind the reach of her beam. "Filou, if that's a squirrel . . ."

Aimée saw a lanyard hanging from the dog's mouth.

"Mon Dieu!" Françoise pulled Filou's leash. "Leave it alone, Filou. There's homeless people sleeping here."

Her phone vibrated. René.

"I have to take this call, Madame," she said, taking a few steps away on the path. "Where's Roland Leseur gone?" she asked René, lowering her voice.

"You tell me, Aimée. I think he discovered the tracker."

Her neck tingled. "Why?"

"No movement."

"Tell me the last tracker location, René."

"Champ de Mars. Hasn't moved for at least seven, maybe nine minutes. Leseur must have wised up, found the tracker and ditched it. There's another expensive piece of tech down the drain . . ."

She'd have hell to pay if she didn't recover René's pricey toy. Up ahead by the bushes near the bench where Françoise had argued with Leseur, Filou was barking nonstop, dragging Françoise on the leash behind him.

"Filou's gone crazy," Françoise said as Aimée caught up, the phone still to her ear. "I don't know what's the matter." She pulled the dog's leash hard, commanded him to heel.

But there was Roland Leseur, sitting on the bench just where Françoise had left him. Determined to get what more she could out of him, she hurried ahead.

"Monsieur Leseur?"

No answer. Then she noticed the way his head slumped on his neck.

"Can you hear me, Monsieur?" In the rising mist tinged by the yellow-orange glow of the Tour Eiffel, she shone her penlight. Blood pooled on the gravel by his shoe. She gasped. Stepped back. Then she stepped closer again and felt for a pulse. None. Her throat caught. His wrist was still warm.

"Deactivate the tracker, René. Now."

"Doing it as we speak. That was an expensive move, Aimée."

"Go call SAMU from the pay phone down

in the café," she said. "Tell them to respond to an incident on the fifth bench up from the corner of rue Marinoni."

"What kind of incident?"

"Roland Leseur's not on the move after all, and he never will be again."

"What?"

"He's dead." She looked down at his chest. The dripping red slit blossoming on his shirt. "A shiv in the ribs."

Like Nicu. A scream behind her, then a frantic voice shouting. "Roland?"

"Call me a taxi for the corner of rue Marinoni and Avenue de la Bourdonnais." She thought again. "No, make it corner of rue Saint-Dominique and Avenue de la Bourdonnais. Quick, René." She clicked off. "Don't look, Françoise. We need to get out of here."

"Roland . . . *Non, non.*" Françoise burst into sobs.

"Don't touch him." Aimée pulled Françoise away, grabbed the leash and pulled the frantic dog away from the corpse. "Let's go. Quickly, move."

"But we can't leave him like that."

"The ambulance and the *flics* are en route."

Françoise struggled and broke away.

Aimée caught up with her and wrapped

her arms around the flailing woman. "They're here somewhere. I don't know how many or who. But we have to get away. Get to safety. Do you understand?"

"But my house is right here, my daughter's waiting at home. The dog."

Didn't the woman understand the danger?

"You're all going to a hotel. With the dog. Just do what I say."

Aimée dragged her by the arm and across the entry to the marionette theater.

Françoise let herself be led, finally. She was breathless and weeping, but she was no longer hysterical. "It was true," she said as Aimée guided her, one arm tight around her shoulders. "Someone's been trying to kill him."

Aimée's gut clenched. This sobbing woman shaking under her arm, the barking dog and a siren screeching closer didn't help.

"Please, can you make it to the corner? There's a taxi waiting."

"I want to go home."

"You can't. We'll call your daughter. They're watching."

"My daughter's deaf." Françoise wiped her tear-stained face. "They won't be watching the servants' entrance. It's round the back."

Françoise fumbled in her trench coat pocket and pulled out a key ring. Tried repeatedly to insert the large old-fashioned key in a metal door of the back gate. The jangling keys were frying Aimée's nerves.

"Here, let me."

On the second try, the key turned. Aimée pushed and the door scraped open. Wet leaves lined the garden's rear service path. Once inside the house's service entrance, she followed Françoise up a musty wooden staircase. Françoise opened the door to a dark pantry, and Aimée wiped her boots and stepped inside behind her. Filou ran to a water bowl and slurped.

They passed through the kitchen and entered a tapestry-lined dining room. Wooden crates and half-filled cardboard boxes gave the room a forlorn feel.

"I'm packing up the house. In the midst of moving everything —"

"Keep the lights off," Aimée interrupted. She immediately wished she'd phrased it more gently. The woman was in shock. "*Désolée*, but you don't have much time. Do you have your passport?"

"But my daughter —"

"Does she have one?"

"Why should I involve my daughter?"

"Diplomatic passports would be even better. Do you both carry them?"

"Of course, but . . . what kind of security are you? I'm through with being a pawn passed between the services. Who do you work for?"

"Explanations later. You and your daughter could be next."

Françoise's mouth tightened. Strands of hair loosened from her ponytail as she shook her head. "I don't believe you."

"So you'd prefer to wait and find out, like Roland did?"

She didn't know if Françoise was actually next. She didn't know what the hell was going on. But she'd made too many mistakes already. Everything in her vibrated with fear and told her to get them out of here.

"What if you were the target?" said Aimée. "But no one counted on you arguing with Roland and taking off, or on me entering the picture. Maybe that saved you — Roland was collateral damage because he suspected or knew too much."

"Mademoiselle, who are you?" her voice rasped. "Security officers don't wear Chanel."

Aimée looked down to see that her windbreaker had come undone to reveal her little black dress. If she didn't come clean, the woman wouldn't cooperate. "A *détective privé,* hired by Nicu Constantin, the son of Pascal Leseur and Djanka Constantin." She flashed her detective license with the post-pregnancy photo — slim and smiling for once. "On Sunday, the woman who raised him after his mother was murdered was abducted from her deathbed because she knew secrets."

Françoise fiddled with the belt on her trench coat. "Secrets . . . what secrets?"

"A cover-up, but it's not exactly clear what's being covered up. And whatever it is these people want to hide, they're ticked off about it. Nicu was murdered yesterday. Knifed in public, quick and dirty, just like Roland."

Françoise gasped.

Aimée moved to the dining room's window, peered from behind the half-drawn damask curtain. The *flics* had arrived. She pulled the curtain closed. "Get your daughter, your diplomatic passports and what you can throw in that Hermès carryall." Aimée pointed to the bag on a chair.

"But our things, *mon Dieu,* I've got so much left to pack and box."

Françoise hadn't moved. Aimée wanted to shake this cosseted woman who either couldn't fathom the danger or . . . Aimée froze. She felt as though a vise was tightening around her throat. What if she'd read this wrong — what if Françoise was in league with them? Whoever "they" were.

The sudden ringing of a telephone on the hall table pierced the silence.

"I wouldn't answer that," said Aimée. And then she had a thought. "Are your husband's things still here?"

"Most of them are packed in his old office. Why?"

The hall phone stopped ringing. The sound was immediately followed by the trilling of a cell phone. Françoise jumped and took it out of her trench coat pocket.

"Wouldn't answer that either," Aimée snapped and took it from her.

Françoise's blue-violet eyes blinked. For the first time, she looked terrified.

"Get your daughter, your passports. Now."

The next moment, she'd disappeared up the wide staircase.

Aimée had to use this time wisely. She didn't know what she was looking for in Gerard Delavigne's office, but Françoise's words — *Your bosses would have done anything to keep my husband quiet* — kept running through her head.

Keep him quiet about what?

She only knew she had precious few minutes before the *flics* would ring the bell.

Delavigne's office was lined with empty bookshelves; the floor was covered in packing boxes and furniture shrouded by sheets. The sodium lights shining on the Champ de Mars gave off just enough light through the tall windows for her to see. Like having a private park outside your house, she thought, except for the flashing red light of the ambulance parked on the *allée* where they'd just been walking. Where Roland Leseur sat dead on the bench.

The musty smell of old paper tickled her nose, and she sneezed. In the corner sat a withered ficus in a Chinese porcelain planter. A large baroque desk with a wooden inlay was bare except for an old framed portrait of Giscard d'Estaing. No drawers.

Think. This man had been Pascal Leseur's classmate. They'd attended the elite *grande école* together, which was a conduit to a ministry position. They were the types who melded for life, kept the power in-house. The old boys' network.

Françoise and Gerard had been sent to faraway postings to get them out of the way. Say Gerard's ambassadorships hinged on what he knew of Pascal's suicide and the cover-up over Djanka. Knowledge so valuable he needed to be kept quiet and in clover? Quick and dirty, but a working theory.

She flicked on her penlight and scanned the boxes — filled with old magazines and books, mostly. Some boxes were labeled PHOTOS or DECORATIONS. She moved toward the empty bookcases. Didn't he have a safe? Most men of his ilk would.

She pressed her fingers along the bookcase ridges and found it on the lowest shelf — an old Fichet-Bauche safe, like her grandfather's. Open and empty.

Of course, Françoise would have packed the valuables for the move. She looked more carefully at the boxes near the bookcase and found one labeled DOCUMENTS, FINANCIALS.

She hated rummaging through people's personal documents. But not enough to stop her from shining the penlight on the box's contents. Kneeling, she flipped through the family birth certificates, marriage certificate, property deeds, Banque de France *livret.* The usual.

But underneath was a distinctive blue folder, legal-size and bearing the insignia of the Ministry of Foreign Affairs. State secrets? But these were old. She thumbed it open. A black-and-white photograph of a half-dressed young boy and a man in what looked like a hotel room; written on the back were the words *Insurance via Pascal.*

"What are you doing in here?"

Aimée's heart jumped to her stomach. She looked up to see Françoise standing in the doorway with a young woman. Their figures were silhouetted against the flashing blue lights from the police car out front, and their faces tinged red from the ambulance lights bleeding in from the Champ de Mars.

Think, she had to think. She slipped the folder under her windbreaker and did it back up, took the penlight out of her mouth and got to her feet.

"What right do you have to go through our things?"

"Maybe I got it wrong, Françoise," she said, edging forward to the door. "Roland was the target, you the bait."

"What in God's name do you mean?"

Aimée wished she could read the woman's expression.

"You're in league with them," Aimée said. "That's why we got away, *n'est-ce pas?*"

Françoise was moving her hands and fingers rapidly. She had turned to face the young woman beside her, who responded, signing with her hands.

"My daughter Janine's deaf," Françoise

said. "But she reads lips, and she says you're lying."

Should she look for another way out and cut her losses? Stall them while she escaped and let them finish whatever game they played? "What do you think, Françoise? Tell me the truth. Before you answer, remember that your daughter's involved now. If she's hurt, they'll only regard her as collateral damage."

"I think you're rude, abrasive and smart," she said. The doorbell rang. "And you're right in only one assumption — that if we don't leave now, we won't leave at all."

"Then how do we get out?"

"This way." Aimée followed Françoise, who had the bulging Hermès carryall tucked under one arm and Filou under the other, back through the dark kitchen and the pantry and out through the servants' door. On the leaf-clogged path to the service gate, Françoise pulled her elbow.

"Over here."

Janine led them through the dark garden. Nestled behind a purple-flowering paulownia tree was a glass-paned hothouse, a winter garden. Janine opened the door and they stepped in; it was filled with orchids and humid air.

Janine took a key from under a flowerpot

and opened the rear glass-paneled door to another door in the stone wall. A click and that door opened to a narrow *allée* — so narrow Aimée's shoulders scraped the stone. A moment later they emerged onto Avenue de la Bourdonnais.

They kept to the shadowed doorways until they reached rue Saint-Dominique. By the time Aimée was sitting in the front passenger seat of a taxi with Filou on her lap, four blue-and-white police cars had whizzed past with their sirens screaming.

"Gare du Nord, *s'il vous plaît,*" she said, panting, to the driver.

Aimée caught her breath as the brightly lit iron lady, the sparkling Tour Eiffel, shrank in the rearview mirror. She thought as quickly as she could. Not counting on their luck to hold, she opened her cell phone's speed-dial contacts and punched the SNCF booking number. She knew it would come in handy someday. Moments later, she'd reserved two seats and Filou's accommodation on the last Eurostar departing for London.

"Françoise, do you remember how many joggers went by the bench?"

"Two, three?" She thought. "*Non,* it was the same one with a headlamp. He went by twice, that's right. I almost ran into him."

Of course. Aimée should have noticed.

The black Seine quivered gel-like below them as they crossed Pont Alexandre III. Aimée would worry about the jogger later. Right now she had to get as much information as she could from Françoise.

"Did you and Roland ever speak about Drina or her sister Djanka?"

"We only ever discussed private issues."

She realized Janine was watching her lips. "Tell Janine this is personal and to close her eyes, *d'accord*?"

The taxi bumped over the cobbles in Place de la Concorde passing the obelisk, a needle-like shadow against the sky.

"I'm waiting, Françoise."

"But I can't talk with the driver listening."

Aimée turned toward the driver, a bearded older man in a plaid scarf, and gestured to the headphones looped around his neck. "Mind wearing those?" She slipped a fifty-franc bill on top of the Discman on his lap.

"*Pas de problème,*" he said and stuck them over his ears. "I love good music. *Les* Temptations — *magnifique.*"

She smiled. Janine had closed her eyes. The taxi driver honked at a bus.

"We've got maybe fifteen minutes, Françoise. Get talking."

Pain clouded those blue-violet eyes. "Roland wanted us to rekindle what we had before. True, I still think he was the love of my life, once. But . . ." Her knuckles whitened on the Hermès bag strap. "I said I'd have to think about it. So much has happened, and my life's in London now."

A sob escaped her.

"Françoise, tell me what you know about Pascal's lover, Djanka. I think it's related."

"Pascal loved her, wouldn't give her or the baby up. Pah — the only decent thing about him."

Did this all boil down to avoiding the scandal that would erupt from a ministry official having an affair with a Gypsy and recognizing their love child?

"What else, Françoise?"

"On the park bench Roland told me he'd been threatened with blackmail. Something about Pascal's death, I don't know."

"By who, Françoise?"

"Didn't say. But Roland knew nothing, had always thought it was suicide."

"An opportunistic journalist who'd twigged Pascal's name in the tell-all memoir?"

"I don't know."

Or the murderer? The taxi passed the church of Saint Madeleine with its spotlit columns and turned onto *les grands boule-vards.*

"But recently Roland had started to think it was murder. He just wanted to protect me."

"Protect you from what?"

"Implications over Gerard? I didn't understand. Didn't care."

"And what had he learned about Pascal's death?"

"A murder, he kept saying. Covered up years ago. Djanka's, too."

"You mean Roland thought they were both murdered to mask their affair, prevent a scandal?"

"He didn't say how or why he thought that. They had a *grand amour,* Djanka and Pascal — Gerard always said that." A shrug. "But I kept asking Roland, why did it matter now? Stupid. What was the point in bringing all this up yet again? Roland said there was a cover-up, a Monsieur X who had pulled strings and who still holds power. He wants to keep the facts from getting out now. He abducted the Gypsy's sister to shut her up."

Monsieur X, a cover-up? She thought back to Thiely's comments at l'École Militaire — *les barbusses,* paramilitary types who did the dirty jobs, leaving no trace so

394

others kept their hands clean. But keeping it covered up, shutting down a police investigation — that meant a lot of corruption and bribery.

So if her father, as a police officer in 1978, had suspected who was behind the hits and been taken off the case . . . the only thing he could do was protect Drina and Nicu, tell them to run. Her father had been drummed out of the force not long after; had that been another loose end in this same tangle? A loose end tied up more finally when he was killed in Place Vendôme?

"Did Roland mention the name Tesla? Or Fifi?"

Françoise shook her head. "Roland said, 'I'm next, and if I tell you any more, you are, too.' " Her shoulders heaved with sobs. "He told me that on the phone. Why didn't I believe him?"

"This Monsieur X, Françoise, any idea who he could be?"

The lit façade of Gare du Nord emerged through the mist.

Françoise shook her head. "That bastard? If I knew, I'd tell you."

After they had dropped the Delavignes at Gare du Nord, Aimée insisted the taxi circle the Île Saint-Louis twice before letting her out. The lights misted over the Seine and leaves blew along the quai as she checked for a surveillance detail, a lone watcher. After what had happened to Roland Leseur, she couldn't be too careful. But the few parked cars showed no window vapor, no figure standing on the corner with an orange-tipped cigarette. The Seine was deserted except for one long barge, colored lights strung on its prow, which sent soft ripples up the river. She still had the taxi let her off around the corner and tipped him extra. She punched the code into the side-street door that led to a back passage from which she accessed her own courtyard.

In the apartment, she set down her keys, kicked off her heels inside her paneled foyer. Sniffed. Warm smells of laundry and . . . garlic?

She'd only called once to check on Chloé since Babette had left the office that afternoon. "Babette, *désolée,*" she called. *Merde,* it was after eleven. She was tired, so tired she almost dropped onto the recamier right there.

She noted folded piles of baby clothes, heard Brahms's "Lullaby" playing softly on the radio she'd found at the flea market.

Babette grinned from the kitchen. "Pot-au-feu?"

Babette, what a jewel!

"Sorry I'm late." She tasted a bite. Heaven. "Don't remember seeing 'master chef' on your résumé."

"Not me. It was Benoît, Gabrielle's *tonton*. He brought it over," she said. "But I took down the recipe."

Fighting down a little disappointment, Aimée smiled at Babette. "I'd say he likes you."

"My fiancé wouldn't go for that," she said, gathering up her sports pack. "He's back from naval maneuvers in Toulon next month."

Toulon. Who was it that had mentioned Toulon recently?

"A nod to the wise," said Babette. "Benoît's returned from Cambodia for an *ethnologie-archéologie* position at the Sorbonne. He's very single." Babette winked.

Aimée felt her neck flush.

In bed that night, she tossed and kicked the silk duvet.

She was exhausted, yet sleep eluded her. She flicked on the lamp beside the baby monitor. Took out the blue file she'd found in Gerard Delavigne's study and stared at the photo. Studied it. From the monogrammed towels, standard furnishings definitely a hotel room: a shirtless young man in his late teens wearing white bell-bottoms and platform boots, à la Saturday Night Fever, leaned over a man in bed. There was something familiar about the man, who was grinning, his middle-aged paunch partially covered by a sheet. She looked closer, gasped. Why hadn't she recognized the face of one of the era's most powerful politicians?

His face had graced every newspaper of the day, and here he was caught in flagrante delicto, or whatever they called it. Explosive if it were leaked to the public. So this was the man, long dead, subject of the tell-all memoir . . . She turned it over, looking at the note on the back again: *Insurance via Pascal.* Also in the folder she'd stolen was a sheet of yellow legal paper with a few names written under the heading COMMISSAIRE BLAUET.

A police *commissaire?* Her mind jumped to the implications: a huge cover-up involving ministries and the police. *More important than money — power.* Cover-ups necessitated strings of payoffs. Supposing Pascal had tried blackmail, but had bitten off more than he could chew?

Miles Davis, curled at her feet, stirred on the duvet. She propped up her feather pillow and hit Martine's number.

"So how's Benoît's *pot-au-feu*?" Martine asked.

Martine amazed her sometimes. "How do you know, telepathy?"

"Babette," she said. "I called about my press pass, and to say goodnight to Chloé. I heard about your leakage incident. Don't worry — he probably found it attractive. Men, for some strange reason, like to protect. They enjoy a minor freakout now and then."

"Minor freakout, Martine? Major, I'd call it. And leaking all over my agnès b. blouse. I almost died."

"No worries," she said. "The Italian cousin's not bad as backup."

"Backup? This Benoît couldn't even look at me, and no wonder. A raccoon-eyed mess, unbuttoned, stockings in shreds."

"Not to mention neurotic," Martine added. "But remember he has a sister — I'm sure she has her moments, too."

Aimée heaved a long sigh. Right across the courtyard, and a hunk. How often did that happen?

Little whistles of sleep came from the baby monitor. For once Chloé slept and she couldn't. Talk about bad timing.

"Melac, that snake, threatened me today.

He was at the lawyer's appointment I missed."

"Missed it? How could you? And give him ammunition?"

Moonlight filtered through the window over her mauve silk duvet.

She explained that she'd been hijacked by the staff at l'Hôtel Matignon, and hadn't much choice in the matter.

"Not so bad, Aimée. You rescheduled with the lawyer, *non*? What's really up?"

With a kick at Chloé's zebra rattle, she gave Martine a condensed version of what had happened in the last few hours.

"Leseur, a *haut fonctionnaire* knifed to death on the Champ de Mars?" Martine sucked in her breath. "Stay away from this, Aimée. Someone's more than desperate."

"Tell me about it," said Aimée. "I got Delavigne and her daughter out on the last Eurostar to London."

"*Mon Dieu!* This'll be spun as an assignation gone wrong, Aimée, you know that. The ministry won't let it blow up in their faces."

"But I have this old file of Gerard Delavigne's, Martine. There's something in it I don't understand."

"That's why you called, eh?"

"Can I fax a photo and an accompanying list over so you can you see what you think?"

A sigh. "Hold on," Martine said, then gave Aimée her *tante*'s shop's fax number. "Give me five minutes to go down to the shop."

By the time Martine called her back, Aimée'd drifted off.

"As I see it, there are two investigations, Aimée," said Martine, yawning. "You started off searching for Drina, and now you're looking for her sister's murderer, from twenty years ago, who might have engineered your father's death."

"One and the same, Martine."

Aimée pulled the duvet around her for warmth. The fretwork of moonlight quivered on the duvet's mauve silk sheen. Miles Davis opened one eye, then the other, and stretched his right paw.

"You're assuming, Aimée. Where's the proof?"

"Drina's last words. And proof in her notebook that she informed for Papa."

"Which you've never seen, and which is missing. You need more than that," said Martine. "At least, I would need more to write a story. No editor would buy it."

"And Gerard Delavigne's file?"

"The photo's incriminating, *bien sûr*: a minister with a young teenager in a hotel. But that's already been squashed — a gag

401

order on publication. It's people in the government and police, that's what you're talking about — the prime minister at l'Hôtel Matignon and the Ministry of Foreign Affairs at d'Orsay. And you have to be very careful what you write about them."

"Djanka's body was discovered in the moat at les Invalides," said Aimée, sitting up, rustling the duvet.

Miles Davis cocked an ear. Stretched and licked his paw.

She studied the file and spread out the crime-scene photos from her father's *procès-verbal,* which she'd brought home. "The military were denied an investigation on their own turf. Doesn't the prime minister trump Foreign Affairs and the Ministry of Defense because he oversees all of them?"

"Aimée, it's all an old boys' club, favors galore. They all went to the *grandes écoles.* Except those from the officer academy at Saint-Cyr, the military elite."

"*Ainsi donc,* they're the outsiders, Martine. The old boys froze out the *armée.*"

"There was a cover-up," said Martine. "What's new? Then and now, it's who you know. Who's got something to lose or to gain by shutting up."

"Pascal Leseur gave this photo to his friend, Gerard Delavigne, as some kind of insurance," Aimée said. She propped up more feather pillows, pulled the duvet tighter against the chill in her bedroom. The rustle of the smooth silk and Chloé's whistles of sleep over the monitor lulled her for a moment.

"Françoise, Gerard's wife, called Pascal a manipulator, out for everything he could get. So I figure he held this over the minister's head and expected favors."

Martine yawned. "Go to sleep."

"Can you ask your friend at *Le Monde* a favor, the one who works in the archives? I need articles on Commissaire Blauet. Anything from 1978. His present whereabouts. Check the obits in case he's dead, too."

A sigh. "Why?"

"If Blauet's alive, I need to reach him. His name's there, Martine. He'd have been the one to shut down my father's investigation."

"*Zut!* And you think, *quoi,* he'll admit it just like that after all this time?"

"You don't think 'pretty please with sugar on top' will work?"

Another yawn. "If I say yes, will you go to sleep?"

If only she could. Miles Davis emitted a snore, and the moon had dipped behind the mansarded rooftops across the river.

"Promise. *Merci,* Martine."

Wednesday Morning

Aimée parked the Gucci-print pod stroller — bought on René's insistence — at the Saint-Germain *piscine.* The humid air was tinged with chlorine.

"Here you go, water baby," she said, handing Chloé to Babette, who was already in the pool. "René or I will meet you at the park later."

The *mamans* in their *maillots de bain* at the baby swim class waved — Aimée had been a part of their group during her maternity leave. She felt a tug of regret at not joining them. "See you next time," smiled one of the *mamans.* The lifeguard, a hunk in a Speedo, whistled for their attention. And scrutiny.

"Enjoy," she called back.

She checked her messages. Maxence had picked up her scooter from Champs de Mars, thank God. But she was waiting to hear what Dussollier had uncovered about Fifi and Tesla, the missing pieces of the puzzle. Nothing. His number answered with an impersonal voice instructing her to leave a message. Why hadn't he gotten back to her yet? Wasn't he taking her request seriously? Maybe he didn't realize how urgent it was.

No news from Martine on her archive query either. Frustrated, she tried René.

"Found another translator for Drina's Romany?"

"Working on it, Aimée." René sighed. "What do I say to my friend about that tracker chip? It was a unique prototype. Valuable."

"So's a human life, René."

Pause. "Aimée, walk away from this." René cleared his throat. "Please, you can't let —"

"Nicu's death go for nothing? *Non,* René, my father wanted me to make it right."

The sidewalk horse chestnut trees bloomed in white and pink as she headed away from Saint-Germain. With almost no warning, the sky opened, as it often did at this time of year — a *giboulée,* a sudden brief downpour followed by sun, characteristic of March. But March was over — where was spring? She ran for cover, ducking into a doorway.

"Won't you help me, René?" she asked when she could hear herself again over the rush of the rain.

His answer was lost as she dropped her phone in the streaming gutter.

Wednesday Morning

From the clanging splash and then buzz on the end of the line, René feared Aimée'd ruined another phone.

He shook his misgivings aside. Rubbed his brow and took a Doliprane for the ache in his hip. Aimée needed him.

Again.

After a second expensive conversation with the *femme* at La Bouteille, he had finally found a Romany translator and made an appointment. Armed with her introduction and an address, he said a prayer to the parking gods — à la Aimée — and plunged into the traffic on the Rive Gauche.

René tried a shortcut. He shifted into first on a rain-slicked street in the warren behind the Musée d'Orsay. Big mistake. Outside Serge Gainsbourg's former house, grafittied with tributes to the dead icon, a delivery truck blocked the street. Fuming, René honked and rolled down his window.

He saw a man in front of the shrine, adding to the graffiti. He looked like the ghost of Gainsbourg himself: tousled hair, cigarette hanging from the corner of his mouth, a day's worth of stubble cultivated on his chin, crisp white shirt, vintage jacket, suede brogues. Harmless, but a man who clearly, René thought, seemed a few slices short of a baguette.

By the time the truck had moved, he had to hurry.

Ten minutes later, the downpour lifted and shoppers filled the boutiques on rue de Sèvres. This was where the fusty 7th bordered the lively 6th, and the streets teemed with life — the damp pavement was thronged, the outdoor cafés bustling. René loved the energy, the crisp morning light sparkling like crystal and dancing as it hit the wet zinc rooftops.

His prayer had worked; the parking gods were smiling, for once. Two minutes later, across Le Bon Marché, he walked into square Boucicaut, which had been built on the site of an ancient cemetery, or was it a medieval leper colony? He could never remember. Light scudded through the plane tree leaves, striking the swollen raindrops clinging to the grass. He passed the statue of Madame Boucicaut, the Bon Marché founder's wife, immortalized in marble beckoning the poor children — offering bread crumbs while she kept the loaf, as the *clochards* used to say. The April breeze blew flurries of twigs and leaves over the gravel. Benches dotted this oasis of calm; the blaring of traffic horns seemed suddenly far away. A few children climbed on the play structure, their parents chatting and keeping an eye on them.

Where was his translator? He punched in the number he'd been given.

"*Désolée,* Monsieur, I can't leave for another hour. Can it wait?"

"There's no time to spare," said René. "I'll come to you."

Annoyed, he made his way around puddles, exited the square and turned left. Past the inviting *terrasse* tables at the café on rue de Babylone. He battled an urge for something warm.

On rue du Bac, he joined the pilgrims entering the Chapel of Our Lady of the Miraculous Medal with its shrine of Saint Catherine Labouré. He followed the cobbled entry past a wall of marble plaques and a religious gift shop selling medals depicting the Virgin's visit to the young Saint Catherine.

He hated crowds, everyone taller than him and no way to see ahead. Nuns shepherded a group of young blue-robed novices, who were speaking to one another in Spanish. A woman paused before the statue of Saint Vincent de Paul, touched his open hand and crossed herself.

Jammed among the worshippers, caught and claustrophobic, he felt like a gnat about to be crushed. Trying not to trip, he moved in the press of people to the whitewashed chapel with its soaring arches, blue murals of the Virgin framing the altar and balconies full of praying supplicants. Ahead he saw a crowd gathered to the right of the main altar. At a door beyond that stood a short nun. She matched the description Madame Bercou at La Bouteille had given him. His translator.

René made his way past the glass case displaying the coffin and incorruptible body of Saint Catherine Labouré, which had been exhumed years after her death in the nineteenth century, still in pristine condition. Shivers ran down his arms when he looked at her wax face framed by a white-peaked wimple, her black rosary trailing over her nun's habit. The body heat of the fervent and the smoke from the melting candles made him light-headed.

Keep going, he had to keep going.

"Monsieur Friant?" asked the nun, only a head taller than he. Petite, she had deep dark eyes and an olive complexion. A simple blue veil was pinned to her dark hair. "You need help translating Romany? I'm Sister Dorothée. Please come this way."

He followed her through a door to a narrow courtyard next to the chapel, then over wet pavers and through another door to another courtyard. From such an oppressive atmosphere, he found himself enveloped in a silent stillness, protected from the wind. The courtyard smelled of damp mowed grass. Sunlight sparkled on the wet chains of a sunken stone well.

"It's much more peaceful here, we can hear ourselves think," said Sister Dorothée as they sat on a bench under the cloister's cold stone arches.

René handed her a hundred-franc note along with the notepad. "My donation," he said.

Sister Dorothée's smile faded. "In the donation box, please."

He'd offended her already. He winced.

"My mother's third cousin's wife asked me to help you," she said. "I do it as one of God's creatures to another. Not all *gens du*

411

voyage want to take your money, Monsieur."

"Please forgive me, Sister Dorothée," he said, ashamed that his prejudice had showed. "I'm told these words contain a curse, and that voicing it would give the words power."

"Some say that, Monsieur Friant," she said. "Others say a curse only has power if you grant it power."

While she read, he gazed at this ancient convent garden, its expanse of lawn lined by fruit trees and blue and purple hydrangeas. A *jardin potager,* a kitchen garden, extended to a wall almost a soccer field away. Vast for the center of Paris. This had all been farms and countryside until Marie de Médicis awarded her land to the convents. The Sisters of Charity convent was just one of many institutions and parcels of land the church owned in the arrondissement.

The tree branches dripped and hung low, heavy with rain.

"C'est privé." A gardener in a blue workcoat emerged from a side path, pushing a wheelbarrow. "The garden's not open to the public," he said sharply to René. "Ah, *pardonnez-moi,* I didn't see you, Sister."

Sister Dorothée nodded.

"Can you make sense of some of it?" René asked.

"It's very sad."

The last thing René expected.

"You're sure you want to know?" she asked.

What could it contain? A dying woman's last words? He nodded.

"*D'accord,* well, some makes no sense," said Sister Dorothée. "But from here it's more coherent. *He covered up my sister's murder by those men. I understood. He couldn't do anything else, he had a daughter. What could I do . . . my people shunned the boy Nicholás, painted me black. He kept the cloak over the guilty. Unfair. That's why we live our own way, with our own kind, only trust our own. But that didn't exist for me. Radu said Djanka was a whore — all family honor gone. I had nothing, so I took his help. When they'd gone too far and he refused to cover up more dirtiness, they blew him up. I saw them. Then we ran and hid, no protector anymore. But he wanted his daughter to know he did it for her, that she should make it right. I owed him that. Tesla, Fifi, I spit in their eyes, on their souls.*"

René bowed his head, sadness flooding him. He and the nun sat in silence. Some pink and white petals of the blooming plum

413

and almond trees had drifted to the ground, joining the pastel carpet of blossoms already covering the vegetable beds. A church bell chimed in the distance. How could he tell Aimée that her father had been part of the cover-up — had died trying to get out of it?

Wednesday Morning

On rue du Pré-aux-Clercs, named for the ancient monk's abbey and once a popular dueling site, a shudder of wind misted Aimée's cheeks with the spring rain. She had salvaged her phone from the gutter, wiped it off, shaken it. Still working. She waited out the second sudden shower under a stone portico. Across the street, a concierge leaned out of her open ground-floor window, talking to the postman huddling in his yellow rain slicker. And just as quickly as the shower burst, it stopped and sunlight broke over the glistening wet pavers.

At the smudged reception window in the *commissariat,* she asked for Commissaire Dejouy, crossing her fingers he hadn't retired.

"In a meeting," said a young recruit, his ironed collar standing at attention.

Great. Her only contact here.

415

"Can you tell him it's Aimée Leduc?"

"Concerning?"

"An investigation."

"Your identification."

She passed over her new PI license. He shook his head.

"Then that's an official visit. You'd need permission from the *commissaire,* and he's in a meeting."

Helpful, this new recruit. And the stale air in here was as bad as his attitude.

"Five minutes, please," she said, glancing at her Tintin watch. "Can you check with the *commissaire?*"

Jojo Dejouy stuck his head round the door. "I'll take care of this, Lelong."

Repressing the urge to smile at the bewildered Lelong, she went through the door Dejouy had opened for her.

Jojo, greyer than she'd remembered and with an expanding waist, led her past institution-green cubicles, through the haze of cigarette smoke and into his office. Brittle fluorescent light highlighted the dust layer on his file cabinet.

He closed the door. "It's good to see you, Aimée," said Jojo. "I appreciate you inviting me to your baby's christening, I'm just sorry I couldn't make it. Your father meant a lot to me. Maybe I didn't show it when they put him against the wall." Jojo shrugged. "I know you're a bigger person than me. You look at the good in people, like he did."

Jojo, like many in the force, had distanced himself from her papa when he'd been fingered for an offense he didn't commit. Years later, her father had said it was the best thing that had ever happened to him; it had driven him to private work. If he could forgive his old team, she'd decided she could, too. And she knew her father would be smiling.

"Here's the card I've been meaning to send." He handed her a baptism card.

"That's sweet, Jojo."

"Got a picture of her?"

"*Bien sûr,* but . . ." She rummaged for her wallet. "Bad mother, *moi.* I took out Chloé's newborns and forgot to put in the ones where she's sitting up."

Jojo smiled. "Your papa would be over the moon."

She nodded. But she hadn't come to socialize. "You're investigating Nicu Constantin's knifing under the Métro at La Motte-Piquet–Grenelle?"

"Same twenty-two-year-old *manouche* questioned about the mercy killing of a patient who disappeared from Hôpital Laennec?" Jojo asked.

417

She nodded, disappointed he would even bring that up now that the real story of Drina's death was public knowledge, splashed all over the papers. "Admit it, Jojo, moot point. A frame-up. Then, right after your men take him in for questioning, he's knifed. A hate crime? I don't think so."

"An angel tell you from on high?"

"Smells like a ripe Roquefort," she said, the *flic* phrase for corruption.

Jojo raised his arm and shrugged as if to say *small-fry.* He rocked on his heels. A nervous habit of his, she remembered. "You should know that we found a *procès-verbal* from 1978 signed by your father in this Nicu Constantin's pocket. A document that should have stayed in-house — *tu comprends?* I was going to call you." He glanced out the office window. "You don't want that getting out, Aimée."

Had Drina been keeping this *procès-verbal* in her notebook? Or had Nicu found this with his birth certificate?

"I don't understand," she said, but she had her suspicions, and wanted him to spell it out. "Why? Nineteen seventy-eight, that's twenty-odd years ago. And it looks like a copy. Why would that *procès-verbal* matter now?"

"Back in 1978, a woman named Djanka

Constantin, whom we have learned was this boy Nicu's mother, was murdered. Your father furnished the homicide-investigation file to the victim's family. That didn't fly, then or now." Jojo paused. "That's why it matters."

It sounded like Jojo was turning this back on her father. Again. But she had to keep pressing him.

"*Alors,* Jojo, what's your investigation turned up apart from that?"

"What's it to you, Aimée?"

"This all goes back to who killed Papa, Jojo," she said. "And you *know* Nicu's homicide wasn't a hate crime."

"I do?" Jojo's phone console lit up. Jojo sighed, his shirt straining.

"His uncle, Roland Leseur, from the Ministry of Foreign Affairs, got knifed the same way on the Champ de Mars last night."

"That's news to me," he said, looking away.

"And that Thomas Dussollier's investigating? That's news to you, too?"

Jojo shook his head. "*Non,* we're in contact," he said, lowering his voice. "I'm working on it, *compris?*"

So Dussollier had acted on her request.

"It's like walking on eggshells, Aimée. If

I'm not careful, everything cracks."

So not like walking on eggshells at all then, Aimée wanted to say, since they crack whether you're careful or not.

Jojo shrugged. "Nicu had a juvenile record but he'd gone Evangelical, the Gypsy version."

Accepted to pursue religious studies at the Sorbonne. Guilt welled up in her stomach. But she needed to hear Jojo's version. "Evangelical, a Bible type?"

"If they haven't found God, they're robbing apartments while the owners visit their country *châteaux,*" said Jojo, "or winching out ATMs with their Mercedes SUVs — those are the ones I see in here. My 'guests.' "

"No surprise your 'guests' like to float in the crème de la crème's *quartier,* Jojo. Rich pickings. Yet as you said, none of that fits Nicu's profile — not these days, anyway."

Jojo rubbed his neck. *"Zut,* I'm just following the *préfecture*'s directives — trying to solve this thing. There's intense media pressure — unheard-of demonstrations near l'Hôtel Matignon, Sciences Po students staging a sit-down at the *mairie."* He rocked again on his feet. "A pain in the neck. And now protests at the Ministry of Health bringing traffic to a standstill."

"Jojo, that's classic — when isn't there a protest bringing traffic to a standstill?"

Bravo, Martine — she must have managed to seed accusations against the Ministry of Health with the right contacts at *Le Monde*. And Rose was rallying the students with her petition. They had been marginalized during their lifetimes, but no one could ignore Drina or Nicu in death.

Small consolation, but something. And maybe a safety net for Aimée. Enough outcry might force a deeper investigation into Nicu's murder.

The officer from reception knocked on the office window. Gestured for Jojo to pick up the phone.

"*Alors*, take that *procès-verbal*, Aimée. It's got no bearing anyway, but *la maison*" — he meant the *préfecture* — "will play by the rules and order an investigation. You cleared your father's name; why get muck on it?" He picked up the phone. "Leave the door open on your way out, *s'il te plaît*." As he started to turn his back on her, he pointed to the yellowed envelope on his desk. "Don't forget that."

It was addressed to Madame Constantin, in what she recognized as her father's faded handwriting. The sight of it seized her heart in a choke hold.

Inside was a copy of the same *procès-verbal* on Djanka's homicide she'd found in her father's files, minus the crime-scene photos.

But as soon as she came out of the *commissariat,* it came flooding back. The memory was ten years old, but she felt it as clearly as if she were reliving it — the twisted, burned metal of the fence around the column in Place Vendôme, her papa's melted watch, the blackened van door gaping open on the cobbles.

Her ringing phone brought her back to the street she was standing on, to the pigeon pecking near her feet. Her father's loss went back to being to a dull ache that never went away.

"Aimée, we're at the park," said Babette. "Chloé's having a big day. Her first tooth's almost here. She'll sleep like a log this afternoon."

Sounded like Babette had it all under control, thank God. The perfect nanny, ready to take her Wednesday afternoon off.

"Put Chloé on," she said.

"*Un moment,* Aimée."

Sounds of gurgling on the line.

"*Ça va, ma puce?* I hear that tooth's about to peek out."

422

More gurgling. Her breath caught at the image of the little rosebud mouth. Babette's voice. "Wet diaper. Need to change it. We're near the slide. See you at the park?"

"I'm on the way, Babette."

Aimée hurried up the Métro stairs at Sully-Morland in the sunshine. Ahead on her right nestled a vestige of the Bastille prison in the wedge-shaped square Henri-Galli. Daffodils blossomed around the lichen-encrusted stone tower base. Spring was here.

Across the quai lay Île Saint-Louis. Children's laughter drifted, the khaki-green Seine rippled. The fragrance of blossoming chestnut trees overlay the diesel fumes from the Number 67 bus. She headed into the square and the play structures inside.

She pictured Chloé and Gabrielle by the slide, Babette pulling out their snacks and juice from a baby bag on the stroller. Pictured taking Chloé home to play with Miles Davis, a long nap.

But neither Chloé nor Gabrielle were by the slide. She jumped at a sudden, loud buzz: a hard hat wearing earphones was using a chainsaw to cut branches off a fallen tree trunk behind a barricade. Sawdust flecks fluttered in the air.

Parents were packing up, enticing toddlers

off swings. The irritating whine of the saw was prompting an exodus. At the far end of the park, Babette was reaching down to settle Gabrielle in her baby backpack. Aimée started to wave but realized Chloé's stroller wasn't there. Nor was Chloé in Babette's other arm. Where was she? Alarmed, she looked around.

Melac and Donatine sat on a bench by the Ping-Pong table, Chloé beside them in her stroller. What was Babette thinking? Livid now, she stomped across the sandy gravel toward them. Babette had strict instructions . . . and that snake Melac had somehow talked her into handing Chloé over?

She'd give Melac and Donatine more than a piece of her mind. She got caught behind two women, who obstructed her view, then a boy riding his bike wove in between them, blocking her way.

Furious now, she contemplated getting that expensive lawyer, who'd done nothing for her so far, on the line to issue a restraining order against these two. *Calm down,* she needed to calm down before she made a scene at the park.

All of a sudden, she heard screeching brakes as the boy's bike skidded. Gravel sprayed, hitting her calf, as the boy swerved to avoid a dog on the path. He veered, lost control and crashed into the flimsy barricade around the fallen tree.

Right where Chloé had been sitting in her stroller. Panic hit her. She broke into a run before she could think, before she could scream a warning to Melac, who was headed toward the garbage can with a diaper. The barricade collapsed against the hard hat, knocking him forward with the chain saw. *Mon Dieu,* the saw, Chloé's stroller! Screaming, she was screaming now. "Chloé! Watch out! Chloé, my baby!"

Donatine, who was sitting on the bench opening a juice carton, looked up when she heard Aimée's screams. In a split second, registering the danger, she shoved Chloé's stroller. But the brakes locked, frozen in place. Time slowed as Aimée saw the chain saw flying through the air toward Chloé's yellow bunny cap. Nothing to stop it. Aimée's heart pounded in her chest. *"Non, non!"* How could this happen?

Donatine bounded off the bench, batting her arms at the saw blade and knocking the stroller over.

A sickening whine. A scream. Chloé's cries. Melac was running and shouting, "Oh, *mon Dieu!*" It all happened so fast: Melac grabbed and switched off the grinding saw, pulled Donatine off Chloé's upset stroller. She heard Chloé's cries and it tore her heart.

Blood dripped from Donatine's sweater, the torn flesh of her arm. Melac whipped Chloé from the stroller.

"Is Chloé all right?" Donatine gasped.

In Melac's arms, Chloé's tear-stained face broke out into a smile.

Later, after Donatine was loaded into the ambulance, Aimée persuaded the attendant to let her in for a moment. Bandaged and connected to an IV, a pale-faced Donatine sat propped on the stretcher. "Chloé's safe, thank God. I'm so sorry. We pressured Babette . . . I crossed the line."

Aimée nodded. "Still, if you hadn't done what you did, Donatine — thrown yourself in the way . . ." said Aimée, taking her hand. Her throat caught.

"This was our fault. How terrible it would have been if . . ." Donatine erupted in tears. "We put Chloé in danger. I didn't have the maternal instincts to protect her. Destroyed any trust we wanted to build, any hope for custody. *Alors.* Please forgive us. Me."

"*Mais non,* what are you saying, Donatine?" Aimée shook her head. "All right, you made a mistake. But your quick reaction saved Chloé. Accidents happen. Freak ones."

Melac, holding Chloé in his arms, joined them. Chloé drooled and fussed. "I think she needs her *maman,*" said a shaken Melac, a lost look on his face. Chloé mewled, gumming his finger. "Oww." Melac winced and pulled out his finger.

That's my girl.

Aimée managed a grin. "I think your daughter just bit you with her first tooth."

Once Chloé was back in her arms, safe and warm, she nuzzled her ear. "I can see Chloé would be safe with you."

Melac looked at Donatine and then back at Aimée. "I'll go with whatever you want, Aimée. But please, it's important I recognize her, put my name on her birth certificate. She's my daughter. Legally it'll give her protection, benefits if something happens to me. The rest, you decide."

Aimée thought back to Nicu's birth certificate, wondering whether having Pascal Leseur's name on there would have changed Nicu's life.

"Then let's forget the lawyers, Melac," she said. "Work things out ourselves."

Aimée reached out for Donatine. She couldn't quite hug her yet, but she squeezed her bruised hand.

■ ■ ■ ■

In her apartment, Aimée settled a freshly changed Chloé on the duvet and kicked off her heels, about to join her for a nap. Miles Davis's ears perked up.

"What's up, Miles Davis?"

He scampered off the bed and beelined it to her desk. Yelped. A low beeping came from her answering machine, which she'd turned down so as not to wake Chloé at night.

The red light blinked. A message. She hit PLAY.

"If you want to keep Chloé safe and unhurt," said a robotic voice, "forget Gerard Delavigne. Burn everything. We'll know." Click. Left fifteen minutes ago, according to the time stamp.

Her heart hammered. She ran barefoot to the kitchen and parted the curtains. Below, a man leaned on the quai wall, smoking and watching her door. A blue van sat parked. The blue van she'd seen before Nicu was knifed at the Métro. It hadn't been there half an hour ago, when they'd returned from the park. Or had it? Her hands shook.

Priorities. She had ignored the warnings, the risks, the bodies piling up. And now they were threatening Chloé. She had to think for this little person with the bunny-ear cap.

Something Morbier had told her long ago came back to her — that her mother hadn't abandoned Aimée as a child; she had left to protect her. Maybe it was true. Could Aimée do the same? Was that a choice she had forced herself to make?

This threat galvanized her into action, her adrenaline coursing. She had to end this. Even if she burned the documents like they asked, even if she and Chloé were safe for today, there'd still be tomorrow or next week. Good God, they'd parked outside her door.

She knew what she had to do. Within five minutes, she'd made two calls and packed up her laptop and essentials for Chloé. Time to travel light.

"Let's go, Miles Davis."

He cocked his ears.

"Chloé and I are taking a vacation. You too, with your favorite concierge." She donned her leather jacket and put a sleeping Chloé in the sling looped over her shoulder.

At Madame Cachou's, she handed over Miles Davis's leash. For once the busybody nodded, no questions asked. "Why, it's just like this spy thriller I'm reading. Espionage, double agents — I'll keep a look out."

"You do that, Madame Cachou. But first go talk to that man smoking over there. Keep him occupied. And keep Miles Davis safe."

Across the courtyard, at Gabrielle's house, Benoît answered the door. He was wearing an apron over jeans and nothing else. Impressive abs.

Flustered, she looked away. Wonderful smells drifted from the kitchen — cilantro, mint, citrus, coconut. She wanted to lick the wooden spoon in his hand.

"More *pot-au-feu*? It was delicious, by the way."

Lame. She sounded like a schoolgirl. But there was no time to worry about that now.

"Lemongrass soup," he said. "I heard what happened at the park," he said. "Babette's so sorry over what happened. She's gutted."

"I know." Aimée cut him off, cradling Chloé in the sling. "I need a favor. It's vital, or I wouldn't ask."

He nodded, giving her his full attention.

"If anyone, I mean *anyone,* asks, you don't know where we've gone. When we're coming back. Can you do that?"

"So it's true, what I've noticed."

He probably figured her for a paranoid

neurotic, based on each of their encounters. "Look, if you could —"

"Say that you've probably taken your baby out of the country, *non*?" He handed her a set of keys. His warm fingers rested on hers, then gripped them. The heat of his hand spread up her wrist like fire.

Down, girl.

"Use my sister's back carriage door downstairs," he said. "Leave them on the ledge."

Michou, René's transvestite neighbor, opened the door and grinned, still in his show makeup. "You brought my sweet pea!" Michou waved them inside. "An emergency, you said, always an emergency with you, *ma chérie. Zut,* I came straight from rehearsal at the club."

While Michou removed his makeup, Aimée put a yawning Chloé down for a nap. Later, over a *cafetière* full of coffee, Aimée explained in detail.

"Chloé won't be out of my sight, Aimée." Michou, a former merchant seaman, held his own and more in a fight. "Or Viard's, when I have a show. He's earned his black belt." Michou gave a big smile. "I'm so proud."

"You two still in the honeymoon stage?"

Michou's lover, Viard, who directed a

crime lab, had moved in after they'd been together for three years. Aimée had introduced them.

Michou rubbed the stubble on his cheek and sighed. "Now we've got a *bébé* to take care of. Wonderful." He paused, arching a plucked eyebrow. "Does René know?"

She shook her head. "Not yet." She needed to keep him out of danger. "I owe you, Michou." Aimée downed the last of her coffee. "Got to go." She hoped Michou hadn't noticed how much her hands were shaking.

"Be careful, *ma chérie.*" His big hands, with purple lacquered nails, closed around hers. "Don't do anything I wouldn't do."

Wednesday Evening

"Reminds me of when we used to do our homework here after school, Aimée, remember?"

Martine made a face at Aimée over her aunt's desk, which was tucked in a closet-sized office in back of the nineteenth-century linen shop on rue du Bac.

"Only we've got laptops instead of pencils, Martine," she said. On her screen was a Leduc proposal she was preparing to return to Maxence. Open beside her was Gerard Delavigne's blue folder, containing the list of names. She'd spent several hours researching them, hoping to trace all the names on the list. But so far her digital search of an outdated police database had only revealed that several on the list were deceased, several others in the police nursing home outside of Paris — in gagaland.

Martine's *Le Monde* contact's archives

had turned up Blauet, the former police *commissaire,* who'd retired to Martinique in 1985 and ran a fishing-boat business. Her phone call reached the canned, impersonal recording on Blauet's answering machine. She'd come up with what she hoped was a plausible story for a police reunion and left him a message with her inquiry. It was a risk, but she decided to leave him the fax number for Martine's aunt's shop. All she could do was keep trying.

The bell on the shop door rang as it opened.

Martine's aunt, all in black YSL and as chic as ever, poked her head into the office. "*Mes filles,* watch the shop for me like good girls, yes?"

"*Oui,* Tante Cybile." Martine stood and kissed her aunt's cheeks. After she left, Martine burst into laughter. "Her *cinq-à-sept amant;* they get younger and younger."

Aimée wished she had Cybile's luck. A vision of Benoît's abs floated in front of her eyes, the warm touch of his hand. She shoved it aside.

"How's your article going, Martine?" she said, passing the plate of pistachio macarons she'd bought across the street at the rue-du-Bac *boulangerie.*

"Making progress." Martine's fingers

434

clicked over the keys. "Got a quote from the Ministry of Health. If I can just get the *clinique* to comment on this Doctor Estienne's violation of the medical-ethics code . . ." She lifted her blouse's neckline and plastered a Nicorette patch on her shoulder. Once a pack-a-day smoker, Martine had quit and gained a kilo, and looked healthy for it.

Aimée scanned Delavigne's list. Two more to locate. The key to all this lay in the police cover-up.

"Gianni's cousin's suggesting dinner Friday," Martine said. "So consider that evening booked — and maybe the rest of the night."

Aimée groaned. "If I make it to Friday."

Her phone rang. An unknown number.

"Aimée, weren't you coming to *la soirée des fiançailles?*" said Thomas Dussollier.

Merde! She'd forgotten his daughter's engagement party. He'd sent the invitation with Chloé's gift.

"*Bien sûr.* Something just came up at work, but . . ."

"We need to talk. I found what you're looking for, *tu comprends?*"

Her blood raced.

"The reception's at the Rodin, right?"

"Get here for the champagne toast," said

Dussollier.

"I'm en route," she said, hanging up.

"Invited to *la soirée des fiançailles?*" Martine said. "Impressive. Usually engagement parties are about the parents meeting each other, the man presenting the ring. He must regard you as family. Not to mention at the Musée Rodin. *Pas mal.*"

"I don't have a gift, or anything to wear."

"My *tante*'s got a shop full of gifts." Martine headed to the register. "I'll be a good girl and ring up a sale for . . . *quoi?* Say, toile de Jouy pillowcases?"

Wasn't that a wedding gift? But if Martine thought it would do, that was good enough for her. *"Parfait."*

"Keep writing, Martine," she said. "Finish the macarons."

Aimée ran up the narrow spiral stairs leading to the living quarters. "I'm borrowing your Versace."

The fastest way to reach the Rodin museum, which was around the corner and up three blocks, was by foot. Even in Martine's red-soled Louboutins. She hurried through the Faubourg Saint-Germain, for once dressed for the occasion. She passed the entrance to the imposing limestone Hôtel Matignon. Noted the guards and security and the old dames who stopped to chat with them. A village all right — for a certain *classe* who kept to themselves.

"Invitation, Mademoiselle?" asked an ex-military security type with a shaved head, one of three at the gate, as he gave her the once-over.

She'd forgotten it. Great.

"Aimée Leduc; please check the guest list."

A moment later he looked up. Smiled.

"Of course, Madame and Monsieur Dussollier's guest. Welcome. The reception's out through the door and in the party tents."

Some big boys and big names here, if this level of security was anything to go by.

Her heels clicked over the cobblestoned courtyard lit by white paper lanterns. A hundred or so friends mingled among Rodin's bronze sculptures and the sentinel-like cypress trees, and crowded into several large, white, candle-lit canvas tents. Not exactly an intimate family affair. Laughter and clinking of glasses accompanied the melodies of a string quartet. Another world.

Wouldn't Morbier be there? But she caught no glimpse of him in the designer-clad crowd. And where was the father of the soon-to-be bride?

She set her gift among the others on a

table covered with a white cloth. Quite a haul — the boxes were all wrapped in Bon Marché or Hermès paper with matching ribbons.

That done, she found the tent serving hors d'oeuvres and helped herself to a sliver of smoked salmon on endive. On the lookout for Dussollier, she caught snatches of conversations drifting in the warm air with the clink of glasses: "*Mais oui,* it's always better to do a dull thing with style than an interesting thing without," came from a woman wearing a large white hat. "How true, Comtesse," nodded another guest who had several strands of pearls around her neck.

Her phone rang. René.

She found a secluded spot behind a cypress tree and answered.

"Chloé's almost decapitated at the park and I don't find out until now?" His voice quivered. "And you're what, out of the country?"

"It would take too long to explain," she said, keeping her voice low. "It's better this way, René."

She still hadn't seen Dussollier. The newly engaged daughter, sporting a sea-foam silk confection and a sparkling diamond ring, was walking arm in arm with her navy blue–

suited fiancé, accepting congratulations from guests on the lawn.

"What's that music?"

"I'm at an engagement party," she said. Suddenly, a wave of anxiety engulfed her. After the van and the smoking man this afternoon, she wasn't sure she should have left Martine's hideout to come to this, no matter how vital Dussollier's information was.

"You pick this time to attend a party?" said René in disbelief. "Who's getting married?"

"A woman wearing Dior. You don't know her. Neither do I. I know her father, and I'm wondering how he can afford a lavish spread like this on a *flic*'s salary."

"He probably inherited the money on his wife's side. Now, Aimée, look —"

She hadn't thought of that. "Tell me you've found something in Drina's notes. Figured out the Romany."

"We'll talk about that later, Aimée," he said.

His voice sounded strange.

"A problem, René?"

"Nothing I can't deal with. You're in Paris, I can tell. And Martine will tell me where."

"*Non,* René, it's not safe —"

"*Attends,* you're at Dussollier's daughter's

big to-do, *non?*"

Why did she always forget how smart he was?

"Shhh, listen, he's Morbier's contact in the seventh. Says he's found what I'm looking for."

"And you believe him, just like that?"

She wasn't sure anymore; there was a bad feeling gnawing at her gut. But this was the man who had attended the police academy with her papa, played cards at their kitchen table throughout her childhood, who came to Chloé's christening and insisted she attend his daughter's engagement reception. Right now, since Morbier had gone to ground, she needed his information. "Security's tighter than an unshucked oyster here."

"Where's Chloé?"

The garden was suddenly filled with notes from a violin quartet.

Dussollier was walking beneath the lanterns on the *terrasse* with his arm around his daughter, accompanied by applause and raised champagne flutes from the guests.

"She's safe. Got to go."

"Welcome, Aimée." Dussollier's flushed face beamed at her. He handed her a fizzing flute of champagne.

"*Félicitations,* your daughter's lovely. A perfect evening." She clinked his glass. "*Santé.*"

"Magical, *non?*" He sipped. "Rodin's sculptures, this garden." Beyond the wall, the gold dome of les Invalides glinted in the last rays of twilight.

She congratulated his wife, a matronly woman in powder blue whom she'd met before. Then she made her way through the receiving line of assorted family, who had come all the way from Toulon in Provence. She smiled through the tedious introductions, burning to take Dussollier aside.

At last, they were through all the relatives. "I don't want to take you from your guests this evening, but . . . you've got something to tell me, *non?*"

He nodded. His face turned serious. "Meet me in five minutes inside the room by the wheelchair ramp on the lower-ground floor, on the Invalides side. That's a quiet place where we can talk."

Aimée passed several catering trucks parked discreetly under the trees against the back wall. A steady flow of white-aproned servers looped back and forth carrying service trays, their feet crunching on the gravel path. She turned the corner and descended the ramp.

The door at the bottom opened at her touch, and she stepped into a hallway. Rough stone walls covered in crumbling grey stucco led to what she figured had once been the boiler room and laundry. A bare bulb illuminated the earthen floor.

She pulled Martine's cashmere shawl tighter, wished she'd borrowed a jacket. Where was Dussollier? Uneasy, she looked back, worried someone had followed her. No one there. But an odd place to meet. Her thoughts were at war inside her. Every nerve was on alert, her instincts telling her she was in danger. But could Dussollier, the warm, avuncular man who had just introduced her to his entire extended family, have invited her here, to his daughter's special day, just to set her up?

She stepped into the vaulted room on her left. Another bare bulb, yellowed with age, hung from a frayed wire in the curved stone ceiling, casting a dim glow over gilt and red satin-backed chairs stacked in piles.

"Mademoiselle Leduc?"

She turned to see the security guard she'd spoken to at the entrance. Her stomach knotted. What was he doing down here?

"Are you lost?" she said, stepping back, her heels sinking into the rough earth.

He shook his head and smiled.

Her hands clenched. "Take a hint and leave. I'm meeting someone." Since he was blocking the door, she moved back toward a sink. "What do you want?"

"You." He lunged, but she was ready, and she sidestepped him. He stumbled, knocking over a stack of chairs. Quick to recover, he gripped her arm and shoved her against the wall. Her shoulders shivered against the cold stone, and crumbling stucco trickled inside the back of her dress and down her spine.

"I like a tigress." He grinned, pulling a roll of duct tape from inside his jacket with his free hand. She saw that he was wearing a shoulder holster.

Her insides crawled. Think. "Why didn't you just say so? Not now, we'll —"

"Shut up." He pinned her to the wall, unwinding a strip of duct tape.

"The host will be here any minute. Don't you understand? Let me go."

The sound of footsteps came from the corridor. Dussollier at last! The guard put his thick hand over her mouth. The footsteps kept going. She bit him hard enough to draw blood.

He pulled back in pain, just far enough for her to wedge her knee up into his groin. He doubled over in a spasm. Then she pushed off from the wall with all her might, knocking him sideways against the sink. Heard the loud crack as his shiny shaved head hit the old porcelain rim. He crumpled to the ground with his eyes rolled up in his head. Knocked out cold.

Shaking, she stumbled and heard static coming from his pocket. His security monitor. "All done?" Static. ". . . taken care of yet?"

The hair rose on the back of her neck. The guard had come down here to subdue her. He had to be acting on Dussollier's orders. She reached into his shoulder holster and took the pistol, a Glock. Stuck it in her clutch. *Merde,* her bag wouldn't snap shut.

And then her phone rang. Martine. She checked the area, saw the corridor was clear. Then edged out, keeping low, intent on finding another exit so she wouldn't be seen leaving. Better take Martine's call to get backup. Security.

"Martine," she said, catching her breath. "Listen, I'm in —"

"A fax just came through from Martinique," she interrupted. "From that Blauet. I think you should hear this."

A bead of perspiration dripped down her neck. "Go ahead."

"He remembers your father fondly. As you

requested, he sent a list of the officers in your father's graduating class."

"*Et . . . ?*" She turned the corner, smack into a storage cellar full of empty boxes. Dead end. She turned and hurried back the way she'd come.

"He liked your idea for some reunion party and gives their nicknames, too, like you asked for."

Her blood ran cold. "Don't tell me, there's a Thomas 'Fifi' Dussollier."

"Right. But isn't that . . . ? Wait, are you in trouble, Aimée?"

"You've got to . . ." Her mouth went dry. The dim corridor light was blocked as Thomas Dussollier swatted the phone out of her hand. It clattered to the stone and he stomped on it. He grabbed her wrists, bent her right hand back in an iron grip. The next moment he'd shoved her forward into the room where the security guard lay. Her clutch fell on the ground.

"Trouble, always trouble, Aimée." He sighed. Shut the door. "Ever since you were small. What your father put up with when you were a teenager, *zut!* I know, we commiserated. I had one too, but look how she turned out."

Pain shot up her hand. *Merde.* A broken finger — if she was lucky.

The man who'd come to Chloé's christening. Whom she'd trusted. She decided to play dumb, give him a way out. "What do you mean? You said to meet here." Distract him, figure out a way to get by him, pray a waiter came by. Start screaming. "*Mon Dieu*, you've got guests upstairs. Let me get my bag and we'll talk in the garden —"

Dussollier shoved her down against the wall, knocking her sprawling onto a broken gilt chair. She lost Martine's left Louboutin in the dirt. He shook his head. "All this nosing around, making problems." Another sigh. "You've got everything the wrong way round. Stubborn. You just haven't wanted to see the reality. You have to know when to let things go."

Let things go?

"All you had to do was keep your nose out of it," he said. "Take a hint once things got difficult. The notebook's been burned. All the proof's gone."

Her eyes darted around, looking for a way out. But Dussollier was blocking the door, and there was no window in this frigid stone cell of a room. Her clutch was just out of her reach on the floor. She had to keep him talking, divert his attention until she could get her hands on the gun.

"Why did this guard appear?" she said,

446

wincing. *Get him explaining.*

Dussollier glanced at the security guard. Shook his head. "I think you've dealt him a permanent blow."

"But he attacked me," she said. *Think.* "*Alors,* I don't understand any of this. Look, if I've gotten things wrong, tell me."

"We're the good guys, remember? We take care of our own."

Anger flared in her. "Like you took care of Papa?"

"Don't you see? Your father was always one of us, Aimée," he said. "Nothing changed. We're family. I've always shown that, haven't I? When others didn't? Sent you gifts every year on Christmas? Always in my thoughts."

Cold seeped into her bare foot from the earth. *Keep this going. Grovel.* "*Mais bien sûr,* I remember. And those Friday night poker games at our kitchen table." Her left hand scrambled, searching in the dirt for her clutch.

He smiled. "The good times, eh?"

Her skin tingled. "What happened, Dussollier?"

"Happened?" He shrugged. "Every so often, word came down the ministerial pipe for your father and me to ignore evidence, to look the other way and back shelve reports." He sighed. "Call us little cogs in the machine. That's all."

That's how he rationalized corruption? By dragging her father into it too?

"My papa in league with you? Never."

"Morbier may have been his first partner, but your father and I went to the police academy together. That's a tie that binds, you know that." A half smile on his face. Wrinkles at the corners of his eyes. He looked old. "Just one more day until I retire. Then this old guy's getting kicked out."

She had to ignore the burning pain in her fingers. Appeal to his vanity and pride. Swallow the bile rising up in her throat.

"She's lovely, your daughter. They make a handsome couple."

"You know, it meant a lot to my wife that you came today. She wants to see the baby." He adjusted his crooked tuxedo collar. "So, are you ready to hear my proposition?"

Nicu. Roland Leseur. He hadn't given them any propositions. Or Djanka Constantin, or Pascal Leseur. She bit her lip, then had to spit out the sour taste of the guard's dirty hand.

"Why me?"

"Pwahh." A lopsided smile. "You're special, Aimée."

Like she believed that.

"I know you'll be reasonable, Aimée. Let's work this out, as I've done with half the crowd upstairs. Let things ride, like your papa did."

He unbuttoned his tuxedo-shirt collar. The hairs on her arms rose. He'd blown her father up in the van in Place Vendôme.

"How many times do I have to prove Papa wasn't on the take?"

"Choose your battles, Aimée. We all did." Dussollier sighed. Rationalizing murder? But it seemed important to him that she see it his way. "With that wild mother of yours, eh? A kid to raise. He made choices. Choices you benefitted from. You kids always need something. Teenagers, well, you'll find out. That high-school year abroad in the US, how do you think he paid for that? Eh, those Texas cowboy boots you couldn't live without?"

Those boots. She'd begged her papa for them.

"So you're saying it's my fault he . . . ?" She couldn't say it. *Non, non.* "You're twisting everything around, Dussollier."

"Kids. Never changes. We do everything for you and it's not enough."

Like this lavish party for his daughter? More like to impress people, stoke his prestige, his craving for power. Hypocrite.

The damp cold crawled up her legs. Dussollier checked his phone. Waiting, she realized, he was waiting for a call — his cohort to back him up? Her finger throbbed. She had to get him to admit it. "So this started twenty years ago with the murders of Pascal Leseur and Djanka Constantin?"

"We didn't kill that blackmailer in the ministry. Or his Gypsy slut . . ." His words trailed off, and after a moment he said, "A real botched job, that one. We just covered it up."

The bare bulb flickered into darkness for a moment, then lit the ground. She inched forward. Her clutch bag was almost in reach. "What do you mean?"

"A fool, that minister who liked little boys." Dussollier waved his hand. "Leseur was blackmailing him for . . . what was it?"

She thought back to the incriminating photo. Françoise's words: "the manipulator."

"He wanted a ministerial post, I think," Dussolier was saying. "Those thugs for hire were just supposed to threaten him. But it went wrong."

"Wrong enough to kill Pascal Leseur and cover it up as a suicide?"

"Not my watch. Blauet, the fool, went along with them. Drunk, the thugs said, roaring drunk. This Pascal fell and hit his head. An accident, but the Gypsy lover walked in and, *enfin,* they couldn't have a witness, could they?"

"So Blauet took Papa off the case to keep it quiet. To shut it down?"

"I worked the investigation with your father." A tired smile. "We cooperated, not for the first time either." Dussollier checked his phone again. She edged back in her chair, scrabbling in the dirt trying to reach her clutch. Her heart hammered. Waiting for Tesla? Would she be able to get away if there were two of them? "That's the way things were done. You should understand, Aimée. Move on."

She put it together now. "But now his brother Roland, aware of the tell-all memoir, suspected Pascal had been murdered, didn't he? He figured out about your cover-up." The puzzle pieces fit; she should have seen it earlier. "You'd be implicated. So you squashed the memoir. Then squashed him. Like Nicu. And Drina because you knew she'd expose the truth. Drina was the key. She saw you. Why didn't you tell me, Dussollier?"

Stupid. All the arrows pointed in the same directions, but she hadn't wanted to follow them — when Nicu had shown up after the

451

baptism, Dussollier must have overheard somehow. Panicked that Drina, after all this time, had returned on the eve of his retirement to threaten his cover-up, to ruin the crowning glory of his daughter's engagement party among his elite cronies and his relatives from Toulon. Toulon — it finally came back to her; the nurse at the clinic had told her the *monsieur* who had posed as ministry security had had a Toulon accent. Dussollier had abducted a dying Drina to keep her quiet, destroyed whatever incriminated him in her notebook, and acted helpful to distract and derail Aimée's progress, while always staying a step ahead . . .

"I'm telling you now, see," he said, a smile breaking on his face. "It's healthy getting things out in the open, you're right. It's all for the best, you'll see. I'm retiring, Chloé will have a little something . . . *non,* a big something for university. Put my gift in the bank now and see how it grows. Jean-Claude would have wanted that."

A bribe? Invoking Chloé's future? How twisted he was, claiming to care for her daughter and threatening her in the same breath.

"Jean-Claude loved you as you love Chloé, Aimée, remember that. He had to pay a price to keep you safe. You want to raise Chloé, don't you?" Dussollier shrugged. "*Alors,* you don't want your baby's ex-*flic* father gaining full custody, do you? A court order declaring you unfit, like your crazy mother, barring you visitation until she's eighteen?"

Her heart thumped. How the hell did he know this, if even she didn't know what had happened to her mother? For a moment his bleary gaze settled on the guard. Her now throbbing hand scrabbled for her clutch, pulled it behind her. She tried to grip the gun's handle. Her finger didn't cooperate.

"Me, I keep a little insurance," said Dussollier. "Know the weaknesses, the dirty secrets that people keep hidden. Judges' drunken car crashes, ministers partying with young girls and boys, diplomats caught with cocaine. We keep it quiet, do our jobs."

"Then you hold all the cards, Dussollier," she said with a sigh. "What do you want me to do?" Could she lull him into thinking she'd cooperate — or would his reflexes have slowed enough for her to threaten him and escape? She wedged the clutch's snap handle aside with her thumb.

Dussollier checked his phone again. His watch. Shook his head. "I can't wait anymore." He took a knife from his pocket. "I don't want to do this, Aimée."

"Then don't," she said, rubbing her hand. "You don't have to. Let's just . . ."

He shook his head. "I'm tired of explaining. Nothing's gotten through to you, has it? You still think we should pay, don't you? Me and Morbier?"

"What?"

A little laugh. "Ask him yourself."

Tremors rippled through her legs. What could he be insinuating?

"Don't fight me now, Aimée, we'll make sure the baby's taken care of," said Dussollier, rubbing his cheek. "I wish you hadn't made me do this."

Gritting her teeth, she flexed her broken finger inside her clutch. Closed her hand around the pistol. "Talk to someone who cares, Dussollier. No one takes my baby. No one smears my papa. Maybe I was a selfish teenager, but I listened to Papa. And the last thing he said to Drina, before you murdered him in the explosion —"

"Don't blame it all on me," said Dussollier, brandishing the knife at her. "I wasn't the only one."

She pulled out the pistol. Aimed it, her hands shaking.

"Can't do it, eh?" Quicker than she could think, Dussollier knocked her hand away

454

and threw her down against the wall.

Her chest clamped; she couldn't breathe. His black tie and tuxedo pressed into her face. Her stinging fingers scrambled on the ground, scratching the beaten earth, trying to feel for the pistol.

"I'll make your excuses upstairs." He knelt on her chest, his knife glinting in the dim light.

"Knifing me at your daughter's engagement reception? How the hell will you hush that up?"

"Easy. The knife shows up in the guard's hands. He was supposed to duct tape you. Hired help, I should have known." His stale breath in her face. "Everyone upstairs is in my pocket, Aimée. They always have been. If they want to hush things up, roadblock or stall an investigation, they come to me."

Sickening.

"You planned this all out, didn't you? Never really meant to give me a choice."

"Details, Aimée — don't they say the devil's in the details?"

Her working finger found the metal of the handle, her fingers inched to the trigger. Breathe, she had to breathe. Get air.

His left hand circled her neck. Squeezed.

She tried to whisper, but no sound came out.

"What's that, Aimée?" he leaned forward, his breath in her face. "You play, you pay, like your papa. But I need to get back to my guests."

"I don't think so, Fifi." She leveled the Glock. Fought through the pain and squeezed.

The crack of her shots reverberated off the stone. Two. Three. The stink of cordite filled the air. Her ears rang with the explosions. She shoved a wide-eyed Dussollier off her, surprise still on his face.

She had minutes to get out of here. On her hands and knees, she gasped for breath. She checked the security guard and found no pulse.

Awkwardly using her left hand, she wiped her prints off the pistol with her shawl. Put the pistol in the guard's hand and fired again twice into Dussollier. She grabbed her clutch from behind the broken chair. Pulled herself up the wall and slipped her wobbling foot into the Louboutin.

She couldn't count on the thick stone walls or the music to have muffled the shots — not with the caterers so nearby, or the waiters sneaking a smoke. Again with her shawl, she turned the handle, opened the door. Looked both ways. Clear.

A phone was ringing behind her. Dussollier's. His partner Tesla checking to see how things had gone? She backed up, hating to do it, to touch him, but she reached into his tuxedo pocket, nonetheless. It was silent now — the call had gone to voice mail.

She stuck the phone in her clutch. Remembered, luckily, to pick up the smashed carcass of her own and stick it besides Dussollier's. She scanned the stone hallway — still clear — then hurried up the ramp into the brisk evening air. She heard a catering truck's engine starting up. The shaking had subsided, but her hand was throbbing. *Focus,* she had to focus and get the hell out of here.

She rounded the corner to see the catering truck's red brake lights: it had paused by the cypress trees while a security guard moved the barricades for it to pull out. She leaped toward it, opened the back door, pulled herself in and crouched down among giant salad bowls and trays. Forced herself to breathe evenly. Keep focused. And prayed the truck would move.

Moments later it did, rumbling forward with the radio turned up high and the driver talking on his cell phone. Then she noticed blood on Martine's dress — Dussollier's blood. *Merde.*

She spit on the bloodstain, then again and

again, remembering from an old forensic manual that saliva enzymes and rubbing took care of the worst. Then she draped her shawl over the damp spot.

She counted to one hundred as the truck turned right onto rue de Varenne, then to two hundred as the driver argued on his cell phone. When the truck stopped at a traffic light, she gritted her teeth at the pain, turned the rear door's handle and slid out. Back on rue du Bac where she'd started. A green neon cross shone at her from across the street: a *pharmacie.*

She stopped for painkillers. Asked the pharmacist to open the pill bottle for her and downed them dry. Anything to stop the pain in her now swelling fingers.

She checked Dussollier's phone with her good hand and guessed his password on the second try — his daughter's name. His contacts were impressive. She hit his voice-mail button. His earlier messages came up and she listened to them one by one. More than impressive — incriminating.

The last one she listened to made her stomach churn.

"I'm waiting. Champ de Mars. Usual place."

She hailed a taxi. En route, she made a call.

■ ■ ■ ■

The figure sat on the bench in the darkness, smoking. The cigarette tip glowed gold-orange and the acrid tang of unfiltered Gauloise hovered in the air. Startled pigeons fluttered from the hydrangea bushes as she approached.

"Dussollier couldn't make it," she said, sitting down.

Morbier turned to look at her. Those basset-hound eyes, the bags under them more pronounced. The thick dark brows.

"I hope he served decent champagne at the reception, Leduc."

"Veuve Clicquot."

"Your favorite." Morbier tossed the cigarette and ground it into the gravel path with his toe. "He told you, didn't he? Cleared the past up."

She waited, her heart thumping, while Morbier took another cigarette from the wrinkled pack in his pocket. Scratched a wooden match against the bench. It lit with a *thupt* and a yellow flare.

"Now everyone involved in what happened to your father is gone," said Morbier. "It's over, Leduc."

"You've lied to me for years, Morbier."

She shook her head, saddened. "Why not just tell me the truth?"

"I think I just did." He glanced at his watch. "Go home and take care of what's important. Chloé."

Zinc rooftops glowed in the light reflected from the Tour Eiffel, just visible through the trees. From the next tree-lined *allée* came the crunch of gravel, the swish of bicycle tires.

"I found proof, Morbier."

"Proof, Leduc? Not this again. Give it up."

"Ten years ago, you met Papa before the explosion."

A snort. "This comes from the Gypsy, *non*? They lie for a living."

"Drina was Papa's lookout under the colonnade at Place Vendôme." Her words caught in her throat. The emotions fought in her chest. "You and Dussollier set Papa up."

Pause.

"It's not like that," Morbier said, shaking his head.

"Look me in the face for once and tell the truth. You're Tesla."

His voice grew cold. "If I tell you what really happened, you're dead, Leduc."

Fear shot through her. "You'd kill me just like that."

"This thing's bigger than you and me," he said. "You'll never know how big. We're just tiny cogs in the big machine."

Cogs in the machine — Dussollier's words.

"Don't try shifting the blame. You can't just claim conspiracy."

"We were all in it, Leduc. All of us."

Her papa . . . *non, non.* She couldn't hear this from Morbier too. "Liar."

"Your insistence on finding your mother." Morbier shook his head. "Good God, do you know how that hurt him? He'd sacrificed his career to get her out of the country. Have you ever thought about the deal he had to make to protect you and her?"

Her cheeks felt wet. She rubbed her face. She couldn't stop the shaking in her legs.

"What do you mean?"

"He cooperated. Otherwise your crazy mother would have ended up in an unmarked grave. He couldn't face that. Or face you."

Realization seared her. The timing — it added up. Her mother vanishing, then Papa helping cover up the Leseur affair? Had he cooperated because he'd struck a deal?

"Your Papa had had enough. Wanted out. So many times I tried to tell you," said Morbier. A sigh. "But I knew you couldn't hear it — would refuse to understand."

461

"That you killed Papa?"

"That I didn't get to Place Vendôme in time," he said. "Couldn't warn him."

Was that true? "And you expect me to believe that?"

"You're like a daughter to me." Morbier's voice choked with emotion. "Don't you think I wanted to stop lying? I've tried to do right, to make it up. When I did they trumped up charges against me, threw me in jail. Remember? You got me out."

"That's history now." Then it hit her. She'd been so stupid. The scene outside her door on the quai after the baptism — she'd been crazed with anger because of Melac's threat at the church. Dussollier had already left — he couldn't have overheard Nicu's plea. She wanted to kick herself. "You overheard Nicu at my door after the baptism, and then you disappeared. It was you who told Dussollier I was on my way. *You* abducted Drina." She grabbed the bench, trying to still her shaking hands. "Then had the gall to come back with cold hands, drink tisane in my kitchen. And when I thought you were having a heart attack you . . . made me promise . . ." Her throat caught.

Morbier's brows knit. "I warned Dussollier, tried to reason with him, but the crazy fool —"

"You went along with Dussollier, always have."

"So did your papa. What does that matter now? Move on."

"I've got the whole list of contacts on Dussollier's phone. Incriminating voice mails. One from you, too."

"You'd do that, Leduc?" His voice, tired and flat.

"Dussollier's out of the picture."

"What do you mean?" His jowls sagged.

"Veuve Cliquot or no, it came down to him or me, Morbier."

He stared at her. Her swollen hand. Understanding suddenly shone in his eyes.

"I never thought I'd do this." Morbier reached for the thick bulge under his jacket. Where he kept his shoulder holster.

"Nor did I, Morbier." She flashed her penlight twice, three times. Almost at once on her signal, the bushes rustled. Three gendarmerie officers from l'École Militaire emerged in blue uniforms, their Uzis leveled.

"Hands up! Nice and slow," barked the lead officer.

Morbier had reached in his pocket. The shot slammed his shoulder. Seconds later they'd grappled him to the ground. Cuffed him, bleeding and facedown on the gravel.

Pulled a shaking Aimée aside.

"What's that in his hand?"

She kneeled down. Shone her penlight. His nicotine-stained fingers clutched the photo of her holding Chloé, smiling at the baptism. His grip slackened, his hand went limp and the photo fell on a trampled hydrangea leaf.

The Seine flowed slick and black under the night sky. The clusters of globed lights strung from the Left Bank to the Right over Pont Alexandre III made her think of a sparkling necklace. Her head leaned against the cold glass of the ambulance's window, which was streaked with her tears.

Loud beeping came from the cardiac monitor. "Step on it," said the medic to the driver.

"Will he make it?"

"That's for the ER to say," said the medic.

They wouldn't let her beyond the swing doors to the operating room. Her last view of him — tubes in his arm, blood-soaked chest, crumpled Gauloise packet, and the basset-hound eyes she loved — was unfocused and brimming with tears.

René met her in the waiting room at l'Hôpital de l'Hôtel-Dieu.

"Let's go, Aimée," he said. "You can't do anything here. They'll call."

She shook her head. How could she live with herself after this?

A surgical nurse in green scrubs came through the swing doors.

Her heart clenched.

"Before we wheeled him into surgery," the nurse said, "he insisted I find you and say, 'You'd be late to your own funeral. Go home to Chloé.'"

ABOUT THE AUTHOR

Cara Black is the *New York Times* bestselling author of 15 books in the Private Investigator Aimée Leduc series, which is set in Paris. Cara has received numerous accolades for her novels, including multiple nominations for the prestigious Anthony and Macavity Awards, a *Washington Post Book World* Book of the Year citation, the Médaille de la Ville de Paris — the Paris City Medal, which is awarded in recognition of contribution to international culture — and invitations to be the Guest of Honor at such noteworthy conferences as the Paris Polar Crime Festival and Left Coast Crime. With more than 400,000 books in print, the Aimée Leduc series has been translated into German, Norwegian, Japanese, French, Spanish, Italian, and Hebrew.

Cara was born in Chicago but has lived in California's Bay Area since she was five years old. Before turning to writing full-time, she tried her hand at a number of jobs: she was a barista in the Basel train station café in Switzerland, taught English in Japan, studied Buddhism in Dharamsala in Northern India, and worked as a bar girl in Bangkok (only pouring drinks!). After studying Chinese history at Sophia University in Tokyo — where she met her husband, Jun, a bookseller, potter, and amateur chef — she obtained her teaching credential at San Francisco State College, and went on to work as a preschool director and then as an agent of the federally funded Head Start program, which sent her into San Francisco's Chinatown to help families there — often sweatshop workers — secure early care and early education for their children. Each of these jobs was amazing and educational in a different way, and the Aimée Leduc books are covered in the fingerprints of Cara's various experiences.

Her love of all things French was kindled by the French-speaking nuns at her Catholic high school, where Cara first encountered French literature and went crazy for the work of Prix Goncourt winner Romain Gary. Her junior year in high school, she wrote him a fan letter — which he answered, and which inspired her to make her first trip to Paris, where her idol took her out for coffee and a cigar. Since then, she has been to Paris many, many times. On each visit she entrenches herself in a different part of the city, learning its secret history.

She has posed as a journalist to sneak into closed areas, trained at a firing range with real Paris flics, gotten locked in a bathroom at the Victor Hugo museum, and — just like Aimee — gone down into the sewers with the rats (she can never pass up an opportunity to see something new, even when the timing isn't ideal — she was headed to a fancy dinner right afterwards and was in a spot of bother with her shoes). For the scoop on real Paris crime, she takes the cops out for drinks and dinner to hear their stories — but it usually turns into a long evening, which is why she sticks with espresso.